CLIFFSCOMPLETE™

Hawthorne's

The Scarlet Letter

Edited and commentary by Karin Jacobson, Ph.D.

Associate Professor

University of Minnesota—Duluth

Complete Text + Commentary + Glossary

T0381062

Hungry Minds™

Hungry Minds, Inc.

New York, NY • Cleveland, OH • Indianapolis, IN

CLIFFSCOMPLETE™

Hawthorne's

The Scarlet Letter

About the Author
Karin Jacobson earned her Ph.D. from The Ohio State University and teaches at the University of Minnesota–Duluth. Her primary academic interests are Shakespeare, Victorian literature, and literary theory.

Cover Illustration:
Private Collection/Bridgeman Art Library. Used under license.

Publisher's Acknowledgments
Editorial
Senior Project Editor: Joan Friedman
Acquisitions Editor: Gregory W. Tubach
Copy Editor: Esmeralda St. Clair
Illustrator: DD Dowden
Editorial Manager: Christine Meloy Beck
Special Help: Jennifer Young
Production
Proofreaders: Corey Bowen, David Faust
Indexer: Rebecca R. Plunkett
Hungry Minds Indianapolis Production Services

CliffsComplete™ Hawthorne's *The Scarlet Letter*
Published by:
Hungry Minds, Inc.
909 Third Avenue
New York, NY 10022
www.hungryminds.com (Hungry Minds Web site)
www.cliffsnotes.com (CliffsNotes Web site)

Library of Congress Control Number: 2001087875

ISBN: 978-0-7645-8724-5

10 9 8 7 6 5 4 3 2 1

1O/QY/QT/QR/IN

Distributed in the United States by Hungry Minds, Inc.

Distributed by CDG Books Canada Inc. for Canada; by Transworld Publishers Limited in the United Kingdom; by IDG Norge Books for Norway; by IDG Sweden Books for Sweden; by IDG Books Australia Publishing Corporation Pty. Ltd. for Australia and New Zealand; by TransQuest Publishers Pte Ltd. for Singapore, Malaysia, Thailand, Indonesia, and Hong Kong; by Gotop Information Inc. for Taiwan; by ICG Muse, Inc. for Japan; by Norma Comunicaciones S.A. for Columbia; by Intersoft for South Africa; by Eyrolles for France; by International Thomson Publishing for Germany, Austria and Switzerland; by Distribuidora Cuspide for Argentina; by LR International for Brazil; by Galileo Libros for Chile; by Ediciones ZETA S.C.R. Ltda. for Peru; by WS Computer Publishing Corporation, Inc., for the Philippines; by Contemporanea de Ediciones for Venezuela; by Express Computer Distributors for the Caribbean and West Indies; by Micronesia Media Distributor, Inc. for Micronesia; by Grupo Editorial Norma S.A. for Guatemala; by Chips Computadoras S.A. de C.V. for Mexico; by Editorial Norma de Panama S.A. for Panama; by American Bookshops for Finland. Authorized Sales Agent: Anthony Rudkin Associates for the Middle East and North Africa.

For general information on Hungry Minds' products and services please contact our Customer Care department; within the U.S. at 800-762-2974, outside the U.S. at 317-572-3993 or fax 317-572-4002.

For sales inquiries and resellers information, including discounts, premium and bulk quantity sales and foreign language translations please contact our Customer Care department at 800-434-3422, fax 317-572-4002 or write to Hungry Minds, Inc., Attn: Customer Care department, 10475 Crosspoint Boulevard, Indianapolis, IN 46256.

For information on licensing foreign or domestic rights, please contact our Sub-Rights Customer Care department at 650-653-7098.

For information on using Hungry Minds' products and services in the classroom or for ordering examination copies, please contact our Educational Sales department at 800-434-2086 or fax 317-572-4005.

Please contact our Public Relations department at 212-884-5163 for press review copies or 212-884-5000 for author interviews and other publicity information or fax 212-884-5400.

For authorization to photocopy items for corporate, personal, or educational use, please contact Copyright Clearance Center, 222 Rosewood Drive, Danvers, MA 01923, or fax 978-750-4470.

Hungry Minds™ is a trademark of Hungry Minds, Inc.

CLIFFSCOMPLETE™

Hawthorne's

The Scarlet Letter

CONTENTS AT A GLANCE

CLIFFSCOMPLETE™

Hawthorne's

The Scarlet Letter

TABLE OF CONTENTS

Nathaniel Hawthorne's

THE SCARLET LETTER

INTRODUCTION TO NATHANIEL HAWTHORNE

Nathaniel Hawthorne was born on July 4, 1804 in Salem, Massachusetts, the only son of Captain Nathaniel Hathorne and Elizabeth Clarke Manning. Hawthorne's ancestors had lived in Salem for almost 200 years, following William Hathorne's arrival in 1630 with Governor Winthrop, the original governor of the Massachusetts Bay Colony. William Hathorne was a strong supporter of Puritan orthodoxy, which led to his cruel, inhumane treatment of anyone who did not fit within Puritan society. For example, he is blamed for sentencing a Quaker woman to public hanging and for brutally beating another woman. Continuing the family's persecution of outsiders, William's son John was one of the judges at the initial hearings of the infamous Salem witch trials in 1692. Partially to separate himself from what he saw as his ancestors' brutality, Nathaniel added a "w" to his name shortly after he graduated from college.

Hawthorne met with tragedy early in life. In 1808, when he was four years old, his father died of yellow fever at Surinam in Dutch Guiana. Following his father's death in 1808, Hawthorne, his mother, and his two sisters (Elizabeth and Maria Louisa) were poverty-stricken and forced to move in with Mrs. Hathorne's relatives, the Mannings. The Hathorne side of his family offered no assistance to the young widow or her children, and this may be another reason Nathaniel chose to add the "w" to his name soon after graduating from college—to differentiate himself from these uncaring relatives. Hawthorne's mother never fully recovered from the loss of her husband and spent most of her life in seclusion, remaining inscrutable even to her children.

Despite the early loss of his father, Hawthorne was blessed with a relatively happy childhood. After hurting his foot in 1813, he was tutored at home and, therefore, was able to read whatever books he liked; some of his favorites included Sir Walter Scott, John Bunyan, and Shakespeare. He traced his love of reading and literature from this phase of his life. In 1818, the family spent most of its time in Raymond, Maine, where Hawthorne developed a love for the wilderness. In fact, he was sorry when his Uncle Robert Manning sent him back to Salem for college preparatory classes.

College and early days of writing

Entering Bowdoin College at Brunswick, Maine, in 1821, Hawthorne was surrounded by classmates who would later become famous. Among the two most influential were Henry Wadsworth Longfellow, later a distinguished poet and Harvard professor, and Franklin Pierce, the future fourteenth president of the United States. Another classmate, Horatio Bridge, later helped convince publishers to produce Hawthorne's first collection of stories.

Although Hawthorne's college career was undistinguished—he graduated in the middle of his class—his college experience helped him solidify his career aspirations. In a letter to his mother he wrote, "I do not want to be a doctor and live by men's diseases, nor a minister to live by their sins, nor a lawyer to live by their quarrels. So, I don't see that there is anything left for me but to be an author. How would you like some day to see a whole shelf full of books, written by your son, with 'Hawthorne's Works' printed on their backs?"

A youthful Hawthorne, painted by Charles Osgood, Essex Institute, Salem.
©Bettmann/CORBIS

Following his graduation in 1825, Hawthorne returned to Salem, lived with his mother for the next 12 years, and began his apprenticeship as an author. Basically a recluse during these 12 solitary years, he had few friends and spent most of his time perfecting his writing and reading New England history, which he used as the basis for many of his works. During this reclusive period, Hawthorne reportedly sent his sister to check out books and magazines for him from the Salem library so he wouldn't need to leave the house.

In 1828, Hawthorne published (at his own expense) his first novel, *Fanshaw: A Tale,* which shows few of the qualities that would later become Hawthorne's distinguishing features. Instead, Hawthorne's first novel, using characters and events from Hawthorne's life at Bowdoin, is a poor imitation of Sir Walter Scott. Analyzing this early work, critic Arlin Turner writes, "Imitation shows on every page; it smacks of a kind of copybook exercise." Hawthorne was almost instantly ashamed of this substandard novel and tried to buy all of the copies so that no one could read it.

Although Hawthorne did not publish another novel for 25 years, he was, in the meantime, perfecting the form for which he was to become famous: the allegorical or symbolic tale. Hawthorne's first published story, "The Hollow of the Three Hills" (1830), shows many of the characteristics that would mark his mature style: an emphasis on evil and suffering, a dark and stunted landscape, and an astute use of metaphor and imagery.

By 1832, many of his most popular stories, including "My Kinsman, Major Molineux" and "Roger Malvin's Burial" had been written. Many of these stories were published in magazines, and, after numerous rejections by publishers, were collected and published in 1837 as the *Twice-Told Tales.* His college friend Horatio Bridge guaranteed the collection's publisher against financial loss. Longfellow and Poe both wrote supportive reviews of the collection, which is now viewed as a standard masterpiece of American literature. In his review, Poe commented on the dearth of worthy writing by Americans, but he placed Hawthorne's tales among the best American stories ever written: "Of Mr. Hawthorne's Tales we would say, emphatically, that they belong to the highest region of Art—an Art subservient to genius of a very lofty order . . . As Americans, we feel proud of the book."

Poe's comments are a reminder that at the time Hawthorne was writing, American literature was still in an infant stage, as American writers attempted to define a unique brand of literature, one that was not a mere imitation of European models. As Poe suggests, Hawthorne accomplishes this. His evocations of Puritan New England accurately capture the often sinister viewpoints of the nation's earliest settlers, along with the details of a specifically American landscape.

Mature years

Soon after the publication of *Twice-Told Tales*, Hawthorne met Sophia Amelia Peabody and, in 1839, they became secretly engaged. From 1839–1841, he worked at the Boston Custom House. When this position took too much of his time away from writing, Hawthorne became interested in a commune in West Roxbury, Massachusetts—the Brook Farm Community. He hoped to find a way to support himself while also finding literary success. But communal living did not agree with Hawthorne and, after living at Brook Farm for only a few months, he left in November of 1841, disillusioned and exhausted. While the Brook Farm experience did not offer him a sustainable new lifestyle, it did provide him with the material for a novel: *The Blithedale Romance* is based primarily on Hawthorne's time in the commune.

With a regular writing job for the *Democratic Review*, Hawthorne finally felt financially secure enough for marriage in 1842. He and Sophia were married on July 9, 1842. After the wedding, they moved into the Old Manse in Concord, where they spent some of the happiest and most productive years of Hawthorne's life. While living in Concord, the Hawthornes were surrounded by some of the most influential thinkers of the time, including Ralph Waldo Emerson, Henry David Thoreau, and Bronson Alcott. Emerson, Thoreau, and their friends regularly got together to discuss transcendentalism, from which Hawthorne learned the value of intuition, rather than reason, as a source of knowledge and truth. Not only did Hawthorne continue writing journalistic articles for the *Democratic Review*, but he also wrote the tales published in *Mosses from an Old Manse* (1846).

Despite this productivity, the Hawthornes were still plagued by financial worries—critical success as a writer did not necessarily translate into financial security. With the birth of the Hawthorne's first two children, Una in 1844 and Julian in 1846, Hawthorne was forced to seek a more financially secure position. Help from his politically savvy Democratic friends landed Hawthorne a more lucrative position as surveyor of the port of Salem during the Polk administration, a role he held from 1847–1849.

Between his family responsibilities and his job as a surveyor, Hawthorne had little time for writing. This situation changed when the Whigs won the election of 1848; when Zachary Taylor became president, Hawthorne lost his position in the Custom-House. His bitterness about this loss is documented in his introduction to *The Scarlet Letter*, "The Custom-House." But as the old cliché tells us, every cloud has its silver lining. Although losing his job was a financial shock to the family, it allowed Hawthorne time to write *The Scarlet Letter*. In fact, after leaving the Salem Custom House, Hawthorne wrote the novels most people consider his best. The publication of *The Scarlet Letter* in 1850 brought Hawthorne fame and reputation, though financial security still eluded him; in fact, only 8,000 copies of the novel sold in Hawthorne's lifetime.

Several other Hawthorne classics soon followed shortly after *The Scarlet Letter*: the novels *The House of the Seven Gables* (1851) and *The Blithedale Romance* (1852), a book of stories called *The Snow-Image and Other Twice-Told Tales* (1851), and a children's book entitled *A Wonder-Book for Girls and Boys* (1852). Together these works solidified Hawthorne's reputation as one of the most respected American authors of his time.

In 1849, the Hawthorne family moved to Lenox, Massachusetts, located in the Berkshire mountains, where the family lived in a "little red house." Here Hawthorne became good friends with Herman Melville, who dedicated *Moby Dick* to him. In reviews of Hawthorne's works, Melville characterized them as having "mystical blackness" and "a touch of Puritanic gloom."

A photograph of Hawthorne taken in 1860 by Mayall, during Hawthorne's stay in England.
©Bettmann/CORBIS

When the Hawthornes' second daughter, Rose, was born, the family moved to West Newton, where Hawthorne wrote *A Life of Pierce*, a campaign biography for his old college friend, Franklin Pierce. In thanks, Pierce gave Hawthorne a position as the U.S. consul in Liverpool, England. The family spent the next seven years in Europe. From 1853 to 1857, they traveled through England, where Hawthorne kept a detailed travel journal. (With information from the journal, he would compile the last book published before his death, *Our Old Home*, sketches of English life published in 1863.) Pierce was not reelected in 1858, so Hawthorne relinquished his position as consul and the family moved to Italy. Here Hawthorne collected material for his *Italian Notebooks* and for a novel, *The Marble Faun* (1860).

Returning to the United States in 1860, Hawthorne's health soon went into decline.

Hawthorne died on May 19, 1864, while on a trip to the White Mountains in New Hampshire with his friend Franklin Pierce. He was buried at Sleepy Hollow Cemetery in Concord.

Hawthorne's style

Although he often described himself as "the obscurest man of letters in America," Hawthorne has become one of the most widely read nineteenth-century American authors. What accounts for his popularity? One of the most significant elements of Hawthorne's achievement is his development of character; in both his stories and his novels, Hawthorne looks deeply at the inner sanctums of the human heart, uncovering our secret motivations, guilt, hopes, and fears. The depth of his understanding of human psychology makes him appealing to readers interested in exploring what it means to be human. Other characteristics of his work that critics have often noted as significant (and that you might look for as you read *The Scarlet Letter*) include:

* mastery of the genre of the romance.
* characters who are a mix of the real and the imaginary.
* clarity of writing style and coherence of structure.
* unity of theme, action, image, and mood.
* insights on the psychology and philosophy of Puritan morality, including questions of sin, guilt, and suffering.
* portrayal of important moral dilemmas and their effects on people's psychological outlook.
* courageous and truthful representation of the dark side of human behavior.
* masterful use of allegory and symbolism.
* dichotomous image clusters that center on dark versus light, natural versus unnatural, sun versus moon, and so on.

INTRODUCTION TO *THE SCARLET LETTER*

Glancing at the looking-glass, we behold—deep within its haunted verge—the smouldering glow of the half-extinguished anthracite, the white moonbeams on the floor, and a repetition of all the gleam and shadow of the picture, with one remove farther from the actual, and nearer to the imaginative. Then, at such an hour, and with this scene before him, if a man, sitting all alone, cannot dream strange things, and make them look like truth, he need never try to write romances.

This passage, taken from "The Custom-House," the essay that introduces *The Scarlet Letter,* provides readers with a clear picture of Hawthorne's view of artistic creation. This passage and the paragraph that precedes it create a sort of artistic manifesto. Hawthorne believes that artists should choose familiar, domestic subjects, but make them unfamiliar by showing their strangeness, as if seen through the glow of moonlight. In this respect, the looking glass is an apt metaphor for the artist's work, which reflects the world, but at a slant. With the light of the moon, Hawthorne also invokes fairy-tales, suggesting that the best romances exist at the point where real and imaginary meet. But they also need a fiery glow, an abundance of passion and tenderness, so that they produce an emotional response. By the dual glow of moonlight and firelight, the artist can make strange things look like the truth.

How does this philosophy relate to *The Scarlet Letter?* The novel depicts a world filled with mysteries and ambiguities. This is not a book that offers its readers a singular truth. Instead, it offers multiple, layered ways of looking at the world, as is seen in the multiple interpretations of the novel's primary symbol, the scarlet "A." This book introduces a spiritual way of looking at the world—a world real enough for readers to relate to but imaginary enough to seem mythical and magical. By briefly exploring the writing of the novel, along with its symbols, themes, and structure, even first-time readers can appreciate the beauty and complexity of Hawthorne's artistry.

The novel's creation

Published in 1850, *The Scarlet Letter* brought Hawthorne instant critical success, although he still lacked the financial security he longed for. The events that led to the writing of the novel are described in "The Custom-House" preface. Not only did he lose his job, but he also lost his mother in 1849; both events had a significant impact on Hawthorne's life and creative identity.

As Hawthorne tells us, the loss of his job was a mixed blessing. His work at the custom house was deadening his soul. While unemployment meant financial hardship, it allowed him to renew and replenish his artistic abilities: "So little adapted is the atmosphere of a Custom House to the delicate harvest of fancy and sensibility, that, had I remained there through ten Presidencies yet to come, I doubt whether the tale of 'The Scarlet Letter' would ever have been brought before the public eye. My imagination is a tarnished mirror."

Obviously, the newly found freedom from public employment was beneficial to his creative development, resulting in one of the most prolific periods of his life. But psychologically, Hawthorne was conflicted about this time of creative growth, due to his ambivalent feelings about the artistic life. Hawthorne seems to have felt a strong push toward financial security, something his writing couldn't provide, and he writes in "The custom house" that the money and stability offered by his government position were seductive. In addition, in "The Custom-House," Hawthorne projects how his ancestors would have perceived his writing—as an idling waste of time. This passage depicts the United States' traditionally negative view of artists: The Puritan work ethic devalues artistic productions, labeling them as pleasure rather than work. Hawthorne internalized some of his ancestors' views, so his position with the custom house offered him the chance to do supposedly "useful" work.

Many critics, such as Nina Baym, have noted that connections exist between Hawthorne and his creation, Hester Prynne: Both are artists, both are rejected by Puritan society, and both value creativity and imagination over law and social rules. In fact, the novel could be viewed as an allegory of the artist's position within American society. Hawthorne places the scarlet letter on his chest in "The Custom-House" and it burns into his flesh, just as it burns into Hester's in the novel. Not only does this incident show their affinity; it also suggests that another interpretation for the scarlet "A" might be "artist" or "author."

Symbols used in the novel

"Artist" and "author" obviously are not the only interpretations of the scarlet letter. Initially, the "A" symbolizes "adultery," a visible sign of Hester's transgression. Later, various people assign meanings such as "able" or "angel" to the letter, as the community's views of Hester change. For Governor Bellingham's servant, the letter signals Hester's upper-class ("aristocratic" or "authoritarian") status. Not only does the scarlet letter's meaning mutate throughout the novel, but the letter itself seems to multiply. For example, Hester's daughter Pearl becomes a living embodiment of the letter, and a version of the letter has apparently been burned into Arthur Dimmesdale's flesh, whether by human or supernatural means. The letter also appears momentarily in the form of a meteor that flashes across the night sky.

The mutability of the letter characterizes all the symbols within the text: All are ambiguous, none can be distilled into a single meaning that is the same for all people and all time. While the Puritans seem to believe that the scarlet letter will universally stigmatize Hester, they overestimate their hold on the symbol's meaning: Neither the Indians nor the sailors nor anyone new to the colonies appears to know what it means. Symbols, like words, take on meanings that are unique to particular cultures and particular individuals.

Lillian Gish starred as Hester Prynne in the 1926 film version of The Scarlet Letter. *Everett Collection*

Hawthorne's brand of romance abounds with such ambiguous yet potent symbols. In this novel, almost everything is a symbol. For example, in the minds of the Puritans, the forest is a symbol of humanity's dark, devilish side, while for Hester and Pearl, it signifies the creativity and imagination the Puritan society forces them to repress. In "The Custom-House," Hawthorne suggests that it has a similar meaning for him, holding an "imaginative delight" he has lost while working within the confines of the custom house.

Colors are also symbolic, with red connoting passion, fire, creativity, and sin, while gray (associated primarily with the Puritans) indicates dreariness, convention, and conformity. The flowers, the brook, and the scaffold are also symbols, as is the meteor that flashes through the sky as Hester, Pearl, and

Dimmesdale stand together on the scaffold at night. This natural event represents Dimmesdale's guilt and Governor Winthrop's death, among other possible interpretations.

Even the novel's characters can be viewed as symbols rather than fully-developed people. Pearl, for example, represents creative freedom and the wildness of the natural world. Arthur, on the other hand, symbolizes the hypocrisy of the Church and all the perversions of the Puritan repression of passion. Hester could represent the artistic, free-spirited nature also repressed by the Puritans.

Themes in *The Scarlet Letter*

As suggested by the brief look at its symbols, this novel introduces a plethora of themes. One of the most central is the clash between the individual and society. The book's opening look at the prison house is a primary example. Although the Puritans had hoped to establish a utopian society in the New World, one where everyone would be united under a shared ideology, their plan appears to have failed before it even began. The prison was one of the first buildings created by the immigrants, suggesting their recognition that certain individuals would inevitably transgress the socially established rules. Unity was impossible. Obviously, Hester's transgression shows the conflict of individual passion with the group's regulations. Pearl, whose entire existence, according to Dimmesdale, is evidence of the "freedom of a broken law," shows no reverence for law or society but lives in a completely self-defined world. So transgressive is Pearl's very existence to Puritan beliefs that Hawthorne ships her off to Europe at the novel's end, showing her inability to live happily within this society's narrow boundaries.

Building on this problem of how individuals should interact with social rules, Hawthorne introduces a cluster of similar questions. For example, who should have the right to judge individuals' behavior? Do the old, desiccated magistrates have the right to judge Hester's passionate action? Does Chillingworth have the right to judge and to administer private vengeance upon Dimmesdale?

The novel also considers the relationship between nature and society. Does nature provide a haven in which the individual can find freedom from society's unjust rules? Does nature's bounty offer solace to humanity, as for example the wild rosebush offers beauty to Hester even when she's confined? Or is nature indifferent to human suffering, much like Pearl seems indifferent to her mother's emotions?

Finally, the novel considers the relationship of specific groups of people to society. What is the role of the artist to society? Are artistic endeavors necessarily individualistic and socially transgressive, because they offer new and different ways of looking at the world? Must artists always minimize their creative powers in order to fit within society's boundaries? Hester is the focus for many of these questions, and her character also introduces

This undated engraving by J.S. King shows a group of Puritans walking to church.
©Bettmann/CORBIS

the theme of women's role within society. Her medi-
ations, along with her apparent suffering, emphasize
women's inequitable position within society. How can
women achieve equality? Must they sacrifice all notions
of female difference in order to be equal? Is the society
Hester dreams of at the novel's end, in which men and
women live happily together, possible?

Other obvious dichotomies within the novel
include Europe versus America, Indian versus Puritan,
magic versus medicine, and so on. Many other the-
matic approaches to this rich novel are possible, but
the questions offered here show the wealth of ideas
sparked simply around the notion of the individual
and society. Hawthorne's approach to writing won't
necessarily lead to a singular answer to any of the questions, but it certainly provokes interesting discussions.

The novel's structure

To readers who return to this novel again and again,
one of the most amazing aspects of Hawthorne's
artistry is his structure. Not only does the novel include
carefully layered symbols and provocative themes, but
it is also minutely crafted. The scaffold scenes are one
of the most obvious structuring devices. Notice that
the novel contains 24 chapters. The first scaffold scene
is contained in chapters 1–3. The second scaffold scene
occurs exactly in the book's middle, at chapter 12.
Chapter 23 contains the last. All of the book's main
characters are present in each of these scenes (although
they play different roles), as is the novel's primary
symbol, the scarlet letter.

In the first scaffold scene, Hester and Pearl stand
alone, publicly humiliated, while Dimmesdale watches
from the side, standing with the other assembled leaders of the community. Emotionally and physically, he
is separate from her, but she bravely bears her solitary
suffering. Presented in all of its beauty, the scarlet letter symbolizes her artistry and imagination, showing
her difference from her more conventional lover.
Dimmesdale's speech in this scene, asking her to reveal
the name of her lover, is filled with double-talk that

shows he lacks the courage to make this revelation
himself. From the sidelines, Chillingworth, Hester's
husband, learns of his wife's transgression. An evil
impulse almost immediately grows within his heart,
as shown by the imagery of the "writhing," snake-like
horror that moves from his face into the "depths of his
nature."

The second scaffold scene contains nearly all the
same elements, although configured slightly differently. Hawthorne brings us back to the market-place,
and all the major characters are here again, including
Governor Bellingham (representing the state) and Mr.
Wilson (representing the church). This time, though,
the scene occurs at night, nearly seven years after the
novel's action begins. Rather than highlighting Hester's suffering, this scene focuses on Dimmesdale's guilt
and remorse, which have led him to the edge of insanity. While in the chapter preceding this one they were
divided, here Hester, Pearl, and Dimmesdale stand
hand-in-hand, forming an "electric chain." Hester
learns the depth of Dimmesdale's punishment by
Chillingworth and makes the important decision to
save him from his enemy. While Dimmesdale has
grown weak and "dim" since his first appearance in the
novel, Hester's strength has expanded, so she now has
sufficient power to confront Chillingworth. Pearl
shows that Dimmesdale's repentance isn't complete by
asking if he'll stand on the scaffold with her and her
mother in the light of day. He won't. The meteor and
the light of Mr. Wilson's lamp provide symbolic richness to this chapter. Of course, Chillingworth, the
embodiment of evil, is present once again on the sidelines. His evil has spread from the "depths of his
nature" and infected his entire being, giving him
almost complete power over Dimmesdale. The scarlet
letter makes an appearance as a glowing light in the
sky, telling Dimmesdale that even nature knows of his
guilt.

The final scaffold scene in some ways replicates
the first. Once again, all the major characters meet in
the marketplace in full daylight. Hester is again the
object of unwanted attention due to the scarlet letter,

him up the scaffold where he can make this revelation. Chillingworth's evil has become full-blown, but his power over Dimmesdale is now gone, because the minister chooses the path of truth. His death frees Pearl from her role as symbol of her parents' guilt, so she can become a compassionate and caring human being. In this scene, the scarlet letter makes its appearance on Dimmesdale's chest.

Numerous other structural devices have been proposed for this novel, and each confirms the book's carefully planned symmetry. No aspect of this novel is irrelevant. Each of the symbols, charac-

A scene from the 1926 MGM film of The Scarlet Letter.
Everett Collection

making her an outcast, while Dimmesdale is exalted as a saint. But this scene is different, because Dimmesdale is dying. Realizing that this is his last opportunity to confess before his death, Dimmesdale finds courage to perform this vital act, if for no other reason than to save his soul. As in the second scaffold scene, Hester's strength is emphasized: Dimmesdale needs her to carry

ters, and themes is presented with consistent, delicately chosen details, creating a beautiful and complex novel that rightfully claims its place as one of the pinnacles of American literature. In writing this novel, the once tarnished mirror of Hawthorne's imagination was carefully polished, creating a book that presents a strange, symbolic, and deeply moving portrait of human life.

CHARACTERS IN THE NOVEL

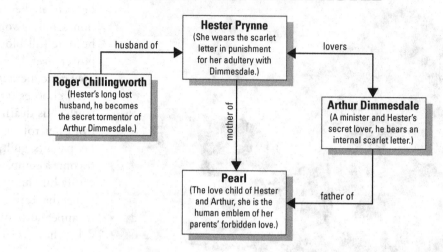

Hester Prynne
(She wears the scarlet letter in punishment for her adultery with Dimmesdale.)

Roger Chillingworth
(Hester's long lost husband, he becomes the secret tormentor of Arthur Dimmesdale.)

Arthur Dimmesdale
(A minister and Hester's secret lover, he bears an internal scarlet letter.)

Pearl
(The love child of Hester and Arthur, she is the human emblem of her parents' forbidden love.)

husband of

lovers

mother of

father of

CLIFFSCOMPLETE

HAWTHORNE'S
THE SCARLET
LETTER

The Custom-House

In this long introductory sketch, Hawthorne gives some autobiographical information, describes the personalities of his coworkers at the custom house in Salem, documents his discovery of the manuscript that was supposedly the basis for the story of *The Scarlet Letter*, and provides his definition of the romance novel.

THE CUSTOM-HOUSE

IT is a little remarkable, that—though disinclined to talk overmuch of myself and my affairs at the fireside, and to my personal friends—an autobiographical impulse should twice in my life have taken possession of me, in addressing the public. The first time was three or four years since, when I favoured the reader—inexcusably, and for no earthly reason that either the indulgent reader or the intrusive author could imagine—with a description of my way of life in the deep quietude of an **Old Manse**. And now—because, beyond my deserts, I was happy enough to find a listener or two on the former occasion—I again seize the public by the button, and talk of my three years' experience in a Custom-House. The example of the famous "**P. P., Clerk of this Parish**," was never more faithfully followed. The truth seems to be, however, that when he casts his leaves forth upon the wind, the author addresses, not the many who will fling aside his volume, or never take it up, but the few who will understand him better than most of his schoolmates or lifemates. Some authors, indeed, do far more than this, and indulge themselves in such confidential depths of revelation as could fittingly be addressed only and exclusively to the one heart and mind of perfect sympathy; as if the printed book, thrown at large on the wide world, were certain to find out the divided segment of the writer's own nature, and complete his circle of existence by bringing him into communion with it. It is scarcely decorous, however, to speak all, even where we speak impersonally. But, as thoughts are frozen and utterance benumbed, unless the speaker stand in some true relation with his audience, it may be pardonable to imagine that a friend, a kind and apprehensive, though not the closest friend, is listening to our talk; and then, a native reserve being thawed by this genial consciousness, we may prate of the circumstances that lie around us, and even of ourself, but still keep the inmost Me behind its veil. To this extent, and within these limits, an author, methinks, may be autobiographical, without violating either the reader's rights or his own.

It will be seen, likewise, that this Custom-House sketch has a certain propriety, of a kind always recognised in literature, as explaining how a large portion of the following pages came into my possession, and as offering proofs of the authenticity of a narrative therein contained. This, in fact—a desire to put myself in my true position as editor, or very little more, of the most prolix among the tales that make up my volume—this, and no other, is my true reason for assuming a personal relation with the public. In accomplishing the main purpose, it has appeared allowable, by a few

NOTES

Old Manse: A manse is the residence of a minister. In 1846, Hawthorne published a collection of short stories called *Mosses from an Old Manse*, which was introduced by an autobiographical sketch, "The Old Manse," similar to "The Custom-House."

"P.P., Clerk of this Parish": "Memoirs of P.P. Clerk of this Parish" was a satirical sketch with a pompous narrator that was written by the Scriblerus Club, founded in 1713 by John Arbuthnot, Alexander Pope, Jonathan Swift, and John Gay.

extra touches, to give a faint representation of a mode of life not heretofore described, together with some of the characters that move in it, among whom the author happened to make one.

In my native town of Salem, at the head of what, half a century ago, in the days of **old King Derby**, was a bustling wharf—but which is now burdened with decayed wooden warehouses, and exhibits few or no symptoms of commercial life; except, perhaps, a bark or brig, half-way down its melancholy length, discharging hides; or, nearer at hand, a Nova Scotia schooner, pitching out her cargo of firewood—at the head, I say, of this dilapidated wharf, which the tide often overflows, and along which, at the base and in the rear of the row of buildings, the track of many languid years is seen in a border of unthrifty grass—here, with a view from its front windows adown this not very enlivening prospect, and thence across the harbour, stands a spacious edifice of brick. From the loftiest point of its roof, during precisely three and a half hours of each forenoon, floats or droops, in breeze or calm, the banner of the republic; but with the thirteen stripes turned vertically, instead of horizontally, and thus indicating that a civil, and not a military, post of Uncle Sam's government is here established. Its front is ornamented with a portico of half-a-dozen wooden pillars, supporting a balcony, beneath which a flight of wide granite steps descends towards the street. Over the entrance hovers an enormous specimen of the American eagle, with outspread wings, a shield before her breast, and, if I recollect aright, a bunch of intermingled thunderbolts and barbed arrows in each claw. With the customary infirmity of temper that characterizes this unhappy fowl, she appears by the fierceness of her beak and eye, and the general truculency of her attitude, to threaten mischief to the inoffensive community; and especially to warn all citizens careful of their safety against intruding on the premises which she overshadows with her wings. Nevertheless, vixenly as she looks, many people are seeking at this very moment to shelter themselves under the wing of the federal eagle; imagining, I presume, that her bosom has all the softness and snugness of an eiderdown pillow. But she has no great tenderness even in her best of moods, and, sooner or later—oftener soon than late—is apt to fling off her nestlings with a scratch of her claw, a dab of her beak, or a rankling wound from her barbed arrows.

The pavement round about the above-described edifice—which we may as well name at once as the Custom-House of the port—has grass enough growing in its chinks to show that it has not, of late days, been worn by any multitudinous resort of business. In some months of the year, however, there often chances a forenoon when affairs move onward with a livelier tread. Such occasions might remind the elderly citizen of that period, before **the last war with England**, when Salem was a port by itself; not scorned, as she is now, by her own merchants and ship-owners, who permit her wharves to crumble to ruin while their ventures go to swell, needlessly and imperceptibly, the mighty flood of commerce at New York or Boston. On some such morning, when three or four vessels

old King Derby: Elias Hasket Derby (1739–1799) was a merchant who established American trade with India and China, for which Salem was famous in the 18th century.

the last war with England: War of 1812.

happen to have arrived at once,—usually from Africa or South America,—or to be on the verge of their departure thitherward, there is a sound of frequent feet passing briskly up and down the granite steps. Here, before his own wife has greeted him, you may greet the sea-flushed shipmaster, just in port, with his vessel's papers under his arm in a tarnished tin box. Here, too, comes his owner, cheerful, sombre, gracious or in the sulks, accordingly as his scheme of the now accomplished voyage has been realized in merchandise that will readily be turned to gold, or has buried him under a bulk of incommodities such as nobody will care to rid him of. Here, likewise,—the germ of the wrinkle-browed, grizzly-bearded, careworn merchant,—we have the smart young clerk, who gets the taste of traffic as a wolf-cub does of blood, and already sends adventures in his master's ships, when he had better be sailing mimic boats upon a mill-pond. Another figure in the scene is the outward-bound sailor, in quest of a protection; or the recently arrived one, pale and feeble, seeking a passport to the hospital. Nor must we forget the captains of the rusty little schooners that bring firewood from the British provinces; a rough-looking set of tarpaulins, without the alertness of the Yankee aspect, but contributing an item of no slight importance to our decaying trade.

Cluster all these individuals together, as they sometimes were, with other miscellaneous ones to diversify the group, and, for the time being, it made the Custom-House a stirring scene. More frequently, however, on ascending the steps, you would discern—in the entry, if it were summer time, or in their appropriate rooms if wintry or inclement weather—a row of venerable figures, sitting in old-fashioned chairs, which were tipped on their hind legs back against the wall. Oftentimes they were asleep, but occasionally might be heard talking together, in voices between a speech and a snore, and with that lack of energy that distinguishes the occupants of almshouses, and all other human beings who depend for subsistence on charity, on monopolized labour, or anything else but their own independent exertions. These old gentlemen—seated, like **Matthew** at the receipt of custom, but not very liable to be summoned thence, like him, for apostolic errands—were Custom-House officers.

Matthew: The apostle Matthew left his job as a tax collector after receiving a calling from Christ.

Furthermore, on the left hand as you enter the front door, is a certain room or office, about fifteen feet square, and of a lofty height, with two of its arched windows commanding a view of the aforesaid dilapidated wharf, and the third looking across a narrow lane, and along a portion of Derby Street. All three give glimpses of the shops of grocers, block-makers, slop-sellers, and ship-chandlers; around the doors of which are generally to be seen, laughing and gossiping, clusters of old salts, and such other wharf-rats as haunt the **Wapping** of a seaport. The room itself is cobwebbed, and dingy with old paint; its floor is strewn with grey sand, in a fashion that has elsewhere fallen into long disuse; and it is easy to conclude, from the general slovenliness of the place, that this is a sanctuary into which womankind, with her tools of magic, the broom and mop, has very infrequent access. In the way of furniture, there is a stove

Wapping: wharf district in London.

with a voluminous funnel; an old pine desk with a three-legged stool beside it; two or three wooden-bottom chairs, exceedingly decrepit and infirm; and—not to forget the library—on some shelves, a score or two of volumes of the Acts of Congress, and a bulky Digest of the Revenue Laws. A tin pipe ascends through the ceiling, and forms a medium of vocal communication with other parts of the edifice. And here, some six months ago,—pacing from corner to corner, or lounging on the long-legged tool, with his elbow on the desk, and his eyes wandering up and down the columns of the morning newspaper,—you might have recognised, honoured reader, the same individual who welcomed you into his cheery little study, where the sunshine glimmered so pleasantly through the willow branches on the western side of the Old Manse. But now, should you go thither to seek him, you would inquire in vain for the **Locofoco Surveyor**. The besom of reform hath swept him out of office, and a worthier successor wears his dignity, and pockets his emoluments.

This old town of Salem—my native place, though I have dwelt much away from it both in boyhood and maturer years—possesses, or did possess, a hold on my affection, the force of which I have never realized during my seasons of actual residence here. Indeed, so far as its physical aspect is concerned, with its flat, unvaried surface, covered chiefly with wooden houses, few or none of which pretend to architectural beauty—its irregularity, which is neither picturesque nor quaint, but only tame,—its long and lazy street, lounging wearisomely through the whole extent of the peninsula, with **Gallows Hill** and **New Guinea** at one end, and a view of the almshouse at the other,—such being the features of my native town, it would be quite as reasonable to form a sentimental attachment to a disarranged checker-board. And yet, though invariably happiest elsewhere, there is within me a feeling for Old Salem, which, in lack of a better phrase, I must be content to call affection. The sentiment is probably assignable to the deep and aged roots which my family has stuck into the soil. It is now nearly two centuries and a quarter since the original Briton, the earliest emigrant of my name, made his appearance in the wild and forest-bordered settlement which has since become a city. And here his descendants have been born and died, and have mingled their earthly substance with the soil, until no small portion of it must necessarily be akin to the mortal frame wherewith, for a little while, I walk the streets. In part, therefore, the attachment which I speak of is the mere sensuous sympathy of dust for dust. Few of my countrymen can know what it is; nor, as frequent transplantation is perhaps better for the stock, need they consider it desirable to know.

But the sentiment has likewise its moral quality. The figure of **that first ancestor**, invested by family tradition with a dim and dusky grandeur, was present to my boyish imagination as far back as I can remember. It still haunts me, and induces a sort of home-feeling with the past, which I scarcely claim in reference to the present phase of the town. I seem to have a stronger claim to a residence here on account of this grave, bearded, sable-cloaked, and steeple-crowned progenitor,—who came so

Locofoco Surveyor: The Locofocos were a radical wing of the Democratic party in the U.S. (c. 1835). Their name refers to a type of self-lighting matches used to light candles extinguished by another faction.

Gallows Hill: a hill in Salem where witches were probably hung following the witch trials of 1692.

New Guinea: a derogatory expression used to designate an area in Salem where immigrants from South Europe had settled.

that first ancestor: William Hathorne (1607–1681), who emigrated to America in 1630 with the founding members of the Massachusetts Bay Colony.

early, with his Bible and his sword, and trode the unworn street with such a stately port, and made so large a figure, as a man of war and peace,—a stronger claim than for myself, whose name is seldom heard and my face hardly known. He was a soldier, legislator, judge; he was a ruler in the Church; he had all the Puritanic traits, both good and evil. He was likewise a bitter persecutor; as witness **the Quakers**, who have remembered him in their histories, and relate an incident of his hard severity towards a woman of their sect, which will last longer, it is to be feared, than any record of his better deeds, although these were many. His son, too, inherited the persecuting spirit, and made himself so conspicuous in the martyrdom of the witches, that their blood may fairly be said to have left a stain upon him. So deep a stain, indeed, that his dry old bones, in the Charter-street burial-ground, must still retain it, if they have not crumbled utterly to dust! I know not whether these ancestors of mine bethought themselves to repent, and ask pardon of Heaven for their cruelties; or whether they are now groaning under the heavy consequences of them in another state of being. At all events, I, the present writer, as their representative, hereby take shame upon myself for their sakes, and pray that any curse incurred by them—as I have heard, and as the dreary and unprosperous condition of the race, for many a long year back, would argue to exist—may be now and henceforth removed.

Doubtless, however, either of these stern and black-browed Puritans would have thought it quite a sufficient retribution for his sins that, after so long a lapse of years, the old trunk of the family tree, with so much venerable moss upon it, should have borne, as its topmost bough, an idler like myself. No aim that I have ever cherished would they recognise as laudable; no success of mine—if my life, beyond its domestic scope, had ever been brightened by success—would they deem otherwise than worthless, if not positively disgraceful. "What is he?" murmurs one grey shadow of my forefathers to the other. "A writer of story books! What kind of business in life—what mode of glorifying God, or being serviceable to mankind in his day and generation—may that be? Why, the degenerate fellow might as well have been a fiddler!" Such are the compliments bandied between my great grandsires and myself, across the gulf of time And yet, let them scorn me as they will, strong traits of their nature have intertwined themselves with mine.

Planted deep, in the town's earliest infancy and childhood, by these two earnest and energetic men, the race has ever since subsisted here; always, too, in respectability; never, so far as I have known, disgraced by a single unworthy member; but seldom or never, on the other hand, after the first two generations, performing any memorable deed, or so much as putting forward a claim to public notice. Gradually, they have sunk almost out of sight; as old houses, here and there about the streets, get covered half-way to the eaves by the accumulation of new soil. From father to son, for above a hundred years, they followed the sea; a grey-headed shipmaster, in each generation, retiring from the quarter-deck to the homestead, while a boy of fourteen took the hereditary place before the mast, confronting the

the Quakers: also called the Society of Friends. A Christian denomination founded in England around 1650 by George Fox, the Quakers have no formal creed, rites, liturgy, or priesthood; and reject violence in human relations, including war. The first Quakers came to Massachusetts in 1656.

salt spray and the gale which had blustered against his sire and grandsire. The boy, also in due time, passed from the forecastle to the cabin, spent a tempestuous manhood, and returned from his world-wanderings, to grow old, and die, and mingle his dust with the natal earth. This long connexion of a family with one spot, as its place of birth and burial, creates a kindred between the human being and the locality, quite independent of any charm in the scenery or moral circumstances that surround him. It is not love but instinct. The new inhabitant—who came himself from a foreign land, or whose father or grandfather came—has little claim to be called a Salemite; he has no conception of the oyster-like tenacity with which an old settler, over whom his third century is creeping, clings to the spot where his successive generations have been embedded. It is no matter that the place is joyless for him; that he is weary of the old wooden houses, the mud and dust, the dead level of site and sentiment, the chill east wind, and the chillest of social atmospheres,—all these, and whatever faults besides he may see or imagine, are nothing to the purpose. The spell survives, and just as powerfully as if the natal spot were an earthly paradise. So has it been in my case. I felt it almost as a destiny to make Salem my home; so that the mould of features and cast of character which had all along been familiar here—ever, as one representative of the race lay down in the grave, another assuming, as it were, his sentry-march along the main street—might still in my little day be seen and recognised in the old town. Nevertheless, this very sentiment is an evidence that the connexion, which has become an unhealthy one, should at last be severed. Human nature will not flourish, any more than a potato, if it be planted and replanted, for too long a series of generations, in the same worn-out soil. My children have had other birthplaces, and, so far as their fortunes may be within my control, shall strike their roots into accustomed earth.

On emerging from the Old Manse, it was chiefly this strange, indolent, unjoyous attachment for my native town that brought me to fill a place in Uncle Sam's brick edifice, when I might as well, or better, have gone somewhere else. My doom was on me. It was not the first time, nor the second, that I had gone away—as it seemed, permanently—but yet returned, like the bad halfpenny, or as if Salem were for me the inevitable centre of the universe. So, one fine morning I ascended the flight of granite steps, with the President's commission in my pocket, and was introduced to the corps of gentlemen who were to aid me in my weighty responsibility as chief executive officer of the Custom-House.

I doubt greatly—or, rather, I do not doubt at all—whether any public functionary of the United States, either in the civil or military line, has ever had such a patriarchal body of veterans under his orders as myself. The whereabouts of the Oldest Inhabitant was at once settled when I looked at them. For upwards of twenty years before this epoch, the independent position of the Collector had kept the Salem Custom-House out of the whirlpool of political vicissitude, which makes the tenure of office generally so fragile. **A soldier,**—New England's most distinguished soldier,—he stood firmly on the pedestal of his gallant services; and,

A soldier: General James F. Miller (1776–1851), who ran the custom house in Salem from 1825–1849.

himself secure in the wise liberality of the successive administrations
through which he had held office, he had been the safety of his subordi-
nates in many an hour of danger and heart-quake. General Miller was
radically conservative; a man over whose kindly nature habit had no
slight influence; attaching himself strongly to familiar faces, and with difficulty moved to change, even when change might have brought unquestionable improvement. Thus, on taking charge of my department, I
found few but aged men. They were ancient sea-captains, for the most
part, who, after being tossed on every sea, and standing up sturdily
against life's tempestuous blast, had finally drifted into this quiet nook,
where, with little to disturb them, except the periodical terrors of a Presi-
dential election, they one and all acquired a new lease of existence.
Though by no means less liable than their fellow-men to age and infirmity, they had evidently some talisman or other that kept death at bay.
Two or three of their number, as I was assured, being gouty and rheumatic, or perhaps bed-ridden, never dreamed of making their appearance
at the Custom-House during a large part of the year; but, after a torpid
winter, would creep out into the warm sunshine of May or June, go lazily
about what they termed duty, and, at their own leisure and convenience,
betake themselves to bed again. I must plead guilty to the charge of
abbreviating the official breath of more than one of these venerable servants of the republic. They were allowed, on my representation, to rest
from their arduous labours, and soon afterwards—as if their sole principle
of life had been zeal for their country's service—as I verily believe it was—
withdrew to a better world. It is a pious consolation to me that, through
my interference, a sufficient space was allowed them for repentance of the
evil and corrupt practices into which, as a matter of course, every Custom-
House officer must be supposed to fall. Neither the front nor the back
entrance of the Custom-House opens on the road to Paradise.

The greater part of my officers were **Whigs**. It was well for their venerable brotherhood that the new Surveyor was not a politician, and though a
faithful Democrat in principle, neither received nor held his office with
any reference to political services. Had it been otherwise—had an active
politician been put into this influential post, to assume the easy task of
making head against a Whig Collector, whose infirmities withheld him
from the personal administration of his office—hardly a man of the old
corps would have drawn the breath of official life within a month after
the exterminating angel had come up the Custom-House steps. According to the received code in such matters, it would have been nothing
short of duty, in a politician, to bring every one of those white heads
under the axe of the guillotine. It was plain enough to discern that the
old fellows dreaded some such discourtesy at my hands. It pained, and at
the same time amused me, to behold the terrors that attended my advent,
to see a furrowed cheek, weather-beaten by half a century of storm, turn
ashy pale at the glance of so harmless an individual as myself; to detect,
as one or another addressed me, the tremor of a voice which, in long-past
days, had been wont to bellow through a speaking-trumpet, hoarsely
enough to frighten **Boreas** himself to silence. They knew, these excellent

Whigs: members of an American party (c. 1834–1856) opposing the Democratic Party and advocating protection of industry and limitation of the power of the executive branch of the government.

Boreas: god of the north wind.

old persons, that, by all established rule—and, as regarded some of them, weighed by their own lack of efficiency for business—they ought to have given place to younger men, more orthodox in politics, and altogether fitter than themselves to serve our common Uncle. I knew it, too, but could never quite find in my heart to act upon the knowledge. Much and deservedly to my own discredit, therefore, and considerably to the detriment of my official conscience, they continued, during my incumbency, to creep about the wharves, and loiter up and down the Custom-House steps. They spent a good deal of time, also, asleep in their accustomed corners, with their chairs tilted back against the walls; awaking, however, once or twice in the forenoon, to bore one another with the several thousandth repetition of old sea-stories and mouldy jokes, that had grown to be passwords and countersigns among them.

The discovery was soon made, I imagine, that the new Surveyor had no great harm in him. So, with lightsome hearts and the happy consciousness of being usefully employed—in their own behalf at least, if not for our beloved country—these good old gentlemen went through the various formalities of office. Sagaciously under their spectacles, did they peep into the holds of vessels! Mighty was their fuss about little matters, and marvellous, sometimes, the obtuseness that allowed greater ones to slip between their fingers! Whenever such a mischance occurred—when a waggon-load of valuable merchandise had been smuggled ashore, at noonday, perhaps, and directly beneath their unsuspicious noses—nothing could exceed the vigilance and alacrity with which they proceeded to lock, and double-lock, and secure with tape and sealing-wax, all the avenues of the delinquent vessel. Instead of a reprimand for their previous negligence, the case seemed rather to require an eulogium on their praiseworthy caution after the mischief had happened; a grateful recognition of the promptitude of their zeal the moment that there was no longer any remedy.

Unless people are more than commonly disagreeable, it is my foolish habit to contract a kindness for them. The better part of my companion's character, if it have a better part, is that which usually comes uppermost in my regard, and forms the type whereby I recognise the man. As most of these old Custom-House officers had good traits, and as my position in reference to them, being paternal and protective, was favourable to the growth of friendly sentiments, I soon grew to like them all. It was pleasant in the summer forenoons—when the fervent heat, that almost liquefied the rest of the human family, merely communicated a genial warmth to their half torpid systems—it was pleasant to hear them chatting in the back entry, a row of them all tipped against the wall, as usual; while the frozen witticisms of past generations were thawed out, and came bubbling with laughter from their lips. Externally, the jollity of aged men has much in common with the mirth of children; the intellect, any more than a deep sense of humour, has little to do with the matter; it is, with both, a gleam that plays upon the surface, and imparts a sunny and cheery aspect alike to the green branch and grey, mouldering trunk. In one case, however, it is real sunshine; in the other, it more resembles the phosphorescent glow of decaying wood.

It would be sad injustice, the reader must understand, to represent all my excellent old friends as in their dotage. In the first place, my coadjutors were not invariably old; there were men among them in their strength and prime, of marked ability and energy, and altogether superior to the sluggish and dependent mode of life on which their evil stars had cast them. Then, moreover, the white locks of age were sometimes found to be the thatch of an intellectual tenement in good repair. But, as respects the majority of my corps of veterans, there will be no wrong done if I characterize them generally as a set of wearisome old souls, who had gathered nothing worth preservation from their varied experience of life. They seemed to have flung away all the golden grain of practical wisdom, which they had enjoyed so many opportunities of harvesting, and most carefully to have stored their memory with the husks. They spoke with far more interest and unction of their morning's breakfast, or yesterday's, to-day's, or tomorrow's dinner, than of the shipwreck of forty or fifty years ago, and all the world's wonders which they had witnessed with their youthful eyes.

The father of the Custom-House—the patriarch, not only of this little squad of officials, but, I am bold to say, of the respectable body of tide-waiters all over the United States—was a certain permanent Inspector. He might truly be termed a legitimate son of the revenue system, dyed in the wool, or rather born in the purple; since his sire, a Revolutionary colonel, and formerly collector of the port, had created an office for him, and appointed him to fill it, at a period of the early ages which few living men can now remember. This Inspector, when I first knew him, was a man of fourscore years, or thereabouts, and certainly one of the most wonderful specimens of winter-green that you would be likely to discover in a lifetime's search. With his florid cheek, his compact figure smartly arrayed in a bright-buttoned blue coat, his brisk and vigorous step, and his hale and hearty aspect, altogether he seemed—not young, indeed—but a kind of new contrivance of Mother Nature in the shape of man, whom age and infirmity had no business to touch. His voice and laugh, which perpetually re-echoed through the Custom-House, had nothing of the tremulous quaver and cackle of an old man's utterance; they came strutting out of his lungs, like the crow of a cock, or the blast of a clarion. Looking at him merely as an animal—and there was very little else to look at—he was a most satisfactory object, from the thorough healthful-ness and wholesomeness of his system, and his capacity, at that extreme age, to enjoy all, or nearly all, the delights which he had ever aimed at or conceived of. The careless security of his life in the Custom-House, on a regular income, and with but slight and infrequent apprehensions of removal, had no doubt contributed to make time pass lightly over him. The original and more potent causes, however, lay in the rare perfection of his animal nature, the moderate proportion of intellect, and the very trifling admixture of moral and spiritual ingredients; these latter qualities, indeed, being in barely enough measure to keep the old gentleman from walking on all-fours. He possessed no power of thought no depth of feeling, no troublesome sensibilities: nothing, in short, but a few commonplace instincts, which, aided by the cheerful temper which grew inevitably out of his physical well-being, did duty very respectably, and to general acceptance, in lieu of a heart. He had been the husband of three wives, all long since dead; the father of twenty children, most of whom, at every age of childhood or maturity, had likewise returned to dust. Here, one would suppose, might have been sorrow enough to imbue the sunniest disposition through and through with a sable tinge. Not so with our old Inspector! One brief sigh sufficed to carry off the entire burden of these dismal reminiscences. The next moment he was as ready for sport as any unbreeched infant: far readier than the Collector's junior clerk, who at nineteen years was much the elder and graver man of the two.

I used to watch and study this patriarchal personage with, I think, livelier curiosity than any other form of humanity there presented to my notice. He was, in truth, a rare phenomenon; so perfect, in one point of view; so shallow, so delusive, so impalpable such an absolute nonentity, in every other. My conclusion was that he had no soul, no heart, no mind; nothing, as I have already said, but instincts; and yet, withal, so cunningly had the few materials of his character been put together that there was no painful perception of deficiency, but, on my part, an entire contentment with what I found in him. It might be difficult—and it was so—to conceive how he should exist hereafter, so earthly and sensuous did he seem; but surely his existence here, admitting that it was to terminate with his last breath, had been not unkindly given; with no higher moral responsibilities than the beasts of the field, but with a larger scope of enjoyment than theirs, and with all their blessed immunity from the dreariness and duskiness of age.

One point in which he had vastly the advantage over his four-footed brethren was his ability to recollect the good dinners which it had made no small portion of the happiness of his life to eat. His gourmandism was a highly agreeable trait; and to hear him talk of roast meat was as appetizing as a pickle or an oyster. As he possessed no higher attribute, and neither sacrificed nor vitiated any spiritual endowment by devoting all his energies and ingenuities to subserve the delight and profit of his maw, it always pleased and satisfied me to hear him expatiate on fish, poultry, and butcher's meat, and the most eligible methods of preparing them for the table. His reminiscences of good cheer, however ancient the date of the actual banquet, seemed to bring the savour of pig or turkey under one's very nostrils. There were flavours on his palate that had lingered there not less than sixty or seventy years, and were still apparently as fresh as that of the mutton chop which he had just devoured for his breakfast. I have heard him smack his lips over dinners, every guest at which, except himself, had long been food for worms. It was marvellous to observe how the ghosts of bygone meals were continually rising up before him—not in anger or retribution, but as if grateful for his former appreciation, and seeking to repudiate an endless series of enjoyment, at once shadowy and sensual. A tender loin of beef, a hind-quarter of veal, a spare-rib of pork, a particular chicken, or a remarkably praiseworthy turkey, which had perhaps adorned his board in the days of **the elder Adams**, would be remembered; while all the subsequent experience of our race, and all the events that brightened or darkened his individual career, had gone over him with as little permanent effect as the passing breeze. The chief tragic event of the old man's life, so far as I could judge, was his mishap with a certain goose, which lived and died some twenty or forty years ago: a goose of most promising figure, but which, at table, proved so inveterately tough, that the carving-knife would make no impression on its carcase, and it could only be divided with an axe and handsaw.

the elder Adams: John Adams (1735–1826), the second president of the U.S.

But it is time to quit this sketch; on which, however, I should be glad to dwell at considerably more length, because of all men whom I have ever known, this individual was fittest to be a Custom-House officer. Most persons, owing to causes which I may not have space to hint at, suffer moral detriment from this peculiar mode of life. The old Inspector was incapable of it; and, were he to continue in office to the end of time, would be just as good as he was then, and sit down to dinner with just as good an appetite.

There is one likeness, without which my gallery of Custom-House portraits would be strangely incomplete, but which my comparatively few opportunities for observation enable me to sketch only in the merest outline. It is that of the Collector, our gallant old General, who, after his brilliant military service, subsequently to which he had ruled over a wild Western territory, had come hither, twenty years before, to spend the decline of his varied and honourable life.

The brave soldier had already numbered, nearly or quite, his three-score years and ten, and was pursuing the remainder of his earthly march, burdened with infirmities which even the martial music of his own spirit-stirring recollections could do little towards lightening. The step was palsied now, that had been foremost in the charge. It was only with the assistance of a servant, and by leaning his hand heavily on the iron balustrade, that he could slowly and painfully ascend the Custom-House steps, and, with a toilsome progress across the floor, attain his customary chair beside the fireplace. There he used to sit, gazing with a somewhat dim serenity of aspect at the figures that came and went, amid the rustle of papers, the administering of oaths, the discussion of business, and the casual talk of the office; all which sounds and circumstances seemed but indistinctly to impress his senses, and hardly to make their way into his inner sphere of contemplation. His countenance, in this repose, was mild and kindly. If his notice was sought, an expression of courtesy and interest gleamed out upon his features, proving that there was light within him, and that it was only the outward medium of the intellectual lamp that obstructed the rays in their passage. The closer you penetrated to the substance of his mind, the sounder it appeared. When no longer called upon to speak or listen—either of which operations cost him an evident effort—his face would briefly subside into its former not uncheerful quietude. It was not painful to behold this look; for, though dim, it had not the imbecility of decaying age. The framework of his nature, originally strong and massive, was not yet crumpled into ruin.

To observe and define his character, however, under such disadvantages, was as difficult a task as to trace out and build up anew, in imagination, an old fortress, like **Ticonderoga**, from a view of its grey and broken ruins. Here and there, perchance, the walls may remain almost complete; but elsewhere may be only a shapeless mound, cumbrous with its very strength, and overgrown, through long years of peace and neglect, with grass and alien weeds.

Ticonderoga: a former fort in northeast New York, taken from the British by the Green Mountain Boys, under the leadership of Ethan Allen, in 1775.

Nevertheless, looking at the old warrior with affection,—for, slight as was the communication between us, my feeling towards him, like that of all bipeds and quadrupeds who knew him, might not improperly be termed so,—I could discern the main points of his portrait. It was marked with the noble and heroic qualities which showed it to be not a mere accident, but of good right, that he had won a distinguished name. His spirit could never, I conceive, have been characterized by an uneasy activity; it must, at any period of his life, have required an impulse to set him in motion; but once stirred up, with obstacles to overcome, and an adequate object to be attained, it was not in the man to give out or fail. The heat that had formerly pervaded his nature, and which was not yet extinct, was never of the kind that flashes and flickers in a blaze; but rather a deep red glow, as of iron in a furnace. Weight, solidity, firmness—this was the expression of his repose, even in such decay as had crept untimely over him at the period of which I speak. But I could imagine, even then, that, under some excitement which should go deeply into his consciousness—roused by a trumpet-peal, loud enough to awaken all of his energies that were not dead, but only slumbering—he was yet capable of flinging off his infirmities like a sick man's gown, dropping the staff of age to seize a battle-sword, and starting up once more a warrior. And, in so intense a moment his demeanour would have still been calm. Such an exhibition, however, was but to be pictured in fancy; not to be anticipated, nor desired. What I saw in him—as evidently as the indestructible ramparts of Old Ticonderoga, already cited as the most appropriate simile—were the features of stubborn and ponderous endurance, which might well have amounted to obstinacy in his earlier days; of integrity, that, like most of his other endowments, lay in a somewhat heavy mass, and was just as unmalleable or unmanageable as a ton of iron ore; and of benevolence, which, fiercely as he led the bayonets on at **Chippewa or Fort Erie**, I take to be of quite as genuine a stamp as what actuates any or all the polemical philanthropists of the age. He had slain men with his own hand, for aught I know—certainly, they had fallen like blades of grass at the sweep of the scythe before the charge to which his spirit imparted its triumphant energy—but, be that as it might, there was never in his heart so much cruelty as would have brushed the down off a butterfly's wing. I have not known the man to whose innate kindliness I would more confidently make an appeal.

Chippewa or Fort Erie: During the War of 1812, American forces crossed the Niagara River to Canada and defeated the British in the Battle of Chippewa. They occupied Fort Erie for a few months before returning to the U.S.

Many characteristics—and those, too, which contribute not the least forcibly to impart resemblance in a sketch—must have vanished, or been obscured, before I met the General. All merely graceful attributes are usually the most evanescent; nor does nature adorn the human ruin with blossoms of new beauty, that have their roots and proper nutriment only in the chinks and crevices of decay, as she sows wallflowers over the ruined fortress of Ticonderoga. Still, even in respect of grace and beauty, there were points well worth noting. A ray of humour, now and then, would make its way through the veil of dim obstruction, and glimmer pleasantly upon our faces. A trait of native elegance, seldom seen in the masculine character after childhood or early youth, was shown in the General's fondness for the sight and fragrance of flowers. An old soldier might be supposed to prize only the bloody laurel on his brow; but here was one who seemed to have a young girl's appreciation of the floral tribe.

There, beside the fireplace, the brave old General used to sit; while the Surveyor—though seldom, when it could be avoided, taking upon himself the difficult task of engaging him in conversation—was fond of standing at a distance, and watching his quiet and almost slumberous countenance. He seemed away from us, although we saw him but a few yards off; remote, though we passed close beside his chair; unattainable, though we might have stretched forth our hands and touched his own. It might be that he lived a more real life within his thoughts than amid the unappropriate environment of the Collector's office. The evolutions of the parade; the tumult of the battle; the flourish of old heroic music, heard thirty years before—such scenes and sounds, perhaps, were all alive before his intellectual sense. Meanwhile, the merchants and ship-masters, the spruce clerks and uncouth sailors, entered and departed; the bustle of his commercial and Custom-House life kept up its little murmur round about him; and neither with the men nor their affairs did the General appear to sustain the most distant relation. He was as much out of place as an old sword—now rusty, but which had flashed once in the battle's front, and showed still a bright gleam along its blade—would have been among the inkstands, paper-folders, and mahogany rulers on the Deputy Collector's desk.

There was one thing that much aided me in renewing and re-creating the stalwart soldier of the Niagara frontier—the man of true and simple energy. It was the recollection of those memorable words of his,—"I'll try, Sir!"—spoken on the very verge of a desperate and heroic enterprise, and breathing the soul and spirit of New England hardihood, comprehending all perils, and encountering all. If, in our country, valour were rewarded by heraldic honour, this phrase—which it seems so easy to speak, but which only he, with such a task of danger and glory before him, has ever spoken—would be the best and fittest of all mottoes for the General's shield of arms.

It contributes greatly towards a man's moral and intellectual health to be brought into habits of companionship with individuals unlike himself, who care little for his pursuits, and whose sphere and abilities he must go out of himself to appreciate. The accidents of my life have often afforded me this advantage, but never with more fulness and variety than during my continuance in office. There was one man, especially, the observation of whose character gave me a new idea of talent. His gifts were emphatically those of a man of business; prompt, acute, clear-minded; with an eye that saw through all perplexities, and a faculty of arrangement that made them vanish as by the waving of an enchanter's wand. Bred up from boyhood in the Custom-House, it was his proper field of activity; and the many intricacies of business, so harassing to the interloper, presented themselves before him with the regularity of a perfectly comprehended system. In my contemplation, he stood as the ideal of his class. He was, indeed, the Custom-House in himself; or, at all events, the mainspring that kept its variously revolving wheels in motion; for, in an institution like this, where its officers are appointed to subserve their own profit and convenience, and seldom with a leading reference to their fitness for the duty to be performed, they must perforce seek elsewhere the dexterity which is not in them. Thus, by an inevitable necessity, as a magnet attracts steel-filings, so did our man of business draw to himself the difficulties which everybody met with. With an easy condescension, and kind forbearance towards our stupidity—which, to his order of mind, must have seemed little short of crime—would he forth-with, by the merest touch of his finger, make the incomprehensible as clear as daylight. The merchants valued him not less than we, his esoteric friends. His integrity was perfect; it was a law of nature with him, rather than a choice or a principle; nor can it be otherwise than the main condition of an intellect so remarkably clear and accurate as his to be honest and regular in the administration of affairs. A stain on his conscience, as to anything that came within the range of his vocation, would trouble such a man very much in the same way, though to a far greater degree, than an error in the balance of an account, or an ink-blot on the fair page of a book of record. Here, in a word—and it is a rare instance in my life—I had met with a person thoroughly adapted to the situation which he held.

Such were some of the people with whom I now found myself connected. I took it in good part, at the hands of Providence, that I was thrown into a position so little akin to my past habits; and set myself seriously to gather from it whatever profit was to be had. After my fellowship of toil and impracticable schemes with the dreamy brethren of **Brook Farm**; after living for three years within the subtle influence of an intellect like **Emerson's**; after those wild, free days on the **Assabeth**, indulging fantastic speculations, beside our fire of fallen boughs, with **Ellery Channing**; after talking with **Thoreau** about pine-trees and Indian relics in his hermitage at **Walden**; after growing fastidious by sympathy with the classic refinement of **Hilliard's** culture; after becoming imbued with poetic sentiment at **Longfellow's** hearthstone—it was time, at length, that I should exercise other faculties of my nature, and nourish myself with food for which I had hitherto had little appetite. Even the old Inspector was

Brook Farm: a utopian commune in Massachusetts established by George Ripley, a Unitarian minister. Hawthorne lived there briefly but became disenchanted and left. His novel *The Blithedale Romance* is based on his experiences there.

Emerson's: Ralph Waldo Emerson (1803–1882), an American essayist, philosopher, and poet who was a leader in the transcendentalist movement.

Assabeth: a river near Concord.

Ellery Channing: Channing (1818–1901) was a moody transcendentalist poet and clergyman.

Thoreau: Henry David Thoreau (1817–1862) was a naturalist influenced by Emerson and the transcendentalists. He is best known for his book *Walden, or Life in the Woods* (1854), published after his two-year stay alone at Walden Pond, near Concord.

Walden: the site of Thoreau's cabin, the place where he wrote *Walden* in 1854.

Hilliard's: George Stillman Hillard (1808–1879) was a Boston lawyer and writer. Hilliard tried to help Hawthorne maintain his position at the custom house.

Longfellow's: Henry Wadsworth Longfellow (1807–1882) was a popular poet during Hawthorne's lifetime. He attended Bowdoin College in Maine with Hawthorne.

desirable, as a change of diet, to a man who had known **Alcott**. I looked upon it as an evidence, in some measure, of a system naturally well balanced, and lacking no essential part of a thorough organization, that, with such associates to remember, I could mingle at once with men of altogether different qualities, and never murmur at the change.

Literature, its exertions and objects, were now of little moment in my regard. I cared not at this period for books; they were apart from me. Nature,—except it were human nature,—the nature that is developed in earth and sky, was, in one sense, hidden from me; and all the imaginative delight wherewith it had been spiritualized passed away out of my mind. A gift, a faculty, if it had not been departed, was suspended and inanimate within me. There would have been something sad, unutterably dreary, in all this, had I not been conscious that it lay at my own option to recall whatever was valuable in the past. It might be true, indeed, that this was a life which could not, with impunity, be lived too long; else, it might make me permanently other than I had been, without transforming me into any shape which it would be worth my while to take. But I never considered it as other than a transitory life. There was always a prophetic instinct, a low whisper in my ear, that within no long period, and whenever a new change of custom should be essential to my good, change would come.

Meanwhile, there I was, a Surveyor of the Revenue, and, so far as I have been able to understand, as good a Surveyor as need be. A man of thought, fancy, and sensibility (had he ten times the Surveyor's proportion of those qualities), may, at any time, be a man of affairs, if he will only choose to give himself the trouble. My fellow-officers, and the merchants and sea-captains with whom my official duties brought me into any manner of connection, viewed me in no other light, and probably knew me in no other character. None of them, I presume, had ever read a page of my inditing, or would have cared a fig the more for me if they had read them all; nor would it have mended the matter, in the least, had those same unprofitable pages been written with a pen like that of **Burns or of Chaucer**, each of whom was a Custom-House officer in his day, as well as I. It is a good lesson—though it may often be a hard one—for a man who has dreamed of literary fame, and of making for himself a rank among the world's dignitaries by such means, to step aside out of the narrow circle in which his claims are recognized and to find how utterly devoid of significance, beyond that circle, is all that he achieves, and all he aims at. I know not that I especially needed the lesson, either in the way of warning or rebuke; but at any rate, I learned it thoroughly: nor, it gives me pleasure to reflect, did the truth, as it came home to my perception, ever cost me a pang, or require to be thrown off in a sigh. In the way of literary talk, it is true, the Naval Officer—an excellent fellow, who came into the office with me, and went out only a little later—would often engage me in a discussion about one or the other of his favourite topics, Napoleon or Shakespeare. The Collector's junior clerk, too,—a young gentleman who, it was whispered occasionally covered a sheet of Uncle Sam's letter paper with what (at the distance of a few yards) looked

Alcott: Amos Bronson Alcott (1799–1888) was called "the most transcendental of the Transcendentalists." An eccentric writer and educator, he was the father of Louisa May Alcott.

Burns or of Chaucer: Robert Burns (1759–1796) and Geoffrey Chaucer (1343–1400) were both poets who also worked as tax collectors, just as Hawthorne did.

very much like poetry—used now and then to speak to me of books, as matters with which I might possibly be conversant. This was my all of lettered intercourse; and it was quite sufficient for my necessities.

No longer seeking or caring that my name should be blasoned abroad on title-pages, I smiled to think that it had now another kind of vogue. The Custom-House marker imprinted it, with a stencil and black paint, on pepper-bags, and baskets of **anatto**, and cigar-boxes, and bales of all kinds of dutiable merchandise, in testimony that these commodities had paid the impost, and gone regularly through the office. Borne on such queer vehicle of fame, a knowledge of my existence, so far as a name conveys it, was carried where it had never been before, and, I hope, will never go again.

But the past was not dead. Once in a great while, the thoughts that had seemed so vital and so active, yet had been put to rest so quietly, revived again. One of the most remarkable occasions, when the habit of bygone days awoke in me, was that which brings it within the law of literary propriety to offer the public the sketch which I am now writing.

In the second storey of the Custom-House there is a large room, in which the brick-work and naked rafters have never been covered with panelling and plaster. The edifice—originally projected on a scale adapted to the old commercial enterprise of the port, and with an idea of subsequent prosperity destined never to be realized—contains far more space than its occupants know what to do with. This airy hall, therefore, over the Collector's apartments, remains unfinished to this day, and, in spite of the aged cobwebs that festoon its dusky beams, appears still to await the labour of the carpenter and mason. At one end of the room, in a recess, were a number of barrels piled one upon another, containing bundles of official documents. Large quantities of similar rubbish lay lumbering the floor. It was sorrowful to think how many days, and weeks, and months, and years of toil had been wasted on these musty papers, which were now only an encumbrance on earth, and were hidden away in this forgotten corner, never more to be glanced at by human eyes. But then, what reams of other manuscripts—filled, not with the dulness of official formalities, but with the thought of inventive brains and the rich effusion of deep hearts—had gone equally to oblivion; and that, moreover, without serving a purpose in their day, as these heaped-up papers had, and—saddest of all—without purchasing for their writers the comfortable livelihood which the clerks of the Custom-House had gained by these worthless scratchings of the pen. Yet not altogether worthless, perhaps, as materials of local history. Here, no doubt, statistics of the former commerce of Salem might be discovered, and memorials of her princely merchants—old King Derby,—**old Billy Gray**,—**old Simon Forrester**—and many another magnate in his day, whose powdered head, however, was scarcely in the tomb before his mountain pile of wealth began to dwindle. The founders of the greater part of the families which now compose the aristocracy of Salem might here be traced, from the petty and obscure beginnings of their traffic, at periods generally much posterior to the Revolution, upward to what their children look upon as long-established rank.

anatto: a reddish yellow dye used to color butter, cheese, varnishes, and so on.

old Billy Gray: William Gray (1750–1825), a successful Salem merchant, who owned a fleet of ships that traded with Russia, India, and China. He also served as lieutenant governor of Massachusetts.

old Simon Forrester: The richest man in Salem, Forrester (1748–1823) was a merchant and ship owner.

Prior to the Revolution there is a dearth of records; the earlier documents and archives of the Custom-House having, probably, been carried off to Halifax, when all the king's officials accompanied the British army in its flight from Boston. It has often been a matter of regret with me; for, going back, perhaps, to the days of **the Protectorate**, those papers must have contained many references to forgotten or remembered men, and to antique customs, which would have affected me with the same pleasure as when I used to pick up Indian arrow-heads in the field near the Old Manse.

But, one idle and rainy day, it was my fortune to make a discovery of some little interest. Poking and burrowing into the heaped-up rubbish in the corner, unfolding one and another document, and reading the names of vessels that had long ago foundered at sea or rotted at the wharves, and those of merchants never heard of now on **'Change**, nor very readily decipherable on their mossy tombstones; glancing at such matters with the saddened, weary, half-reluctant interest which we bestow on the corpse of dead activity,—and exerting my fancy, sluggish with little use, to raise up from these dry bones an image of the old town's brighter aspect, when India was a new region, and only Salem knew the way thither—I chanced to lay my hand on a small package, carefully done up in a piece of ancient yellow parchment. This envelope had the air of an official record of some period long past, when clerks engrossed their stiff and formal chirography on more substantial materials than at present. There was something about it that quickened an instinctive curiosity, and made me undo the faded red tape that tied up the package, with the sense that a treasure would here be brought to light. Unbending the rigid folds of the parchment cover, I found it to be a commission, under the hand and seal of **Governor Shirley**, in favour of one **Jonathan Pue**, as Surveyor of His Majesty's Customs for the Port of Salem, in the Province of Massachusetts Bay. I remembered to have read (probably in **Felt's "Annals"**) a notice of the decease of Mr. Surveyor Pue, about fourscore years ago; and likewise, in a newspaper of recent times, an account of the digging up of his remains in the little graveyard of St. Peter's Church, during the renewal of that edifice. Nothing, if I rightly call to mind, was left of my respected predecessor, save an imperfect skeleton, and some fragments of apparel, and a wig of majestic frizzle, which, unlike the head that it once adorned, was in very satisfactory preservation. But, on examining the papers which the parchment commission served to envelop, I found more traces of Mr. Pue's mental part, and the internal operations of his head, than the frizzled wig had contained of the venerable skull itself.

They were documents, in short, not official, but of a private nature, or, at least, written in his private capacity, and apparently with his own hand. I could account for their being included in the heap of Custom-House lumber only by the fact that Mr. Pue's death had happened suddenly, and that these papers, which he probably kept in his official desk, had never come to the knowledge of his heirs, or were supposed to relate to the business of the revenue. On the transfer of the archives to Halifax, this package, proving to be of no public concern, was left behind, and had remained ever since unopened.

the Protectorate: During the English interregnum (1653–1659), Oliver Cromwell served as the Lord Protectorate.

'Change: the Boston Merchants' Exchange.

Governor Shirley: William Shirley (1694–1771) served as colonial governor from 1741–1749 and from 1753–1756.

Jonathan Pue: According to Felt's *Annals of Salem,* Jonathan Pue became surveyor of the custom house in 1752.

Felt's "Annals": The Annals of Salem from its First Settlement (1827), published by Joseph B. Felt.

The ancient Surveyor—being little molested, I suppose, at that early day, with business pertaining to his office—seems to have devoted some of his many leisure hours to researches as a local antiquarian, and other inquisitions of a similar nature. These supplied material for petty activity to a mind that would otherwise have been eaten up with rust. A portion of his facts, by the by, did me good service in the preparation of the article entitled **"MAIN STREET,"** included in the present volume. The remainder may perhaps be applied to purposes equally valuable hereafter, or not impossibly may be worked up, so far as they go, into a regular history of Salem, should my veneration for the natal soil ever impel me to so pious a task. Meanwhile, they shall be at the command of any gentleman, inclined and competent, to take the unprofitable labour off my hands. As a final disposition, I contemplate depositing them with the **Essex Historical Society**.

But the object that most drew my attention to the mysterious package was a certain affair of fine red cloth, much worn and faded. There were traces about it of gold embroidery, which, however, was greatly frayed and defaced, so that none, or very little, of the glitter was left. It had been wrought, as was easy to perceive, with wonderful skill of needlework; and the stitch (as I am assured by ladies conversant with such mysteries) gives evidence of a now forgotten art, not to be discovered even by the process of picking out the threads. This rag of scarlet cloth—for time, and wear, and a sacrilegious moth had reduced it to little other than a rag—on careful examination, assumed the shape of a letter.

It was the capital letter A. By an accurate measurement, each limb proved to be precisely three inches and a quarter in length. It had been intended, there could be no doubt, as an ornamental article of dress; but how it was to be worn, or what rank, honour, and dignity, in by-past times, were signified by it, was a riddle which (so evanescent are the fashions of the world in these particulars) I saw little hope of solving. And yet it strangely interested me. My eyes fastened themselves upon the old scarlet letter, and would not be turned aside. Certainly there was some deep meaning in it most worthy of interpretation, and which, as it were, streamed forth from the mystic symbol, subtly communicating itself to my sensibilities, but evading the analysis of my mind.

While thus perplexed—and cogitating, among other hypotheses, whether the letter might not have been one of those decorations which the white men used to contrive in order to take the eyes of Indians—I happened to place it on my breast. It seemed to me—the reader may smile, but must not doubt my word—it seemed to me, then, that I experienced a sensation not altogether physical, yet almost so, as of burning heat, and as if the letter were not of red cloth, but red-hot iron. I shuddered, and involuntarily let it fall upon the floor.

In the absorbing contemplation of the scarlet letter, I had hitherto neglected to examine a small roll of dingy paper, around which it had been twisted. This I now opened, and had the satisfaction to find recorded by the old Surveyor's pen, a reasonably complete explanation of the whole

"MAIN STREET": a sketch written by Hawthorne that he meant to publish with *The Scarlet Letter* but, instead, published in *The Snow-Image* (1852).

Essex Historical Society: Begun in 1821, the society became the Essex Institute in 1848. The town of Salem is located in Essex County, Massachusetts.

affair. There were several foolscap sheets, containing many particulars respecting the life and conversation of one Hester Prynne, who appeared to have been rather a noteworthy personage in the view of our ancestors. She had flourished during the period between the early days of Massachusetts and the close of the seventeenth century. Aged persons, alive in the time of Mr. Surveyor Pue, and from whose oral testimony he had made up his narrative, remembered her, in their youth, as a very old, but not decrepit woman, of a stately and solemn aspect. It had been her habit, from an almost immemorial date, to go about the country as a kind of voluntary nurse, and doing whatever miscellaneous good she might; taking upon herself, likewise, to give advice in all matters, especially those of the heart, by which means—as a person of such propensities inevitably must—she gained from many people the reverence due to an angel, but, I should imagine, was looked upon by others as an intruder and a nuisance. Prying further into the manuscript, I found the record of other doings and sufferings of this singular woman, for most of which the reader is referred to the story entitled "The Scarlet Letter"; and it should be borne carefully in mind that the main facts of that story are authorized and authenticated by the document of Mr. Surveyor Pue. The original papers, together with the scarlet letter itself—a most curious relic—are still in my possession, and shall be freely exhibited to whomsoever, induced by the great interest of the narrative, may desire a sight of them. I must not be understood affirming that, in the dressing up of the tale, and imagining the motives and modes of passion that influenced the characters who figure in it, I have invariably confined myself within the limits of the old Surveyor's half-a-dozen sheets of foolscap. On the contrary, I have allowed myself, as to such points, nearly, or altogether, as much license as if the facts had been entirely of my own invention. What I contend for is the authenticity of the outline.

This incident recalled my mind, in some degree, to its old track. There seemed to be here the groundwork of a tale. It impressed me as if the ancient Surveyor, in his garb of a hundred years gone by, and wearing his immortal wig—which was buried with him, but did not perish in the grave—had bet me in the deserted chamber of the Custom-House. In his port was the dignity of one who had borne His Majesty's commission, and who was therefore illuminated by a ray of the splendour that shone so dazzlingly about the throne. How unlike alas the hangdog look of a republican official, who, as the servant of the people, feels himself less than the least, and below the lowest of his masters. With his own ghostly hand, the obscurely seen, but majestic, figure had imparted to me the scarlet symbol and the little roll of explanatory manuscript. With his own ghostly voice he had exhorted me, on the sacred consideration of my filial duty and reverence towards him—who might reasonably regard himself as my official ancestor—to bring his mouldy and moth-eaten lucubrations before the public. "Do this," said the ghost of Mr. Surveyor Pue, emphatically nodding the head that looked so imposing within its memorable wig; "do this, and the profit shall be all your own. You will shortly need it; for it is not in your days as it was in mine, when a man's office was a life-lease, and oftentimes an heirloom. But I charge you, in this matter of old Mistress Prynne, give to your predecessor's memory the credit which will be rightfully due!" And I said to the ghost of Mr. Surveyor Pue,—"I will!"

On Hester Prynne's story, therefore, I bestowed much thought. It was the subject of my meditations for many an hour, while pacing to and fro across my room, or traversing, with a hundredfold repetition, the long extent from the front door of the Custom-House to the side entrance, and back again. Great were the weariness and annoyance of the old Inspector and the Weighers and Gaugers, whose slumbers were disturbed by the unmercifully lengthened tramp of my passing and returning footsteps. Remembering their own former habits, they used to say that the Surveyor was walking the quarter-deck. They probably fancied that my sole object—and, indeed, the sole object for which a sane man could ever put himself into voluntary motion—was to get an appetite for dinner. And, to say the truth, an appetite, sharpened by the east wind that generally blew along the passage, was the only valuable result of so much indefatigable exercise. So little adapted is the atmosphere of a Custom-house to the delicate harvest of fancy and sensibility, that, had I remained there through ten Presidencies yet to come, I doubt whether the tale of "The Scarlet Letter" would ever have been brought before the public eye. My imagination was a tarnished mirror. It would not reflect, or only with miserable dimness, the figures with which I did my best to people it. The characters of the narrative would not be warmed and rendered malleable by any heat that I could kindle at my intellectual forge. They would take neither the glow of passion nor the tenderness of sentiment, but retained all the rigidity of dead corpses, and stared me in the face with a fixed and ghastly grin of contemptuous defiance. "What have you to do with us?" that expression seemed to say. "The little power you might have once possessed over the tribe of unrealities is gone You have bartered it for a pittance of the public gold. Go then, and earn your wages!" In short, the almost torpid creatures of my own fancy twitted me with imbecility, and not without fair occasion.

It was not merely during the three hours and a half which Uncle Sam claimed as his share of my daily life that this wretched numbness held possession of me. It went with me on my sea-shore walks and rambles into the country, whenever—which was seldom and reluctantly—I bestirred myself to seek that invigorating charm of Nature which used to give me such freshness and activity of thought, the moment that I stepped across the threshold of the Old Manse. The same torpor, as regarded the capacity for intellectual effort, accompanied me home, and weighed upon me in the chamber which I most absurdly termed my study. Nor did it quit me when, late at night, I sat in the deserted parlour, lighted only by the glimmering coal-fire and the moon, striving to picture forth imaginary scenes, which, the next day, might flow out on the brightening page in many-hued description.

If the imaginative faculty refused to act at such an hour, it might well be deemed a hopeless case. Moonlight, in a familiar room, falling so white upon the carpet, and showing all its figures so distinctly—making every object so minutely visible, yet so unlike a morning or noontide visibility—is a medium the most suitable for a romance-writer to get acquainted with his illusive guests. There is the little domestic scenery of the well-known apartment; the chairs, with each its separate individuality; the centre-table, sustaining a work-basket, a volume or two, and an extinguished lamp; the sofa; the book-case; the picture on the wall—all these details, so completely seen, are so spiritualised by the unusual light, that they seem to lose their actual substance, and become things of intellect. Nothing is too small or too trifling to undergo this change, and acquire dignity thereby. A child's shoe; the doll, seated in her little wicker carriage; the hobby-horse—whatever, in a word, has been used or played with during the day is now invested with a quality of strangeness and remoteness, though still almost as vividly present as by daylight. Thus, therefore, the floor of our familiar room has become a neutral territory, somewhere between the real world and fairy-land, where the Actual and the Imaginary may meet, and each imbue itself with the nature of the other. Ghosts might enter here without affrighting us. It would be too much in keeping with the scene to excite surprise, were we to look about us and discover a form, beloved, but gone hence, now sitting quietly in a streak of this magic moonshine, with an aspect that would make us doubt whether it had returned from afar, or had never once stirred from our fireside.

The somewhat dim coal fire has an essential influence in producing the effect which I would describe. It throws its unobtrusive tinge throughout the room, with a faint ruddiness upon the walls and ceiling, and a reflected gleam upon the polish of the furniture. This warmer light mingles itself with the cold spirituality of the moon-beams, and communicates, as it were, a heart and sensibilities of human tenderness to the forms which fancy summons up. It converts them from snow-images into men and women. Glancing at the looking-glass, we behold—deep within its haunted verge—the smouldering glow of the half-extinguished **anthracite**, the white moon-beams on the floor, and a repetition of all the gleam and shadow of the picture, with one remove further from the actual, and nearer to the imaginative. Then, at such an hour, and with this scene before him, if a man, sitting all alone, cannot dream strange things, and make them look like truth, he need never try to write romances.

anthracite: hard coal, which gives much heat with little flame and smoke.

But, for myself, during the whole of my Custom-House experience, moonlight and sunshine, and the glow of firelight, were just alike in my regard; and neither of them was of one whit more avail than the twinkle of a tallow-candle. An entire class of susceptibilities, and a gift connected with them—of no great richness or value, but the best I had—was gone from me.

It is my belief, however, that had I attempted a different order of composition, my faculties would not have been found so pointless and inefficacious. I might, for instance, have contented myself with writing out the narratives of a veteran shipmaster, one of the Inspectors, whom I should be most ungrateful not to mention, since scarcely a day passed that he did not stir me to laughter and admiration by his marvelous gifts as a story-teller. Could I have preserved the picturesque force of his style, and the humourous colouring which nature taught him how to throw over his descriptions, the result, I honestly believe, would have been something new in literature. Or I might readily have found a more serious task. It was a folly, with the materiality of this daily life pressing so intrusively upon me, to attempt to fling myself back into another age, or to insist on creating the semblance of a world out of airy matter, when, at every moment, the impalpable beauty of my soap-bubble was broken by the rude contact of some actual circumstance. The wiser effort would have been to diffuse thought and imagination through the opaque substance of to-day, and thus to make it a bright transparency; to spiritualise the burden that began to weigh so heavily; to seek, resolutely, the true and inde-structible value that lay hidden in the petty and wearisome incidents, and ordinary characters with which I was now conversant. The fault was mine. The page of life that was spread out before me seemed dull and common-place only because I had not fathomed its deeper import. A better book than I shall ever write was there; leaf after leaf presenting itself to me, just as it was written out by the reality of the flitting hour, and vanishing as fast as written, only because my brain wanted the insight, and my hand the cunning, to transcribe it. At some future day, it may be, I shall remem-ber a few scattered fragments and broken paragraphs, and write them down, and find the letters turn to gold upon the page.

These perceptions had come too late. At the instant, I was only conscious that what would have been a pleasure once was now a hopeless toil. There was no occasion to make much moan about this state of affairs. I had ceased to be a writer of tolerably poor tales and essays, and had become a tolerably good Surveyor of the Customs. That was all. But, nevertheless, it is anything but agreeable to be haunted by a suspicion that one's intellect is dwindling away, or exhaling, without your con-sciousness, like ether out of a phial; so that, at every glance, you find a smaller and less volatile residuum. Of the fact there could be no doubt and, examining myself and others, I was led to conclusions, in reference to the effect of public office on the character, not very favourable to the mode of life in question. In some other form, perhaps, I may hereafter develop these effects. Suffice it here to say that a Custom-House officer of long continuance can hardly be a very praiseworthy or respectable per-sonage, for many reasons; one of them, the tenure by which he holds his situation, and another, the very nature of his business, which—though, I trust, an honest one—is of such a sort that he does not share in the united effort of mankind.

An effect—which I believe to be observable, more or less, in every indi-vidual who has occupied the position—is, that while he leans on the mighty arm of the Republic, his own proper strength, departs from him. He loses, in an extent proportioned to the weakness or force of his original nature, the capability of self-support. If he possesses an unusual share of native energy, or the enervating magic of place do not operate too long upon him, his forfeited powers may be redeemable. The ejected officer—fortunate in the unkindly shove that sends him forth betimes, to struggle amid a struggling world—may return to himself, and become all that he has ever been. But this seldom happens. He usually keeps his ground just long enough for his own ruin, and is then thrust out, with sinews all unstrung, to totter along the difficult footpath of life as he best may. Conscious of his own infirmity—that his tempered steel and elasticity are lost—he for ever afterwards looks wistfully about him in quest of support external to himself. His pervading and continual hope—a hallucination, which, in the face of all discouragement, and making light of impossibilities, haunts him while he lives, and, I fancy, like the convulsive throes of the cholera, torments him for a brief space after death—is, that finally, and in no long time, by some happy coincidence of circumstances, he shall be restored to office. This faith, more than anything else, steals the pith and availability out of whatever enterprise he may dream of undertaking. Why should he toil and moil, and be at so much trouble to pick himself up out of the mud, when, in a little while hence, the strong arm of his Uncle will raise and support him? Why should he work for his living here, or go to dig gold in California, when he is so soon to be made happy, at monthly intervals, with a little pile of glittering coin out of his Uncle's pocket? It is sadly curious to observe how slight a taste of office suffices to infect a poor fellow with this singular disease. Uncle Sam's gold—meaning no disrespect to the worthy old gentleman—has, in this respect, a quality of enchantment like that of the devil's wages. Whoever touches it should look well to himself, or he may find the bargain to go hard against him, involving, if not his soul, yet many of its better attributes; its sturdy force, its courage and constancy, its truth, its self-reliance, and all that gives the emphasis to manly character.

Here was a fine prospect in the distance. Not that the Surveyor brought the lesson home to himself, or admitted that he could be so utterly undone, either by continuance in office or ejectment. Yet my reflections were not the most comfortable. I began to grow melancholy and restless; continually prying into my mind, to discover which of its poor properties were gone, and what degree of detriment had already accrued to the remainder. I endeavoured to calculate how much longer I could stay in the Custom-House, and yet go forth a man. To confess the truth, it was my greatest apprehension—as it would never be a measure of policy to turn out so quiet an individual as myself; and it being hardly in the nature of a public officer to resign—it was my chief trouble, therefore, that I was likely to grow grey and decrepit in the Surveyorship, and become much such another animal as the old Inspector. Might it not, in the tedious lapse of official life that lay before me, finally be with me as it was with this venerable friend—to make the dinner-hour the nucleus of the day, and to spend the rest of it, as an old dog spends it, asleep in the sunshine or in the shade? A dreary look-forward, this, for a man who felt it to be the best definition of happiness to live throughout the whole range of his faculties and sensibilities! But, all this while, I was giving myself very unnecessary alarm. Providence had meditated better things for me than I could possibly imagine for myself.

A remarkable event of the third year of my Surveyorship—to adopt the tone of "P. P."—was the election of **General Taylor** to the Presidency. It is essential, in order to a complete estimate of the advantages of official life, to view the incumbent at the in-coming of a hostile administration. His position is then one of the most singularly irksome, and, in every contingency, disagreeable, that a wretched mortal can possibly occupy; with seldom an alternative of good on either hand, although what presents itself to him as the worst event may very probably be the best. But it is a strange experience, to a man of pride and sensibility, to know that his interests are within the control of individuals who neither love nor understand him, and by whom, since one or the other must needs happen, he would rather be injured than obliged. Strange, too, for one who has kept his calmness throughout the contest, to observe the bloodthirstiness that is developed in the hour of triumph, and to be conscious that he is himself among its objects! There are few uglier traits of human nature than this tendency—which I now witnessed in men no worse than their neighbours—to grow cruel, merely because they possessed the power of inflicting harm. If the guillotine, as applied to office-holders, were a literal fact, instead of one of the most apt of metaphors, it is my sincere belief that the active members of the victorious party were sufficiently excited to have chopped off all our heads, and have thanked Heaven for the opportunity! It appears to me—who have been a calm and curious observer, as well in victory as defeat—that this fierce and bitter spirit of malice and revenge has never distinguished the many triumphs of my own party as it now did that of the Whigs. The Democrats take the offices, as a general rule, because they need them, and because the practice of many years has made it the law of political warfare, which unless a different system be proclaimed, it was weakness and cowardice to murmur at. But the long habit of victory has made them generous. They know how to spare when they see occasion; and when they strike, the axe may be sharp indeed, but its edge is seldom poisoned with ill-will; nor is it their custom ignominiously to kick the head which they have just struck off.

In short, unpleasant as was my predicament, at best, I saw much reason to congratulate myself that I was on the losing side rather than the triumphant one. If, heretofore, I had been none of the warmest of partisans, I began now, at this season of peril and adversity, to be pretty acutely sensible with which party my predilections lay; nor was it without something like regret and shame that, according to a reasonable calculation of chances, I saw my own prospect of retaining office to be better than those of my democratic brethren. But who can see an inch into futurity beyond his nose? My own head was the first that fell!

The moment when a man's head drops off is seldom or never, I am inclined to think, precisely the most agreeable of his life. Nevertheless, like

General Taylor: Zachary Taylor (1784–1850) was the 12th president of the U.S. When he assumed office, Hawthorne lost his position in the custom house.

the greater part of our misfortunes, even so serious a contingency brings its remedy and consolation with it, if the sufferer will but make the best rather than the worst, of the accident which has befallen him. In my particular case the consolatory topics were close at hand, and, indeed, had suggested themselves to my meditations a considerable time before it was requisite to use them. In view of my previous weariness of office, and vague thoughts of resignation, my fortune somewhat resembled that of a person who should entertain an idea of committing suicide, and although beyond his hopes, meet with the good hap to be murdered. In the Custom-House, as before in the Old Manse, I had spent three years—a term long enough to rest a weary brain: long enough to break off old intellectual habits, and make room for new ones: long enough, and too long, to have lived in an unnatural state, doing what was really of no advantage nor delight to any human being, and withholding myself from toil that would, at least, have stilled an unquiet impulse in me. Then, moreover, as regarded his unceremonious ejectment, the late Surveyor was not altogether ill-pleased to be recognised by the Whigs as an enemy; since his inactivity in political affairs—his tendency to roam, at will, in that broad and quiet field where all mankind may meet, rather than confine himself to those narrow paths where brethren of the same household must diverge from one another— had sometimes made it questionable with his brother Democrats whether he was a friend. Now, after he had won the crown of martyrdom (though with no longer a head to wear it on), the point might be looked upon as settled. Finally, little heroic as he was, it seemed more decorous to be overthrown in the downfall of the party with which he had been content to stand than to remain a forlorn survivor, when so many worthier men were falling: and at last, after subsisting for four years on the mercy of a hostile administration, to be compelled then to define his position anew, and claim the yet more humiliating mercy of a friendly one.

Meanwhile, the press had taken up my affair, and kept me for a week or two careering through the public prints, in my decapitated state, like **Irving's Headless Horseman**, ghastly and grim, and longing to be buried, as a political dead man ought. So much for my figurative self. The real human being all this time, with his head safely on his shoulders, had brought himself to the comfortable conclusion that everything was for the best; and making an investment in ink, paper, and steel pens, had opened his long-disused writing desk, and was again a literary man.

Now it was that the lucubrations of my ancient predecessor, Mr. Surveyor Pue, came into play. Rusty through long idleness, some little space was requisite before my intellectual machinery could be brought to work upon the tale with an effect in any degree satisfactory. Even yet, though my thoughts were ultimately much absorbed in the task, it wears, to my eye, a stern and sombre aspect: too much ungladdened by genial sunshine; too little relieved by the tender and familiar influences which soften almost every scene of nature and real life, and undoubtedly should soften every picture of them. This uncaptivating effect is perhaps due to the period of hardly accomplished revolution, and still seething turmoil,

Irving's Headless Horseman: from the story "The Legend of Sleepy Hollow" by Washington Irving, published in *The Sketch Book* (1819–1820).

in which the story shaped itself. It is no indication, however, of a lack of cheerfulness in the writer's mind: for he was happier while straying through the gloom of these sunless fantasies than at any time since he had quitted the Old Manse. Some of the briefer articles, which contribute to make up the volume, have likewise been written since my involuntary withdrawal from the toils and honours of public life, and the remainder are gleaned from annuals and magazines, of such antique date, that they have gone round the circle, and come back to novelty again. Keeping up the metaphor of the political guillotine, the whole may be considered as the POSTUMOUS PAPERS OF A DECAPITATED SURVEYOR; and the sketch which I am now bringing to a close, if too autobiographical for a modest person to publish in his lifetime, will readily be excused in a gentleman who writes from beyond the grave. Peace be with all the world! My blessing on my friends My forgiveness to my enemies! For I am in the realm of quiet!

The life of the Custom-House lies like a dream behind me. The old Inspector—who, by the bye, I regret to say, was overthrown and killed by a horse some time ago, else he would certainly have lived for ever—he, and all those other venerable personages who sat with him at the receipt of custom, are but shadows in my view: white-headed and wrinkled images, which my fancy used to sport with, and has now flung aside for ever. The merchants—Pingree, Phillips, Shepard, Upton, Kimball, Bertram, Hunt—these and many other names, which had such classic familiarity for my ear six months ago,—these men of traffic, who seemed to occupy so important a position in the world—how little time has it required to disconnect me from them all, not merely in act, but recollection! It is with an effort that I recall the figures and appellations of these few. Soon, likewise, my old native town will loom upon me through the haze of memory, a mist brooding over and around it; as if it were no portion of the real earth, but an overgrown village in cloud-land, with only imaginary inhabitants to people its wooden houses and walk its homely lanes, and the unpicturesque prolixity of its main street. Henceforth it ceases to be a reality of my life; I am a citizen of somewhere else. My good townspeople will not much regret me, for—though it has been as dear an object as any, in my literary efforts, to be of some importance in their eyes, and to win myself a pleasant memory in this abode and burial-place of so many of my forefathers—there has never been, for me, the genial atmosphere which a literary man requires in order to ripen the best harvest of his mind. I shall do better amongst other faces; and these familiar ones, it need hardly be said, will do just as well without me.

It may be, however—oh, transporting and triumphant thought!—that the great-grandchildren of the present race may sometimes think kindly of the scribbler of bygone days, when the antiquary of days to come, among the sites memorable in the town's history, shall point out the locality of **THE TOWN PUMP**.

THE TOWN PUMP: Another sketch written by Hawthorne, "A Rill from the Town Pump," was published in Hawthorne's *Twice-told Tales* (1837).

COMMENTARY

Hawthorne's goals in this introduction to the novel are to present some of his ideas about writing and about the romance genre in particular; to provide the reader with background about his job as surveyor of the Salem custom house and about his Puritan ancestors; and to explain how he discovered the manuscript of this novel. Hawthorne begins by telling us that he writes this section out of an autobiographical impulse. A few years earlier, he wrote a similar autobiographical piece, "The Old Manse," which was used to introduce his book of stories *Mosses from an Old Manse* (1846). That essay was well received by readers, so he decided to try it again.

Hawthorne's philosophy of writing

Although he is writing autobiographically in this section, Hawthorne explains that he doesn't approve of some writers, whose text is so intimate that it makes readers uncomfortable. He suggests that writers should imagine that they are speaking to a friend, a person who is "kind and apprehensive, though not the closest friend." In this way, the writer personalizes his writing but doesn't risk revealing his innermost self. (This seems to be Hawthorne's technique in *The Scarlet Letter*, where we find a friendly, obtrusive narrator who guides our reading like a sympathetic friend, offering explanation and interpretation to deepen our understanding.) Hawthorne also explains his goal of positioning himself as the editor, rather than the originator, of this story. By pretending that he has discovered the manuscript of the story in an unused room of the custom house, Hawthorne adds an element of authenticity to his tale.

In addition to explaining Hawthorne's view of the proper relationship between reader and writer, this introduction also reveals his ideas about romance, the genre of *The Scarlet Letter*. According to Hawthorne, the perfect place for writing a romance is in a familiar room in the evening, with the moonlight making every object visible. Unlike the glare of sunshine, the moonlight "spiritualizes" the room, erasing its physical substance and endowing it with "strangeness and remoteness." Even the smallest objects gain a new dignity through this process. In moonlight, the real and fairy-tale worlds may meet and interweave. A dim coal fire also contributes to this process. This warm light of the fire mixes with the cold spirituality of the moonlight to add heart and tenderness to the imagination's more spiritual productions. The fire converts the shadowy figures of the imagination into real human beings.

This description of how a romantic writer should work offers the reader insight on how to approach this novel. It, too, is a story told in this blend of moonlight and coal fire, in which intellectual ideas mix with human passions. The reader should look for moments where the real and fairy-tale worlds meet in *The Scarlet Letter.* How does Hawthorne make the real seem fantastic, or the fantastic appear real? Hawthorne critiques his novel for being too somber, for having too few soft, tender human influences. He suggests that he may have spent too much time in the moonlight when writing it—he needed more fire!

The custom house in Salem, Massachusetts.
©Kevin Fleming/CORBIS

Hawthorne's role as surveyor

Hawthorne's second goal in this preface is to explain his role as surveyor of the custom house. His descriptions of the government and of his fellow employees are highly critical, reflecting his bitterness at having lost his position when the Democrats were voted out of office in 1848. In describing the hardness of the American eagle, Hawthorne's symbol for the federal government, Hawthorne issues a warning to anyone who plans to find shelter by having a government position: Sooner or later, the eagle will "fling off her nestlings with a scratch of her claw, a dab of her beak, or a rankling from her barbed arrows." Hawthorne alludes here to his perceived mistreatment as an employee of the custom house. Later he describes the way that he has been "swept out of office" and replaced by a "worthier successor."

Yet Hawthorne doesn't seem to have liked his job, nor does he show much respect for his fellow employees. Hawthorne's scathing sketches of the Inspector and the Collector who he worked with at the custom house were criticized in the Salem newspapers when the novel was published. The Inspector, for example, is represented as a man without morals, intellect, or feeling, whose primary interest in life is food. In a telling example, Hawthorne writes that although he rarely regrets the deaths of his three wives and numerous children, the Inspector fondly remembers roast beef that he ate 20 or 40 years ago.

Unaccustomed to such unintellectual company, Hawthorne tells the reader that he is more at home with Emerson, Thoreau, and Longfellow, famous writers of his time, than with the dullards at the custom house. Although he claims to like this "change of diet" and believes that he could "mingle at once with men of altogether different qualities," his self-assessment is clearly mistaken: His condescension toward these men he considers to be his inferiors is apparent. In opposition to them, Hawthorne presents himself as a man of "thought, fancy, and sensibility."

His time in the custom house does have the humbling effect of showing Hawthorne how little impact his literary success matters to the world in general; only those within his limited literary circle have any respect for his talents or support his dreams. Through this depiction of his conflicts with the mundane world of the custom house, Hawthorne shows the difficulty artists and other imaginative people (represented in this novel by Hester and Pearl) often have with America's more utilitarian values.

Hawthorne's Puritan heritage

Another goal of this introduction is to offer the reader background information on Hawthorne's family's history in Salem, which accounts, in part, for his interest in exploring the Puritan mentality in the novel. Although Hawthorne is "happiest elsewhere," he has recently discovered that he also has an affectionate attachment to his birthplace of Salem, perhaps because of his family's deep roots in the town. His ancestor, Major William Hathorne, arrived in Massachusetts in 1630 and made a big impact on Salem as a soldier, legislator, and judge. Family legends about this man have affected Hawthorne, leading to his fascination with the Puritan mentality, a recurrent theme in his stories and in this novel. But his feelings toward his Puritan ancestors aren't wholly positive. He describes them as "dim and dusky," as "grave, bearded, sable-cloaked, and steeple-crowned" men, whose "better deeds" will be completely overshadowed by their crueler actions. He acknowledges that they were narrow-minded and bitter persecutors of anyone whose ideas differed from theirs, such as the Quakers. One of his relatives participated in the Salem witch trials, again showing the family's intolerance and cruelty.

Hawthorne says that he will take his ancestors' shame upon himself—perhaps this novel is an attempt to rid himself of some of this shame by presenting an accurate, and critical, picture of the Puritans. Notice how often the novel's narrator critiques their intolerance, lack of imagination, and severity. Hawthorne also recognizes that, as a writer, his successes would not seem admirable to his Puritan ancestors, who had no interest in artistic pursuits and would have called him an "idler," a worthless "writer of story books."

The origins of this novel

A final goal of this introduction to the novel is to explain the manner in which Hawthorne supposedly discovered the manuscript of the novel and a cloth scarlet letter "A." Critics have not been able to find evidence that either the letter or the manuscript actually existed, so this is probably just a ploy to add an element of historical authenticity to the novel.

Hawthorne's description of the letter in this preface is significant. First, he tells us that the signification of the letter is not immediately apparent, showing the relativity of all symbols by which our culture makes meaning. Although he can't guess the meaning, Hawthorne assumes that it is deep and worthy of interpretation. In fact, he attributes an almost mystical power to this strange letter, as if it is communicating directly with his subconscious even though its meaning evades his rational mind. His comments suggest that the story of this scarlet letter will be almost mythical, a story perennially relevant to humanity because it is constantly repeated, though in different forms.

The continuing popularity of the novel suggests that Hawthorne is right, as new generations of readers always seem to find some way to relate to this tale of suffering and betrayal. The letter's effect isn't just spiritual, but also physical; Hawthorne claims that when he places it upon his breast, he has the sensation of red-hot iron burning his flesh. This tale will obviously have a deep and potent impact on the human heart.

In order to increase the veracity of his narrative, Hawthorne assures us that the documents accompanying the letter have all been verified and authenticated by a previous surveyor, Jonathan Pue. Although he assures us that he will follow the "outline" of the story contained in these documents, Hawthorne has added his own ideas about the "motives and modes of passion" that influenced the characters involved. While his familial ancestors have bequeathed him his Puritan heritage, this "official ancestor"(Pue) has bestowed the story of the scarlet letter to him, making it his "filial duty" to publish the tale—this is his inheritance and responsibility as a custom house officer.

The mirror of imagination

Unfortunately, Hawthorne's job at the custom house seems to have dulled his imagination, which he describes as "a tarnished mirror." (Hawthorne often uses mirrors to symbolize the workings of the creative process. For example, in this novel, Pearl, the most creative and imaginative character, will often be shown reflected in pools of water.) Hawthorne also admits that his inner thoughts tell him that he's sold his creative soul in order to earn a living, and he'll need to quit the job at the custom house in order to rediscover his artistic abilities. Having a full-time job and achieving artistic success don't blend.

Fortunately for Hawthorne, and for the reader, the Democrats lose the 1848 election to the Whigs, and Hawthorne loses his surveyor position. Although he is upset about this event, referring to the Whigs as a cruel bunch of guillotiners, the loss of his job leads Hawthorne back to writing, back to his imagination. The once tarnished mirror of imagination becomes polished and bright once again as Hawthorne creates *The Scarlet Letter.*

Chapter I

A group of drably dressed townspeople stands outside the prison where Hester Prynne is serving her term for adultery. A wild rosebush grows just outside the prison door, symbolizing the human frailty and suffering that will be the topic of this novel.

CHAPTER I: THE PRISON DOOR

NOTES

A throng of bearded men, in sad-coloured garments and grey steeple-crowned hats, inter-mixed with women, some wearing hoods, and others bareheaded, was assembled in front of a wooden edifice, the door of which was heavily timbered with oak, and studded with iron spikes.

The founders of a new colony, whatever **Utopia** of human virtue and happiness they might originally project, have invariably recognised it among their earliest practical necessities to allot a portion of the virgin soil as a cemetery, and another portion as the site of a prison. In accordance with this rule it may safely be assumed that the forefathers of Boston had built the first prison-house somewhere in the vicinity of **Cornhill**, almost as seasonably as they marked out the first burial-ground, on **Isaac Johnson's lot**, and round about his grave, which subsequently became the nucleus of all the congregated sepulchres in the old churchyard of **King's Chapel**. Certain it is that, some fifteen or twenty years after the settlement of the town, the wooden jail was already marked with weather-stains and other indications of age, which gave a yet darker aspect to its beetle-browed and gloomy front. The rust on the ponderous iron-work of its oaken door looked more antique than anything else in the New World. Like all that pertains to crime, it seemed never to have known a youthful era. Before this ugly edifice, and between it and the wheel-track of the street, was a grass-plot, much overgrown with burdock, pig-weed, apple-peru, and such unsightly vegetation, which evidently found something congenial in the soil that had so early borne the black flower of civilised society, a prison. But on one side of the portal, and rooted almost at the threshold, was a wild rose-bush, covered, in this month of June, with its delicate gems, which might be imagined to offer their fragrance and fragile beauty to the prisoner as he went in, and to the condemned criminal as he came forth to his doom, in token that the deep heart of Nature could pity and be kind to him.

This rose-bush, by a strange chance, has been kept alive in history; but whether it had merely survived out of the stern old wilderness, so long after the fall of the gigantic pines and oaks that originally overshadowed it, or whether, as there is far authority for believing, it had sprung up under the footsteps of the sainted **Ann Hutchinson** as she entered the prison-door, we shall not take upon us to determine. Finding it so directly on the threshold of our narrative, which is now about to issue from that inauspicious portal, we could hardly do otherwise than pluck one of its flowers, and present it to the reader. It may serve, let us hope, to symbolise some sweet moral blossom that may be found along the track, or relieve the darkening close of a tale of human frailty and sorrow.

Utopia: an imaginary island described in a book of the same name written in 1516 by Sir Thomas More. Utopia is described as having a perfect political and social system.

Cornhill: a street in Boston, now Washington Street.

Isaac Johnson's lot: He died a few months after arriving in New England from Charleston.

King's Chapel: the first Episcopalian church in New England.

Ann Hutchinson: Hutchinson (1591–1643) emigrated to Massachusetts in 1634. An influential religious leader, she was viewed as a threat and banished from the colony. She moved to Rhode Island and then New York, where she was killed by Native Americans.

COMMENTARY

From the opening description of the townspeople in this chapter, readers have a clear image of life in a Puritan New England town. For example, the clothing of all the spectators standing outside the prison door is "sad-colored" and "gray," illustrating the Puritans' rejection of anything frivolous or colorful. These people are somber and serious; fun and festivity do not intrude in their lives. In their practicality, the first institutions they created after settling this new, supposedly utopian, community were a cemetery and a prison. Although the Puritans hoped to create a more perfect life in the new world, the old problems of death and crime still plague them. Implicitly, the narrator questions the possibility of creating a utopian society: Will humans ever be able to create the world of virtue and happiness dreamed of by these early New England settlers? This narrator thinks not. Notice how strongly he presents his ideas to the reader through his choice of words. By emphasizing in the novel's opening sentence the dark, dreary, overly-serious attitude of the Puritans, he implicitly critiques their repressive lifestyle. The narrator's interpretive intrusions into the text become more explicit by the end of this chapter.

Along with a description of the townspeople, the novel's opening sentence paints a clear picture of the prison door. "[H]eavily timbered" and "studded with iron spikes," the prison door is ominously associated with torture and oppression. Like the men's clothing, the prison is presented as "dark" and "gloomy," an effect that has only been heightened by age. That this gloomy edifice of punishment was one of the first buildings created by the Puritan settlers suggests their punitive, almost despotic approach to life. Clearly, difference is not tolerated by this culture. The narrator tells us that the rust on the prison door looks more antique than any other aspect of the new world, implying that crime and punishment are ancient, unavoidable elements of human life—things that can't be escaped even in the new world's supposedly "virgin soil." Even nature seems to recognize the oppressiveness of this building, so the vegetation growing near the prison is ominous and ugly: Burdock, pig-weed, and other unattractive weeds grow in the grass plot near the prison, helping to make it the "black flower of civilized society." What images are conjured up by this notion of a "black flower"? Something that doesn't exist in nature, the black flower represents a blighting of the natural world, an ugly and unsightly tumor.

Overall, the imagery in these first paragraphs of the novel indicates a world that is gloomy, ugly, and unnatural. Certainly, the narrator appears critical of this society, and he is setting us up to like Hester, the prisoner lurking behind the iron door, in contrast to her severe wardens.

The contrast between Hester and the townspeople is first suggested with the introduction of the wild rosebush. In contrast to all the ugliness of the prison and the people, this fragrant bush grows on one side of the door to the prison. An important symbol, the wild rose connotes beauty, the natural world, and morality. Unlike the unsightly weeds growing in front of the prison, this beautiful bush is covered with "delicate gems" and offers "fragrance and fragile beauty" to the criminal condemned to life in the "black flower" of the prison. Many readers think that the narrator associates the rose's wild beauty with Hester. The narrator theorizes that the "deep heart of Nature" is perhaps offering this gift to humanity and, in particular, to Hester, who will see its beauty each time she walks out of the prison door. A contrast is therefore created between the black flower—the unnatural and ugly creation of humanity—and the beautiful rose created by nature. While civilization is corrupting and unsympathetic toward human frailty, nature is bountiful and forgiving.

The wild rosebush growing next to the prison door.

The rosebush has further connotations: It is associated with the "sainted Ann Hutchinson," under whose step it sprung when she, like Hester, walked through the prison door. Like Hester, Hutchinson was shunned and rejected by Puritan society, which believes that absolute conformity is necessary for public safety in the New World. A woman preacher and an *antinomian* (a believer in the Christian doctrine that faith alone is important for salvation, not obedience to institutional or moral law), Hutchinson was a threat to the Puritanical belief in absolute obedience to law. By invoking Hutchinson, the narrator implicitly asks the reader to question whether Puritan law was justified in condemning Hester. (Hutchinson would probably say "no," and she might ask who is judging the judges.) That the narrator sides with Hutchinson against the Puritan community is obvious: He refers to her as "sainted." Both Hester and Ann Hutchinson, two female renegades, are associated with the wild beauty of the rosebush, a relationship that allows the narrator to create reader sympathy for Hester's situation even before she's officially entered the novel.

Finally, the narrator symbolically plucks a bloom from this beautiful, fragrant bush and offers it to the reader as an image of "some sweet moral blossom." This symbol will remind us of beauty, of morality, and of the wholesomeness of the natural world as we read this dark story of human sorrow. In associating morality with a wild, natural blossom, the narrator implies that his view of morality may differ from that of the Puritans, who glean their ideas of morality from the Bible rather than from the natural beauty that surrounds them.

The narrator explicitly tells the reader how to interpret the symbol of the bloom. Why has Hawthorne created a narrator who so often intrudes on the story? First, he may have felt that narrative explanation was necessary because his story is set in such a distant time: Without the narrator's comments, a modern reader might not catch the full significance of the story's symbols. In addition, the narrator's direct comments to the reader give the story a conversational feel, as if the reader is sitting in front of a fire listening to the story being told by an older and wiser friend.

Although short, this first chapter accomplishes a great deal. It introduces the Puritan community, which it links with images of oppression, darkness, and gloom. It provides us with an important symbol—the wild rosebush—that is linked with Hester, beauty, morality, and nature. Finally, it introduces us to the fairly intrusive narrator who will guide our reading experience by offering us both implicit and explicit commentary on and interpretation of the events described in the novel.

Chapter II

As Hester emerges from the prison door with the scarlet "A" for adultery emblazoned on her dress, several townswomen self-righteously criticize her. Hester is led to the scaffold where she stands on display as punishment for the sin of adultery. Humiliated but still strong, she contemplates her past and imagines a dreary, shamed future.

CHAPTER II: THE MARKET-PLACE

THE grass-plot before the jail, in Prison Lane, on a certain summer morning, not less than two centuries ago, was occupied by a pretty large number of the inhabitants of Boston, all with their eyes intently fastened on the iron-clamped oaken door. Amongst any other population, or at a later period in the history of New England, the grim rigidity that petrified the bearded physiognomies of these good people would have augured some awful business in hand. It could have betokened nothing short of the anticipated execution of some rioted culprit, on whom the sentence of a legal tribunal had but confirmed the verdict of public sentiment. But, in that early severity of the Puritan character, an inference of this kind could not so indubitably be drawn. It might be that a sluggish bond-servant, or an undutiful child, whom his parents had given over to the civil authority, was to be corrected at the whipping-post. It might be that an **Antinomian**, a Quaker, or other heterodox religionist, was to be scourged out of the town, or an idle or vagrant Indian, whom the white man's fire-water had made riotous about the streets, was to be driven with stripes into the shadow of the forest. It might be, too, that a witch, like old **Mistress Hibbins**, the bitter-tempered widow of the magistrate, was to die upon the gallows. In either case, there was very much the same solemnity of demeanour on the part of the spectators, as befitted a people among whom religion and law were almost identical, and in whose character both were so thoroughly interfused, that the mildest and severest acts of public discipline were alike made venerable and awful. Meagre, indeed, and cold, was the sympathy that a transgressor might look for, from such bystanders, at the scaffold. On the other hand, a penalty which, in our days, would infer a degree of mocking infamy and ridicule, might then be invested with almost as stern a dignity as the punishment of death itself.

It was a circumstance to he noted on the summer morning when our story begins its course, that the women, of whom there were several in the crowd, appeared to take a peculiar interest in whatever penal infliction might be expected to ensue. The age had not so much refinement, that any sense of impropriety restrained the wearers of petticoat and farthingale from stepping forth into the public ways, and wedging their not unsubstantial persons, if occasion were, into the throng nearest to the scaffold at an execution. Morally, as well as materially, there was a coarser fibre in those wives and maidens of old English birth and breeding than in their fair descendants, separated from them by a series of six or seven

Antinomian: a believer in the Christian doctrine that faith alone, not obedience to the moral law, is necessary for salvation.

Mistress Hibbins: Ann Hibbins, accused of witchcraft and hanged in 1656.

generations; for, throughout that chain of ancestry, every successive mother had transmitted to her child a fainter bloom, a more delicate and briefer beauty, and a slighter physical frame, if not character of less force and solidity than her own. The women who were now standing about the prison-door stood within less than half a century of the period when the **man-like Elizabeth** had been the not altogether unsuitable representative of the sex. They were her countrywomen: and the beef and ale of their native land, with a moral diet not a whit more refined, entered largely into their composition. The bright morning sun, therefore, shone on broad shoulders and well-developed busts, and on round and ruddy cheeks, that had ripened in the far-off island, and had hardly yet grown paler or thinner in the atmosphere of New England. There was, more-over, a boldness and rotundity of speech among these matrons, as most of them seemed to be, that would startle us at the present day, whether in respect to its purport or its volume of tone.

man-like Elizabeth: Queen Elizabeth I ruled in England from 1558 to 1603. She was referred to as "man-like" because she was in a position of power unusual for a woman.

"Goodwives," said a hard-featured dame of fifty, "I'll tell ye a piece of my mind. It would be greatly for the public behoof if we women, being of mature age and church-members in good repute, should have the han-dling of such malefactresses as this Hester Prynne. What think ye, gos-sips? If the hussy stood up for judgment before us five, that are now here in a knot together, would she come off with such a sentence as the wor-shipful magistrates have awarded? Marry, I trow not!"

"People say," said another, "that the Reverend Master Dimmesdale, her godly pastor, takes it very grievously to heart that such a scandal should have come upon his congregation."

"The magistrates are God-fearing gentlemen, but merciful overmuch—that is a truth," added a third autumnal matron. "At the very least, they should have put the brand of a hot iron on Hester Prynne's forehead. Madame Hester would have winced at that, I warrant me. But she—the naughty baggage—little will she care what they put upon the bodice of her gown. Why, look you, she may cover it with a brooch, or such like, heathenish adornment, and so walk the streets as brave as ever."

"Ah, but," interposed, more softly, a young wife, holding a child by the hand, "let her cover the mark as she will, the pang of it will be always in her heart."

"What do we talk of marks and brands, whether on the bodice of her gown or the flesh of her forehead?" cried another female, the ugliest as well as the most pitiless of these self-constituted judges. "This woman has brought shame upon us all, and ought to die; Is there not law for it? Truly there is, both in the Scripture and the statute-book. Then let the magistrates, who have made it of no effect, thank themselves if their own wives and daughters go astray."

"Mercy on us, goodwife," exclaimed a man in the crowd, "is there no virtue in woman, save what springs from a wholesome fear of the gal-lows? That is the hardest word yet. Hush now, gossips for the lock is turning in the prison-door, and here comes Mistress Prynne herself."

The door of the jail being flung open from within there appeared, in the first place, like a black shadow emerging into sunshine, the grim and gristly presence of the town-beadle, with a sword by his side, and his staff of office in his hand. This personage prefigured and represented in his aspect the whole dismal severity of the Puritanic code of law, which it was his business to administer in its final and closest application to the offender. Stretching forth the official staff in his left hand, he laid his right upon the shoulder of a young woman, whom he thus drew forward, until, on the threshold of the prison-door, she repelled him, by an action marked with natural dignity and force of character, and stepped into the open air as if by her own free will. She bore in her arms a child, a baby of some three months old, who winked and turned aside its little face from the too vivid light of day; because its existence, heretofore, had brought it acquaintance only with the grey twilight of a dungeon, or other darksome apartment of the prison.

When the young woman—the mother of this child—stood fully revealed before the crowd, it seemed to be her first impulse to clasp the infant closely to her bosom; not so much by an impulse of motherly affection, as that she might thereby conceal a certain token, which was wrought or fastened into her dress. In a moment, however, wisely judging that one token of her shame would but poorly serve to hide another, she took the baby on her arm, and with a burning blush, and yet a haughty smile, and a glance that would not be abashed, looked around at her townspeople and neighbours. On the breast of her gown, in fine red cloth, surrounded with an elaborate embroidery and fantastic flourishes of gold thread, appeared the letter A. It was so artistically done, and with so much fertility and gorgeous luxuriance of fancy, that it had all the effect of a last and fitting decoration to the apparel which she wore, and which was of a splendour in accordance with the taste of the age, but greatly beyond what was allowed by the sumptuary regulations of the colony.

The young woman was tall, with a figure of perfect elegance on a large scale. She had dark and abundant hair, so glossy that it threw off the sunshine with a gleam; and a face which, besides being beautiful from regularity of feature and richness of complexion, had the impressiveness belonging to a marked brow and deep black eyes. She was ladylike, too, after the manner of the feminine gentility of those days; characterised by a certain state and dignity, rather than by the delicate, evanescent, and indescribable grace which is now recognised as its indication. And never had Hester Prynne appeared more ladylike, in the antique interpretation of the term, than as she issued from the prison. Those who had before known her, and had expected to behold her dimmed and obscured by a disastrous cloud, were astonished, and even startled, to perceive how her beauty shone out, and made a halo of the misfortune and ignominy in which she was enveloped. It may be true that, to a sensitive observer, there was some thing exquisitely painful in it. Her attire, which indeed, she had wrought for the occasion in prison, and had modelled much after her own fancy, seemed to express the attitude of her spirit, the desperate recklessness of her mood, by its wild and picturesque peculiarity. But the point which drew all eyes, and, as it were, transfigured the wearer—so that both men and women who had been familiarly acquainted with Hester Prynne were now impressed as if they beheld her for the first time—was that SCARLET LETTER, so fantastically embroidered and illuminated upon her bosom. It had the effect of a spell, taking her out of the ordinary relations with humanity, and enclosing her in a sphere by herself.

"She hath good skill at her needle, that's certain," remarked one of her female spectators; "but did ever a woman, before this brazen hussy, contrive such a way of showing it? Why, gossips, what is it but to laugh in the faces of our godly magistrates, and make a pride out of what they, worthy gentlemen, meant for a punishment?"

"It were well," muttered the most iron-visaged of the old dames, "if we stripped Madame Hester's rich gown off her dainty shoulders; and as for the red letter which she hath stitched so curiously, I'll bestow a rag of mine own rheumatic flannel to make a fitter one!"

"Oh, peace, neighbours—peace!" whispered their youngest companion; "do not let her hear you! Not a stitch in that embroidered letter but she has felt it in her heart."

The grim beadle now made a gesture with his staff. "Make way, good people—make way, in the King's name!" cried he. "Open a passage; and I promise ye, Mistress Prynne shall be set where man, woman, and child may have a fair sight of her brave apparel from this time till an hour past **meridian**. A blessing on the righteous colony of the Massachusetts, where iniquity is dragged out into the sunshine! Come along, Madame Hester, and show your scarlet letter in the market-place!"

meridian: noon.

A lane was forthwith opened through the crowd of spectators. Preceded by the beadle, and attended by an irregular procession of stern-browed men and unkindly visaged women, Hester Prynne set forth towards the place appointed for her punishment. A crowd of eager and curious schoolboys, understanding little of the matter in hand, except that it gave them a half-holiday, ran before her progress, turning their heads continually to stare into her face and at the winking baby in her arms, and at the ignominious letter on her breast. It was no great distance, in those days, from the prison door to the market-place. Measured by the prisoner's experience, however, it might be reckoned a journey of some length; for haughty as her demeanour was, she perchance underwent an agony from every footstep of those that thronged to see her, as if her heart had been flung into the street for them all to spurn and trample upon. In our nature, however, there is a provision, alike marvellous and merciful, that the sufferer should never know the intensity of what he endures by its present torture, but chiefly by the pang that rankles after it. With almost a serene deportment, therefore, Hester Prynne passed through this portion of her ordeal, and came to a sort of scaffold, at the western extremity of the market-place. It stood nearly beneath the eaves of Boston's earliest church, and appeared to be a fixture there.

In fact, this scaffold constituted a portion of a penal machine, which now, for two or three generations past, has been merely historical and traditionary among us, but was held, in the old time, to be as effectual an agent, in the promotion of good citizenship, as ever was the guillotine among the terrorists of France. It was, in short, the platform of the pillory; and above it rose the framework of that instrument of discipline, so fashioned as to confine the human head in its tight grasp, and thus hold it up to the public gaze. The very ideal of ignominy was embodied and made manifest in this contrivance of wood and iron. There can be no outrage, methinks, against our common nature—whatever be the delinquencies of the individual—no outrage more flagrant than to forbid the culprit to hide his face for shame; as it was the essence of this punishment to do. In Hester Prynne's instance, however, as not unfrequently in other cases, her sentence bore that she should stand a certain time upon the platform, but without undergoing that gripe about the neck and confinement of the head, the proneness to which was the most devilish characteristic of this ugly engine. Knowing well her part, she ascended a flight of wooden steps, and was thus displayed to the surrounding multitude, at about the height of a man's shoulders above the street.

Had there been a Papist among the crowd of Puritans, he might have seen in this beautiful woman, so picturesque in her attire and mien, and with the infant at her bosom, an object to remind him of the **image of Divine Maternity**, which so many illustrious painters have vied with one another to represent; something which should remind him, indeed, but only by contrast, of that sacred image of sinless motherhood, whose infant was to redeem the world. Here, there was the taint of deepest sin in the most sacred quality of human life, working such effect, that the world was only the darker for this woman's beauty, and the more lost for the infant that she had borne.

image of Divine Maternity: Some critics see this reference as evidence of Hawthorne's fascination with Roman Catholicism. They also suggest that Hester is associated with Mary to show her connection with the rich and elegant Old World rejected by the austere Puritans.

The scene was not without a mixture of awe, such as must always invest the spectacle of guilt and shame in a fellow-creature, before society shall have grown corrupt enough to smile, instead of shuddering at it. The witnesses of Hester Prynne's disgrace had not yet passed beyond their simplicity. They were stern enough to look upon her death, had that been the sentence, without a murmur at its severity, but had none of the heartlessness of another social state, which would find only a theme for jest in an exhibition like the present. Even had there been a disposition to turn the matter into ridicule, it must have been repressed and overpowered by the solemn presence of men no less dignified than the governor, and several of his counsellors, a judge, a general, and the ministers of the town, all of whom sat or stood in a balcony of the meeting-house, looking down upon the platform. When such personages could constitute a part of the spectacle, without risking the majesty, or reverence of rank and office, it was safely to be inferred that the infliction of a legal sentence would have an earnest and effectual meaning. Accordingly, the crowd was sombre and grave. The unhappy culprit sustained herself as best a woman might, under the heavy weight of a thousand unrelenting eyes, all fastened upon her, and concentrated at her bosom. It was almost intolerable to be borne. Of an impulsive and passionate nature, she had fortified herself to encounter the stings and venomous stabs of public contumely, wreaking itself in every variety of insult; but there was a quality so much more terrible in the solemn mood of the popular mind, that she longed rather to behold all those rigid countenances contorted with scornful merriment, and herself the object. Had a roar of laughter burst from the multitude—each man, each woman, each little shrill-voiced child, contributing their individual parts—Hester Prynne might have repaid them all with a bitter and disdainful smile. But, under the leaden infliction which it was her doom to endure, she felt, at moments, as if she must needs shriek out with the full power of her lungs, and cast herself from the scaffold down upon the ground, or else go mad at once.

Yet there were intervals when the whole scene, in which she was the most conspicuous object, seemed to vanish from her eyes, or, at least, glimmered indistinctly before them, like a mass of imperfectly shaped and spectral images. Her mind, and especially her memory, was preternaturally active, and kept bringing up other scenes than this roughly hewn street of a little town, on the edge of the western wilderness: other faces than were lowering upon her from beneath the brims of those steeple-crowned hats. Reminiscences, the most trifling and immaterial, passages of infancy and school-days, sports, childish quarrels, and the little domestic traits of her maiden years, came swarming back upon her, intermingled with recollections of whatever was gravest in her subsequent life; one picture precisely as vivid as another; as if all were of similar importance, or all alike a play. Possibly, it was an instinctive device of her spirit to relieve itself by the exhibition of these phantasmagoric forms, from the cruel weight and hardness of the reality.

Be that as it might, the scaffold of the pillory was a point of view that revealed to Hester Prynne the entire track along which she had been treading, since her happy infancy. Standing on that miserable eminence, she saw again her native village, in Old England, and her paternal home: a decayed house of grey stone, with a poverty-stricken aspect, but retaining a half obliterated shield of arms over the portal, in token of antique gentility. She saw her father's face, with its bold brow, and reverend white beard that flowed over the old-fashioned Elizabethan ruff; her mother's, too, with the look of heedful and anxious love which it always wore in her remembrance, and which, even since her death, had so often laid the impediment of a gentle remonstrance in her daughter's pathway. She saw her own face, glowing with girlish beauty, and illuminating all the interior of the dusky mirror in which she had been wont to gaze at it. There she beheld another countenance, of a man well stricken in years, a pale, thin, scholar-like visage, with eyes dim and bleared by the lamp-light that had served them to pore over many ponderous books. Yet those same bleared optics had a strange, penetrating power, when it was their owner's purpose to read the human soul. This figure of the study and the cloister,

as Hester Prynne's womanly fancy failed not to recall, was slightly
deformed, with the left shoulder a trifle higher than the right. Next rose
before her in memory's picture-gallery, the intricate and narrow thor-
oughfares, the tall, grey houses, the huge cathedrals, and the public edi-
fices, ancient in date and quaint in architecture, of a continental city;
where new life had awaited her, still in connexion with the misshapen
scholar: a new life, but feeding itself on time-worn materials, like a tuft of
green moss on a crumbling wall. Lastly, in lieu of these shifting scenes,
came back the rude market-place of the Puritan settlement, with all the
townspeople assembled, and levelling their stern regards at Hester
Prynne—yes, at herself—who stood on the scaffold of the pillory, an
infant on her arm, and the letter A, in scarlet, fantastically embroidered
with gold thread, upon her bosom.

Could it be true? She clutched the child so fiercely to her breast that it
sent forth a cry; she turned her eyes downward at the scarlet letter, and
even touched it with her finger, to assure herself that the infant and the
shame were real. Yes!—these were her realities—all else had vanished!

COMMENTARY

While the description of the Puritans, the prison, and
the wild rosebush in the previous scene set the
general tone of the novel, the opening paragraph in this
chapter places the events of the novel in a specific time
and place: This is Puritan Boston, two centuries before
Hawthorne wrote the novel. This chapter offers further
insight into the character and beliefs of the Puritans by
emphasizing the severity of the people; here their faces
are "petrified" with "grim rigidity," and they are "iron-
visaged" and "unkindly-visaged." Hawthorne skillfully
piles on images that portray the severe, inflexible attitude
of the early Puritans, who are dour in even the most
casual situations. Part of their inflexibility grows from the
fact that law and religion are inseparable for these people. Indeed, so deep is their reliance on religion and law
that even the mildest transgression meets with discipline
that is "venerable and awful." The Puritans' rigid sense
of law also leaves them unable to feel compassion for
anyone who has the misfortune to transgress their rigid
legal code, partly because they believe that any transgression of law is also a transgression against God. As in
the previous chapter, the narrator's tone once again
implicitly criticizes the "early severity" of our Puritan forefathers by emphasizing their intolerance.

After painting this grim picture of the people gathered
outside the prison door, the narrator narrows his focus,
examining the women in the group. He notes that the
audience is made up primarily of women, who seem to
take a particular interest in the criminal who is about to
step out of the prison door. Their conversation reveals
that the prisoner's name is Hester Prynne and that she
must wear a marking on her breast. The reader also gains
insight on the characters of these Puritan women.
According to the narrator, these women are both morally
and physically coarser, or tougher, than the women of
today. For them, for example, it was natural to watch a
hanging or any other type of "penal infliction." Indeed,
their lack of sympathy for Hester makes them appear
inhumanly tough. In the narrator's opinion, each new
generation of New England women has been more delicate, having less character and force, than these sturdy,
first-generation immigrants. He connects them with the
"man-like" Queen Elizabeth I, "the not altogether unsuitable representative of the sex," who ruled England from
1558 to 1603. Their firm, sturdy physical appearance—
broad shoulders and "well-developed busts"—is
matched by a "boldness and rotundity" in their speech,
which is both loud and tactless. These sturdy women

argue that Hester's punishment was too lenient. Rather than the scarlet letter on her breast, they would like to see a brand on her forehead. Only one woman, a young wife, feels any sympathy for Hester; she recognizes that Hester's self-punishment will always be greater than anything the legal authorities can dole out.

The conversation of these women offers more specific insight on the thoughts and beliefs of the early New Englanders, along with the narrator's views of gender differences and differences between the peasant inhabitants of England and the colonists in the New World. Obviously, these women feel morally superior to Hester and, therefore, feel they can condemn her actions. Perhaps they are even harsher critics than the male magistrates because Hester's sin could be used to suggest women's generally sinful and passionate nature (an association made in Chapter V), which makes all women look suspect.

Finally, the prison door opens and Hester, the novel's protagonist, is about to enter the novel. Before she appears, though, this chapter offers another look at a representative of Puritan legal authority: the town beadle. Charged with administering all legal punishments, this man is like a "black shadow"—"grim and grisly." Once again, the darkness of Puritan punishment is emphasized and critiqued. Can a society that creates a cruel criminal system be just or fair? According to the narrator, the dismal beadle represents the severity of Puritan law. By presenting this man in such a negative light, the narrator creates additional sympathy for Hester, the prisoner of this legal system.

Just behind this man walks Hester with her three-month-old baby in her arms. From the first glimpse of her, the reader immediately sees the strength and beauty of Hester's appearance and character. Even while walking across the scaffold at this moment of public disgrace, Hester smiles haughtily and looks unabashed. Unlike the women in the audience, depicted as large and matronly, Hester is a figure of "perfect elegance." Her dark and abundant hair gleams in the sunshine, her face is beautiful and impressive, and her stature is lady-like and dignified. Her beauty is not delicate; it is regal and solid. The narrator emphasizes that prison and disgrace seem to have enhanced Hester's beauty, rather than dimming or diminishing it, again emphasizing the strength of her character.

Meg Foster as Hester Prynne in a 1979 PBS production of The Scarlet Letter. Everett Collection

The terms associated with Hester—beauty, grace, and dignity—provide a strong, positive contrast to the terms used to describe the other inhabitants of Boston. But there is also an edge to her attractiveness: Just as the beauty of the rosebush sprung partially from its wild nature, Hester's spirit shows "desperate recklessness" and "wild and picturesque peculiarity." Both her beauty and her personality brand her as a rebel and an individual in a community that tolerates only absolute conformity.

Hester's free spirit is exemplified in the symbol of the scarlet letter, which Hester must wear indefinitely as part of her punishment for adultery. Not the austere and simple "A" that might be expected of a Puritan woman, Hester's red "A" is embroidered with "fantastic flourishes of gold thread" and with "fertility and gorgeous luxuriance of fancy" that demonstrate her imagination. These attributes also indicate an embrace of excess—an impulsivity and passion that combat the severe austerity of the Puritan imagination. Remember from the previous chapter that the people surrounding the prison door were dressed in "sad-colored," gray clothing: Obviously, Hester's flamboyant red and gold contrasts with communal norms. Later in this chapter, the narrator tells us that all of Hester's clothing is made in her unique style.

The scarlet letter places a sort of spell upon the crowd, removing Hester from the community and placing her in a sphere by herself. Again, the narrator emphasizes Hester's difference—her inability to conform with the rules of the Puritan community. The word *spell* implicitly links her with men and women who were accused of witchcraft, primarily because of their nonconformity.

Of course, the female spectators in the crowd don't look favorably upon Hester's flamboyant "A." In their opinion, her fantastic design is a symbol of pride that makes a mockery of her punishment. Their comments, together with the description of the letter, suggest the different meanings associated with the letter by the community and by Hester: For them it is a sign of humiliation and loss of identity, while for her it symbolizes artistry, pride, and individuality.

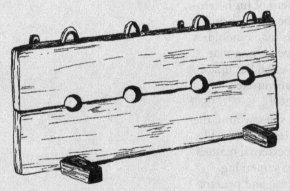

The pillory.

After this first glimpse of Hester, the scene's focus shifts back to the legal authorities and to the machinery of penal authority: the scaffold and the pillory. These wood and iron devices were the symbols of crime and punishment to a society in which all legal transgressions were publicly punished and the body of the criminal was the focus of punishment. For example, the pillory kept the criminal's head firmly confined, so that he or she was unable to hide it in shame. While Hester's punishment does not involve this particular implement of torture, she is required to stand on the platform of the scaffold as a public symbol of shame and dishonor. But the image of Hester on the platform does not invoke exactly the negative feelings the Puritan fathers might have hoped for. In her beauty and dignity, she could, the narrator suggests, be compared to the Virgin Mary.

All the weightiness that was earlier attributed to the wooden doors of the prison has now become invested in the looks of the spectators who stare at Hester with "heavy," "unrelenting," "leaden" eyes. Although the gazes of the spectators discompose Hester, she is, at moments, able to distance herself from this uncomfortable scene. In particular, she remembers her early life in England, offering additional insights into her character. For example, her family, once part of the upper classes, fell on hard times. Hester's recollections also reveal that she married an older man, a scholar whose eyes have a "strange, penetrating power" that allows him to read into the human soul. (This detail foreshadows the arrival of her husband, an odd, deformed man, and signals the role he will play in the drama of Hester's life.) After their marriage, the couple lived in Amsterdam, which offered Hester a new life, but one that fed "on time-worn materials, like a tuft of green moss on a crumbling wall." In creating this contrast between new and old, between green moss and crumbling wall, the narrator hints at the problem in Hester's marriage: Her older husband lived on dusty scholarship, while the youthful Hester longed for fresh, new ideas. The details gleaned through Hester's reminiscing infer that Hester was forced into an unhappy marriage due to her family's poverty.

Chapter III

As Hester stands on the scaffold, she suddenly notices a deformed, older man in the crowd. When he sees her, his face blanches in horror. Meanwhile, the ministers of the town try to make Hester reveal the identity of her baby's father. She refuses to tell them.

CHAPTER III: THE RECOGNITION

FROM this intense consciousness of being the object of severe and universal observation, the wearer of the scarlet letter was at length relieved, by discerning, on the outskirts of the crowd, a figure which irresistibly took possession of her thoughts. An Indian in his native garb was standing there; but the red men were not so infrequent visitors of the English settlements that one of them would have attracted any notice from Hester Prynne at such a time; much less would he have excluded all other objects and ideas from her mind. By the Indian's side, and evidently sustaining a companionship with him, stood a white man, clad in a strange disarray of civilized and savage costume.

He was small in stature, with a furrowed visage, which as yet could hardly be termed aged. There was a remarkable intelligence in his features, as of a person who had so cultivated his mental part that it could not fail to mould the physical to itself and become manifest by unmistakable tokens. Although, by a seemingly careless arrangement of his heterogeneous garb, he had endeavoured to conceal or abate the peculiarity, it was sufficiently evident to Hester Prynne that one of this man's shoulders rose higher than the other. Again, at the first instant of perceiving that thin visage, and the slight deformity of the figure, she pressed her infant to her bosom with so convulsive a force that the poor babe uttered another cry of pain. But the mother did not seem to hear it.

At his arrival in the market-place, and some time before she saw him, the stranger had bent his eyes on Hester Prynne. It was carelessly at first, like a man chiefly accustomed to look inward, and to whom external matters are of little value and import, unless they bear relation to something within his mind. Very soon, however, his look became keen and penetrative. A writhing horror twisted itself across his features, like a snake gliding swiftly over them, and making one little pause, with all its wreathed intervolutions in open sight. His face darkened with some powerful emotion, which, nevertheless, he so instantaneously controlled by an effort of his will, that, save at a single moment, its expression might have passed for calmness. After a brief space, the convulsion grew almost imperceptible, and finally subsided into the depths of his nature. When he found the eyes of Hester Prynne fastened on his own, and saw that she appeared to recognize him, he slowly and calmly raised his finger, made a gesture with it in the air, and laid it on his lips.

Then touching the shoulder of a townsman who stood near to him, he addressed him in a formal and courteous manner:

"I pray you, good Sir," said he, "who is this woman?—and wherefore is she here set up to public shame?"

"You must needs be a stranger in this region, friend," answered the townsman, looking curiously at the questioner and his savage companion, "else you would surely have heard of Mistress Hester Prynne and her evil doings. She hath raised a great scandal, I promise you, in godly Master Dimmesdale's church."

"You say truly," replied the other: "I am a stranger, and have been a wanderer, sorely against my will. I have met with grievous mishaps by sea and land, and have been long held in bonds among the heathen-folk to the southward; and am now brought hither by this Indian to be redeemed out of my captivity. Will it please you, therefore, to tell me of Hester Prynne's—have I her name rightly?—of this woman's offences, and what has brought her to yonder scaffold?"

"Truly, friend; and methinks it must gladden your heart, after your troubles and sojourn in the wilderness," said the townsman, "to find yourself at length in a land where iniquity is searched out and punished in the sight of rulers and people, as here in our godly New England. Yonder woman, Sir, you must know, was the wife of a certain learned man, English by birth, but who had long ago dwelt in Amsterdam, whence some good time agone he was minded to cross over and cast in his lot with us of the Massachusetts. To this purpose he sent his wife before him, remaining himself to look after some necessary affairs. Marry, good Sir, in some two years, or less, that the woman has been a dweller here in Boston, no tidings have come of this learned gentleman, Master Prynne; and his young wife, look you, being left to her own misguidance—"

"Ah!—aha!—I conceive you," said the stranger with a bitter smile. "So learned a man as you speak of should have learned this too in his books. And who, by your favour, Sir, may be the father of yonder babe—it is some three or four months old, I should judge—which Mistress Prynne is holding in her arms?"

"Of a truth, friend, that matter remaineth a riddle; and the **Daniel** who shall expound it is yet a-wanting," answered the townsman. "Madame Hester absolutely refuseth to speak, and the magistrates have laid their heads together in vain. Peradventure the guilty one stands looking on at this sad spectacle, unknown of man, and forgetting that God sees him."

"The learned man," observed the stranger with another smile, "should come himself to look into the mystery."

"It behoves him well if he be still in life," responded the townsman. "Now, good Sir, our Massachusetts magistracy, bethinking themselves that this woman is youthful and fair, and doubtless was strongly tempted to her fall, and that, moreover, as is most likely, her husband may be at the bottom of the sea, they have not been bold to put in force the extremity of our righteous law against her. The penalty thereof is death.

Daniel: a biblical prophet who was able to interpret dreams and a mysterious writing on the wall of King Balthazar.

But in their great mercy and tenderness of heart they have doomed Mistress Prynne to stand only a space of three hours on the platform of the pillory, and then and thereafter, for the remainder of her natural life to wear a mark of shame upon her bosom."

"A wise sentence," remarked the stranger, gravely, bowing his head. "Thus she will be a living sermon against sin, until the ignominious letter be engraved upon her tombstone. It irks me, nevertheless, that the partner of her iniquity should not at least, stand on the scaffold by her side. But he will be known—he will be known!—he will be known!"

He bowed courteously to the communicative townsman, and whispering a few words to his Indian attendant, they both made their way through the crowd.

While this passed, Hester Prynne had been standing on her pedestal, still with a fixed gaze towards the stranger—so fixed a gaze that, at moments of intense absorption, all other objects in the visible world seemed to vanish, leaving only him and her. Such an interview, perhaps, would have been more terrible than even to meet him as she now did, with the hot mid-day sun burning down upon her face, and lighting up its shame; with the scarlet token of infamy on her breast; with the sin-born infant in her arms; with a whole people, drawn forth as to a festival, staring at the features that should have been seen only in the quiet gleam of the fireside, in the happy shadow of a home, or beneath a matronly veil at church. Dreadful as it was, she was conscious of a shelter in the presence of these thousand witnesses. It was better to stand thus, with so many betwixt him and her, than to greet him face to face—they two alone. She fled for refuge, as it were, to the public exposure, and dreaded the moment when its protection should be withdrawn from her. Involved in these thoughts, she scarcely heard a voice behind her until it had repeated her name more than once, in a loud and solemn tone, audible to the whole multitude.

"Hearken unto me, Hester Prynne!" said the voice.

It has already been noticed that directly over the platform on which Hester Prynne stood was a kind of balcony, or open gallery, appended to the meeting-house. It was the place whence proclamations were wont to be made, amidst an assemblage of the magistracy, with all the ceremonial that attended such public observances in those days. Here, to witness the scene which we are describing, sat **Governor Bellingham** himself with four sergeants about his chair, bearing **halberds**, as a guard of honour. He wore a dark feather in his hat, a border of embroidery on his cloak, and a black velvet tunic beneath—a gentleman advanced in years, with a hard experience written in his wrinkles. He was not ill-fitted to be the head and representative of a community which owed its origin and progress, and its present state of development, not to the impulses of youth, but to the stern and tempered energies of manhood and the sombre sagacity of age; accomplishing so much, precisely because it imagined and hoped so little. The other eminent characters by whom the chief ruler was surrounded were distinguished by a dignity of mien, belonging

Governor Bellingham: Richard Bellingham (1592–1672) emigrated to New England in 1634 and served as the governor of Massachusetts.

halberds: combination spears and battle axes used in the fifteenth and sixteenth centuries.

to a period when the forms of authority were felt to possess the sacredness of Divine institutions. They were, doubtless, good men, just and sage. But, out of the whole human family, it would not have been easy to select the same number of wise and virtuous persons, who should be less capable of sitting in judgment on an erring woman's heart, and disentangling its mesh of good and evil, than the sages of rigid aspect towards whom Hester Prynne now turned her face. She seemed conscious, indeed, that whatever sympathy she might expect lay in the larger and warmer heart of the multitude; for, as she lifted her eyes towards the balcony, the unhappy woman grew pale, and trembled.

The voice which had called her attention was that of the reverend and famous **John Wilson**, the eldest clergyman of Boston, a great scholar, like most of his contemporaries in the profession, and withal a man of kind and genial spirit. This last attribute, however, had been less carefully developed than his intellectual gifts, and was, in truth, rather a matter of shame than self-congratulation with him. There he stood, with a border of grizzled locks beneath his skull-cap, while his grey eyes, accustomed to the shaded light of his study, were winking, like those of Hester's infant, in the unadulterated sunshine. He looked like the darkly engraved portraits which we see prefixed to old volumes of sermons, and had no more right than one of those portraits would have to step forth, as he now did, and meddle with a question of human guilt, passion, and anguish.

John Wilson: An influential preacher at Boston's First Church until his death, Wilson (1590–1667) emigrated to the colonies in 1630.

"Hester Prynne," said the clergyman, "I have striven with my young brother here, under whose preaching of the Word you have been privileged to sit"—here Mr. Wilson laid his hand on the shoulder of a pale young man beside him—"I have sought, I say, to persuade this godly youth, that he should deal with you, here in the face of Heaven, and before these wise and upright rulers, and in hearing of all the people, as touching the vileness and blackness of your sin. Knowing your natural temper better than I, he could the better judge what arguments to use, whether of tenderness or terror, such as might prevail over your hardness and obstinacy, insomuch that you should no longer hide the name of him who tempted you to this grievous fall. But he opposes to me—with a young man's over-softness, albeit wise beyond his years—that it were wronging the very nature of woman to force her to lay open her heart's secrets in such broad daylight, and in presence of so great a multitude. Truly, as I sought to convince him, the shame lay in the commission of the sin, and not in the showing of it forth. What say you to it, once again, brother Dimmesdale? Must it be thou, or I, that shall deal with this poor sinner's soul?"

There was a murmur among the dignified and reverend occupants of the balcony; and Governor Bellingham gave expression to its purport, speaking in an authoritative voice, although tempered with respect towards the youthful clergyman whom he addressed:

"Good Master Dimmesdale," said he, "the responsibility of this woman's soul lies greatly with you. It behoves you; therefore, to exhort her to repentance and to confession, as a proof and consequence thereof."

The directness of this appeal drew the eyes of the whole crowd upon the Reverend Mr. Dimmesdale—young clergyman, who had come from one of the great English universities, bringing all the learning of the age into our wild forest land. His eloquence and religious fervour had already given the earnest of high eminence in his profession. He was a person of very striking aspect, with a white, lofty, and impending brow; large, brown, melancholy eyes, and a mouth which, unless when he forcibly compressed it, was apt to be tremulous, expressing both nervous sensibility and a vast power of self restraint. Notwithstanding his high native gifts and scholar-like attainments, there was an air about this young minister—an apprehensive, a startled, a half-frightened look—as of a being who felt himself quite astray, and at a loss in the pathway of human existence, and could only be at ease in some seclusion of his own. Therefore, so far as his duties would permit, he trod in the shadowy by-paths, and thus kept himself simple and childlike, coming forth, when occasion was, with a freshness, and fragrance, and dewy purity of thought, which, as many people said, affected them like the speech of an angel.

Such was the young man whom the Reverend Mr. Wilson and the Governor had introduced so openly to the public notice, bidding him speak, in the hearing of all men, to that mystery of a woman's soul, so sacred even in its pollution. The trying nature of his position drove the blood from his cheek, and made his lips tremulous.

"Speak to the woman, my brother," said Mr. Wilson. "It is of moment to her soul, and, therefore, as the worshipful Governor says, momentous to thine own, ill whose charge hers is. Exhort her to confess the truth!"

The Reverend Mr. Dimmesdale bent his head, silent prayer, as it seemed, and then came forward.

"Hester Prynne," said he, leaning over the balcony and looking down steadfastly into her eyes, "thou hearest what this good man says, and seest the accountability under which I labour. If thou feelest it to be for thy soul's peace, and that thy earthly punishment will thereby be made more effectual to salvation, I charge thee to speak out the name of thy fellow-sinner and fellow-sufferer! Be not silent from any mistaken pity and tenderness for him; for, believe me, Hester, though he were to step down from a high place, and stand there beside thee, on thy pedestal of shame, yet better were it so than to hide a guilty heart through life. What can thy silence do for him, except it tempt him—yea, compel him, as it were—to add hypocrisy to sin? Heaven hath granted thee an open ignominy, that thereby thou mayest work out an open triumph over the evil within thee and the sorrow without. Take heed how thou deniest to him—who, perchance, hath not the courage to grasp it for himself—the bitter, but wholesome, cup that is now presented to thy lips!"

The young pastor's voice was tremulously sweet, rich, deep, and broken. The feeling that it so evidently manifested, rather than the direct purport of the words, caused it to vibrate within all hearts, and brought the listeners into one accord of sympathy. Even the poor baby at Hester's bosom was affected by the same influence, for it directed its hitherto vacant gaze towards Mr. Dimmesdale, and held up its little arms with a half-pleased, half-plaintive murmur. So powerful seemed the minister's appeal that the people could not believe but that Hester Prynne would speak out the guilty name, or else that the guilty one himself in whatever high or lowly place he stood, would be drawn forth by an inward and inevitable necessity, and compelled to ascend the scaffold.

Hester shook her head.

"Woman, transgress not beyond the limits of Heaven's mercy!" cried the Reverend Mr. Wilson, more harshly than before. "That little babe hath been gifted with a voice, to second and confirm the counsel which thou hast heard. Speak out the name! That, and thy repentance, may avail to take the scarlet letter off thy breast."

"Never," replied Hester Prynne, looking, not at Mr. Wilson, but into the deep and troubled eyes of the younger clergyman. "It is too deeply branded. Ye cannot take it off. And would that I might endure his agony as well as mine!"

"Speak, woman!" said another voice, coldly and sternly, proceeding from the crowd about the scaffold, "Speak; and give your child a father!"

"I will not speak!" answered Hester, turning pale as death, but responding to this voice, which she too surely recognised. "And my child must seek a heavenly father; she shall never know an earthly one!"

"She will not speak!" murmured Mr. Dimmesdale, who, leaning over the balcony, with his hand upon his heart, had awaited the result of his appeal. He now drew back with a long respiration. "Wondrous strength and generosity of a woman's heart! She will not speak!"

Discerning the impracticable state of the poor culprit's mind, the elder clergyman, who had carefully prepared himself for the occasion, addressed to the multitude a discourse on sin, in all its branches, but with continual reference to the ignominious letter. So forcibly did he dwell upon this symbol, for the hour or more during which his periods were rolling over the people's heads, that it assumed new terrors in their imagination, and seemed to derive its scarlet hue from the flames of the infernal pit. Hester Prynne, meanwhile, kept her place upon the pedestal of shame, with glazed eyes, and an air of weary indifference. She had borne that morning all that nature could endure; and as her temperament was not of the order that escapes from too intense suffering by a swoon, her spirit could only shelter itself beneath a stony crust of insensibility, while the faculties of animal life remained entire. In this state, the voice of the preacher thundered remorselessly, but unavailingly, upon her ears. The infant, during the latter portion of her ordeal, pierced the air with its wailings and screams; she strove to hush it mechanically, but seemed scarcely to sympathise with its trouble. With the same hard demeanour, she was led back to prison, and vanished from the public gaze within its iron-clamped portal. It was whispered by those who peered after her that the scarlet letter threw a lurid gleam along the dark passage-way of the interior.

COMMENTARY

From remembrances of her life in England, Hester's focus in this chapter shifts to awareness of a particular member of the crowd surrounding the scaffold: a white man clad in a mixture of "civilized and savage" clothing. The description of this man emphasizes the intelligence obvious in his face but also the fact that he lives on the boundary between two cultures, European and Native American. Although he has tried to cover it, Hester notices a slight deformity in the man's body: One shoulder is higher than the other. Immediately, the reader is reminded of the older man hinted at in the previous chapter who was, perhaps still is, Hester's husband. This instance of recognition exemplifies the fact that each detail of the plot is essential—each has a role to play in the overall movement of the novel.

This odd man in the crowd seems equally interested in Hester. After glancing at her, his gaze becomes "keen and penetrative"; even more surprising, his face is twisted with a "writhing horror," as if a snake had glided across it. Each detail provides insight on this man, who is soon revealed to be Hester's husband, Roger Chillingworth. His mixture of clothing is symbolic of his personality: Although he appears to be an intelligent, educated man, he also has a savage, malicious side. (Note that Hawthorne's equation of Native Americans with "savageness" is a racial slur typical of his day. As you read passages like this, consider whether such racial comments make this novel less valid to modern readers.) Indeed, later in the book Chillingworth will seem almost satanic, an element of his personality prefigured here in the image of the snake gliding across his face. The snake is associated with sin, specifically with Eve's sexual transgression in the Garden of Eden. Notice that Chillingworth quickly hides this horrific facial expression, absorbing it into "the depths of his nature." He internalizes his rage, but its effects will be evident as the novel progresses and he becomes obsessed with his need to avenge himself upon Hester's lover.

From Chillingworth's conversation with a townsman, the reader discovers more about Hester's past. Not only was she unhappily married to an older, scholarly man, but this man decided to move to New England and sent Hester ahead to the New World by herself. In the two years that Hester has lived in Massachusetts, no word has come from this man, so the townsfolk assume he must have perished at sea. Both Chillingworth and the townsman suggest that Hester's husband should have learned more about human nature in his studies, and should have known better than to leave a young woman alone in a New World. This conversation also reveals that the identity of the father of Hester's baby is unknown. Death is the typical punishment for adultery, but Hester has been spared because the Massachusetts magistrates believe she was probably seduced and recognize that the long absence of her husband has made her especially vulnerable.

The conversation between Chillingworth and the townsman shows the strength of Hester's character again: Although the judges have tried to force her to reveal the identity of the baby's father, she has resisted all their efforts, just as she repelled the town beadle in the previous chapter. In addition, this conversation gives a clear picture of the factors that led to Hester's fall: Not only was she unhappily married, but her husband seemed to have disappeared on his voyage to the colonies and was presumed dead.

Hawthorne's goal in this novel isn't to provide a simple moral judgment about adultery, but to examine adultery's psychological impact on everyone involved. Chillingworth's comments add a new shade of meaning to the scarlet letter. He suggests that the letter will make Hester "a living sermon against sin." As the bearer of the scarlet letter, she will lose her individuality, functioning as a symbol of morality, a potent antidote to inappropriate sexuality among members of the community.

In addition to offering further insight on the characters of Hester and Chillingworth, this chapter also offers a description of Boston's leaders. Governor Bellingham is an older man, a fit leader for this community, which was formed not with the impulses of youth but with the stern and somber wisdom of age. The narrator's analysis suggests that the colony accomplishes little because it dreams of little. The narrator indicates that the other men in the group, although good and just, are probably the least capable people to judge "an erring woman's heart": These old men have lost sight of the importance or meaning of passion, if they ever understood it. They are men like the Reverend John Wilson, who has developed his intellect more than his sympathy; he looks like "a darkly engraved portrait" that might accompany a volume of sermons but has no more right to judge a question of human passion and sorrow than one of those portraits. Wilson's sermon in this chapter expatiates on the scarlet letter, adding new depth and meaning to the symbol.

According to Wilson, the letter seems to have gained its scarlet color from the flames of hell. As in previous chapters, the narrator takes Hester's side rather than that of the Puritan leaders, once again pointing to their conservatism, narrow-mindedness, and lack of imagination.

Only the Reverend Arthur Dimmesdale, the unnamed father of Hester's baby, seems to have any understanding of Hester's needs, and his understanding is selfishly motivated. While the elderly magistrates believe that Hester should reveal the name of her lover in this public forum, Dimmesdale convinces them that it would be opposing the "nature of woman" to lay her "heart's secrets" open in such a public manner. Ironically, Hester's soul is said to be Dimmesdale's responsibility, yet he shares her sin.

In this chapter, Dimmesdale's great eloquence and religious fervor is revealed, but the fact that his body is frail and has a tendency to tremble is also brought to light. He is full of nervous energy that reflects his great capacity for self-restraint. For example, his nervous habit of placing his hand over his heart indicates that his guilt is branding him with its own scarlet letter, though one that isn't visible to the public eye. Overall, his personality is defined by "an apprehensive, a startled, a half-frightened look." Ironically, his parishioners see Dimmesdale as "simple and childlike," with an angelic "dewy purity of thought." The narrator implicitly critiques the Puritans for misreading Dimmesdale, for seeing this adulterer as an angel.

Knowing that Dimmesdale is Hester's lover and Pearl's father, the reader is aware of the double meanings of his speech to Hester. The speech, which is meant to uncover the identity of Pearl's father, reveals as much about Dimmesdale as it does about Hester. Publicly, he holds the position of advisor to her spiritual growth; privately, he was her lover. In this scene, Hawthorne emphasizes the huge gap that often separates our private and public lives.

The ironies in Dimmesdale's speech to Hester are apparent, for example, when he tells her that her lover would be better to share her pedestal of shame than to live with the secret of his guilty heart. Her silence only compels him to add hypocrisy to his list of sins—though, of course, the question could be raised as to why Hester has the sole responsibility to reveal his name. Shouldn't Dimmesdale have the moral courage to admit his fault, as Hester has been forced to do? The narrator suggests that public shame is more acceptable than private sin.

Although the Puritan leaders tell her that if she identifies her lover they will allow her to remove the scarlet letter from her breast, Hester rejects their appeals, exemplifying her ethical and moral strength. She says that she feels strong enough to bear her lover's pain along with her own. Obviously, she loves this man for whom she is sacrificing so much. Although Hawthorne never provides the reader with any details about their relationship, it is apparent that Hester and Dimmesdale shared a deep connection. Even Dimmesdale recognizes that Hester is capable of "wondrous strength and generosity." As she returns back through the doorway, the scarlet letter is said to throw "a lurid gleam" in the dark passageway—a light into the interior of the prison—that the spectators associate with the fires of hell.

Chapter IV

When she returns to her prison cell, Hester becomes hysterical, overwhelmed by the humiliation of her public punishment. That evening, the older man she saw in the crowd visits her cell. He is her long-lost husband, Roger Chillingworth, who vows to discover the identity of the baby's father despite Hester's continuing refusal to reveal this information. Hester promises to keep Chillingworth's identity a secret, even though it may mean the destruction of her soul.

CHAPTER IV: THE INTERVIEW

AFTER her return to the prison, Hester Prynne was found to be in a state of nervous excitement, that demanded constant watchfulness, lest she should perpetrate violence on herself, or do some half-frenzied mischief to the poor babe. As night approached, it proving impossible to quell her insubordination by rebuke or threats of punishment, Master Brackett, the jailer, thought fit to introduce a physician. He described him as a man of skill in all Christian modes of physical science, and likewise familiar with whatever the savage people could teach in respect to medicinal herbs and roots that grew in the forest. To say the truth, there was much need of professional assistance, not merely for Hester herself, but still more urgently for the child—who, drawing its sustenance from the maternal bosom, seemed to have drank in with it all the turmoil, the anguish and despair, which pervaded the mother's system. It now writhed in convulsions of pain, and was a forcible type, in its little frame, of the moral agony which Hester Prynne had borne throughout the day.

Closely following the jailer into the dismal apartment, appeared that individual, of singular aspect whose presence in the crowd had been of such deep interest to the wearer of the scarlet letter. He was lodged in the prison, not as suspected of any offence, but as the most convenient and suitable mode of disposing of him, until the magistrates should have conferred with the Indian **sagamores** respecting his ransom. His name was announced as Roger Chillingworth. The jailer, after ushering him into the room, remained a moment, marvelling at the comparative quiet that followed his entrance; for Hester Prynne had immediately become as still as death, although the child continued to moan.

sagamores: chiefs of second rank among Native Americans in New England.

"Prithee, friend, leave me alone with my patient," said the practitioner. "Trust me, good jailer, you shall briefly have peace in your house; and, I promise you, Mistress Prynne shall hereafter be more amenable to just authority than you may have found her heretofore."

"Nay, if your worship can accomplish that," answered Master Brackett, "I shall own you for a man of skill, indeed! Verily, the woman hath been like a possessed one; and there lacks little that I should take in hand, to drive Satan out of her with stripes."

The stranger had entered the room with the characteristic quietude of the profession to which he announced himself as belonging. Nor did his demeanour change when the withdrawal of the prison keeper left him face to face with the woman, whose absorbed notice of him, in the crowd, had intimated so close a relation between himself and her. His first care was given to the child, whose cries, indeed, as she lay writhing on the trundle-bed, made it of peremptory necessity to postpone all other business to the task of soothing her. He examined the infant carefully, and then proceeded to unclasp a leathern case, which he took from beneath his dress. It appeared to contain medical preparations, one of which he mingled with a cup of water.

"My old studies in **alchemy**," observed he, "and my sojourn, for above a year past, among a people well versed in the kindly properties of simples, have made a better physician of me than many that claim the medical degree. Here, woman! The child is yours—she is none of mine—neither will she recognise my voice or aspect as a father's. Administer this draught, therefore, with thine own hand."

Hester repelled the offered medicine, at the same time gazing with strongly marked apprehension into his face. "Wouldst thou avenge thyself on the innocent babe?" whispered she.

"Foolish woman!" responded the physician, half coldly, half soothingly. "What should ail me to harm this misbegotten and miserable babe? The medicine is potent for good, and were it my child—yea, mine own, as well as thine!—I could do no better for it."

As she still hesitated, being, in fact, in no reasonable state of mind, he took the infant in his arms, and himself administered the draught. It soon proved its efficacy, and redeemed the leech's pledge. The moans of the little patient subsided; its convulsive tossings gradually ceased; and in a few moments, as is the custom of young children after relief from pain, it sank into a profound and dewy slumber. The physician, as he had a fair right to be termed, next bestowed his attention on the mother. With calm and intent scrutiny, he felt her pulse, looked into her eyes—a gaze that made her heart shrink and shudder, because so familiar, and yet so strange and cold—and, finally, satisfied with his investigation, proceeded to mingle another draught.

"I know not **Lethe nor Nepenthe**," remarked he; "but I have learned many new secrets in the wilderness, and here is one of them—a recipe that an Indian taught me, in requital of some lessons of my own, that were as old as **Paracelsus**. Drink it! It may be less soothing than a sinless conscience. That I cannot give thee. But it will calm the swell and heaving of thy passion, like oil thrown on the waves of a tempestuous sea."

He presented the cup to Hester, who received it with a slow, earnest look into his face; not precisely a look of fear, yet full of doubt and questioning as to what his purposes might be. She looked also at her slumbering child.

"I have thought of death," said she,—"have wished for it—would even have prayed for it, were it fit that such as I should pray for anything. Yet, if death be in this cup, I bid thee think again, ere thou beholdest me quaff it. See! It is even now at my lips."

alchemy: an early form of chemistry with magical and philosophic associations, studied in the Middle Ages. Its aims were to change base metals into gold and to discover the secret of eternal life.

Lethe nor Nepenthe: Lethe was the river of forgetfulness flowing through Hades, whose water produces loss of memory in those who drink it; Nepenthe was a drug thought by the ancient Greeks to cause forgetfulness of sorrow.

Paracelsus: Philippus Aureolus Theophrastus Bombastus von Hohenheim (1493–1541), a controversial Swiss physician and alchemist, often called the father of chemistry.

"Drink, then," replied he, still with the same cold composure. "Dost thou know me so little, Hester Prynne? Are my purposes wont to be so shallow? Even if I imagine a scheme of vengeance, what could I do better for my object than to let thee live—than to give thee medicines against all harm and peril of life—so that this burning shame may still blaze upon thy bosom?" As he spoke, he laid his long fore-finger on the scarlet letter, which forthwith seemed to scorch into Hester's breast, as if it had been red hot. He noticed her involuntary gesture, and smiled. "Live, therefore, and bear about thy doom with thee, in the eyes of men and women—in the eyes of him whom thou didst call thy husband—in the eyes of yonder child! And, that thou mayest live, take off this draught."

Without further expostulation or delay, Hester Prynne drained the cup, and, at the motion of the man of skill, seated herself on the bed, where the child was sleeping; while he drew the only chair which the room afforded, and took his own seat beside her. She could not but tremble at these preparations; for she felt that—having now done all that humanity, or principle, or, if so it were, a refined cruelty, impelled him to do for the relief of physical suffering—he was next to treat with her as the man whom she had most deeply and irreparably injured.

"Hester," said he, "I ask not wherefore, nor how thou hast fallen into the pit, or say, rather, thou hast ascended to the pedestal of infamy on which I found thee. The reason is not far to seek. It was my folly, and thy weakness. I—a man of thought—the book-worm of great libraries—a man already in decay, having given my best years to feed the hungry dream of knowledge—what had I to do with youth and beauty like thine own? Misshapen from my birth-hour, how could I delude myself with the idea that intellectual gifts might veil physical deformity in a young girl's fantasy? Men call me wise. If sages were ever wise in their own behoof, I might have foreseen all this. I might have known that, as I came out of the vast and dismal forest, and entered this settlement of Christian men, the very first object to meet my eyes would be thyself, Hester Prynne, standing up, a statue of ignominy, before the people. Nay, from the moment when we came down the old church-steps together, a married pair, I might have beheld the bale-fire of that scarlet letter blazing at the end of our path!"

"Thou knowest," said Hester—for, depressed as she was, she could not endure this last quiet stab at the token of her shame—"thou knowest that I was frank with thee. I felt no love, nor feigned any."

"True," replied he. "It was my folly! I have said it. But, up to that epoch of my life, I had lived in vain. The world had been so cheerless! My heart was a habitation large enough for many guests, but lonely and chill, and without a household fire. I longed to kindle one! It seemed not so wild a dream—old as I was, and sombre as I was, and misshapen as I was—that the simple bliss, which is scattered far and wide, for all mankind to gather up, might yet be mine. And so, Hester, I drew thee into my heart, into its innermost chamber, and sought to warm thee by the warmth which thy presence made there!"

"I have greatly wronged thee," murmured Hester.

"We have wronged each other," answered he. "Mine was the first wrong, when I betrayed thy budding youth into a false and unnatural relation with my decay. Therefore, as a man who has not thought and philosophised in vain, I seek no vengeance, plot no evil against thee. Between thee and me, the scale hangs fairly balanced. But, Hester, the man lives who has wronged us both! Who is he?"

"Ask me not!" replied Hester Prynne, looking firmly into his face. "That thou shalt never know!"

"Never, sayest thou?" rejoined he, with a smile of dark and self-relying intelligence. "Never know him! Believe me, Hester, there are few things whether in the outward world, or, to a certain depth, in the invisible sphere of thought—few things hidden from the man who devotes himself earnestly and unreservedly to the solution of a mystery. Thou mayest cover up thy secret from the prying multitude. Thou mayest conceal it, too, from the ministers and magistrates, even as thou didst this day, when they sought to wrench the name out of thy heart, and give thee a partner on thy pedestal. But, as for me, I come to the inquest with other senses than they possess. I shall seek this man, as I have sought truth in books: as I have sought gold in alchemy. There is a sympathy that will make me conscious of him. I shall see him tremble. I shall feel myself shudder, suddenly and unawares. Sooner or later, he must needs be mine."

The eyes of the wrinkled scholar glowed so intensely upon her, that Hester Prynne clasped her hand over her heart, dreading lest he should read the secret there at once.

"Thou wilt not reveal his name? Not the less he is mine," resumed he, with a look of confidence, as if destiny were at one with him. "He bears no letter of infamy wrought into his garment, as thou dost, but I shall read it on his heart. Yet fear not for him! Think not that I shall interfere with Heaven's own method of retribution, or, to my own loss, betray him to the gripe of human law. Neither do thou imagine that I shall contrive aught against his life; no, nor against his fame, if as I judge, he be a man of fair repute. Let him live! Let him hide himself in outward honour, if he may! Not the less he shall be mine!"

"Thy acts are like mercy," said Hester, bewildered and appalled; "but thy words interpret thee as a terror!"

"One thing, thou that wast my wife, I would enjoin upon thee," continued the scholar. "Thou hast kept the secret of thy paramour. Keep, likewise, mine! There are none in this land that know me. Breathe not to any human soul that thou didst ever call me husband! Here, on this wild outskirt of the earth, I shall pitch my tent; for, elsewhere a wanderer, and isolated from human interests, I find here a woman, a man, a child, amongst whom and myself there exist the closest ligaments. No matter whether of love or hate: no matter whether of right or wrong! Thou and thine, Hester Prynne, belong to me. My home is where thou art and where he is. But betray me not!"

"Wherefore dost thou desire it?" inquired Hester, shrinking, she hardly knew why, from this secret bond. "Why not announce thyself openly, and cast me off at once?"

"It may be," he replied, "because I will not encounter the dishonour that besmirches the husband of a faithless woman. It may be for other reasons. Enough, it is my purpose to live and die unknown. Let, therefore, thy husband be to the world as one already dead, and of whom no tidings shall ever come. Recognise me not, by word, by sign, by look! Breathe not the secret, above all, to the man thou wottest of. Shouldst thou fail me in this, beware! His fame, his position, his life will be in my hands. Beware!"

"I will keep thy secret, as I have his," said Hester.

"Swear it!" rejoined he.

And she took the oath.

"And now, Mistress Prynne," said old Roger Chillingworth, as he was hereafter to be named, "I leave thee alone: alone with thy infant and the scarlet letter! How is it, Hester? Doth thy sentence bind thee to wear the token in thy sleep? Art thou not afraid of nightmares and hideous dreams?"

"Why dost thou smile so at me?" inquired Hester, troubled at the expression of his eyes. "Art thou like **the Black Man** that haunts the forest round about us? Hast thou enticed me into a bond that will prove the ruin of my soul?"

"Not thy soul," he answered, with another smile. "No, not thine!"

the Black Man: the devil.

COMMENTARY

Following her day of public humiliation, Hester is hysterical and in danger of hurting herself or her baby. To calm her down, the jailer brings a doctor, a man skilled in both Western and Native American medicine, into her cell. This man turns out to be the strange man Hester was watching in the crowd, her husband, Roger Chillingworth. When she sees his eyes, Hester is amazed to find them both familiar and "strange and cold." This description of his eyes hints at Chillingworth's negative function in the novel: His coldness will lead him to exact a chilly vengeance against Dimmesdale. From his discussion with Hester about medicine, the reader learns that Chillingworth was a student of alchemy in the Old World and has learned to use herbs in the new, which suggests his knowledge of esoteric, almost magical ways of healing. Although he separates himself from the powers of the Greek gods—he claims that he knows neither Lethe nor Nepenthe, which in Greek mythology are the waters that

could lead to forgetfulness and banish grief—the recipe he has learned from the Native Americans is "as old as Paracelsus," a medieval astrologer and alchemist. As in the previous chapter, Chillingworth is represented as inhabiting the border between two cultures: He understands ancient Western knowledge along with Native American methods.

Although his efforts to relieve the suffering of Hester and her child seem admirable, readers might question the honesty of Chillingworth's intentions: Is he preserving Hester only because he wants to increase her suffering? Is he practicing humanitarianism or refined cruelty? As her husband, he is the person most deeply wronged by her adultery—does this give him the right to exact vengeance upon her? As the book progresses, the narrator will try to answer these questions through his depiction and analysis of Chillingworth's character.

In this initial introduction to Chillingworth, the reader is led to sympathize with him. For example, Chillingworth immediately takes the blame for Hester's fall: He was too devoted to his studies and did not spend enough time with her; he was too old for a young girl; he was "misshapen" and, therefore, unattractive to her. Selfishly, he married her despite all these objections, because he wanted to create "a household fire" in his lonely life. His name suggests the impossibility of his efforts to find love with Hester: His chilly personality could never enflame this spirited younger woman. Even though she married him, Hester never pretended to love Chillingworth.

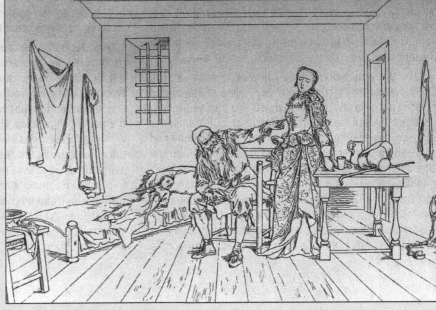

An illustration of Chillingworth and Hester in the prison cell by Felix Octavius Carr Darley (1821–1888).
Photo courtesy of The Darley Society, Inc.

In presenting Chillingworth's thoughts in this chapter, the narrative complicates the situation of Hester's adultery by emphasizing Hester's vulnerability and Chillingworth's recognition of his role in her downfall. There are no easy answers here; blame cannot be easily apportioned, despite the Puritans' efforts to divide the moral universe into clearly defined categories of right and wrong. When Hester admits she has wronged him, Chillingworth correctly posits that they have wronged each other. In some sense, his "decay" has betrayed her "budding youth." In these meditations, Chillingworth appears to be a thoughtful, reasonable man, one who will not seek senseless or violent retribution.

But Chillingworth's generosity does not extend to the father of Hester's baby. When Hester refuses to tell him the identity of this mysterious man, a more dangerous side of Chillingworth's personality emerges. As a man of science, Chillingworth believes that nothing can remain a secret if it is earnestly sought. Uncovering the seeming secrets of existence was his goal as an alchemist, and his goal now will be to find the solution to this mystery. Much like Hawthorne, Chillingworth plans to expose the secret workings of the heart. Chillingworth creates a link between his current project and reading: He will seek the man just as he has looked for truth in books. He will "read" the secret in this man's heart. The fact that the two men bear the same "sympathy" for Hester, they both love her, will offer Chillingworth additional help in discovering his identity. This is not a purely intellectual endeavor. Chillingworth will also read the adulterer's emotional and physical reactions—he will see him tremble and feel himself "shudder."

Hester is so convinced of her husband's powers that she fears he will read the secret written on her own heart. In Chillingworth's opinion, a visible sign, such as Hester's letter, is not necessary for revealing guilt: Our bodies themselves betray our shame. The penetrating power of his eyes indicates his ability to look beyond a person's physical body and into his interior psychology.

Unlike the Puritans, Chillingworth will not exact his revenge on Hester's lover by public punishment, yet the man will still suffer. Perhaps this private punishment is actually more heinous than the overt penal machinery of the Puritan colony. Hester seems to suggest that this is the case when she says Chillingworth's acts are merciful but his words show his true evil.

Sins confessed lose their terror. But secret sins have the ability to rip our souls to pieces. Chillingworth insists upon secrecy, upon the anguish inflicted on a guilty soul that is not allowed to confess its sins. He demands that Hester not reveal his identity to anyone in the community so that he will be effectively dead to the world. Having relinquished his identity, Chillingworth has virtually released all connections with humanity: He is now free to pursue whatever actions necessary to solve the mystery of the identity of Hester's lover. He is now accountable only to himself.

Like the antinomians (see Chapter I commentary), Chillingworth tacitly rejects society's laws of ethics and creates his own law. In some sense, we can see a connection between the actions of Hester and Chillingworth: Like him, she rejected the laws of the Puritan colony and pursued an adulterous affair. But are there also differences between their actions? Hester's adultery was presumably based on a need for love and connection. (We can't say this for certain because Hawthorne does not give us any information about the past relations between Hester and Dimmesdale, although she must love him because she has kept his identity secret.) Chillingworth's vow to secretly uncover Hester's lover signals a rejection of connection: His goal is the destruction of a human soul, while her actions created one.

Although she accepts her husband's terms, Hester recognizes the moral irresponsibility of his plan and believes that she is entering a devil's pact. In fact, she wonders if Chillingworth might be the "Black Man" himself, a connection that will become more pronounced as the novel progresses. Here she also connects the devil with the forests that surround the city. For the Puritans, the natural world was not an idyllic haven but a place of evil and danger where one might encounter Satan. Implicitly, Hester's words connect the devil with the Native American inhabitants of the forests. Indeed, the Puritans believed the natives were children of the devil, a racist idea that still haunts the relationship of Europeans and Native Americans.

Chapter V

After being freed from prison, Hester and her baby, Pearl, move to a seaside cottage on the outskirts of town. She makes a living doing needlework. Her craftsmanship is so excellent that her work is in high demand for all public ceremonies, except weddings. Although she is respected as a seamstress and also donates much of her work to the poor, Hester is treated as an outcast.

CHAPTER V: HESTER AT HER NEEDLE

HESTER Prynne's term of confinement was now at an end. Her prison-door was thrown open, and she came forth into the sunshine, which, falling on all alike, seemed, to her sick and morbid heart, as if meant for no other purpose than to reveal the scarlet letter on her breast. Perhaps there was a more real torture in her first unattended footsteps from the threshold of the prison than even in the procession and spectacle that have been described, where she was made the common infamy, at which all mankind was summoned to point its finger. Then, she was supported by an unnatural tension of the nerves, and by all the combative energy of her character, which enabled her to convert the scene into a kind of lurid triumph. It was, moreover, a separate and insulated event, to occur but once in her lifetime, and to meet which, therefore, reckless of economy, she might call up the vital strength that would have sufficed for many quiet years. The very law that condemned her—a giant of stern features but with vigour to support, as well as to annihilate, in his iron arm—had held her up through the terrible ordeal of her ignominy. But now, with this unattended walk from her prison door, began the daily custom; and she must either sustain and carry it forward by the ordinary resources of her nature, or sink beneath it. She could no longer borrow from the future to help her through the present grief. Tomorrow would bring its own trial with it; so would the next day, and so would the next: each its own trial, and yet the very same that was now so unutterably grievous to be borne. The days of the far-off future would toil onward, still with the same burden for her to take up, and bear along with her, but never to fling down; for the accumulating days and added years would pile up their misery upon the heap of shame. Throughout them all, giving up her individuality, she would become the general symbol at which the preacher and moralist might point, and in which they might vivify and embody their images of woman's frailty and sinful passion. Thus the young and pure would be taught to look at her, with the scarlet letter flaming on her breast—at her, the child of honourable parents—at her, the mother of a babe that would hereafter be a woman—at her, who had once been innocent—as the figure, the body, the reality of sin. And over her grave, the infamy that she must carry thither would be her only monument.

It may seem marvellous that, with the world before her—kept by no restrictive clause of her condemnation within the limits of the Puritan settlement, so remote and so obscure—free to return to her birth-place, or to any other European land, and there hide her character and identity under a new exterior, as completely as if emerging into another state of being—and having also the passes of the dark, inscrutable forest open to her, where the wildness of her nature might assimilate itself with a people whose customs and life were alien from the law that had condemned her—it may seem marvellous that this woman should still call that place her home, where, and where only, she must needs be the type of shame. But there is a fatality, a feeling so irresistible and inevitable that it has the force of doom, which almost invariably compels human beings to linger around and haunt, ghost-like, the spot where some great and marked event has given the colour to their lifetime; and, still the more irresistibly, the darker the tinge that saddens it. Her sin, her ignominy, were the roots which she had struck into the soil. It was as if a new birth, with stronger assimilations than the first, had converted the forest-land, still so uncongenial to every other pilgrim and wanderer, into Hester Prynne's wild and dreary, but life-long home. All other scenes of earth—even that village of rural England, where happy infancy and stainless maidenhood seemed yet to be in her mother's keeping, like garments put off long ago—were foreign to her, in comparison. The chain that bound her here was of iron links, and galling to her inmost soul, but could never be broken.

It might be, too—doubtless it was so, although she hid the secret from herself, and grew pale whenever it struggled out of her heart, like a serpent from its hole—it might be that another feeling kept her within the scene and pathway that had been so fatal. There dwelt, there trode, the feet of one with whom she deemed herself connected in a union that, unrecognised on earth, would bring them together before the bar of final judgment, and make that their marriage-altar, for a joint futurity of endless retribution. Over and over again, the tempter of souls had thrust this idea upon Hester's contemplation, and laughed at the passionate and desperate joy with which she seized, and then strove to cast it from her. She barely looked the idea in the face, and hastened to bar it in its dungeon. What she compelled herself to believe—what, finally, she reasoned upon as her motive for continuing a resident of New England—was half a truth, and half a self-delusion. Here, she said to herself had been the scene of her guilt, and here should be the scene of her earthly punishment; and so, perchance, the torture of her daily shame would at length purge her soul, and work out another purity than that which she had lost: more saint-like, because the result of martyrdom.

Hester Prynne, therefore, did not flee. On the outskirts of the town, within the verge of the peninsula, but not in close vicinity to any other habitation, there was a small thatched cottage. It had been built by an earlier settler, and abandoned, because the soil about it was too sterile for cultivation, while its comparative remoteness put it out of the sphere of that social activity which already marked the habits of the emigrants. It stood on the shore, looking across a basin of the sea at the forest-covered hills, towards the west. A clump of scrubby trees, such as alone grew on the peninsula, did not so much conceal the cottage from view, as seem to denote that here was some object which would fain have been, or at least ought to be, concealed. In this little lonesome dwelling, with some slender means that she possessed, and by the licence of the magistrates, who still kept an inquisitorial watch over her, Hester established herself, with her infant child. A mystic shadow of suspicion immediately attached itself to the spot. Children, too young to comprehend wherefore this woman should be shut out from the sphere of human charities, would creep nigh enough to behold her plying her needle at the cottage-window, or standing in the doorway, or labouring in her little garden, or coming forth along the pathway that led townward, and, discerning the scarlet letter on her breast, would scamper off with a strange contagious fear.

Lonely as was Hester's situation, and without a friend on earth who dared to show himself, she, however, incurred no risk of want. She possessed an art that sufficed, even in a land that afforded comparatively little scope for its exercise, to supply food for her thriving infant and herself. It was the art, then, as now, almost the only one within a woman's grasp—of needle-work. She bore on her breast, in the curiously embroidered letter, a specimen of her delicate and imaginative skill, of which the dames of a court might gladly have availed themselves, to add the richer and more spiritual adornment of human ingenuity to their fabrics of silk and gold. Here, indeed, in the sable simplicity that generally characterised the Puritanic modes of dress, there might be an infrequent call for the finer productions of her handiwork. Yet the taste of the age, demanding whatever was elaborate in compositions of this kind, did not fail to extend its influence over our stern progenitors, who had cast behind them so many fashions which it might seem harder to dispense with.

Public ceremonies, such as ordinations, the installation of magistrates, and all that could give majesty to the forms in which a new government manifested itself to the people, were, as a matter of policy, marked by a stately and well-conducted ceremonial, and a sombre, but yet a studied magnificence. Deep ruffs, painfully wrought bands, and gorgeously embroidered gloves, were all deemed necessary to the official state of men assuming the reins of power, and were readily allowed to individuals dignified by rank or wealth, even while sumptuary laws forbade these and similar extravagances to the plebeian order. In the array of funerals, too—whether for the apparel of the dead body, or to typify, by manifold emblematic devices of sable cloth and snowy lawn, the sorrow of the survivors—there was a frequent and characteristic demand for such labour as Hester Prynne could supply. Baby-linen—for babies then wore robes of state—afforded still another possibility of toil and emolument.

By degrees, not very slowly, her handiwork became what would now be termed the fashion. Whether from commiseration for a woman of so miserable a destiny; or from the morbid curiosity that gives a fictitious value even to common or worthless things; or by whatever other intangible circumstance was then, as now, sufficient to bestow, on some persons, what others might seek in vain; or because Hester really filled a gap which must otherwise have remained vacant; it is certain that she had ready and fairly equited employment for as many hours as she saw fit to occupy with her needle. Vanity, it may be, chose to mortify itself, by putting on, for ceremonials of pomp and state, the garments that had been wrought by her sinful hands. Her needle-work was seen on the ruff of the Governor; military men wore it on their scarfs, and the minister on his band; it decked the baby's little cap; it was shut up, to be mildewed and moulder away, in the coffins of the dead. But it is not recorded that, in a single instance, her skill was called in to embroider the white veil which was to cover the pure blushes of a bride. The exception indicated the ever relentless vigour with which society frowned upon her sin.

Hester sought not to acquire anything beyond a subsistence, of the plainest and most ascetic description, for herself, and a simple abundance for her child. Her own dress was of the coarsest materials and the most sombre hue, with only that one ornament—the scarlet letter—which it was her doom to wear. The child's attire, on the other hand, was distinguished by a fanciful, or, we may rather say, a fantastic ingenuity, which served, indeed, to heighten the airy charm that early began to develop itself in the little girl, but which appeared to have also a deeper meaning. We may speak further of it hereafter. Except for that small expenditure in the decoration of her infant, Hester bestowed all her superfluous means in charity, on wretches less miserable than herself, and who not unfrequently insulted the hand that fed them. Much of the time, which she might readily have applied to the better efforts of her art, she employed in making coarse garments for the poor. It is probable that there was an idea of penance in this mode of occupation, and that she offered up a real sacrifice of enjoyment in devoting so many hours to such rude handiwork. She had in her nature a rich, voluptuous, Oriental characteristic—a taste for the gorgeously beautiful, which, save in the exquisite productions of her needle, found nothing else, in all the possibilities of her life, to exercise itself upon. Women derive a pleasure, incomprehensible to the other sex, from the delicate toil of the needle. To Hester Prynne it might have been a mode of expressing, and therefore soothing, the passion of her life. Like all other joys, she rejected it as sin. This morbid meddling of conscience with an immaterial matter betokened, it is to be feared, no genuine and steadfast penitence, but something doubtful, something that might be deeply wrong beneath.

In this matter, Hester Prynne came to have a part to perform in the world. With her native energy of character and rare capacity, it could not entirely cast her off, although it had set a mark upon her, more intolerable to a woman's heart than that which branded **the brow of Cain**. In all her intercourse with society, however, there was nothing that made her feel as if she belonged to it. Every gesture, every word, and even the silence of those with whom she came in contact, implied, and often expressed, that she was banished, and as much alone as if she inhabited another sphere, or communicated with the common nature by other organs and senses than the rest of human kind. She stood apart from

the brow of Cain: Genesis 4:15, "And the Lord put a mark on Cain, lest any who came upon him should kill him."

moral interests, yet close beside them, like a ghost that revisits the familiar fireside, and can no longer make itself seen or felt; no more smile with the household joy, nor mourn with the kindred sorrow; or, should it succeed in manifesting its forbidden sympathy, awakening only terror and horrible repugnance. These emotions, in fact, and its bitterest scorn besides, seemed to be the sole portion that she retained in the universal heart. It was not an age of delicacy; and her position, although she understood it well, and was in little danger of forgetting it, was often brought before her vivid self-perception, like a new anguish, by the rudest touch upon the tenderest spot. The poor, as we have already said, whom she sought out to be the objects of her bounty, often reviled the hand that was stretched forth to succour them. Dames of elevated rank, likewise, whose doors she entered in the way of her occupation, were accustomed to distil drops of bitterness into her heart; sometimes through that alchemy of quiet malice, by which women can concoct a subtle poison from ordinary trifles; and sometimes, also, by a coarser expression, that fell upon the sufferer's defenceless breast like a rough blow upon an ulcerated wound. Hester had schooled herself long and well; and she never responded to these attacks, save by a flush of crimson that rose irrepressibly over her pale cheek, and again subsided into the depths of her bosom. She was patient—a martyr, indeed—but she forebore to pray for enemies, lest, in spite of her forgiving aspirations, the words of the blessing should stubbornly twist themselves into a curse.

Continually, and in a thousand other ways, did she feel the innumerable throbs of anguish that had been so cunningly contrived for her by the undying, the ever-active sentence of the Puritan tribunal. Clergymen paused in the streets, to address words of exhortation, that brought a crowd, with its mingled grin and frown, around the poor, sinful woman. If she entered a church, trusting to share the Sabbath smile of the Universal Father, it was often her mishap to find herself the text of the discourse. She grew to have a dread of children; for they had imbibed from their parents a vague idea of something horrible in this dreary woman gliding silently through the town, with never any companion but one only child. Therefore, first allowing her to pass, they pursued her at a distance with shrill cries, and the utterances of a word that had no distinct purport to their own minds, but was none the less terrible to her, as proceeding from lips that babbled it unconsciously. It seemed to argue so wide a diffusion of her shame, that all nature knew of it; it could have caused her no deeper pang had the leaves of the trees whispered the dark story among themselves—had the summer breeze murmured about it—had the wintry blast shrieked it aloud! Another peculiar torture was felt in the gaze of a new eye. When strangers looked curiously at the scarlet letter—and none ever failed to do so—they branded it afresh in Hester's soul; so that, oftentimes, she could scarcely refrain, yet always did refrain, from covering the symbol with her hand. But then, again, an accustomed eye had likewise its own anguish to inflict. Its cool stare of familiarity was intolerable. From first to last, in short, Hester Prynne had always this dreadful agony in feeling a human eye upon the token; the spot never grew callous; it seemed, on the contrary, to grow more sensitive with daily torture.

But sometimes, once in many days, or perchance in many months, she felt an eye—a human eye—upon the ignominious brand, that seemed to give a momentary relief, as if half of her agony were shared. The next instant, back it all rushed again, with still a deeper throb of pain; for, in that brief interval, she had sinned anew. Had Hester sinned alone?

Her imagination was somewhat affected, and, had she been of a softer moral and intellectual fibre would have been still more so, by the strange and solitary anguish of her life. Walking to and fro, with those lonely footsteps, in the little world with which she was outwardly connected, it now and then appeared to Hester—if altogether fancy, it was nevertheless too potent to be resisted—she felt or fancied, then, that the scarlet letter had endowed her with a new sense. She shuddered to believe, yet could not help believing, that it gave her a sympathetic knowledge of the hidden sin in other hearts. She was terror-stricken by the revelations that were thus made. What were they? Could they be other than the insidious whispers of the bad angel, who would fain have persuaded the struggling woman, as yet only half his victim, that the outward guise of purity was but a lie, and that, if truth were everywhere to be shown, a scarlet letter would blaze forth on many a bosom besides Hester Prynne's? Or, must she receive those intimations—so obscure, yet so distinct—as truth? In all her miserable experience, there was nothing else so awful and so loathsome as this sense. It perplexed, as well as shocked her, by the irreverent inopportuneness of the occasions that brought it into vivid action. Sometimes the red infamy upon her breast would give a sympathetic throb, as she passed near a venerable minister or magistrate, the model of piety and justice, to whom that age of antique reverence looked up, as to a mortal man in fellowship with angels. "What evil thing is at hand?" would Hester say to herself. Lifting her reluctant eyes, there would be nothing human within the scope of view, save the form of this earthly saint! Again a mystic sisterhood would contumaciously assert itself, as she met the sanctified frown of some matron, who, according to the rumour of all tongues, had kept cold snow within her bosom throughout life. That unsunned snow in the matron's bosom, and the burning shame on Hester Prynne's—what had the two in common? Or, once more, the electric thrill would give her warning—"Behold Hester, here is a companion!" and, looking up, she would detect the eyes of a young maiden glancing at the scarlet letter, shyly and aside, and quickly averted, with a faint, chill crimson in her cheeks as if her purity were somewhat sullied by that momentary glance. O Fiend, whose talisman was that fatal symbol, wouldst thou leave nothing, whether in youth or age, for this poor sinner to revere?—such loss of faith is ever one of the saddest results of sin. Be it accepted as a proof that all was not corrupt in this poor victim of her own frailty, and man's hard law, that Hester Prynne yet struggled to believe that no fellow-mortal was guilty like herself.

The vulgar, who, in those dreary old times, were always contributing a grotesque horror to what interested their imaginations, had a story about the scarlet letter which we might readily work up into a terrific legend. They averred that the symbol was not mere scarlet cloth, tinged in an earthly dye-pot, but was red-hot with infernal fire, and could be seen glowing all alight whenever Hester Prynne walked abroad in the night-time. And we must needs say it seared Hester's bosom so deeply, that perhaps there was more truth in the rumour than our modern incredulity may be inclined to admit.

COMMENTARY

Chapter V offers additional insight on Hester's psychology and develops the various symbolic meanings associated with the scarlet letter. The sun is shining on the day of Hester's release from prison, but she cannot enjoy its warmth. Instead, she feels the sun's only goal is to form a spotlight on the scarlet letter. Until this moment, the law has held her up within the strength of its "iron arm," but now she must resume her daily life with only her own resources to support her. Hester realizes that she can no longer look to the future for solace, because she feels that she has no future: All comfort must come from the present moment, from living day by day. These thoughts prove that Hester is an insightful woman, one who has considered carefully the implications of her transgressions.

This chapter documents the various humiliations that Hester faces as she reenters the Puritan community that refuses to forget her sin: Children shun her, ministers use her as the subject of their sermons, and everyone feels they have the right to criticize her. Indeed, she begins to feel that all of nature knows her shame and shrieks it into the wind.

The symbol of the scarlet letter is developed in this chapter, and a variety of meanings become associated with it. For example, a legend grows in the town that the letter isn't simply a scarlet cloth but is red-hot with the fires of hell and glows in the dark. The narrator tells us there is a certain element of truth in this rumor: The letter has seared more deeply into Hester's heart than a simple piece of red cloth could. As the bearer of the scarlet letter, Hester will lose her individuality and become a pure symbol: an emblem of woman's frailty and sinful passion. No longer will sin be merely an idea; it will now have a body and a reality. By gazing upon Hester, the Puritans will be reminded not to transgress the laws of their God.

But the letter serves a different purpose for Hester, offering her a new, almost paranormal ability to know and understand the hidden sins in other people's hearts. Therefore, the letter leads her to greater understanding of human psychology and a clear recognition of the vast gulf between public virtue and private transgression. From the insights offered by the letter, Hester discovers that the outward show of purity by her fellow Puritans is often only a disguise. She learns that almost every person in Boston has committed a transgression as dire as hers, so almost every breast in Boston should blaze forth with a similar scarlet letter. These comments point to the narrator's own fairly negative view of human frailty and Puritan hypocrisy; it appears these people need to punish Hester as a method of keeping their own sins hidden. She is a scapegoat created by the town to appease God's need to punish sinners, and the obviousness of her sin—pregnancy—makes her a clearly defined target. The narrator also suggests that the scarlet letter is the devil's talisman, revealing other people's sins in order to chip away at Hester's belief in human purity and goodness. Despite the growing evidence of the sinful nature of all humans, Hester struggles to believe that she is the only guilty member of the community.

Besides offering Hester psychological insights on fellow members of the community, the letter also indicates her skill as a needle-worker—her delicate and imaginative artistic abilities. In a blatant display of hypocrisy, the members of the community allow Hester to embroider their garments while rejecting her presence. Hester's magnificent embroidery would be valued even by aristocratic women back in England, but the plain clothing worn by the Puritans makes it inappropriate for everyday wear in the New World. Hester's work instead graces the ceremonial garments used for public occasions in which her creations are appropriate. In another example of

F.O.C. Darley's illustration of Hester's release from prison.
Photo courtesy of The Darley Society, Inc.

beliefs. Coarse, plain, and somber except for the blazing red letter, it contrasts sharply with Pearl's clothing, which is described as "fanciful," a "fantastic ingenuity," and an "airy charm." Thus, the narrator presents Hester's conflicted nature: An imaginative, passionate woman, she is forced to live a repressed and lonely life.

Why, the narrator wonders, does Hester not leave the village of Boston? Why remain and be subjected to the town's enmity? She could return to England or escape into the depths of the forest; no one is making her remain at the site of her infamy. The narrator suggests that the wildness of her nature might fit more closely with that of the Native Americans who live beyond the boundaries of Puritan law. Peering into human psychology, the narrator offers several possible reasons for Hester's inertia. First, she may feel mentally chained to Boston—rooted to the spot of her disgrace—precisely because of the sin she has committed. Another possible reason for her inability to leave is that she loves Dimmesdale; even though they can't be together, she does get to see and hear him every day. Finally, living through the daily shame may allow her to purify her soul, to become more saint-like because of the martyrdom she experiences. By analyzing Hester's thoughts on this issue, the narrator emphasizes her complexity: Like most people, her sense of morality and correct action is tinged with both lofty ideals and trivial hopes. This is a book concerned less with plot than with delving into the secret workings of the human heart.

Hester is positioned between the village and the forest like Chillingworth, who lives on the border between the Europeans and the Native Americans. Her cottage is situated in an isolated borderland on the outskirts of town, separate from any other dwelling. The description of her home emphasizes her isolation and her association with the threat of contamination. Children, too young to understand the nature of her sin, scamper away when they get

narrow-mindedness, the townsfolk allow Hester to embroider garments for all ceremonies except weddings—as if her sin would infect the new bride but not any other member of the community. Hester uses her spare time to fashion rough clothing for the poor; in return, they give her criticism and condemnation. These incidents prove Hester's strength of character, which allows her to continue working despite constant criticism.

By examining Hester's work, which reflects her character, the narrator is able to give the reader a deeper understanding of her psychological makeup. "[R]ude handiwork" does not come naturally to Hester, whose nature is rich, voluptuous, and exotic, preferring the "gorgeously beautiful" to the simple and plain. The narrator suggests that Hester's exquisite needlework could be the one way she expresses her passion for life; all of the energy she might have invested in love, she now expends in creativity. Indeed, all of Hester's creativity seems invested in her work and in her daughter's attire. Although Hester's inward passion and energy signal her difference from the other members of the Puritan community, she outwardly follows all their moral injunctions. For example, she feels her needlework is sinful because it gives her pleasure. Her clothing connotes her Puritanical too close to her cottage, as if afraid that her presence might defile them. Even the scrubby trees that surround the cottage denote that it houses an object that ought to be concealed. An "inquisitorial" watch is kept over her by the colony's magistrates, and a "mystic shadow of suspicion" attaches to the cottage, as if Hester's presence has spread a contagion throughout the landscape near where she lives.

Thus, immediately after Hester's release from prison, Hester and her scarlet letter connote fear, contagion, and suspicion. This connotation infects Hester herself, so that she feels separate from society, as if she inhabits a different sphere. The emotional impact of her isolation is contained in the image of a series of lonely footsteps moving in solitary anguish toward a future that offers no hope of change or growth.

Chapter VI

Hester is amazed by the loveliness of her daughter, Pearl. Hester wonders how such beauty could have grown out of sin. But Pearl is also a difficult child, wild and temperamental. Hester sometimes thinks that her daughter might be possessed by the devil, especially after Pearl denies having a Heavenly Father.

CHAPTER VI: PEARL

WE have as yet hardly spoken of the infant; that little creature, whose innocent life had sprung, by the inscrutable decree of Providence, a lovely and immortal flower, out of the rank luxuriance of a guilty passion. How strange it seemed to the sad woman, as she watched the growth, and the beauty that became every day more brilliant, and the intelligence that threw its quivering sunshine over the tiny features of this child! Her Pearl—for so had Hester called her; not as a name expressive of her aspect, which had nothing of the calm, white, unimpassioned lustre that would be indicated by the comparison. But she named the infant "Pearl," as being **of great price**—purchased with all she had—her mother's only treasure! How strange, indeed! Man had marked this woman's sin by a scarlet letter, which had such potent and disastrous efficacy that no human sympathy could reach her, save it were sinful like herself. God, as a direct consequence of the sin which man thus punished, had given her a lovely child, whose place was on that same dishonoured bosom, to connect her parent for ever with the race and descent of mortals, and to be finally a blessed soul in heaven! Yet these thoughts affected Hester Prynne less with hope than apprehension. She knew that her deed had been evil; she could have no faith, therefore, that its result would be good. Day after day she looked fearfully into the child's expanding nature, ever dreading to detect some dark and wild peculiarity that should correspond with the guiltiness to which she owed her being.

Certainly there was no physical defect. By its perfect shape, its vigour, and its natural dexterity in the use of all its untried limbs, the infant was worthy to have been brought forth in Eden: worthy to have been left there to be the plaything of the angels after the world's first parents were driven out. The child had a native grace which does not invariably co-exist with faultless beauty; its attire, however simple, always impressed the beholder as if it were the very garb that precisely became it best. But little Pearl was not clad in rustic weeds. Her mother, with a morbid purpose that may be better understood hereafter, had bought the richest tissues that could be procured, and allowed her imaginative faculty its full play in the arrangement and decoration of the dresses which the child wore before the public eye. So magnificent was the small figure when thus arrayed, and such was the splendour of Pearl's own proper beauty, shining through the gorgeous robes which might have extinguished a paler loveliness, that there was an absolute circle of radiance around her on the darksome cottage floor. And yet a russet gown, torn and soiled

of great price: Matthew 13:45–46. A parable of Christ in which a merchant sells all he owns to buy a single pearl, signifying heavenly salvation.

with the child's rude play, made a picture of her just as perfect. Pearl's aspect was imbued with a spell of infinite variety; in this one child there were many children, comprehending the full scope between the wild-flower prettiness of a peasant-baby, and the pomp, in little, of an infant princess. Throughout all, however, there was a trait of passion, a certain depth of hue, which she never lost; and if in any of her changes, she had grown fainter or paler, she would have ceased to be herself—it would have been no longer Pearl!

This outward mutability indicated, and did not more than fairly express, the various properties of her inner life. Her nature appeared to possess depth, too, as well as variety; but—or else Hester's fears deceived her—it lacked reference and adaptation to the world into which she was born. The child could not be made amenable to rules. In giving her existence a great law had been broken; and the result was a being whose elements were perhaps beautiful and brilliant, but all in disorder, or with an order peculiar to themselves, amidst which the point of variety and arrange-ment was difficult or impossible to be discovered. Hester could only account for the child's character—and even then most vaguely and imperfectly—by recalling what she herself had been during that momen-tous period while Pearl was imbibing her soul from the spiritual world, and her bodily frame from its material of earth. The mother's impas-sioned state had been the medium through which were transmitted to the unborn infant the rays of its moral life; and, however white and clear originally, they had taken the deep stains of crimson and gold, the fiery lustre, the black shadow, and the untempered light of the intervening substance. Above all, the warfare of Hester's spirit at that epoch was per-petuated in Pearl. She could recognize her wild, desperate, defiant mood, the flightiness of her temper, and even some of the very cloud-shapes of gloom and despondency that had brooded in her heart. They were now illuminated by the morning radiance of a young child's disposition, but, later in the day of earthly existence, might be prolific of the storm and whirlwind.

The discipline of the family in those days was of a far more rigid kind than now. The frown, the harsh rebuke, the frequent application of the rod, enjoined by Scriptural authority, were used, not merely in the way of punishment for actual offences, but as a wholesome regimen for the growth and promotion of all childish virtues. Hester Prynne, neverthe-less, the loving mother of this one child, ran little risk of erring on the side of undue severity. Mindful, however, of her own errors and misfor-tunes, she early sought to impose a tender but strict control over the infant immortality that was committed to her charge. But the task was beyond her skill. After testing both smiles and frowns, and proving that neither mode of treatment possessed any calculable influence, Hester was ultimately compelled to stand aside and permit the child to be swayed by her own impulses. Physical compulsion or restraint was effectual, of course, while it lasted. As to any other kind of discipline, whether addressed to her mind or heart, little Pearl might or might not be within its reach, in accordance with the caprice that ruled the moment. Her mother, while Pearl was yet an infant, grew acquainted with a certain peculiar look, that warned her when it would be labour thrown away to insist, persuade or plead.

It was a look so intelligent, yet inexplicable, perverse, sometimes so malicious, but generally accompanied by a wild flow of spirits, that Hester could not help questioning at such moments whether Pearl was a human child. She seemed rather an airy sprite, which, after playing its fantastic sports for a little while upon the cottage floor, would flit away with a mocking smile. Whenever that look appeared in her wild, bright, deeply black eyes, it invested her with a strange remoteness and intangibility: it was as if she were hovering in the air, and might vanish, like a glimmering light that comes we know not whence and goes we know not whither. Beholding it, Hester was constrained to rush towards the child—to pursue the little elf in the flight which she invariably began—to snatch her to her bosom with a close pressure and earnest kisses—not so much from overflowing love as to assure herself that Pearl was flesh and blood, and not utterly delusive. But Pearl's laugh, when she was caught, though full of merriment and music, made her mother more doubtful than before.

Heart-smitten at this bewildering and baffling spell, that so often came between herself and her sole treasure, whom she had bought so dear, and who was all her world, Hester sometimes burst into passionate tears. Then, perhaps—for there was no foreseeing how it might affect her— Pearl would frown, and clench her little fist, and harden her small features into a stern, unsympathising look of discontent. Not seldom she would laugh anew, and louder than before, like a thing incapable and unintelligent of human sorrow. Or—but this more rarely happened—she would be convulsed with rage of grief and sob out her love for her mother in broken words, and seem intent on proving that she had a heart by breaking it. Yet Hester was hardly safe in confiding herself to that gusty tenderness: it passed as suddenly as it came. Brooding over all these matters, the mother felt like one who has evoked a spirit, but, by some irregularity in the process of conjuration, has failed to win the master-word that should control this new and incomprehensible intelligence. Her only real comfort was when the child lay in the placidity of sleep. Then she was sure of her, and tasted hours of quiet, sad, delicious happiness; until—perhaps with that perverse expression glimmering from beneath her opening lids—little Pearl awoke!

How soon—with what strange rapidity, indeed did Pearl arrive at an age that was capable of social intercourse beyond the mother's ever-ready smile and nonsense-words! And then what a happiness would it have been could Hester Prynne have heard her clear, bird-like voice mingling with the uproar of other childish voices, and have distinguished and unravelled her own darling's tones, amid all the entangled outcry of a group of sportive children. But this could never be. Pearl was a born outcast of the infantile world. An imp of evil, emblem and product of sin, she had no right among christened infants. Nothing was more remarkable than the instinct, as it seemed, with which the child comprehended her loneliness: the destiny that had drawn an inviolable circle round about her: the whole peculiarity, in short, of her position in respect to other children. Never since her release from prison had Hester met the public gaze without her. In all her walks about the town, Pearl, too, was there: first as the babe in arms, and afterwards as the little girl, small companion of her mother, holding a forefinger with her whole grasp, and tripping along at the rate of three or four footsteps to one of Hester's. She saw the children of the settlement on the grassy margin of the street, or at the domestic thresholds, disporting themselves in such grim fashions as the Puritanic nurture would permit; playing at going to church, perchance; or at scourging Quakers; or taking scalps in a sham fight with the Indians; or scaring one another with freaks of imitative witchcraft. Pearl saw, and gazed intently, but never sought to make acquaintance. If spoken to, she would not speak again. If the children gathered about her, as they sometimes did, Pearl would grow positively terrible in her puny wrath, snatching up stones to fling at them, with shrill, incoherent exclamations, that made her mother tremble, because they had so much the sound of a witch's anathemas in some unknown tongue.

The truth was, that the little Puritans, being of the most intolerant brood that ever lived, had got a vague idea of something outlandish, unearthly, or at variance with ordinary fashions, in the mother and child, and therefore scorned them in their hearts, and not unfrequently reviled them with their tongues. Pearl felt the sentiment, and requited it with the bitterest hatred that can be supposed to rankle in a childish bosom. These outbreaks of a fierce temper had a kind of value, and even comfort for the mother; because there was at least an intelligible earnestness in the mood, instead of the fitful caprice that so often thwarted her in the child's manifestations. It appalled her, nevertheless, to discern here, again, a shadowy reflection of the evil that had existed in herself. All this enmity and passion had Pearl inherited, by inalienable right, out of Hester's heart. Mother and daughter stood together in the same circle of seclusion from human society; and in the nature of the child seemed to be perpetuated those unquiet elements that had distracted Hester Prynne before Pearl's birth, but had since begun to be soothed away by the softening influences of maternity.

At home, within and around her mother's cottage, Pearl wanted not a wide and various circle of acquaintance. The spell of life went forth from her ever-creative spirit, and communicated itself to a thousand objects, as a torch kindles a flame wherever it may be applied. The unlikeliest materials—a stick, a bunch of rags, a flower—were the puppets of Pearl's witchcraft, and, without undergoing any outward change, became spiritually adapted to whatever drama occupied the stage of her inner world. Her one baby-voice served a multitude of imaginary personages, old and young, to talk withal. The pine-trees, aged, black, and solemn, and flinging groans and other melancholy utterances on the breeze, needed little transformation to figure as Puritan elders; the ugliest weeds of the garden were their children, whom Pearl smote down and uprooted most unmercifully. It was wonderful, the vast variety of forms into which she threw her intellect, with no continuity, indeed, but darting up and dancing, always in a state of preternatural activity—soon sinking down, as if exhausted by so rapid and feverish a tide of life—and succeeded by other shapes of a similar wild energy. It was like nothing so much as the phantasmagoric play of **the northern lights**. In the mere exercise of the fancy, however, and the sportiveness of a growing mind, there might be a little more than was observable in other children of bright faculties; except as Pearl, in the dearth of human playmates, was thrown more upon the visionary throng which she created. The singularity lay in the hostile feelings with which the child regarded all these offsprings of her own heart and mind. She never created a friend, but seemed always to be sowing broadcast **the dragon's teeth**, whence sprung a harvest of armed enemies, against whom she rushed to battle. It was inexpressibly sad—then what depth of sorrow to a mother, who felt in her own heart the cause—to observe, in one so young, this constant recognition of an adverse world, and so fierce a training of the energies that were to make good her cause in the contest that must ensue.

Gazing at Pearl, Hester Prynne often dropped her work upon her knees, and cried out with an agony which she would fain have hidden, but which made utterance for itself betwixt speech and a groan—"O Father in Heaven—if Thou art still my Father—what is this being which I have brought into the world?" And Pearl, overhearing the ejaculation, or aware through some more subtle channel, of those throbs of anguish, would turn her vivid and beautiful little face upon her mother, smile with sprite-like intelligence, and resume her play.

One peculiarity of the child's deportment remains yet to be told. The very first thing which she had noticed in her life, was—what?—not the mother's smile, responding to it, as other babies do, by that faint, embryo smile of the little mouth, remembered so doubtfully afterwards, and with such fond discussion whether it were indeed a smile. By no means! But that first object of which Pearl seemed to become aware was—shall we say it?—the scarlet letter on Hester's bosom! One day, as her mother stooped over the cradle, the infant's eyes had been caught by the glimmering of the gold embroidery about the letter; and putting up her little hand she grasped at it, smiling, not doubtfully, but with a decided gleam, that gave her face the look of a much older child. Then, gasping for breath, did Hester Prynne clutch the fatal token, instinctively endeavouring to tear it away, so infinite was the torture inflicted by the intelligent touch of Pearl's baby-hand. Again, as if her mother's agonised gesture were meant only to make sport for her, did little Pearl look into her eyes, and smile. From that epoch, except when the child was asleep, Hester had never felt a moment's safety: not a moment's calm enjoyment of her. Weeks, it is true, would sometimes elapse, during which Pearl's gaze might never once be fixed upon the scarlet letter; but then, again, it would come at unawares, like the stroke of sudden death, and always with that peculiar smile and odd expression of the eyes.

the northern lights: Aurora Borealis—irregular, luminous phenomena, such as streamers, visible at night in a zone surrounding the north magnetic pole and produced in the ionosphere when atomic particles strike and excite atoms.

the dragon's teeth: In Greek mythology, Cadmus kills a dragon and sows its teeth, from which many armed men rise, fighting each other, until only five of them are left to help him build the city of Thebes.

Cadmus and the dragon.

Once this freakish, elvish cast came into the child's eyes while Hester was looking at her own image in them, as mothers are fond of doing; and suddenly for women in solitude, and with troubled hearts, are pestered with unaccountable delusions she fancied that she beheld, not her own miniature portrait, but another face in the small black mirror of Pearl's eye. It was a face, fiend-like, full of smiling malice, yet bearing the semblance of features that she had known full well, though seldom with a smile, and never with malice in them. It was as if an evil spirit possessed the child, and had just then peeped forth in mockery. Many a time afterwards had Hester been tortured, though less vividly, by the same illusion.

In the afternoon of a certain summer's day, after Pearl grew big enough to run about, she amused herself with gathering handfuls of wild flowers, and flinging them, one by one, at her mother's bosom; dancing up and down like a little elf whenever she hit the scarlet letter. Hester's first motion had been to cover her bosom with her clasped hands. But whether from pride or resignation, or a feeling that her penance might best be wrought out by this unutterable pain, she resisted the impulse, and sat erect, pale as death, looking sadly into little Pearl's wild eyes. Still came the battery of flowers, almost invariably hitting the mark, and covering the mother's breast with hurts for which she could find no balm in this world, nor knew how to seek it in another. At last, her shot being all expended, the child stood still and gazed at Hester, with that little laughing image of a fiend peeping out—or, whether it peeped or no, her mother so imagined it—from the unsearchable abyss of her black eyes.

"Child, what art thou?" cried the mother.

"Oh, I am your little Pearl!" answered the child.

But while she said it, Pearl laughed, and began to dance up and down with the humoursome gesticulation of a little imp, whose next freak might be to fly up the chimney.

"Art thou my child, in very truth?" asked Hester.

Nor did she put the question altogether idly, but, for the moment, with a portion of genuine earnestness; for, such was Pearl's wonderful intelligence, that her mother half doubted whether she were not acquainted with the secret spell of her existence, and might not now reveal herself.

"Yes; I am little Pearl!" repeated the child, continuing her antics.

"Thou art not my child! Thou art no Pearl of mine!" said the mother half playfully; for it was often the case that a sportive impulse came over her in the midst of her deepest suffering. "Tell me, then, what thou art, and who sent thee hither?"

"Tell me, mother!" said the child, seriously, coming up to Hester, and pressing herself close to her knees. "Do thou tell me!"

"Thy Heavenly Father sent thee!" answered Hester Prynne.

But she said it with a hesitation that did not escape the acuteness of the child. Whether moved only by her ordinary freakishness, or because an evil spirit prompted her, she put up her small forefinger and touched the scarlet letter.

"He did not send me!" cried she, positively. "I have no Heavenly Father!"

"Hush, Pearl, hush! Thou must not talk so!" answered the mother, suppressing a groan. "He sent us all into the world. He sent even me, thy mother. Then, much more thee! Or, if not, thou strange and elfish child, whence didst thou come?"

"Tell me! Tell me!" repeated Pearl, no longer seriously, but laughing and capering about the floor. "It is thou that must tell me!"

But Hester could not resolve the query, being herself in a dismal labyrinth of doubt. She remembered—betwixt a smile and a shudder—the talk of the neighbouring townspeople, who, seeking vainly elsewhere for the child's paternity, and observing some of her odd attributes, had given out that poor little Pearl was **a demon offspring**: such as, ever since old Catholic times, had occasionally been seen on earth, through the agency of their mother's sin, and to promote some foul and wicked purpose. **Luther**, according to the scandal of his monkish enemies, was a brat of that hellish breed; nor was Pearl the only child to whom this inauspicious origin was assigned among the New England Puritans.

a demon offspring: The Puritans view Pearl as a child of Satan, which implicitly makes Dimmesdale the devil.

Luther: Martin Luther (1483–1546), a German theologian and translator of the Bible, who led the Protestant Reformation in Germany.

COMMENTARY

From the careful description of Hester in the previous chapter, the narrator moves to an equally in-depth look at her daughter Pearl in Chapter VI. The description begins by focusing on Pearl's contradictory nature: She is a "lovely and immortal flower," but one that has grown out of "rank luxuriance" and "guilty passion." The narrator continues to use the flower imagery that began in the first chapter with his description of the black flower and the wild rosebush. Pearl's name does not evoke the calm, white, unimpassioned beauty of the gem but instead bespeaks the pearl of great price, a biblical reference to Matthew 13:45–46. Like the merchant in the Bible who sells everything he has in order to purchase a single pearl, Hester has sold everything that was valuable to her—her reputation, her status in the community, and all manner of social acceptability and contact—for this one treasure, her daughter.

No single meaning can fully capture Pearl's significance, and critics have spent hundreds of pages arguing about different interpretations of her name; as the narrator tells us, inside this one child there are "many children." Most argue that Pearl should most properly be viewed as a symbol, rather than as a character. First, she is a symbol of the scarlet letter itself, and all the descriptions of her in the book emphasize this connection. For example, when we first see Pearl, as her mother steps out of the prison door, Hester tries to use the baby to cover the scarlet letter on her breast; the narrator tells us that both Pearl and the letter share a place on the "same dishonored bosom." Hester expects her daughter's nature to correspond with the sin that brought her into the world. Every day Hester looks for a "dark and wild peculiarity" in Pearl's personality. These images of darkness and wildness reoccur throughout the novel.

Pearl can also be viewed as God's blessing on Hester. At times, Hester recognizes the discrepancy between the treatment she has received from man and that she has received from God: While man has marked her with the heinous scarlet letter and separated her from all human sympathy, God has sent her a lovely child, who will connect Hester to humanity and will someday become a "blessed soul in heaven." Although Hester does not have much faith in this logic—because her deed was evil, she believes the product of it, Pearl, must also be evil—these musings again imply the narrator's critique of Puritan hypocrisy and narrow-mindedness. What right do these cold men have to condemn Hester's passion, especially when God has seen fit to reward her with such a beautiful child?

Just as Hester has fashioned the scarlet letter to be fanciful and imaginative—a fit emblem of her passionate adultery—Pearl is also adorned in clothes that emphasize her connection with a bohemian luxury. Pearl's clothing is made of the richest material Hester can find and reflects the heights of her imagination. Pearl is thus surrounded by a magnificent circle of radiance that expresses her mother's own repressed nature.

Within the darkness of their lonely cottage, Pearl's light shines. But it doesn't shine with just one kind of light. Her look varies from the simple "wild-flower prettiness" of a peasant baby to the luxurious excess of a young princess. One constant, though, is Pearl's passion, which adds a depth to her personality that she never loses. The variety of Pearl's outward appearance is a fitting emblem for her equally mutable inner life, which lacks any understanding of the nature of human laws. Hester believes that the child's nature grew out of Hester's mood while she was pregnant: Pearl has absorbed the "deep stains of crimson and gold, the fiery lustre, the black shadow, and the untempered light" of her mother's feelings and the wild, defiant, and flighty aspects of her mood. A product of sin, of passion, and of love, Pearl has an understandably contradictory nature. She is a symbol of her mother's imagination, passion, vision, and capriciousness: all qualities Puritan society rejects. In some sense, Pearl can be seen as Hester's double, as the carrier of all the characteristics Hester must repress in order to fit within the boundaries of the Puritan worldview. Although these features now emerge from Pearl's personality as "morning radiance," Hester worries they will be transformed into "storm and whirlwind" when Pearl ages.

Given Pearl's capricious and wild nature, Hester finds it difficult to discipline her. The Puritans advocated the harsh discipline of children, just as they advocated severe punishment of adult transgressions. Born of intolerant parents, other children in town learn early in life to revile difference and, therefore, treat Hester and Pearl as outcasts. Even the games of these children show their repressed and severe nature: They play at going to church, scouring Quakers, or taking Indian scalps in fake fights. But Hester is incapable of using strict discipline with Pearl. Pearl is associated with a "wild flow of spirits" and "an airy sprite." She has an "intangibility," like a "glimmering light," which could vanish at any moment.

To the Puritans, Pearl is a symbol of sin and a child of the devil, so she is not allowed to interact with the other children in the village. When they try to surround her, Pearl shouts at them in a terrible manner that reminds Hester of a witch's curse. To Hester, this behavior reflects a strand of the evil from which Pearl was born. Pearl's creative spirit is in touch with "the spell of life," and she applies her "witchcraft" to the objects around her. Using her wild imagination, she recreates everything around her so it becomes a participant in her fantastic drama. Her intellect is like the "phantasmagoric play of the northern lights." Thus, Pearl is associated with passion, imagination, magic, and intensity.

Another oddity of Pearl's life is that the first thing she noticed as a child wasn't her mother's smile, but the scarlet letter. When Pearl stares at the letter, a "freakish, elfish cast" comes into her eyes, and Hester fears that she sees a "fiend-like" visage in Pearl's face. Although Hester interprets Pearl's fascination with the letter as symbolic of her impishness, her pleasure in the bright gold and red of the embroidery might have a much simpler explanation: Most children are fascinated by bright colors and vivid images. But Hester's Puritan indoctrination causes her to fear that the child is inherently evil because she was born out of an unlawful relationship. Pearl's fascination with the letter does serve as a constant corrective to Hester: It prevents her mother from ever forgetting the letter's presence.

Chapter VII

Worried that her sinful past makes Hester an unfit mother, some of Boston's most influential townspeople try to take Pearl away from her. Hester makes a trip to the governor's home to plead for her child.

CHAPTER VII: THE GOVERNOR'S HALL

HESTER Prynne went one day to the mansion of Governor Bellingham, with a pair of gloves which she had fringed and embroidered to his order, and which were to be worn on some great occasion of state; for, though the chances of a popular election had caused this former ruler to descend a step or two from the highest rank, he still held an honourable and influential place among the colonial magistracy.

Another and far more important reason than the delivery of a pair of embroidered gloves, impelled Hester, at this time, to seek an interview with a personage of so much power and activity in the affairs of the settlement. It had reached her ears that there was a design on the part of some of the leading inhabitants, cherishing the more rigid order of principles in religion and government, to deprive her of her child. On the supposition that Pearl, as already hinted, was of demon origin, these good people not unreasonably argued that a Christian interest in the mother's soul required them to remove such a stumbling-block from her path. If the child, on the other hand, were really capable of moral and religious growth, and possessed the elements of ultimate salvation, then, surely, it would enjoy all the fairer prospect of these advantages by being transferred to wiser and better guardianship than Hester Prynne's. Among those who promoted the design, Governor Bellingham was said to be one of the most busy. It may appear singular, and, indeed, not a little ludicrous, that an affair of this kind, which in later days would have been referred to no higher jurisdiction than that of the select men of the town, should then have been a question publicly discussed, and on which statesmen of eminence took sides. At that epoch of pristine simplicity, however, matters of even slighter public interest, and of far less intrinsic weight than the welfare of Hester and her child, were strangely mixed up with the deliberations of legislators and acts of state. The period was hardly, if at all, earlier than that of our story, when a dispute concerning the right of **property in a pig** not only caused a fierce and bitter contest in the legislative body of the colony, but resulted in an important modification of the framework itself of the legislature.

Full of concern, therefore—but so conscious of her own right that it seemed scarcely an unequal match between the public on the one side, and a lonely woman, backed by the sympathies of nature, on the other— Hester Prynne set forth from her solitary cottage. Little Pearl, of course, was her companion. She was now of an age to run lightly along by her mother's side, and, constantly in motion from morn till sunset, could have accomplished a much longer journey than that before her. Often, nevertheless, more from caprice than necessity, she demanded to be taken

property in a pig: In 1642, a member of the colony was accused of stealing a pig, leading to a split in the views of the elected officials. Hawthorne uses this example to emphasize that many of the Puritan leaders were more influenced by monetary than spiritual values.

up in arms; but was soon as imperious to be let down again, and frisked onward before Hester on the grassy pathway, with many a harmless trip and tumble. We have spoken of Pearl's rich and luxuriant beauty—a beauty that shone with deep and vivid tints, a bright complexion, eyes possessing intensity both of depth and glow, and hair already of a deep, glossy brown, and which, in after years, would be nearly akin to black. There was fire in her and throughout her: she seemed the unpremeditated offshoot of a passionate moment. Her mother, in contriving the child's garb, had allowed the gorgeous tendencies of her imagination their full play, arraying her in a crimson velvet tunic of a peculiar cut, abundantly embroidered in fantasies and flourishes of gold thread. So much strength of colouring, which must have given a wan and pallid aspect to cheeks of a fainter bloom, was admirably adapted to Pearl's beauty, and made her the very brightest little jet of flame that ever danced upon the earth.

But it was a remarkable attribute of this garb, and indeed, of the child's whole appearance, that it irresistibly and inevitably reminded the beholder of the token which Hester Prynne was doomed to wear upon her bosom. It was the scarlet letter in another form: the scarlet letter endowed with life! The mother herself—as if the red ignominy were so deeply scorched into her brain that all her conceptions assumed its form—had carefully wrought out the similitude, lavishing many hours of morbid ingenuity to create an analogy between the object of her affection and the emblem of her guilt and torture. But, in truth, Pearl was the one as well as the other; and only in consequence of that identity had Hester contrived so perfectly to represent the scarlet letter in her appearance.

As the two wayfarers came within the precincts of the town, the children of the Puritans looked up from their player what passed for play with those sombre little urchins—and spoke gravely one to another:

"Behold, verily, there is the woman of the scarlet letter: and of a truth, moreover, there is the likeness of the scarlet letter running along by her side! Come, therefore, and let us fling mud at them!"

But Pearl, who was a dauntless child, after frowning, stamping her foot, and shaking her little hand with a variety of threatening gestures, suddenly made a rush at the knot of her enemies, and put them all to flight. She resembled, in her fierce pursuit of them, an infant pestilence—the scarlet fever, or some such half-fledged angel of judgment—whose mission was to punish the sins of the rising generation. She screamed and shouted, too, with a terrific volume of sound, which, doubtless, caused the hearts of the fugitives to quake within them. The victory accomplished, Pearl returned quietly to her mother, and looked up, smiling, into her face. Without further adventure, they reached the dwelling of Governor Bellingham. This was a large wooden house, built in a fashion of which there are specimens still extant in the streets of our older towns now moss-grown, crumbling to decay, and melancholy at heart with the many sorrowful or joyful occurrences, remembered or forgotten, that have happened and passed away within their dusky chambers. Then, however, there was the freshness of the passing year on its exterior, and the cheerfulness, gleaming forth from the sunny windows, of a human habitation, into which death had never entered. It had, indeed, a very cheery aspect, the walls being overspread with a kind of stucco, in which fragments of broken glass were plentifully intermixed; so that, when the sunshine fell aslant-wise over the front of the edifice, it glittered and sparkled as if diamonds had been flung against it by the double handful. The brilliancy might have be fitted **Aladdin's palace** rather than the mansion of a grave old Puritan ruler. It was further decorated with strange and seemingly **cabalistic** figures and diagrams, suitable to the quaint taste of the age which had been drawn in the stucco, when newly laid on, and had now grown hard and durable, for the admiration of after times.

Aladdin's palace: A boy in *The Arabian Nights,* Aladdin discovers a magical lamp and ring that bring him everything he wishes for.

cabalistic: an occult philosophy of some Jewish rabbis, especially in the Middle Ages, based on a mystical interpretation of the Scriptures.

Pearl, looking at this bright wonder of a house began to caper and dance, and imperatively required that the whole breadth of sunshine should be stripped off its front, and given her to play with.

"No, my little Pearl!" said her mother; "thou must gather thine own sunshine. I have none to give thee!"

They approached the door, which was of an arched form, and flanked on each side by a narrow tower or projection of the edifice, in both of which were lattice-windows, the wooden shutters to close over them at need. Lifting the iron hammer that hung at the portal, Hester Prynne gave a summons, which was answered by one of the Governor's bond servants, a free-born Englishman, but now a seven years' slave. During that term he was to be the property of his master, and as much a commodity of bargain and sale as an ox, or a joint-stool. The serf wore the customary garb of serving-men at that period, and long before, in the old hereditary halls of England.

"Is the worshipful Governor Bellingham within?" inquired Hester.

"Yea, forsooth," replied the bond-servant, staring with wide-open eyes at the scarlet letter, which, being a new-comer in the country, he had never before seen. "Yea, his honourable worship is within. But he hath a godly minister or two with him, and likewise a **leech**. Ye may not see his worship now."

leech: a physician.

"Nevertheless, I will enter," answered Hester Prynne; and the bondservant, perhaps judging from the decision of her air, and the glittering symbol in her bosom, that she was a great lady in the land, offered no opposition.

So the mother and little Pearl were admitted into the hall of entrance. With many variations, suggested by the nature of his building materials, diversity of climate, and a different mode of social life, Governor Bellingham had planned his new habitation after the residences of gentlemen of fair estate in his native land. Here, then, was a wide and reasonably lofty hall, extending through the whole depth of the house, and forming a medium of general communication, more or less directly, with all the other apartments. At one extremity, this spacious room was lighted by the windows of the two towers, which formed a small recess on either side of the portal. At the other end, though partly muffled by a curtain, it was more powerfully illuminated by one of those embowed hall windows which we read of in old books, and which was provided with a deep and cushion seat. Here, on the cushion, lay a folio tome, probably of the **Chronicles of England**, or other such substantial literature; even as, in our own days, we scatter gilded volumes on the centre table, to be turned over by the casual guest. The furniture of the hall consisted of some ponderous chairs, the backs of which were elaborately carved with wreaths of oaken flowers; and likewise a table in the same taste, the whole being of the Elizabethan age, or perhaps earlier, and heirlooms, transferred hither from the Governor's paternal home. On the table—in token that the sentiment of old English hospitality had not been left behind—stood a large pewter tankard, at the bottom of which, had Hester or Pearl peeped into it, they might have seen the frothy remnant of a recent draught of ale.

On the wall hung a row of portraits, representing the forefathers of the Bellingham lineage, some with armour on their breasts, and others with stately ruffs and robes of peace. All were characterised by the sternness and severity which old portraits so invariably put on, as if they were the ghosts, rather than the pictures, of departed worthies, and were gazing with harsh and intolerant criticism at the pursuits and enjoyments of living men.

At about the centre of the oaken panels that lined the hall was suspended a suit of mail, not, like the pictures, an ancestral relic, but of the most modern date; for it had been manufactured by a skilful armourer in London, the same year in which Governor Bellingham came over to New England. There was a steel head-piece, a **cuirass**, a **gorget** and **greaves**, with a pair of **gauntlets** and a sword hanging beneath; all, and especially the helmet and breastplate, so highly burnished as to glow with white radiance, and scatter an illumination everywhere about upon the floor. This bright panoply was not meant for mere idle show, but had been worn by the Governor on many a solemn muster and draining field, and had glittered, moreover, at the head of a regiment in the **Pequod war**. For, though bred a lawyer, and accustomed to speak of **Bacon, Coke, Noye, and Finch**, as his professional associates, the exigencies of this new country had transformed Governor Bellingham into a soldier, as well as a statesman and ruler.

Little Pearl, who was as greatly pleased with the gleaming armour as she had been with the glittering frontispiece of the house, spent some time looking into the polished mirror of the breastplate.

"Mother," cried she, "I see you here. Look! look!"

Hester looked by way of humouring the child; and she saw that, owing to the peculiar effect of this convex mirror, the scarlet letter was represented in exaggerated and gigantic proportions, so as to be greatly the most prominent feature of her appearance. In truth, she seemed absolutely hidden behind it. Pearl pointed upwards also, at a similar picture in the head-piece; smiling at her mother, with the elfish intelligence that was so familiar an expression on her small physiognomy. That look

Chronicles of England: published by Holinshed in 1577.

cuirass: a piece of closefitting armor for protecting the breast and back.

gorget: a piece of armor to protect the throat.

greaves: armor for the leg from the ankle to the knee.

gauntlets: medieval gloves, usually made of leather covered with metal plates, worn by knights in armor to protect their hands in combat.

Pequod war: The Pequot lived in a territory in northeast New York and east Connecticut. In 1636, the settlers of Massachusetts claimed a Pequot murdered a member of the colony. As a result, they burned a Pequot village in revenge. In 1637, the colonists slaughtered the Pequot in their fort on the Mystic River in Connecticut, burning alive 600–700 men, women, and children. Any remaining Pequot were sold into slavery in Bermuda.

Bacon, Coke, Noye, and Finch: all famous legal scholars who made important contributions to British Common Law.

of naughty merriment was likewise reflected in the mirror, with so much breadth and intensity of effect, that it made Hester Prynne feel as if it could not be the image of her own child, but of an imp who was seeking to mould itself into Pearl's shape.

"Come along, Pearl," said she, drawing her away, "Come and look into this fair garden. It may be we shall see flowers there; more beautiful ones than we find in the woods."

Pearl accordingly ran to the bow-window, at the further end of the hall, and looked along the vista of a garden walk, carpeted with closely-shaven grass, and bordered with some rude and immature attempt at shrubbery. But the proprietor appeared already to have relinquished as hopeless, the effort to perpetuate on this side of the Atlantic, in a hard soil, and amid the close struggle for subsistence, the native English taste for ornamental gardening. Cabbages grew in plain sight; and a pumpkin-vine, rooted at some distance, had run across the intervening space, and deposited one of its gigantic products directly beneath the hall window, as if to warn the Governor that this great lump of vegetable gold was as rich an ornament as New England earth would offer him. There were a few rose-bushes, however, and a number of apple-trees, probably the descendants of those planted by the **Reverend Mr. Blackstone**, the first settler of the peninsula; that half mythological personage who rides through our early annals, seated on the back of a bull.

Pearl, seeing the rose-bushes, began to cry for a red rose, and would not be pacified.

"Hush, child, hush!" said her mother, earnestly. "Do not cry, dear little Pearl! I hear voices in the garden. The Governor is coming, and gentlemen along with him."

In fact, adown the vista of the garden-avenue, a number of persons were seen approaching towards the house. Pearl, in utter scorn of her mother's attempt to quiet her, gave an eldritch scream, and then became silent, not from any motion of obedience, but because the quick and mobile curiosity of her disposition was excited by the appearance of those new personages.

Reverend Mr. Blackstone: William Blackstone (1595–1675) was the first white settler in the area where Boston now stands. Because he didn't like the Puritans, Blackstone later moved away to Rhode Island.

COMMENTARY

In this chapter, Hester and Pearl momentarily leave their secluded cottage and enter the impressive abode of Governor Bellingham. They make this journey into town because the townspeople have requested that Pearl be taken away from her mother. How do they justify separating a mother and child? On the one hand, they claim that because Pearl is the devil's offspring, she is an impediment to her mother's salvation. On the other hand, they argue that the child could possibly profit from moral guidance; Hester is not the right guardian for Pearl, given

her own fallen nature. In presenting the townspeople's arguments, the narrator offers additional insight into their beliefs, revealing once again the limitations of their reasoning. To illustrate the pettiness of their interference, the narrator tells us that the townspeople recently disputed "the right of property in a pig" (explained in this chapter's Notes), an argument that has caused a "fierce and bitter" fight in the legislature.

Again, the narrator focuses on Pearl's beauty, which is "rich and luxuriant": Her eyes have "depth and glow," her hair is "deep, glossy brown," and a fire permeates her being that indicates the passionate moment from which she was born. Similar to the scarlet letter, Pearl's clothing is made of a crimson velvet and is embroidered with "fantasies and flourishes of gold thread," making her look like a bright "jet of flame." So close is her appearance to the scarlet letter that the narrator writes: "It was the scarlet letter in another form; the scarlet letter endowed with life!" Hester has consciously created this likeness between her beloved child and the "emblem of her guilt and torture," and, in truth, Pearl is both: a loved object of affection and the symbol of her mother's suffering. Even the children playing on the street recognize that Pearl is "the likeness of the scarlet letter" running by Hester's side. And Pearl's anger with these children when they threaten to throw mud at her is much like a "scarlet fever" or an "angel of judgment" whose goal is to punish the sins of this infant generation.

Hester and Pearl are jeered by children in this F.O.C. Darley illustration.
Photo courtesy of The Darley Society, Inc.

The narrator shows in this chapter that the significance of the letter—just like the significance of Pearl—is not inherently negative. When Hester knocks on the door of Governor Bellingham's house, a servant new to the country answers. Not knowing the significance of the scarlet letter, he assumes its elegance marks Hester as a respected member of the community. This incident shows the arbitrariness of the significance of Hester's "A": To someone unfamiliar with the Puritan's view of life, the letter is not necessarily associated with evil.

Chapter VII also shows a new side of Governor Bellingham. In contrast with the austere prison or the dark and dreary townspeople, the governor's home is notable primarily for its combination of newness and Old World charm. His home is so new that no one has yet died in it. It boasts cheerful, sun-filled windows, and its stucco is studded with broken glass that looks like diamonds when the sun shines on it. Indeed, the brilliance of the mansion seems out of place in the Puritan settlement, more typical of Aladdin's magical palace than the home of a grave and stern Puritan ruler. In addition, the house is decorated with strange, apparently cabalistic diagrams. The only element of the house that does not reflect the governor's English ancestry is the garden; the harsh New England soil will not support the ornamental gardens so popular in England, so the governor has, instead, planted cabbages and pumpkins, vegetables native to the land. In contrast to the general cheerfulness of the house are the portraits of Bellingham's ancestors that line the walls; these representations of the governor's forefathers appear stern, severe, harsh, and intolerant. They offer a reminder of the types of viewpoints and attitudes upon which Puritan austerity was founded, showing the deeply negative foundation of much American thought.

Most intriguing to Pearl is a suit of armor, which Bellingham wore when he defended the country during the Pequot War. Reference to this conflagration, in which the Indians—men, women, and children—were senselessly slaughtered, offers another image of the violence and intolerance that underlies the seeming compassion and peacefulness of these Christian folk. When Hester sees her reflection in the suit of armor, she appears to be dwarfed behind the scarlet letter. Pearl's reflection is also disconcerting: Her "elfish intelligence" and "look of naughty merriment" make Hester believe she is an imp, rather than her child. This incident symbolizes the manner in which the governor and his stern laws have exaggerated Hester's crimes, making her little more than a body to bear the scarlet letter, and have also turned a happy, creative child into the offspring of the devil. Is this natural? Aren't the governor's crimes against these women and against the Pequot equally atrocious? The narrator reveals the limitations in the Puritan elders' views, which pervert minor human failings into embodiments of evil, just as the coat of armor magnifies the scarlet letter until Hester is almost completely obscured.

Chapter VIII

To be certain that Pearl is being raised correctly, Rev. Wilson tests her biblical knowledge by asking her who made her. Although Pearl knows the correct answer, she mischievously tells Wilson that her mother plucked her from the rosebush outside her prison door. The minister and governor are shocked, but Dimmesdale convinces them that Hester is the best mother for Pearl, who was given to Hester as a gift from God and as a reminder of her sin.

CHAPTER VIII: THE ELF-CHILD AND THE MINISTER

GOVERNOR Bellingham, in a loose gown and easy cap—such as elderly gentlemen loved to endue themselves with, in their domestic privacy—walked foremost, and appeared to be showing off his estate, and expatiating on his projected improvements. The wide circumference of an elaborate ruff, beneath his grey beard, in the antiquated fashion of **King James's** reign, caused his head to look not a little like that of **John the Baptist** in a charger. The impression made by his aspect, so rigid and severe, and frost-bitten with more than autumnal age, was hardly in keeping with the appliances of worldly enjoyment wherewith he had evidently done his utmost to surround himself. But it is an error to suppose that our great forefathers—though accustomed to speak and think of human existence as a state merely of trial and warfare, and though unfeignedly prepared to sacrifice goods and life at the behest of duty—made it a matter of conscience to reject such means of comfort, or even luxury, as lay fairly within their grasp. This creed was never taught, for instance, by the venerable pastor, John Wilson, whose beard, white as a snow-drift, was seen over Governor Bellingham's shoulders, while its wearer suggested that pears and peaches might yet be naturalised in the New England climate, and that purple grapes might possibly be compelled to flourish against the sunny garden-wall. The old clergyman, nurtured at the rich bosom of the English Church, had a long established and legitimate taste for all good and comfortable things, and however stern he might show himself in the pulpit, or in his public reproof of such transgressions as that of Hester Prynne, still, the genial benevolence of his private life had won him warmer affection than was accorded to any of his professional contemporaries.

Behind the Governor and Mr. Wilson came two other guests: one, the Reverend Arthur Dimmesdale, whom the reader may remember as having taken a brief and reluctant part in the scene of Hester Prynne's disgrace; and, in close companionship with him, old Roger Chillingworth, a person of great skill in physic, who for two or three years past had been settled in the town. It was understood that this learned man was the physician as well as friend of the young minister, whose health had severely suffered of late by his too unreserved self-sacrifice to the labours and duties of the pastoral relation.

King James's: King James I was the King of England from 1603–1625.

John the Baptist: In the Bible, Salome demanded the head of John the Baptist on a platter. She got her wish.

The Governor, in advance of his visitors, ascended one or two steps, and, throwing open the leaves of the great hall window, found himself close to little Pearl. The shadow of the curtain fell on Hester Prynne, and partially concealed her.

"What have we here?" said Governor Bellingham, looking with surprise at the scarlet little figure before him. "I profess, I have never seen the like since my days of vanity, in old King James's time, when I was wont to esteem it a high favour to be admitted to a court mask! There used to be a swarm of these small apparitions in holiday time, and we called them children of the **Lord of Misrule**. But how gat such a guest into my hall?"

"Ay, indeed!" cried good old Mr. Wilson. "What little bird of scarlet plumage may this be? Methinks I have seen just such figures when the sun has been shining through a richly painted window, and tracing out the golden and crimson images across the floor. But that was in the old land. Prithee, young one, who art thou, and what has ailed thy mother to bedizen thee in this strange fashion? Art thou a Christian child—ha? Dost know thy catechism? Or art thou one of those naughty elfs or fairies whom we thought to have left behind us, with other relics of Papistry, in merry old England?"

"I am mother's child," answered the scarlet vision, "and my name is Pearl!"

"Pearl?—Ruby, rather—or Coral!—or Red Rose, at the very least, judging from thy hue!" responded the old minister, putting forth his hand in a vain attempt to pat little Pearl on the cheek. "But where is this mother of thine? Ah! I see," he added; and, turning to Governor Bellingham, whispered, "This is the selfsame child of whom we have held speech together; and behold here the unhappy woman, Hester Prynne, her mother!"

"Sayest thou so?" cried the Governor. "Nay, we might have judged that such a child's mother must needs be a scarlet woman, and a worthy type of **her of Babylon**! But she comes at a good time, and we will look into this matter forthwith."

Governor Bellingham stepped through the window into the hall, followed by his three guests.

"Hester Prynne," said he, fixing his naturally stern regard on the wearer of the scarlet letter, "there hath been much question concerning thee of late. The point hath been weightily discussed, whether we, that are of authority and influence, do well discharge our consciences by trusting an immortal soul, such as there is in yonder child, to the guidance of one who hath stumbled and fallen amid the pitfalls of this world. Speak thou, the child's own mother! Were it not, thinkest thou, for thy little one's temporal and eternal welfare that she be taken out of thy charge, and clad soberly, and disciplined strictly, and instructed in the truths of heaven and earth? What canst thou do for the child in this kind?"

"I can teach my little Pearl what I have learned from this!" answered Hester Prynne, laying her finger on the red token.

Lord of Misrule: a position appointed by the court to superintend Christmas festivities at the end of the 15th and beginning of the 16th centuries.

her of Babylon: a reference to the "Whore of Babylon" (Revelation 17:3–5). Also a derogatory term used by the early Puritans to refer to the Roman Catholic Church.

"Woman, it is thy badge of shame!" replied the stern magistrate. "It is because of the stain which that letter indicates that we would transfer thy child to other hands."

"Nevertheless," said the mother, calmly, though growing more pale, "this badge hath taught me—it daily teaches me—it is teaching me at this moment—lessons whereof my child may be the wiser and better, albeit they can profit nothing to myself."

"We will judge warily," said Bellingham, "and look well what we are about to do. Good Master Wilson, I pray you, examine this Pearl—since that is her name—and see whether she hath had such Christian nurture as befits a child of her age."

The old minister seated himself in an arm-chair and made an effort to draw Pearl betwixt his knees. But the child, unaccustomed to the touch or familiarity of any but her mother, escaped through the open window, and stood on the upper step, looking like a wild tropical bird of rich plumage, ready to take flight into the upper air. Mr. Wilson, not a little astonished at this outbreak—for he was a grandfatherly sort of personage, and usually a vast favourite with children—essayed, however, to proceed with the examination.

"Pearl," said he, with great solemnity, "thou must take heed to instruction, that so, in due season, thou mayest wear in thy bosom the pearl of great price. Canst thou tell me, my child, who made thee?"

Now Pearl knew well enough who made her, for Hester Prynne, the daughter of a pious home, very soon after her talk with the child about her Heavenly Father, had begun to inform her of those truths which the human spirit, at whatever stage of immaturity, imbibes with such eager interest. Pearl, therefore—so large were the attainments of her three years' lifetime—could have borne a fair examination in the **New England Primer**, or the first column of the **Westminster Catechisms**, although unacquainted with the outward form of either of those celebrated works. But that perversity, which all children have more or less of, and of which little Pearl had a tenfold portion, now, at the most inopportune moment, took thorough possession of her, and closed her lips, or impelled her to speak words amiss. After putting her finger in her mouth, with many ungracious refusals to answer good Mr. Wilson's question, the child finally announced that she had not been made at all, but had been plucked by her mother off the bush of wild roses that grew by the prison-door.

This phantasy was probably suggested by the near proximity of the Governor's red roses, as Pearl stood outside of the window, together with her recollection of the prison rose-bush, which she had passed in coming hither.

Old Roger Chillingworth, with a smile on his face, whispered something in the young clergyman's ear. Hester Prynne looked at the man of skill, and even then, with her fate hanging in the balance, was startled to

New England Primer: a famous schoolbook used to teach reading, which contained moral texts and an alphabet illustrated with rhyming couplets.

Westminster Catechisms: probably the shorter Catechism of the Westminster Assembly of Divines, published in 1647.

perceive what a change had come over his features—how much uglier they were, how his dark complexion seemed to have grown duskier, and his figure more misshapen—since the days when she had familiarly known him. She met his eyes for an instant, but was immediately constrained to give all her attention to the scene now going forward.

"This is awful!" cried the Governor, slowly recovering from the astonishment into which Pearl's response had thrown him. "Here is a child of three years old, and she cannot tell who made her! Without question, she is equally in the dark as to her soul, its present depravity, and future destiny! Methinks, gentlemen, we need inquire no further."

Hester caught hold of Pearl, and drew her forcibly into her arms, confronting the old Puritan magistrate with almost a fierce expression. Alone in the world, cast off by it, and with this sole treasure to keep her heart alive, she felt that she possessed indefeasible rights against the world, and was ready to defend them to the death.

"God gave me the child!" cried she. "He gave her in requital of all things else which ye had taken from me. She is my happiness—she is my torture, none the less! Pearl keeps me here in life! Pearl punishes me, too! See ye not, she is the scarlet letter, only capable of being loved, and so endowed with a millionfold the power of retribution for my sin? Ye shall not take her! I will die first!"

"My poor woman," said the not unkind old minister, "the child shall be well cared for—far better than thou canst do for it."

"God gave her into my keeping!" repeated Hester Prynne, raising her voice almost to a shriek. "I will not give her up!" And here by a sudden impulse, she turned to the young clergyman, Mr. Dimmesdale, at whom, up to this moment, she had seemed hardly so much as once to direct her eyes. "Speak thou for me!" cried she. "Thou wast my pastor, and hadst charge of my soul, and knowest me better than these men can. I will not lose the child! Speak for me! Thou knowest—for thou hast sympathies which these men lack—thou knowest what is in my heart, and what are a mother's rights, and how much the stronger they are when that mother has but her child and the scarlet letter! Look thou to it! I will not lose the child! Look to it!"

At this wild and singular appeal, which indicated that Hester Prynne's situation had provoked her to little less than madness, the young minister at once came forward, pale, and holding his hand over his heart, as was his custom whenever his peculiarly nervous temperament was thrown into agitation. He looked now more careworn and emaciated than as we described him at the scene of Hester's public ignominy; and whether it were his failing health, or whatever the cause might be, his large dark eyes had a world of pain in their troubled and melancholy depth.

"There is truth in what she says," began the minister, with a voice sweet, tremulous, but powerful, insomuch that the hall re-echoed and the hollow armour rang with it—"truth in what Hester says, and in the feeling which inspires her! God gave her the child, and gave her, too, an instinctive knowledge of its nature and requirements—both seemingly so peculiar—which no other mortal being can possess. And, moreover, is there not a quality of awful sacredness in the relation between this mother and this child?"

"Ay!—how is that, good Master Dimmesdale?" interrupted the Governor. "Make that plain, I pray you!"

"It must be even so," resumed the minister. "For, if we deem it otherwise, do we not hereby say that the Heavenly Father, the creator of all flesh, hath lightly recognised a deed of sin, and made of no account the distinction between unhallowed lust and holy love? This child of its father's guilt and its mother's shame has come from the hand of God, to work in many ways upon her heart, who pleads so earnestly and with such bitterness of spirit the right to keep her. It was meant for a blessing—for the one blessing of her life! It was meant, doubtless, the mother herself hath told us, for a retribution, too; a torture to be felt at many an unthought of moment; a pang, a sting, an ever-recurring agony, in the midst of a troubled joy! Hath she not expressed this thought in the garb of the poor child, so forcibly reminding us of that red symbol which sears her bosom?"

"Well said again!" cried good Mr. Wilson. "I feared the woman had no better thought than to make a **mountebank** of her child!"

"Oh, not so!—not so!" continued Mr. Dimmesdale. "She recognises, believe me, the solemn miracle which God hath wrought in the existence of that child. And may she feel, too—what, methinks, is the very truth—that this boon was meant, above all things else, to keep the mother's soul alive, and to preserve her from blacker depths of sin into which Satan might else have sought to plunge her! Therefore it is good for this poor, sinful woman, that she hath an infant immortality, a being capable of eternal joy or sorrow, confided to her care—to be trained up by her to righteousness, to remind her, at every moment, of her fall,—but yet to teach her, as if it were by the Creator's sacred pledge, that, if she bring the child to heaven, the child also will bring its parents thither! Herein is the sinful mother happier than the sinful father. For Hester Prynne's sake, then, and no less for the poor child's sake, let us leave them as Providence hath seen fit to place them!"

"You speak, my friend, with a strange earnestness," said old Roger Chillingworth, smiling at him.

"And there is a weighty import in what my young brother hath spoken," added the Reverend Mr. Wilson.

"What say you, worshipful Master Bellingham? Hath he not pleaded well for the poor woman?"

"Indeed hath he," answered the magistrate; "and hath adduced such arguments, that we will even leave the matter as it now stands; so long, at least, as there shall be no further scandal in the woman. Care must be

mountebank: a charlatan or quack.

had nevertheless, to put the child to due and stated examination in the catechism, at thy hands or Master Dimmesdale's. Moreover, at a proper season, the **tithing-men** must take heed that she go both to school and to meeting."

The young minister, on ceasing to speak had withdrawn a few steps from the group, and stood with his face partially concealed in the heavy folds of the window-curtain; while the shadow of his figure, which the sunlight cast upon the floor, was tremulous with the vehemence of his appeal. Pearl, that wild and flighty little elf stole softly towards him, and taking his hand in the grasp of both her own, laid her cheek against it; a caress so tender, and withal so unobtrusive, that her mother, who was looking on, asked herself—"Is that my Pearl?" Yet she knew that there was love in the child's heart, although it mostly revealed itself in passion, and hardly twice in her lifetime had been softened by such gentleness as now. The minister—for, save the long-sought regards of woman, nothing is sweeter than these marks of childish preference, accorded spontaneously by a spiritual instinct, and therefore seeming to imply in us something truly worthy to be loved—the minister looked round, laid his hand on the child's head, hesitated an instant, and then kissed her brow. Little Pearl's unwonted mood of sentiment lasted no longer; she laughed, and went capering down the hall so airily, that old Mr. Wilson raised a question whether even her tiptoes touched the floor.

"The little baggage hath witchcraft in her, I profess," said he to Mr. Dimmesdale. "She needs no old woman's broomstick to fly withal!"

"A strange child!" remarked old Roger Chillingworth. "It is easy to see the mother's part in her. Would it be beyond a philosopher's research, think ye, gentlemen, to analyse that child's nature, and, from it make a mould, to give a shrewd guess at the father?"

"Nay; it would be sinful, in such a question, to follow the clue of profane philosophy," said Mr. Wilson. "Better to fast and pray upon it; and still better, it may be, to leave the mystery as we find it, unless Providence reveal it of its own accord. Thereby, every good Christian man hath a title to show a father's kindness towards the poor, deserted babe."

The affair being so satisfactorily concluded, Hester Prynne, with Pearl, departed from the house. As they descended the steps, it is averred that the lattice of a chamber-window was thrown open, and forth into the sunny day was thrust the face of Mistress Hibbins, Governor Bellingham's bitter-tempered sister, and the same who, a few years later, was executed as a witch.

"Hist, hist!" said she, while her ill-omened physiognomy seemed to cast a shadow over the cheerful newness of the house. "Wilt thou go with us to-night? There will be a merry company in the forest; and I well-nigh promised the Black Man that comely Hester Prynne should make one."

"Make my excuse to him, so please you!" answered Hester, with a triumphant smile. "I must tarry at home, and keep watch over my little

tithing-men: in England, a unit of civil administrators originally consisting of ten families. Here, the men who collect church taxes.

Pearl. Had they taken her from me, I would willingly have gone with thee into the forest, and signed my name in the Black Man's book too, and that with mine own blood!"

"We shall have thee there anon!" said the witch-lady, frowning, as she drew back her head.

But here—if we suppose this interview betwixt Mistress Hibbins and Hester Prynne to be authentic, and not a parable—was already an illustration of the young minister's argument against sundering the relation of a fallen mother to the offspring of her frailty. Even thus early had the child saved her from Satan's snare.

COMMENTARY

Although the Puritan clergymen appear stern in public, their private lives aren't quite so austere. For example, John Wilson enjoys all "good and comfortable things." Although he is strict when disciplining transgressors such as Hester, he shows much more benevolence in his private life. As in previous chapters, the difference between the public and private lives of the Puritans is highlighted here.

When Hester and Pearl enter the governor's home, the Reverend Arthur Dimmesdale and Roger Chillingworth are present. Dimmesdale and Chillingworth take on larger roles in the subsequent narrative. Gathering together all the novel's major characters, Chapter VIII highlights, through conversation, the changes these characters have undergone since their previous meeting on the scaffold two or three years earlier. The psychological connections between the major characters are complex.

Upon first seeing Pearl, the governor is reminded of his days in the court of King James, when such prettily dressed children were often seen at court parties. He associates Pearl with the Lord of Misrule, a character connected with the Christmas season and assumed to be the perpetrator of a variety of mischievous acts. Of course, Pearl is also linked in the governor's mind with another type of misrule: the extramarital affair that led to her birth. Wilson compares Pearl to a bird covered with "scarlet plumage," like the images reflected on the floor when light shines through stained glass—notice, again, that this is an image drawn from the Old World rather than the new. Indeed, Pearl is associated with the festive beauty and ceremony of old England, elements of the Old World that the Puritans tried to erase in their austere colonial environment. Later in the chapter, the narrator makes a similar connection, labeling Pearl a "wild,

tropical bird, of rich plumage, ready to take flight into the upper air." Pearl is associated with the soul, with freedom, and with beauty. Her imagination is as wild, as free, and as untamed as a bird. She is like one of the naughty elves or fairies, also thought to have been left behind in merry old England. Wilson calls her a witch and suggests that "Ruby" or "Coral" might be a better name for this magnificently dressed child than Pearl.

Pearl's capriciousness and instinctive dislike of authority is evident during Wilson's interrogation. When Wilson asks the three-year-old who made her, Pearl playfully answers that she was plucked off the wild rosebush that grows by the prison door. Although her answer surprises the clergyman, it is accurate in a metaphorical sense. The wild and beautiful Pearl is associated with this natural bounty and, like the rose, she grows in close proximity to human frailty and suffering.

Hester hasn't seen Chillingworth since he spoke with her in prison, and she is stunned by how much he has changed in the two or three years since that meeting. He has become Dimmesdale's personal physician, supposedly helping the young clergyman improve his chronically poor health but obviously also making some progress in his revenge against Hester's lover. In Hester's opinion, Chillingworth has become uglier. His already dark complexion has become duskier, and his misshapen body seems more contorted. These physical changes point to an inward change in Chillingworth: Although we now recognize this way of thinking as racist and narrow-minded, in earlier times, ugliness, darkness, and deformities were often viewed as signs of moral degeneration.

Throughout the conversation, Chillingworth makes subtle digs at Dimmesdale, who he obviously knows is Pearl's father. For example, he suggests that a careful researcher could analyze the child's nature and from it make a mold in order to guess the identity of the father. He also notes the "weighty import" with which Dimmesdale defends Hester's right to keep Pearl. These small, subtle statements point to Chillingworth's under-handed methods of slowly escalating Dimmesdale's guilt, tearing apart his soul by tiny shreds. Wilson argues that it would be sinful to follow a clue offered by "profane philoso-phy" in order to identify Pearl's father; the secret of his iden-tity must remain unless Provi-dence reveals it. The fact that Chillingworth is taking the situ-ation into his own hands and not looking to Providence to reveal the identity emphasizes his moral depravity. The reader senses that his attack on Dimmesdale's soul will be ruthless.

An F.O.C. Darley illustration of the gathering in the governor's mansion.
Photo courtesy of The Darley Society, Inc.

His plan is having an effect on Dimmesdale, whose health has suffered since the last time we saw him: He looks careworn and emaciated; his large dark eyes have a "troubled and melancholy depth" that reveals his pain; and he covers his heart with his hand whenever he feels anxious, which seems to be often. Hester's wild appeal to him for support in defending her right to keep Pearl causes him to immediately place his hand over his heart. The child seems to have an instinctive knowledge of her father's identity, running to him after he has made his appeal for Hester and placing her cheek gently against his hand.

Hester defends her claim to Pearl by arguing that God gave Pearl to her in exchange for everything the magis-trates have taken from her. Not only is all her happiness focused on Pearl, but Pearl's presence actually keeps her alive. Pearl also punishes her. In Hester's mind, Pearl *is* the scarlet letter, which must be loved in retribution for Hester's sins. Dimmesdale supports her claim, saying that Hester seems to have an instinctive knowledge of Pearl's idiosyncrasies and that an "awful sacredness" exists

between the mother and child. In his opinion, the child is both a blessing and a retribution, a fact Hester makes apparent through the manner in which she has dressed Pearl—a manner reminiscent of the red symbol that sears Hester's breast. Through the child, he argues, the mother's soul has been saved, and she's been kept from plunging into "blacker" depths of sin.

The governor and Wilson are persuaded by Dimmes-dale and agree to let Pearl stay with her mother. As Hes-ter and Pearl leave the mansion, Mistress Hibbins asks Hester to join her at a witches' meeting that night in the forest. Hester says that without Pearl to keep her com-pany, she would willingly have joined the witches who dance nightly in the woods. The narrator wonders if Hes-ter's conversation with Mistress Hibbins really occurred; by having the narrator question the authenticity of this exchange, Hawthorne heightens the reader's belief in the narrator's truthfulness. But whether the exchange occurred or not, the narrator believes that it shows the truth of the minister's statements: Pearl has kept her mother from Satan's lair. Mistress Hibbins' appearance at the end of the chapter is a reminder of how many dark powers lurk around Hester and proves her ability to dodge them.

Chapter IX

Dimmesdale's health is quickly failing, so Chillingworth, with his vast knowledge of local healing herbs and roots, becomes his physician. Not knowing of Chillingworth's true identity, Dimmesdale allows his new doctor to live with him. As he becomes more involved in Dimmesdale's life, Chillingworth's face becomes increasingly evil and ugly. Rumors begin to circulate through the town that Chillingworth is practicing black magic on the minister.

CHAPTER IX: THE LEECH

UNDER the appellation of Roger Chillingworth, the reader will remember, was hidden another name, which its former wearer had resolved should never more be spoken. It has been related, how, in the crowd that witnessed Hester Prynne's ignominious exposure, stood a man, elderly, travel-worn, who, just emerging from the perilous wilderness, beheld the woman, in whom he hoped to find embodied the warmth and cheerfulness of home, set up as a type of sin before the people. Her matronly fame was trodden under all men's feet. Infamy was babbling around her in the public market-place. For her kindred, should the tidings ever reach them, and for the companions of her unspotted life, there remained nothing but the contagion of her dishonour; which would not fail to be distributed in strict accordance and proportion with the intimacy and sacredness of their previous relationship. Then why—since the choice was with himself—should the individual, whose connexion with the fallen woman had been the most intimate and sacred of them all, come forward to vindicate his claim to an inheritance so little desirable? He resolved not to be pilloried beside her on her pedestal of shame. Unknown to all but Hester Prynne, and possessing the lock and key of her silence, he chose to withdraw his name from the roll of mankind, and, as regarded his former ties and interest, to vanish out of life as completely as if he indeed lay at the bottom of the ocean, whither rumour had long ago consigned him. This purpose once effected, new interests would immediately spring up, and likewise a new purpose; dark, it is true, if not guilty, but of force enough to engage the full strength of his faculties.

In pursuance of this resolve, he took up his residence in the Puritan town as Roger Chillingworth, without other introduction than the learning and intelligence of which he possessed more than a common measure. As his studies, at a previous period of his life, had made him extensively acquainted with the medical science of the day, it was as a physician that he presented himself and as such was cordially received. Skilful men, of the medical and chirurgical profession, were of rare occurrence in the colony. They seldom, it would appear, partook of the religious zeal that brought other emigrants across the Atlantic. In their researches into the human frame, it may be that the higher and more subtile faculties of such men were materialised, and that they lost the spiritual view of existence amid the intricacies of that wondrous mechanism, which seemed to involve art enough to comprise all of life within itself. At all events, the health of the good town of Boston, so far as medicine had aught to do with it, had hitherto lain in the guardianship of an aged deacon and apothecary, whose piety and godly deportment were stronger testimonials in his favour than any that he could have produced in the shape of a diploma. The only surgeon was one who combined the occasional exercise of that noble art with the daily and habitual flourish of a razor. To such a professional body Roger Chillingworth was a brilliant acquisition. He soon manifested his familiarity with the ponderous and imposing machinery of antique physic; in which every remedy contained a multitude of far-fetched and heterogeneous ingredients, as elaborately compounded as if the proposed result had been the **Elixir of Life**. In his Indian captivity, moreover, he had gained much knowledge of the properties of native herbs and roots; nor did he conceal from his patients that these simple medicines, Nature's boon to the untutored savage, had quite as large a share of his own confidence as the European Pharmacopoeia, which so many learned doctors had spent centuries in elaborating.

Elixir of Life: a hypothetical substance sought by medieval alchemists to prolong life indefinitely.

Elixir of Life.

This learned stranger was exemplary as regarded at least the outward forms of a religious life; and early after his arrival, had chosen for his spiritual guide the Reverend Mr. Dimmesdale. The young divine, whose scholar-like renown still lived in Oxford, was considered by his more fervent admirers as little less than a heavenly ordained apostle, destined, should he live and labour for the ordinary term of life, to do as great deeds, for the now feeble New England Church, as the early Fathers had achieved for the infancy of the Christian faith. About this period, however, the health of Mr. Dimmesdale had evidently begun to fail. By those best acquainted with his habits, the paleness of the young minister's cheek was accounted for by his too earnest devotion to study, his scrupulous fulfilment of parochial duty, and more than all, to the fasts and vigils of which he made a frequent practice, in order to keep the grossness of this earthly state from clogging and obscuring his spiritual lamp. Some declared, that if Mr. Dimmesdale were really going to die, it was cause enough that the world was not worthy to be any longer trodden by his feet. He himself, on the other hand, with characteristic humility, avowed his belief that if Providence should see fit to remove him, it would be because of his own unworthiness to perform its humblest mission here on earth. With all this difference of opinion as to the cause of his decline, there could be no question of the fact. His form grew emaciated; his voice, though still rich and sweet, had a certain melancholy prophecy of decay in it; he was often observed, on any slight alarm or other sudden accident, to put his hand over his heart with first a flush and then a paleness, indicative of pain.

Such was the young clergyman's condition, and so imminent the prospect that his dawning light would be extinguished, all untimely, when Roger Chillingworth made his advent to the town. His first entry on the scene, few people could tell whence, dropping down as it were out of the sky or starting from the nether earth, had an aspect of mystery, which was easily heightened to the miraculous. He was now known to be a man of skill; it was observed that he gathered herbs and the blossoms of wild-flowers, and dug up roots and plucked off twigs from the forest-trees like one acquainted with hidden virtues in what was valueless to common eyes. He was heard to speak of **Sir Kenelm Digby** and other famous men— whose scientific attainments were esteemed hardly less than supernatural— as having been his correspondents or associates. Why, with such rank in the learned world, had he come hither? What, could he, whose sphere was in great cities, be seeking in the wilderness? In answer to this query, a rumour gained ground—and however absurd, was entertained by some very sensible people—that Heaven had wrought an absolute miracle, by transporting an eminent Doctor of Physic from a German university bodily through the air and setting him down at the door of Mr. Dimmesdale's study! Individuals of wiser faith, indeed, who knew that Heaven promotes its purposes without aiming at the stage-effect of what is called miraculous interposition, were inclined to see a providential hand in Roger Chillingworth's so opportune arrival.

Sir Kenelm Digby: (1603–1665) a Catholic natural philosopher, astrologer, and alchemist, famous for his interest in botany and chemistry.

This idea was countenanced by the strong interest which the physician ever manifested in the young clergyman; he attached himself to him as a parishioner, and sought to win a friendly regard and confidence from his naturally reserved sensibility. He expressed great alarm at his pastor's state of health, but was anxious to attempt the cure, and, if early undertaken, seemed not despondent of a favourable result. The elders, the deacons, the motherly dames, and the young and fair maidens of Mr. Dimmesdale's flock, were alike importunate that he should make trial of the physician's frankly offered skill. Mr. Dimmesdale gently repelled their entreaties.

"I need no medicine," said he.

But how could the young minister say so, when, with every successive Sabbath, his cheek was paler and thinner, and his voice more tremulous than before—when it had now become a constant habit, rather than a casual gesture, to press his hand over his heart? Was he weary of his labours? Did he wish to die? These questions were solemnly propounded to Mr. Dimmesdale by the elder ministers of Boston, and the deacons of his church, who, to use their own phrase, "dealt with him," on the sin of rejecting the aid which Providence so manifestly held out. He listened in silence, and finally promised to confer with the physician.

"Were it God's will," said the Reverend Mr. Dimmesdale, when, in fulfilment of this pledge, he requested old Roger Chillingworth's professional advice, "I could be well content that my labours, and my sorrows, and my sins, and my pains, should shortly end with me, and what is earthly of them be buried in my grave, and the spiritual go with me to my eternal state, rather than that you should put your skill to the proof in my behalf."

"Ah," replied Roger Chillingworth, with that quietness, which, whether imposed or natural, marked all his deportment, "it is thus that a young clergyman is apt to speak. Youthful men, not having taken a deep root, give up their hold of life so easily! And saintly men, who walk with God on earth, would fain be away, to walk with him on the golden pavements of the New Jerusalem."

"Nay," rejoined the young minister, putting his hand to his heart, with a flush of pain flitting over his brow, "were I worthier to walk there, I could be better content to toil here."

"Good men ever interpret themselves too meanly," said the physician.

In this manner, the mysterious old Roger Chillingworth became the medical adviser of the Reverend Mr. Dimmesdale. As not only the disease interested the physician, but he was strongly moved to look into the character and qualities of the patient, these two men, so different in age, came gradually to spend much time together. For the sake of the minister's health, and to enable the leech to gather plants with healing balm in them, they took long walks on the sea-shore, or in the forest; mingling various walks with the splash and murmur of the waves, and the solemn wind-anthem among the tree-tops. Often, likewise, one was the guest of the other in his place of study and retirement. There was a fascination for the minister in the company of the man of science, in whom he recognised an intellectual cultivation of no moderate depth or scope; together with a range and freedom of ideas, that he would have vainly looked for among the members of his own profession. In truth, he was startled, if not shocked, to find this attribute in the physician. Mr. Dimmesdale was a true priest, a true religionist, with the reverential sentiment largely developed, and an order of mind that impelled itself powerfully along the track of a creed, and wore its passage continually deeper with the lapse of time. In no state of society would he have been what is called a man of liberal views; it would always be essential to his peace to feel the pressure of a faith about him, supporting, while it confined him within its iron framework. Not the less, however, though with a tremulous enjoyment, did he feel the occasional relief of looking at the universe through the medium of another kind of intellect than those with which he habitually held converse. It was as if a window were thrown open, admitting a freer atmosphere into the close and stifled study, where his life was wasting itself away, amid lamp-light, or obstructed day-beams, and the musty fragrance, be it sensual or moral, that exhales from books. But the air was too fresh and chill to be long breathed with comfort. So the minister, and the physician with him, withdrew again within the limits of what their Church defined as orthodox.

Thus Roger Chillingworth scrutinised his patient carefully, both as he saw him in his ordinary life, keeping an accustomed pathway in the range of thoughts familiar to him, and as he appeared when thrown amidst other moral scenery, the novelty of which might call out something new to the surface of his character. He deemed it essential, it would seem, to know the man, before attempting to do him good. Wherever there is a heart and an intellect, the diseases of the physical frame are tinged with the peculiarities of these. In Arthur Dimmesdale, thought and imagination were so active, and sensibility so intense, that the bodily infirmity would be likely to have its groundwork there. So Roger Chillingworth—the man of skill, the kind and friendly physician—strove to go deep into his patient's bosom, delving among his principles, prying into his recollections, and probing everything with a cautious touch, like a treasure-seeker in a dark cavern. Few secrets can escape an investigator, who has opportunity and license to undertake such a quest, and skill to follow it up. A man burdened with a secret should especially avoid the intimacy of his physician. If the latter possess native sagacity, and a name-less something more,—let us call it intuition; if he show no intrusive ego-tism, nor disagreeable prominent characteristics of his own; if he have the power, which must be born with him, to bring his mind into such affin-ity with his patient's, that this last shall unawares have spoken what he imagines himself only to have thought; if such revelations be received without tumult, and acknowledged not so often by an uttered sympathy as by silence, an inarticulate breath, and here and there a word to indicate that all is understood; if to these qualifications of a confidant be joined the advantages afforded by his recognised character as a physician;—then, at some inevitable moment, will the soul of the sufferer be dis-solved, and flow forth in a dark but transparent stream, bringing all its mysteries into the daylight.

Roger Chillingworth possessed all, or most, of the attributes above enu-merated. Nevertheless, time went on; a kind of intimacy, as we have said, grew up between these two cultivated minds, which had as wide a field as the whole sphere of human thought and study to meet upon; they dis-cussed every topic of ethics and religion, of public affairs, and private character; they talked much, on both sides, of matters that seemed per-sonal to themselves; and yet no secret, such as the physician fancied must exist there, ever stole out of the minister's consciousness into his compan-ion's ear. The latter had his suspicions, indeed, that even the nature of Mr. Dimmesdale's bodily disease had never fairly been revealed to him. It was a strange reserve!

After a time, at a hint from Roger Chillingworth, the friends of Mr. Dimmesdale effected an arrangement by which the two were lodged in the same house; so that every ebb and flow of the minister's life-tide might pass under the eye of his anxious and attached physician. There was much joy throughout the town when this greatly desirable object was attained. It was held to be the best possible measure for the young clergy-man's welfare; unless, indeed, as often urged by such as felt authorised to do so, he had selected some one of the many blooming damsels, spiritu-ally devoted to him, to become his devoted wife. This latter step, how-ever, there was no present prospect that Arthur Dimmesdale would be prevailed upon to take; he rejected all suggestions of the kind, as if priestly celibacy were one of his articles of Church discipline. Doomed by his own choice, therefore, as Mr. Dimmesdale so evidently was, to eat his unsavoury morsel always at another's board, and endure the life-long chill which must be his lot who seeks to warm himself only at another's fireside, it truly seemed that this sagacious, experienced, benevolent old physician, with his concord of paternal and reverential love for the young pastor, was the very man, of all mankind, to be constantly within reach of his voice.

The new abode of the two friends was with a pious widow, of good social rank, who dwelt in a house covering pretty nearly the site on which the venerable structure of King's Chapel has since been built. It had the graveyard, originally Isaac Johnson's home-field, on one side, and so was well adapted to call up serious reflections, suited to their respective employments, in both minister and man of physic. The motherly care of the good widow assigned to Mr. Dimmesdale a front apartment, with a sunny exposure, and heavy window-curtains, to create a noontide shadow when desirable. The walls were hung round with tapestry, said to be from the **Gobelin looms**, and, at all events, representing the Scriptural story of **David and Bathsheba**, and **Nathan the Prophet**, in colours still unfaded, but which made the fair woman of the scene almost as grimly picturesque as the woe-denouncing seer. Here the pale clergyman piled up his library, rich with parchment-bound folios of the Fathers, and the lore of Rabbis, and monkish erudition, of which the Protestant divines, even while they vilified and decried that class of writers, were yet constrained often to avail themselves. On the other side of the house, old Roger Chillingworth arranged his study and laboratory: not such as a modern man of science would reckon even tolerably complete, but provided with a distilling apparatus and the means of compounding drugs and chemicals, which the practised alchemist knew well how to turn to purpose. With such commodiousness of situation, these two learned persons sat themselves down, each in his own domain, yet familiarly passing from one apartment to the other, and bestowing a mutual and not incurious inspection into one another's business.

And the Reverend Arthur Dimmesdale's best discerning friends, as we have intimated, very reasonably imagined that the hand of Providence had done all this for the purpose—besought in so many public and domestic and secret prayers—of restoring the young minister to health. But, it must now be said, another portion of the community had latterly begun to take its own view of the relation betwixt Mr. Dimmesdale and the mysterious old physician. When an uninstructed multitude attempts to see with its eyes, it is exceedingly apt to be deceived. When, however, it forms its judgment, as it usually does, on the intuitions of its great and warm heart, the conclusions thus attained are often so profound and so unerring as to possess the character of truth supernaturally revealed. The people, in the case of which we speak, could justify its prejudice against Roger Chillingworth by no fact or argument worthy of serious refutation. There was an aged handicraftsman, it is true, who had been a citizen of London at the period of **Sir Thomas Overbury's murder**, now some thirty years agone; he testified to having seen the physician, under some other name, which the narrator of the story had now forgotten, in

Gobelin looms: a reference to the Gobelin family of France, famous manufacturers of tapestries beginning in the 15th century.

David and Bathsheba: Samuel 2:11. King David seduced Bathsheba, the wife of Uriah, then had Uriah murdered.

Nathan the Prophet: Samuel 2:12. Because he was angry with David, God sent Nathan to trick David into condemning himself by telling him the parable of the rich man.

Sir Thomas Overbury's murder: Overbury (1581–1613) was poisoned by Frances Howard, Countess of Essex, because he opposed her marriage to Robert Carr, Earl of Rochester.

company with **Dr. Forman**, the famous old conjurer, who was implicated in the affair of Overbury. Two or three individuals hinted that the man of skill, during his Indian captivity, had enlarged his medical attainments by joining in the incantations of the savage priests, who were universally acknowledged to be powerful enchanters, often performing seemingly miraculous cures by their skill in the black art. A large number—and many of these were persons of such sober sense and practical observation that their opinions would have been valuable in other matters—affirmed that Roger Chillingworth's aspect had undergone a remarkable change while he had dwelt in town, and especially since his abode with Mr. Dimmesdale. At first, his expression had been calm, meditative, scholar-like. Now there was something ugly and evil in his face, which they had not previously noticed, and which grew still the more obvious to sight the oftener they looked upon him. According to the vulgar idea, the fire in his laboratory had been brought from the lower regions, and was fed with infernal fuel; and so, as might be expected, his visage was getting sooty with the smoke.

To sum up the matter, it grew to be a widely diffused opinion that the Reverend Arthur Dimmesdale, like many other personages of special sanctity, in all ages of the Christian world, was haunted either by Satan himself or Satan's emissary, in the guise of old Roger Chillingworth. This diabolical agent had the Divine permission, for a season, to burrow into the clergyman's intimacy, and plot against his soul. No sensible man, it was confessed, could doubt on which side the victory would turn. The people looked, with an unshaken hope, to see the minister come forth out of the conflict transfigured with the glory which he would unquestionably win. Meanwhile, nevertheless, it was sad to think of the perchance mortal agony through which he must struggle towards his triumph.

Alas, to judge from the gloom and terror in the depth of the poor minister's eyes, the battle was a sore one, and the victory anything but secure.

Dr. Forman: Simon Forman (1552–1611), a quack doctor who helped prepare the poison for Sir Thomas Overbury's murder. He died before his trial, but letters implicating him for the murder were found in his chambers.

COMMENTARY

Like the Puritan elders, Roger Chillingworth possesses more than average learning and intelligence—not necessarily an asset in this novel, where all of the educated members of society seem the most hypocritical and the least admirable. Medical men are rare in the New England colonies; they don't seem to share the religious zeal of the Puritans, so the colonists are happy to have Chillingworth in their community. Unlike many of the colonists, Chillingworth believes that Native American remedies are as efficacious as European pharmaceuticals, which leads some members of this racist community to be suspicious of him.

Chillingworth's sudden arrival in Boston has an aura of mystery that the superstitious Puritans quickly associate with the miraculous. His behavior is somewhat odd to them because he gathers herbs and roots, obviously able to find their hidden virtues. He also speaks of other metaphysicians, whose powers are viewed as supernatural, as his peers. Piecing these fragments of information together, many members of the community decide that Chillingworth was brought to town as a heavenly miracle in order to save Reverend Arthur Dimmesdale. Dimmesdale's parishioners view their pastor as an apostle who might one day bring as much glory to New England as the early Christian fathers brought to the infant religion. But Dimmedale's health is fading rapidly, due supposedly to his overly ardent studying and fasting, though the reader knows that it is actually due to his guilt. Again, the Puritans' interpretation of events proves wrong, as they've misjudged both Dimmesdale and Chillingworth.

Having discovered Dimmesdale's secret, Chillingworth is not interested primarily in Dimmesdale's physical health but in his character and psychological qualities. Similarly, Dimmesdale is intrigued by the depth of his doctor's intellectual attainments and with the liberality of his ideas, something Dimmesdale would not find among his fellow clergymen. Dimmesdale, a conformist, finds many of Chillingworth's notions shocking. In this chapter, the reader learns that Dimmesdale is the type of man who needs to feels himself locked within the "iron framework" of a particular creed, rather than ranging freely through a variety of ideas. But the complexity of his psychological makeup is also apparent. Despite his stringent beliefs, he feels that Chillingworth's ideas are like an open window, bringing freshness into his tightly confined life. As his name suggests, Dimmesdale is associated with dim lights, with candles and curtained rooms, with the musty fragrance that comes from books. Still, the air surrounding Chillingworth is too "fresh and chill" to be breathed for long. Obviously, similarities exist between these two intellectual men. Yet, Dimmesdale's character has a moral underpinning that Chillingworth's lacks, and Chillingworth has an intellectual freedom and imagination unknown to Dimmesdale.

Chapter IX also reveals Chillingworth's views of human psychology and disease. For example, Chillingworth believes that mind and body are inextricable: Whenever a heart and intellect are involved, they necessarily influence the body. Therefore, many seemingly physical diseases are actually spiritually or psychologically based. In order to discover the cause of these internal ailments, the doctor becomes a "treasure-seeker" delving into the "dark cavern" of the human heart and soul. In

Chillingworth's opinion, "few secrets can escape an investigator, who has opportunity and license to undertake such a quest, and skill to follow it up." Eventually, the soul of the patient will flow forth in a dark stream, and all its mysteries will emerge into the daylight. Chillingworth is like the treasure-seekers who desecrate ancient, sacred ruins simply for personal satisfaction or gain, much like the looters who steal relics from Egyptian tombs or from Native American burial grounds. Does Chillingworth have the right to penetrate someone else's soul? In the previous chapter, John Wilson suggested that only God has this right. Are Chillingworth's tactics actually more damaging than the Puritan leaders' public methods of punishment? The narrator seems to say "yes." By referring to him as a "leech," Hawthorne emphasizes the negative effect of Chillingworth's doctoring, which is literally sucking the life right out of his patient.

Some members of the community also seem to recognize Chillingworth's nefarious intentions. For example, he's thought to be an enchanter like the shamans among the Native Americans, who were believed to create miraculous cures based on their knowledge of magical arts. As we've seen in other chapters, the Puritans' opinion of Native Americans was not high. More remarkably, Chillingworth's appearance has suffered a major change since he came to town: Although he had appeared calm and meditative, he now looks ugly and evil. Some townspeople suspect that Chillingworth is Satan himself or one of Satan's emissaries. They claim that his laboratory is fueled with the fires of hell, which leave a sooty residue on the doctor's face, accounting for his awful appearance.

Throughout this chapter we are presented with images of good and evil battling. The struggle is obviously taking a toll on Dimmesdale, and the "gloom and terror" in his eyes show that the battle is fierce. As the novel progresses, Chillingworth is taking on attributes of the devil, slowly and methodically stealing Dimmesdale's soul.

Chapter X

Having insinuated himself into Dimmesdale's life by pretending to be his friend and physician, Chillingworth secretly prods the heart and soul of the minister, subtly reminding him of his equal guilt in Hester's crime. When the two men see Hester and Pearl out walking, they agree that sins are best revealed rather than concealed. One day, finding Dimmesdale asleep on a chair, Chillingworth pulls aside the minister's vestment; he sees something on Dimmesdale's chest that causes him both joy and horror. Exactly what he sees is never revealed to the reader.

CHAPTER X: THE LEECH AND HIS PATIENT

OLD Roger Chillingworth, throughout life, had been calm in temperament, kindly, though not of warm affections, but ever, and in all his relations with the world, a pure and upright man. He had begun an investigation, as he imagined, with the severe and equal integrity of a judge, desirous only of truth, even as if the question involved no more than the air-drawn lines and figures of a geometrical problem, instead of human passions, and wrongs inflicted on himself. But, as he proceeded, a terrible fascination, a kind of fierce, though still calm, necessity, seized the old man within its gripe, and never set him free again until he had done all its bidding. He now dug into the poor clergyman's heart, like a miner searching for gold; or, rather, like a sexton delving into a grave, possibly in quest of a jewel that had been buried on the dead man's bosom, but likely to find nothing save mortality and corruption. Alas, for his own soul, if these were what he sought!

Sometimes a light glimmered out of the physician's eyes, burning blue and ominous, like the reflection of a furnace, or, let us say, like one of those gleams of ghastly fire that darted from **Bunyan's awful doorway** in the hillside, and quivered on the pilgrim's face. The soil where this dark miner was working had perchance shown indications that encouraged him.

"This man," said he, at one such moment, to himself, "pure as they deem him—all spiritual as he seems—hath inherited a strong animal nature from his father or his mother. Let us dig a little further in the direction of this vein!"

Then after long search into the minister's dim interior, and turning over many precious materials, in the shape of high aspirations for the welfare of his race, warm love of souls, pure sentiments, natural piety, strengthened by thought and study, and illuminated by revelation—all of which invaluable gold was perhaps no better than rubbish to the seeker—he would turn back, discouraged, and begin his quest towards another point. He groped along as stealthily, with as cautious a tread, and as wary an outlook, as a thief entering a chamber where a man lies only half asleep—or, it may be, broad awake—with purpose to steal the very treasure which this man guards as the apple of his eye. In spite of his premeditated carefulness, the floor would now and then creak; his garments

Bunyan's awful doorway: the door in John Bunyan's Christian allegory, *Pilgrim's Progress* (1678). The pilgrim is shown the entrance to hell, through which traitors and hypocrites supposedly passed.

would rustle; the shadow of his presence, in a forbidden proximity, would be thrown across his victim. In other words, Mr. Dimmesdale, whose sensibility of nerve often produced the effect of spiritual intuition, would become vaguely aware that something inimical to his peace had thrust itself into relation with him. But Old Roger Chillingworth, too, had perceptions that were almost intuitive; and when the minister threw his startled eyes towards him, there the physician sat; his kind, watchful, sympathising, but never intrusive friend.

Yet Mr. Dimmesdale would perhaps have seen this individual's character more perfectly, if a certain morbidness, to which sick hearts are liable, had not rendered him suspicious of all mankind. Trusting no man as his friend, he could not recognize his enemy when the latter actually appeared. He therefore still kept up a familiar intercourse with him, daily receiving he old physician in his study, or visiting the laboratory, and, for recreation's sake, watching the processes by which weeds were converted into drugs of potency.

One day, leaning his forehead on his hand, and his elbow on the sill of the open window, that looked towards the grave-yard, he talked with Roger Chillingworth, while the old man was examining a bundle of unsightly plants.

"Where," asked he, with a look askance at them—for it was the clergyman's peculiarity that he seldom, now-a-days, looked straight forth at any object, whether human or inanimate,—"where, my kind doctor, did you gather those herbs, with such a dark, flabby leaf?"

"Even in the graveyard here at hand," answered the physician, continuing his employment. "They are new to me. I found them growing on a grave, which bore no tombstone, no other memorial of the dead man, save these ugly weeds, that have taken upon themselves to keep him in remembrance. They grew out of his heart, and typify, it may be, some hideous secret that was buried with him, and which he had done better to confess during his lifetime."

"Perchance," said Mr. Dimmesdale, "he earnestly desired it, but could not."

"And wherefore?" rejoined the physician.

"Wherefore not; since all the powers of nature call so earnestly for the confession of sin, that these black weeds have sprung up out of a buried heart, to make manifest, an outspoken crime?"

"That, good sir, is but a phantasy of yours," replied the minister. "There can be, if I forbode aright, no power, short of the Divine mercy, to disclose, whether by uttered words, or by type or emblem, the secrets that may be buried in the human heart. The heart, making itself guilty of such secrets, must perforce hold them, until the day when all hidden things shall be revealed. Nor have I so read or interpreted Holy Writ, as to understand that the disclosure of human thoughts and deeds, then to be made, is intended as a part of the retribution. That, surely, were a shallow view of it. No; these revelations, unless I greatly err, are meant merely to promote the intellectual satisfaction of all intelligent beings, who will stand waiting, on that day, to see the dark problem of this life made plain. A knowledge of men's hearts will be needful to the completest solution of that problem. And, I conceive moreover, that the hearts holding such miserable secrets as you speak of, will yield them up, at that last day, not with reluctance, but with a joy unutterable."

"Then why not reveal it here?" asked Roger Chillingworth, glancing quietly aside at the minister. "Why should not the guilty ones sooner avail themselves of this unutterable solace?"

"They mostly do," said the clergyman, griping hard at his breast, as if afflicted with an importunate throb of pain. "Many, many a poor soul hath given its confidence to me, not only on the death-bed, but while strong in life, and fair in reputation. And ever, after such an outpouring, oh, what a relief have I witnessed in those sinful brethren! even as in one who at last draws free air, after a long stifling with his own polluted breath. How can it be otherwise? Why should a wretched man—guilty, we will say, of murder—prefer to keep the dead corpse buried in his own heart, rather than fling it forth at once, and let the universe take care of it!"

"Yet some men bury their secrets thus," observed the calm physician.

"True; there are such men," answered Mr. Dimmesdale. "But not to suggest more obvious reasons, it may be that they are kept silent by the very constitution of their nature. Or—can we not suppose it?—guilty as they may be, retaining, nevertheless, a zeal for God's glory and man's welfare, they shrink from displaying themselves black and filthy in the view of men; because, thenceforward, no good can be achieved by them; no evil of the past be redeemed by better service. So, to their own unutterable torment, they go about among their fellow-creatures, looking pure as new-fallen snow, while their hearts are all speckled and spotted with iniquity of which they cannot rid themselves."

"These men deceive themselves," said Roger Chillingworth, with somewhat more emphasis than usual, and making a slight gesture with his forefinger. "They fear to take up the shame that rightfully belongs to them. Their love for man, their zeal for God's service—these holy impulses may or may not coexist in their hearts with the evil inmates to which their guilt has unbarred the door, and which must needs propagate a hellish breed within them. But, if they seek to glorify God, let them not lift heavenward their unclean hands! If they would serve their fellowmen, let them do it by making manifest the power and reality of conscience, in constraining them to penitential self-abasement! Would thou have me to believe, O wise and pious friend, that a false show can be better—can be more for God's glory, or man's welfare—than God's own truth? Trust me, such men deceive themselves!"

"It may be so," said the young clergyman, indifferently, as waiving a discussion that he considered irrelevant or unseasonable. He had a ready faculty, indeed, of escaping from any topic that agitated his too sensitive and nervous temperament.—"But, now, I would ask of my well-skilled physician, whether, in good sooth, he deems me to have profited by his kindly care of this weak frame of mine?"

Before Roger Chillingworth could answer, they heard the clear, wild laughter of a young child's voice, proceeding from the adjacent burial-ground. Looking instinctively from the open window—for it was summer-time—the minister beheld Hester Prynne and little Pearl passing along the footpath that traversed the enclosure. Pearl looked as beautiful as the day, but was in one of those moods of perverse merriment which, whenever they occurred, seemed to remove her entirely out of the sphere of sympathy or human contact. She now skipped irreverently from one grave to another; until coming to the broad, flat, armorial tombstone of a departed worthy—perhaps of Isaac Johnson himself—she began to dance upon it. In reply to her mother's command and entreaty that she would behave more decorously, little Pearl paused to gather the prickly burrs from a tall burdock which grew beside the tomb. Taking a handful of these, she arranged them along the lines of the scarlet letter that decorated the maternal bosom, to which the burrs, as their nature was, tenaciously adhered. Hester did not pluck them off.

Roger Chillingworth had by this time approached the window and smiled grimly down.

"There is no law, nor reverence for authority, no regard for human ordinances or opinions, right or wrong, mixed up with that child's composition," remarked he, as much to himself as to his companion. "I saw her, the other day, bespatter the Governor himself with water at the cattle-trough in Spring Lane. What, in heaven's name, is she? Is the imp altogether evil? Hath she affections? Hath she any discoverable principle of being?"

"None, save the freedom of a broken law," answered Mr. Dimmesdale, in a quiet way, as if he had been discussing the point within himself. "Whether capable of good, I know not."

The child probably overheard their voices, for, looking up to the window with a bright, but naughty smile of mirth and intelligence, she threw one of the prickly burrs at the Reverend Mr. Dimmesdale. The sensitive clergyman shrank, with nervous dread, from the light missile. Detecting his emotion, Pearl clapped her little hands in the most extravagant ecstacy. Hester Prynne, likewise, had involuntarily looked up, and all these four persons, old and young, regarded one another in silence, till the child laughed aloud, and shouted—"Come away, mother! Come away, or yonder old Black Man will catch you! He hath got hold of the minister already. Come away, mother or he will catch you! But he cannot catch little Pearl!"

So she drew her mother away, skipping, dancing, and frisking fantastically among the hillocks of the dead people, like a creature that had nothing in common with a bygone and buried generation, nor owned herself akin to it. It was as if she had been made afresh out of new elements, and must perforce be permitted to live her own life, and be a law unto herself without her eccentricities being reckoned to her for a crime.

"There goes a woman," resumed Roger Chillingworth, after a pause, "who, be her demerits what they may, hath none of that mystery of hidden sinfulness which you deem so grievous to be borne. Is Hester Prynne the less miserable, think you, for that scarlet letter on her breast?"

"I do verily believe it," answered the clergyman. "Nevertheless, I cannot answer for her. There was a look of pain in her face which I would gladly have been spared the sight of. But still, methinks, it must needs be better for the sufferer to be free to show his pain, as this poor woman Hester is, than to cover it up in his heart."

There was another pause, and the physician began anew to examine and arrange the plants which he had gathered.

"You inquired of me, a little time agone," said he, at length, "my judgment as touching your health."

"I did," answered the clergyman, "and would gladly learn it. Speak frankly, I pray you, be it for life or death."

"Freely then, and plainly," said the physician, still busy with his plants, but keeping a wary eye on Mr. Dimmesdale, "the disorder is a strange one; not so much in itself nor as outwardly manifested,—in so far, at least as the symptoms have been laid open to my observation. Looking daily at you, my good sir, and watching the tokens of your aspect now for months gone by, I should deem you a man sore sick, it may be, yet not so sick but that an instructed and watchful physician might well hope to cure you. But I know not what to say, the disease is what I seem to know, yet know it not."

"You speak in riddles, learned sir," said the pale minister, glancing aside out of the window.

"Then, to speak more plainly," continued the physician, "and I crave pardon, sir, should it seem to require pardon, for this needful plainness of my speech. Let me ask as your friend, as one having charge, under Providence, of your life and physical well being, hath all the operations of this disorder been fairly laid open and recounted to me?"

"How can you question it?" asked the minister. "Surely it were child's play to call in a physician and then hide the sore!"

"You would tell me, then, that I know all?" said Roger Chillingworth, deliberately, and fixing an eye, bright with intense and concentrated intelligence, on the minister's face. "Be it so! But again! He to whom only the outward and physical evil is laid open, knoweth, oftentimes, but half the evil which he is called upon to cure. A bodily disease, which we look upon as whole and entire within itself, may, after all, be but a symptom of some ailment in the spiritual part. Your pardon once again, good sir, if my speech give the shadow of offence. You, sir, of all men whom I have known, are he whose body is the closest conjoined, and imbued, and identified, so to speak, with the spirit whereof it is the instrument."

"Then I need ask no further," said the clergyman, somewhat hastily rising from his chair. "You deal not, I take it, in medicine for the soul!"

"Thus, a sickness," continued Roger Chillingworth, going on, in an unaltered tone, without heeding the interruption, but standing up and confronting the emaciated and white-cheeked minister, with his low, dark, and misshapen figure,—"a sickness, a sore place, if we may so call it, in your spirit hath immediately its appropriate manifestation in your bodily frame. Would you, therefore, that your physician heal the bodily evil? How may this be unless you first lay open to him the wound or trouble in your soul?"

"No,—not to thee!—not to an earthly physician!" cried Mr. Dimmesdale, passionately, and turning his eyes, full and bright, and with a kind of fierceness, on old Roger Chillingworth. "Not to thee! But, if it be the soul's disease, then do I commit myself to the one Physician of the soul! He, if it stand with His good pleasure, can cure, or he can kill. Let Him do with me as, in His justice and wisdom, He shall see good. But who art thou, that meddlest in this matter?—that dares thrust himself between the sufferer and his God?"

With a frantic gesture, he rushed out of the room.

"It is as well to have made this step," said Roger Chillingworth to himself, looking after the minister, with a grave smile. "There is nothing lost. We shall be friends again anon. But see, now, how passion takes hold upon this man, and hurrieth him out of himself! As with one passion so with another. He hath done a wild thing ere now, this pious Master Dimmesdale, in the hot passion of his heart."

It proved not difficult to re-establish the intimacy of the two companions, on the same footing and in the same degree as heretofore. The young clergyman, after a few hours of privacy, was sensible that the disorder of his nerves had hurried him into an unseemly outbreak of temper, which there had been nothing in the physician's words to excuse or palliate. He marvelled, indeed, at the violence with which he had thrust back the kind old man, when merely proffering the advice which it was his duty to bestow, and which the minister himself had expressly sought. With these remorseful feelings, he lost no time in making the amplest apologies, and besought his friend still to continue the care which, if not successful in restoring him to health, had, in all probability, been the means of prolonging his feeble existence to that hour. Roger Chillingworth readily assented, and went on with his medical supervision of the minister; doing his best for him, in all good faith, but always quitting the patient's apartment, at the close of the professional interview, with a mysterious and puzzled smile upon his lips. This expression was invisible in Mr. Dimmesdale's presence, but grew strongly evident as the physician crossed the threshold.

"A rare case," he muttered. "I must needs look deeper into it. A strange sympathy betwixt soul and body! Were it only for the art's sake, I must search this matter to the bottom."

It came to pass, not long after the scene above recorded, that the Reverend Mr. Dimmesdale, noon-day, and entirely unawares, fell into a deep, deep slumber, sitting in his chair, with a large black-letter volume open before him on the table. It must have been a work of vast ability in the somniferous school of literature. The profound depth of the minister's repose was the more remarkable, inasmuch as he was one of those persons whose sleep ordinarily is as light as fitful, and as easily scared away, as a small bird hopping on a twig. To such an unwonted remoteness, however, had his spirit now withdrawn into itself that he stirred not in his chair when old Roger Chillingworth, without any extraordinary precaution, came into the room. The physician advanced directly in front of his patient, laid his hand upon his bosom, and thrust aside the vestment, that hitherto had always covered it even from the professional eye.

Then, indeed, Mr. Dimmesdale shuddered, and slightly stirred.

After a brief pause, the physician turned away.

But with what a wild look of wonder, joy, and honor! With what a ghastly rapture, as it were, too mighty to be expressed only by the eye and features, and therefore bursting forth through the whole ugliness of his figure, and making itself even riotously manifest by the extravagant gestures with which he threw up his arms towards the ceiling, and stamped his foot upon the floor! Had a man seen old Roger Chillingworth, at that moment of his ecstasy, he would have had no need to ask how Satan comports himself when a precious human soul is lost to heaven, and won into his kingdom.

But what distinguished the physician's ecstasy from Satan's was the trait of wonder in it!

COMMENTARY

This chapter builds on the last, continuing to develop the complicated relationship that has flourished between Chillingworth and Dimmesdale. Here we clearly see the devilish character of Chillingworth's efforts and the minister's mighty battle to save his own soul.

The narrator begins by filling us in on some background information about Chillingworth. In the past, he has been a pure, upstanding, and kind man, although not particularly affectionate. He began his investigation into Dimmesdale's heart with the pure intentions of a judge, believing that he could objectively discover the truth about Hester's lover. But he should have recognized the depth of passion and guilt involved in his investigation. Somewhere along the way, he lost the purity of his intentions, and his investigations into the clergyman's soul have gained the ferocity of a miner searching for gold or, more aptly, of a graverobber digging up a grave in search

of a jewel buried with the dead man. This image, which shows the deeply corrupt and underhanded nature of Chillingworth's investigation into Dimmesdale's soul, is reaffirmed later in the chapter when Chillingworth is compared with a thief who sneaks into a room where a man lies half-asleep. By comparing Chillingworth with a thief and a graverobber, the narrator emphasizes that the doctor's methods have lost all sense of objectivity or ethics. Of course, Chillingworth's own soul is in grave danger for undertaking this violation of another human being. The light emanating from the doctor's eyes indicates his evil intentions: It glows blue and ominous, like the fire burning in the doorway to hell.

Chillingworth vows to continue searching in this "vein," a term that connotes miners digging through the earth but also a term that refers to the doctor digging into the minister's heart. Much of the language used here

Although Dimmesdale rec-
ognizes the value of purg-
ing one's guilt by revealing
secrets, he cannot confess his
own silent guilt because such
a revelation will remove from
him the power of doing good
for others. Chillingworth dis-
agrees with this argument: Can
a false show be better than
truth? For example, is Hester
worse off for the scarlet letter on her breast? Through
their conversations, Chillingworth intentionally and contin-
uously pricks at Dimmesdale's
soul, intensifying the minister's
already extreme guilt.

Chillingworth's philosophy
is that a disease of the body
cannot be completely understood without also under-
standing the patient's spiritual

Dimmesdale and Chillingworth in an illustration by F.O.C. Darley.
Photo courtesy of The Darley Society, Inc.

connotes mining and also reminds us of Chillingworth's earlier life as an alchemist, attempting to change rock into gold: He searches through Dimmesdale's "dim interior" to find the "precious materials" hidden inside, and the "gold" he discovers there—such as Dimmesdale's good intentions toward the human race—is pure rubbish to Chillingworth. His purpose is to steal Dimmesdale's most valuable treasure. (Remember that Pearl was earlier referred to as Hester's treasure; the irony is that this pre-cious child is Hester's treasure, but Dimmesdale's secret.)

We see many examples here of Chillingworth's meth-ods. Primarily, he uses the tools of innuendo and exam-ple to catch the minister in his verbal trap. For example, when Dimmesdale asks where Chillingworth found a par-ticular dark, thick leaf, the doctor says it came from the graveyard, where it grew out of the heart of a dead man and may exemplify some ominous secret that was buried with him. Suggesting that all of nature so earnestly desires the confession of sin that it created these black weeds to make manifest an unspoken crime, Chilling-worth taunts the poor minister further. As earlier in the book, flowers and weeds are used to signify good and evil. Dimmesdale rejects this philosophy, arguing that only God can reveal human guilt, whether through unspoken words or an emblem.

and psychological sides, as mind and body cannot be separated. This is particularly true in the case of Dimmes-dale, who has almost killed his body because he feels so spiritually diseased. Dimmesdale refuses to reveal his spiritual wound, so Chillingworth utilizes subtle methods to trick him into revealing the secret. While their conver-sation does not specifically evoke a verbal confession, Chillingworth reads the messages displayed in Dimmes-dale's actions: His show of passion suggests that the minister has probably done other wild things in the "hot passion of his heart." The doctor believes that Dimmes-dale has a strong animal or physical nature, which he stringently represses through his spiritual practice.

Chillingworth's investigations show his astute under-standing of human psychology. In particular, his probings reveal a certain consistency in human behavior, so that our personalities are revealed through each of our seemingly unrelated actions. The connections between Dimmesdale's soul and body fascinate Chillingsworth, claiming that he would want to analyze this man if only for the "art's sake." (Is he suggesting the dark art of necromancy or the medical art of investigating human psychology?) Throughout the novel, the characters' actions have this symbolic intent; nothing is without sig-nificance, as all physical bodily acts have a correspon-ding spiritual meaning.

As Dimmesdale and Chillingworth pursue their conversation, Hester and Pearl pass by on the street below. Pearl is in one of her crazy, capricious moods that makes her seem removed from all human community. She skips, even dances, irreverently through the graveyard. Pearl's dancing suggests that she has nothing in common with previous generations of humans but has been made afresh, a law unto herself. Chillingworth notes that Pearl seems to exist beyond the bounds of human law or authority, outside the confines of good and evil. Dimmesdale agrees, suggesting that the only principle of Pearl's nature is "the freedom of a broken law." As Hester argued earlier, both men seem to believe that Pearl's illegitimate status has somehow infected her personality—because she was born outside of marriage, her entire life will somehow exist beyond the boundaries of Puritan authority.

Pearl's ability to intuit the hidden relationships between people is also apparent in this chapter. Instinctively, Pearl recognizes the perverse relationship between Chillingworth and Dimmesdale, claiming that Chillingworth is indeed the devil who has managed to capture Dimmesdale's soul.

At the end of this chapter, fantasy blends with reality—a typical occurrence in the romance genre—as Chillingworth looks at Dimmesdale's chest after the minister has fallen into an unnaturally deep sleep. He sees an unspecified something that causes a look of wild "joy, and horror" and leads to "extravagant gestures," "riotous" actions, and a "ghastly rapture." Perhaps he feels ecstasy similar to that which Satan feels when he wins a new soul, but the narrator notes that there is also an element of wonder in Chillingworth's joy. This event foreshadows later events in the novel and suggests that Chillingworth has received the proof he was looking for. Has he also become the devil himself?

Chapter XI   **Mistaking Dimmesdale's melancholy and suffering for holiness, his parishioners adulate him. For them, his humility and vague references to his own sins are signs of saintliness. Dimmesdale realizes that he could end his suffering by publicly announcing that he is Pearl's father, but he is unable to do this. Instead, he resorts to self-punishment, whipping himself bloody, fasting, and maintaining all-night vigils.**

CHAPTER XI: THE INTERIOR OF A HEART

AFTER the incident last described, the intercourse between the clergyman and the physician, though externally the same, was really of another character than it had previously been. The intellect of Roger Chillingworth had now a sufficiently plain path before it. It was not, indeed, precisely that which he had laid out for himself to tread. Calm, gentle, passionless, as he appeared, there was yet, we fear, a quiet depth of malice, hitherto latent, but active now, in this unfortunate old man, which led him to imagine a more intimate revenge than any mortal had ever wreaked upon an enemy. To make himself the one trusted friend, to whom should be confided all the fear, the remorse, the agony, the ineffectual repentance, the backward rush of sinful thoughts, expelled in vain! All that guilty sorrow, hidden from the world, whose great heart would have pitied and forgiven, to be revealed to him, the Pitiless—to him, the Unforgiving! All that dark treasure to be lavished on the very man, to whom nothing else could so adequately pay the debt of vengeance!

The clergyman's shy and sensitive reserve had balked this scheme. Roger Chillingworth, however, was inclined to be hardly, if at all, less satisfied with the aspect of affairs, which Providence—using the avenger and his victim for its own purposes, and, perchance, pardoning, where it seemed most to punish—had substituted for his black devices. A revelation, he could almost say, had been granted to him. It mattered little for his object, whether celestial or from what other region. By its aid, in all the subsequent relations betwixt him and Mr. Dimmesdale, not merely the external presence, but the very inmost soul of the latter, seemed to be brought out before his eyes, so that he could see and comprehend its every movement. He became, thenceforth, not a spectator only, but a chief actor in the poor minister's interior world. He could play upon him as he chose. Would he arouse him with a throb of agony? The victim was for ever on the rack; it needed only to know the spring that controlled the engine: and the physician knew it well. Would he startle him with sudden fear? As at the waving of a magician's wand, uprose a grisly phantom,—uprose a thousand phantoms,—in many shapes, of death, or more awful shame, all flocking round-about the clergyman, and pointing with their fingers at his breast!

All this was accomplished with a subtlety so perfect, that the minister, though he had constantly a dim perception of some evil influence watching over him, could never gain a knowledge of its actual nature. True, he looked doubtfully, fearfully—even, at times, with horror and the bitterness of hatred—at the deformed figure of the old physician. His gestures, his gait, his grizzled beard, his slightest and most indifferent acts, the very fashion of his garments, were odious in the clergyman's sight; a token implicitly to be relied on of a deeper antipathy in the breast of the latter than he was willing to acknowledge to himself. For, as it was impossible to assign a reason for such distrust and abhorrence, so Mr. Dimmesdale, conscious that the poison of one morbid spot was infecting his heart's entire substance, attributed all his presentiments to no other cause. He took himself to task for his bad sympathies in reference to Roger Chillingworth, disregarded the lesson that he should have drawn from them, and did his best to root them out. Unable to accomplish this, he nevertheless, as a matter of principle, continued his habits of social familiarity with the old man, and thus gave him constant opportunities for perfecting the purpose to which—poor forlorn creature that he was, and more wretched than his victim—the avenger had devoted himself.

While thus suffering under bodily disease, and gnawed and tortured by some black trouble of the soul, and given over to the machinations of his deadliest enemy, the Reverend Mr. Dimmesdale had achieved a brilliant popularity in his sacred office. He won it indeed, in great part, by his sorrows. His intellectual gifts, his moral perceptions, his power of experiencing and communicating emotion, were kept in a state of preternatural activity by the prick and anguish of his daily life. His fame, though still on its upward slope, already overshadowed the soberer reputations of his fellow-clergymen, eminent as several of them were. There are scholars among them, who had spent more years in acquiring abstruse lore, connected with the divine profession, than Mr. Dimmesdale had lived; and who might well, therefore, be more profoundly versed in such solid and valuable attainments than their youthful brother. There were men, too, of a sturdier texture of mind than his, and endowed with a far greater share of shrewd, hard iron, or granite understanding; which, duly mingled with a fair proportion of doctrinal ingredient, constitutes a highly respectable, efficacious, and unamiable variety of the clerical species. There were others again, true saintly fathers, whose faculties had been elaborated by weary toil among their books, and by patient thought, and etherealised, moreover, by spiritual communications with the better world, into which their purity of life had almost introduced these holy personages, with their garments of mortality still clinging to them. All that they lacked was, the gift that descended upon the chosen disciples at **Pentecost**, in tongues of flame; symbolising, it would seem, not the power of speech in foreign and unknown languages, but that of addressing the whole human brotherhood in the heart's native language. These fathers, otherwise so apostolic, lacked Heaven's last and rarest attestation of their office, the Tongue of Flame. They would have vainly sought—had they ever dreamed of seeking—to express the highest truths through the humblest medium of familiar words and images. Their voices came down, afar and indistinctly, from the upper heights where they habitually dwelt.

Pentecost: On Pentecost, the seventh Sunday of Easter, the Holy Spirit descended into the 12 apostles and gave them the power to speak in tongues.

Not improbably, it was to this latter class of men that Mr. Dimmesdale, by many of his traits of character, naturally belonged. To the high mountain peaks of faith and sanctity he would have climbed, had not the tendency been thwarted by the burden, whatever it might be, of crime or anguish, beneath which it was his doom to totter. It kept him down on a level with the lowest; him, the man of ethereal attributes, whose voice the angels might else have listened to and answered! But this very burden it was that gave him sympathies so intimate with the sinful brotherhood of mankind; so that his heart vibrated in unison with theirs, and received their pain into itself and sent its own throb of pain through a thousand other hearts, in gushes of sad, persuasive eloquence. Oftenest persuasive, but sometimes terrible! The people knew not the power that moved them thus. They deemed the young clergyman a miracle of holiness. They fancied him the mouth-piece of Heaven's messages of wisdom, and rebuke, and love. In their eyes, the very ground on which he trod was sanctified. The virgins of his church grew pale around him, victims of a passion so imbued with religious sentiment, that they imagined it to be all religion, and brought it openly, in their white bosoms, as their most acceptable sacrifice before the altar. The aged members of his flock, beholding Mr. Dimmesdale's frame so feeble, while they were themselves so rugged in their infirmity, believed that he would go heavenward before them, and enjoined it upon their children that their old bones should be buried close to their young pastor's holy grave. And all this time, perchance, when poor Mr. Dimmesdale was thinking of his grave, he questioned with himself whether the grass would ever grow on it, because an accursed thing must there be buried!

It is inconceivable, the agony with which this public veneration tortured him. It was his genuine impulse to adore the truth, and to reckon all things shadow-like, and utterly devoid of weight or value, that had not its divine essence as the life within their life. Then what was he?—a substance?—or the dimmest of all shadows? He longed to speak out from his own pulpit at the full height of his voice, and tell the people what he was. "I, whom you behold in these black garments of the priesthood—I, who ascend the sacred desk, and turn my pale face heavenward, taking upon myself to hold communion in your behalf with the Most High Omniscience—I, in whose daily life you discern the **sanctity of Enoch**—I, whose footsteps, as you suppose, leave a gleam along my earthly track, whereby the Pilgrims that shall come after me may be guided to the regions of the blest—I, who have laid the hand of baptism upon your children—I, who have breathed the parting prayer over your dying friends, to whom the Amen sounded faintly from a world which they had quitted—I, your pastor, whom you so reverence and trust, am utterly a pollution and a lie!"

More than once, Mr. Dimmesdale had gone into the pulpit, with a purpose never to come down its steps until he should have spoken words like the above. More than once he had cleared his throat, and drawn in the long, deep, and tremulous breath, which, when sent forth again, would come burdened with the black secret of his soul. More than once—nay,

sanctity of Enoch: Genesis 5:24. Because he was so virtuous, Enoch was taken to heaven by God without having died.

more than a hundred times—he had actually spoken! Spoken! But how? He had told his hearers that he was altogether vile, a viler companion of the vilest, the worst of sinners, an abomination, a thing of unimaginable iniquity, and that the only wonder was that they did not see his wretched body shrivelled up before their eyes by the burning wrath of the Almighty! Could there be plainer speech than this? Would not the people start up in their seats, by a simultaneous impulse, and tear him down out of the pulpit which he defiled? Not so, indeed! They heard it all, and did but reverence him the more. They little guessed what deadly purport lurked in those self-condemning words. "The godly youth!" said they among themselves. "The saint on earth! Alas! if he discern such sinfulness in his own white soul, what horrid spectacle would he behold in thine or mine!" The minister well knew—subtle, but remorseful hypocrite that he was!—the light in which his vague confession would be viewed. He had striven to put a cheat upon himself by making the avowal of a guilty conscience, but had gained only one other sin, and a self-acknowledged shame, without the momentary relief of being self-deceived. He had spoken the very truth, and transformed it into the veriest falsehood. And yet, by the constitution of his nature, he loved the truth, and loathed the lie, as few men ever did. Therefore, above all things else, he loathed his miserable self!

His inward trouble drove him to practices more in accordance with the old, corrupted faith of Rome than with the better light of the church in which he had been born and bred. In Mr. Dimmesdale's secret closet, under lock and key, there was a bloody scourge. Oftentimes, this Protestant and Puritan divine had plied it on his own shoulders, laughing bitterly at himself the while, and smiting so much the more pitilessly because of that bitter laugh. It was his custom, too, as it has been that of many other pious Puritans, to fast—not however, like them, in order to purify the body, and render it the fitter medium of celestial illumination—but rigorously, and until his knees trembled beneath him, as an act of penance. He kept vigils, likewise, night after night, sometimes in utter darkness, sometimes with a glimmering lamp, and sometimes, viewing his own face in a looking-glass, by the most powerful light which he could throw upon it. He thus typified the constant introspection wherewith he tortured, but could not purify himself. In these lengthened vigils, his brain often reeled, and visions seemed to flit before him; perhaps seen doubtfully, and by a faint light of their own, in the remote dimness of the chamber, or more vividly and close beside him, within the looking-glass. Now it was a herd of diabolic shapes, that grinned and mocked at the pale minister, and beckoned him away with them; now a group of shining angels, who flew upward heavily, as sorrow-laden, but grew more ethereal as they rose. Now came the dead friends of his youth, and his white-bearded father, with a saint-like frown, and his mother turning her face away as she passed by Ghost of a mother—thinnest fantasy of a mother—methinks she might yet have thrown a pitying glance towards her son! And now, through the chamber which these spectral thoughts had made so ghastly, glided Hester Prynne leading along little Pearl, in her scarlet garb, and pointing her forefinger, first at the scarlet letter on her bosom, and then at the clergyman's own breast.

None of these visions ever quite deluded him. At any moment, by an effort of his will, he could discern substances through their misty lack of substance, and convince himself that they were not solid in their nature, like yonder table of carved oak, or that big, square, leather-bound and brazen-clasped volume of divinity. But, for all that, they were, in one sense, the truest and most substantial things which the poor minister now dealt with. It is the unspeakable misery of a life so false as his, that it steals the pith and substance out of whatever realities there are around us, and which were meant by Heaven to be the spirit's joy and nutriment. To the untrue man, the whole universe is false—it is impalpable—it shrinks to nothing within his grasp. And he himself in so far as he shows himself in a false light, becomes a shadow, or, indeed, ceases to exist. The only truth that continued to give Mr. Dimmesdale a real existence on this earth was the anguish in his inmost soul, and the undissembled expression of it in his aspect. Had he once found power to smile, and wear a face of gaiety, there would have been no such man!

On one of those ugly nights, which we have faintly hinted at, but forborne to picture forth, the minister started from his chair. A new thought had struck him. There might be a moment's peace in it. Attiring himself with as much care as if it had been for public worship, and precisely in the same manner, he stole softly down the staircase, undid the door, and issued forth.

COMMENTARY

This chapter offers further insights into the characters of Chillingworth and Dimmesdale. First, we learn more about Chillingworth's secret and pernicious methods of revenge. We also discover that because Dimmesdale is living a lie, the light of his soul is becoming "dim"; he is losing his identity.

The incidents of the previous chapter have proven that Chillingworth's actions are driven by malice. He is pursuing an "intimate revenge" that exposes him to all of Dimmesdale's deepest thoughts. Rather than seek a public exposure of the minister, which would subject him to immediate censure and, therefore, end his guilt and suffering, Chillingworth pursues a prolonged and private revenge. The narrator calls Chillingworth "Pitiless" and "Unforgiving," because his goal is to deprive Dimmesdale of his "dark treasure," the secrets of his soul that should be revealed only to God or to those who would pity and forgive him.

Whatever Chillingworth saw on Dimmesdale's chest at the end of Chapter X has given the doctor access to Dimmesdale's soul and laid bare his private motivations. From now on, Chillingworth won't be merely a spectator but also an actor in Dimmesdale's inner life. With proof that Dimmesdale is Pearl's father, which the vision at the end of Chapter X seems to have provided, Chillingworth can now pursue his revenge confidently. The language used to describe the doctor's treatment of his victim evokes the cruelty of the Spanish Inquisition: Dimmesdale is on the "rack"—an instrument that inflicts slow, cruel pain on its victim—and Chillingworth controls this machinery of horror. Like the members of the Inquisition, who kept their faces hooded while they conducted their investigations, Chillingworth pursues his revenge without Dimmesdale's conscious knowledge. Other imagery associated with Chillingworth uses the language of magic. Like a magician, he waves his wand to invoke a thousand phantoms that will play on the minister's guilt. Ironically, because Chillingworth's machinations are so underhanded, they do not provide him with comfort but, instead, leave him "more wretched than his victim."

Dimmesdale's suffering actually increases the number of followers within his congregation. His constant inner torture hones his intelligence and also offers him the compassion and psychological understanding he needs in order to relate to the suffering of his parishioners. The narrator explains that some spiritual leaders become almost pure spirit, "etherealized" by their communications with the spiritual world. Dimmesdale is not one of them; he is very much connected to this earth because of his sin and his guilt. Ironically, though, Dimmesdale has a rare gift that these "etherealized" leaders lack, which allows him to connect with all people. The narrator explains that the "tongue of flame" is a gift that even spiritual leaders who live in absolute purity often do not have. The "tongue of flame" is defined as symbolizing the ability to speak to "the whole human brotherhood in the heart's native language"—to speak with the sinner as well as the pure of heart in a language that addresses humanity's corporeal weaknesses. The spiritual men that Dimmesdale idolizes often lack the ability to connect with the average person; they speak, instead, using the abstract language of their profession. But Dimmesdale, because of his sin, is able to speak the language of average, sinful mankind. His ability to understand and sympathize with his parishioners' pain makes him the more effective minister, despite Dimmesdale's limited view of religion that does not allow him to recognize the value of his suffering.

Dimmesdale is tortured by the schism between his public and private persona, which has almost erased his identity. He is now only "the dimmest of shadows"—because he is living a lie, Dimmesdale feels that he has no true identity and is, therefore, "dim." His weak and vague attempts to confess his guilt just add to the lie, because his listeners interpret these attempts as further signs of his humility and sainthood. Ironically, his need to atone for his sins leads Dimmesdale to secretly scourge himself, and this practice further dims the light of his character. His excessive fasting and nightly vigils result in visions: Demons, angels, friends, parents, and Hester all appear in these reveries. Because of the minister's failure to confess his sin, his world has become insubstantial, inhabited by shadows and visions. By appearing in public only in a false light, Dimmesdale has become a shadow and lost his identity.

Chapter XII

One night, Dimmesdale's guilt becomes overwhelming, so he walks out to the scaffold. As he stands there, guilty because he hasn't been publicly shamed or punished, he sees Hester and Pearl returning home from Governor Winthrop's deathbed. They join him, and as the three stand hand-in-hand on the scaffold, a meteor illuminates the sky. In the light of the meteor, Pearl points out Roger Chillingworth who is also returning from Winthrop's deathbed. Those townspeople who see the meteor believe it flashed an "A" on the sky, which they interpret as meaning "Angel."

CHAPTER XII: THE MINISTER'S VIGIL

WALKING in the shadow of a dream, as it were, and perhaps actually under the influence of a species of somnambulism, Mr. Dimmesdale reached the spot where, now so long since, Hester Prynne had lived through her first hours of public ignominy. The same platform or scaffold, black and weather-stained with the storm or sunshine of seven long years, and foot-worn, too, with the tread of many culprits who had since ascended it, remained standing beneath the balcony of the meeting-house. The minister went up the steps.

It was an obscure night in early May. An unwearied pall of cloud muffled the whole expanse of sky from zenith to horizon. If the same multitude which had stood as eye-witnesses while Hester Prynne sustained her punishment could now have been summoned forth, they would have discerned no face above the platform nor hardly the outline of a human shape, in the dark grey of the midnight. But the town was all asleep. There was no peril of discovery. The minister might stand there, if it so pleased him, until morning should redden in the east, without other risk than that the dank and chill night air would creep into his frame, and stiffen his joints with rheumatism, and clog his throat with catarrh and cough; thereby defrauding the expectant audience of to-morrow's prayer and sermon. No eye could see him, save that ever-wakeful one which had seen him in his closet, wielding the bloody scourge. Why, then, had he come hither? Was it but the mockery of penitence? A mockery, indeed, but in which his soul trifled with itself! A mockery at which angels blushed and wept, while fiends rejoiced with jeering laughter! He had been driven hither by the impulse of that Remorse which dogged him everywhere, and whose own sister and closely linked companion was that Cowardice which invariably drew him back, with her tremulous gripe, just when the other impulse had hurried him to the verge of a disclosure. Poor, miserable man! what right had infirmity like his to burden itself with crime? Crime is for the iron-nerved, who have their choice either to endure it, or, if it press too hard, to exert their fierce and savage strength for a good purpose, and fling it off at once! This feeble and most sensitive of spirits could do neither, yet continually did one thing or another, which intertwined, in the same inextricable knot, the agony of heaven-defying guilt and vain repentance.

And thus, while standing on the scaffold, in this vain show of expiation, Mr. Dimmesdale was overcome with a great horror of mind, as if the universe were gazing at a scarlet token on his naked breast, right over his heart. On that spot, in very truth, there was, and there had long been, the gnawing and poisonous tooth of bodily pain. Without any effort of his will, or power to restrain himself, he shrieked aloud: an outcry that went pealing through the night, and was beaten back from one house to another, and reverberated from the hills in the background; as if a company of devils, detecting so much misery and terror in it, had made a plaything of the sound, and were bandying it to and fro.

"It is done!" muttered the minister, covering his face with his hands. "The whole town will awake and hurry forth, and find me here!"

But it was not so. The shriek had perhaps sounded with a far greater power, to his own startled ears, than it actually possessed. The town did not awake; or, if it did, the drowsy slumberers mistook the cry either for something frightful in a dream, or for the noise of witches, whose voices, at that period, were often heard to pass over the settlements or lonely cottages, as they rode with Satan through the air. The clergyman, therefore, hearing no symptoms of disturbance, uncovered his eyes and looked about him. At one of the chamber-windows of Governor Bellingham's mansion, which stood at some distance, on the line of another street, he beheld the appearance of the old magistrate himself with a lamp in his hand, a white night-cap on his head, and a long white gown enveloping his figure. He looked like a ghost evoked unseasonably from the grave. The cry had evidently startled him. At another window of the same house, moreover, appeared old Mistress Hibbins, the Governor's sister, also with a lamp, which even thus far off revealed the expression of her sour and discontented face. She thrust forth her head from the lattice, and looked anxiously upward. Beyond the shadow of a doubt, this venerable witch-lady had heard Mr. Dimmesdale's outcry, and interpreted it, with its multitudinous echoes and reverberations, as the clamour of the fiends and night-hags, with whom she was well known to make excursions in the forest.

Detecting the gleam of Governor Bellingham's lamp, the old lady quickly extinguished her own, and vanished. Possibly, she went up among the clouds. The minister saw nothing further of her motions. The magistrate, after a wary observation of the darkness—into which, nevertheless, he could see but little further than he might into a mill-stone—retired from the window.

The minister grew comparatively calm. His eyes, however, were soon greeted by a little glimmering light, which, at first a long way off, was approaching up the street. It threw a gleam of recognition, on here a post, and there a garden fence, and here a latticed window-pane, and there a pump, with its full trough of water, and here again an arched door of oak, with an iron knocker, and a rough log for the door-step. The Reverend Mr. Dimmesdale noted all these minute particulars, even while firmly convinced that the doom of his existence was stealing onward, in the footsteps which he now heard; and that the gleam of the lantern would fall upon him in a few moments more, and reveal his long-hidden secret. As the light drew nearer, be beheld, within its illuminated circle, his brother clergyman—or, to speak more accurately, his professional father, as well as highly valued friend—the Reverend Mr. Wilson, who, as Mr. Dimmesdale now conjectured, had been praying at the bedside of some dying man. And so he had. The good old minister came freshly from the death-chamber of **Governor Winthrop**, who had passed from earth to heaven within that very hour. And now surrounded, like the saint-like personage of olden times, with a radiant halo, that glorified him amid this gloomy night of sin—as if the departed Governor had left him an inheritance of his glory, or as if he had caught upon himself the distant shine of the celestial city, while looking thitherward to see the triumphant pilgrim pass within its gates—now, in short, good Father Wilson was moving homeward, aiding his footsteps with a lighted lantern! The glimmer of this luminary suggested the above conceits to Mr. Dimmesdale, who smiled—nay, almost laughed at them—and then wondered if he was going mad.

As the Reverend Mr. Wilson passed beside the scaffold, closely muffling his Geneva cloak about him with one arm, and holding the lantern before his breast with the other, the minister could hardly restrain himself from speaking.

"A good evening to you, venerable Father Wilson. Come up hither, I pray you, and pass a pleasant hour with me!"

Good Heavens! Had Mr. Dimmesdale actually spoken? For one instant he believed that these words had passed his lips. But they were uttered only within his imagination. The venerable Father Wilson continued to step slowly onward, looking carefully at the muddy pathway before his feet, and never once turning his head towards the guilty platform. When the light of the glimmering lantern had faded quite away, the minister discovered, by the faintness which came over him, that the last few moments had been a crisis of terrible anxiety, although his mind had made an involuntary effort to relieve itself by a kind of lurid playfulness.

Shortly afterwards, the like grisly sense of the humorous again stole in among the solemn phantoms of his thought. He felt his limbs growing stiff with the unaccustomed chilliness of the night, and doubted whether he should be able to descend the steps of the scaffold. Morning would break and find him there. The neighbourhood would begin to rouse itself. The earliest riser, coming forth in the dim twilight, would perceive a vaguely-defined figure aloft on the place of shame; and half-crazed betwixt alarm and curiosity, would go knocking from door to door, summoning all the people to behold the ghost—as he needs must think it—of some defunct transgressor. A dusky tumult would flap its wings from one house to another. Then—the morning light still waxing stronger—old patriarchs would rise up in great haste, each in his flannel gown, and matronly dames, without pausing to put off their night-gear. The whole tribe of decorous personages, who had never heretofore been seen with a

Governor Winthrop: John Winthrop (1588–1649) was the first governor of the Massachusetts Bay Colony and was elected before the colonists left England.

single hair of their heads awry, would start into public view with the disorder of a nightmare in their aspects. Old Governor Bellingham would come grimly forth, with his King James' ruff fastened askew, and Mistress Hibbins, with some twigs of the forest clinging to her skirts, and looking sourer than ever, as having hardly got a wink of sleep after her night ride; and good Father Wilson too, after spending half the night at a death-bed, and liking ill to be disturbed, thus early, out of his dreams about the glorified saints. Hither, likewise, would come the elders and deacons of Mr. Dimmesdale's church, and the young virgins who so idolized their minister, and had made a shrine for him in their white bosoms, which now, by-the-bye, in their hurry and confusion, they would scantly have given themselves time to cover with their kerchiefs. All people, in a word, would come stumbling over their thresholds, and turning up their amazed and horror-stricken visages around the scaffold. Whom would they discern there, with the red eastern light upon his brow? Whom, but the Reverend Arthur Dimmesdale, half-frozen to death, overwhelmed with shame, and standing where Hester Prynne had stood!

Carried away by the grotesque horror of this picture, the minister, unawares, and to his own infinite alarm, burst into a great peal of laughter. It was immediately responded to by a light, airy, childish laugh, in which, with a thrill of the heart—but he knew not whether of exquisite pain, or pleasure as acute—he recognised the tones of little Pearl.

"Pearl! Little Pearl!" cried he, after a moment's pause; then, suppressing his voice—"Hester! Hester Prynne! Are you there?"

"Yes; it is Hester Prynne!" she replied, in a tone of surprise; and the minister heard her footsteps approaching from the side-walk, along which she had been passing. "It is I, and my little Pearl."

"Whence come you, Hester?" asked the minister. "What sent you hither?"

"I have been watching at a death-bed," answered Hester Prynne,—"at Governor Winthrop's death-bed, and have taken his measure for a robe, and am now going homeward to my dwelling."

"Come up hither, Hester, thou and Little Pearl," said the Reverend Mr. Dimmesdale. "Ye have both been here before, but I was not with you. Come up hither once again, and we will stand all three together."

She silently ascended the steps, and stood on the platform, holding little Pearl by the hand. The minister felt for the child's other hand, and took it. The moment that he did so, there came what seemed a tumultuous rush of new life, other life than his own, pouring like a torrent into his heart, and hurrying through all his veins, as if the mother and the child were communicating their vital warmth to his half-torpid system. The three formed an electric chain.

"Minister!" whispered little Pearl.

"What wouldst thou say, child?" asked Mr. Dimmesdale.

"Wilt thou stand here with mother and me, to-morrow noontide?" inquired Pearl.

"Nay; not so, my little Pearl," answered the minister; for, with the new energy of the moment, all the dread of public exposure, that had so long been the anguish of his life, had returned upon him; and he was already trembling at the conjunction in which—with a strange joy, nevertheless—he now found himself—"not so, my child. I shall, indeed, stand with thy mother and thee one other day, but not to-morrow."

Pearl laughed, and attempted to pull away her hand. But the minister held it fast.

"A moment longer, my child!" said he.

"But wilt thou promise," asked Pearl, "to take my hand, and mother's hand, to-morrow noontide?"

"Not then, Pearl," said the minister; "but another time."

"And what other time?" persisted the child.

"At the great judgment day," whispered the minister; and, strangely enough, the sense that he was a professional teacher of the truth impelled him to answer the child so. "Then, and there, before the judgment-seat, thy mother, and thou, and I must stand together. But the daylight of this world shall not see our meeting!"

Pearl laughed again.

But before Mr. Dimmesdale had done speaking, a light gleamed far and wide over all the muffled sky. It was doubtless caused by one of those meteors, which the night-watcher may so often observe burning out to waste, in the vacant regions of the atmosphere. So powerful was its radiance, that it thoroughly illuminated the dense medium of cloud betwixt the sky and earth. The great vault brightened, like the dome of an immense lamp. It showed the familiar scene of the street with the distinctness of mid-day, but also with the awfulness that is always imparted to familiar objects by an unaccustomed light. The wooden houses, with their jutting storeys and quaint gable-peaks; the doorsteps and thresholds with the early grass springing up about them; the garden-plots, black with freshly-turned earth; the wheel-track, little worn, and even in the market-place margined with green on either side—all were visible, but with a singularity of aspect that seemed to give another moral interpretation to the things of this world than they had ever borne before. And there stood the minister, with his hand over his heart; and Hester Prynne, with the embroidered letter glimmering on her bosom; and little Pearl, herself a symbol, and the connecting link between those two. They stood in the noon of that strange and solemn splendour, as if it were the light that is to reveal all secrets, and the daybreak that shall unite all who belong to one another.

There was witchcraft in little Pearl's eyes; and her face, as she glanced upward at the minister, wore that naughty smile which made its expression frequently so elvish. She withdrew her hand from Mr. Dimmesdale's, and pointed across the street. But he clasped both his hands over his breast, and cast his eyes towards the zenith.

Nothing was more common, in those days, than to interpret all meteoric appearances, and other natural phenomena that occurred with less regularity than the rise and set of sun and moon, as so many revelations from a supernatural source. Thus, a blazing spear, a sword of flame, a bow, or a sheaf of arrows seen in the midnight sky, prefigured Indian warfare. Pestilence was known to have been foreboded by a shower of crimson light. We doubt whether any marked event, for good or evil, ever befell New England, from its settlement down to revolutionary times, of which the inhabitants had not been previously warned by some spectacle of its nature. Not seldom, it had been seen by multitudes. Oftener, however, its credibility rested on the faith of some lonely eye-witness, who beheld the wonder through the coloured, magnifying, and distorted medium of his imagination, and shaped it more distinctly in his after-thought. It was, indeed, a majestic idea that the destiny of nations should be revealed, in these awful hieroglyphics, on the cope of heaven. A scroll so wide might not be deemed too expensive for Providence to write a people's doom upon. The belief was a favourite one with our forefathers, as betokening that their infant commonwealth was under a celestial guardianship of peculiar intimacy and strictness. But what shall we say, when an individual discovers a revelation addressed to himself alone, on the same vast sheet of record. In such a case, it could only be the symptom of a highly disordered mental state, when a man, rendered morbidly self-contemplative by long, intense, and secret pain, had extended his egotism over the whole expanse of nature, until the firmament itself should appear no more than a fitting page for his soul's history and fate.

We impute it, therefore, solely to the disease in his own eye and heart that the minister, looking upward to the zenith, beheld there the appearance of an immense letter—the letter A—marked out in lines of dull red light. Not but the meteor may have shown itself at that point, burning duskily through a veil of cloud, but with no such shape as his guilty imagination gave it, or, at least, with so little definiteness, that another's guilt might have seen another symbol in it.

There was a singular circumstance that characterised Mr. Dimmesdale's psychological state at this moment. All the time that he gazed upward to the zenith, he was, nevertheless, perfectly aware that little Pearl was hinting her finger towards old Roger Chillingworth, who stood at no great distance from the scaffold. The minister appeared to see him, with the same glance that discerned the miraculous letter. To his feature as to all other objects, the meteoric light imparted a new expression; or it might well be that the physician was not careful then, as at all other times, to hide the malevolence with which he looked upon his victim. Certainly, if the meteor kindled up the sky, and disclosed the earth, with an awfulness that admonished Hester Prynne and the clergyman of the day of judgment, then might Roger Chillingworth have passed with them for the arch-fiend, standing there with a smile and scowl, to claim his own. So vivid was the expression, or so intense the minister's perception of it, that it seemed still to remain painted on the darkness after the meteor had vanished, with an effect as if the street and all things else were at once annihilated.

"Who is that man, Hester?" gasped Mr. Dimmesdale, overcome with terror. "I shiver at him! Dost thou know the man? I hate him, Hester!"

She remembered her oath, and was silent.

"I tell thee, my soul shivers at him!" muttered the minister again. "Who is he? Who is he? Canst thou do nothing for me? I have a nameless horror of the man!"

"Minister," said little Pearl, "I can tell thee who he is!"

"Quickly, then, child!" said the minister, bending his ear close to her lips. "Quickly, and as low as thou canst whisper."

Pearl mumbled something into his ear that sounded, indeed, like human language, but was only such gibberish as children may be heard amusing themselves with by the hour together. At all events, if it involved any secret information in regard to old Roger Chillingworth, it was in a tongue unknown to the erudite clergyman, and did but increase the bewilderment of his mind. The elvish child then laughed aloud.

"Dost thou mock me now?" said the minister.

"Thou wast not bold!—thou wast not true!" answered the child. "Thou wouldst not promise to take my hand, and mother's hand, to-morrow noon-tide!"

"Worthy sir," answered the physician, who had now advanced to the foot of the platform—"pious Master Dimmesdale! can this be you? Well, well, indeed! We men of study, whose heads are in our books, have need to be straitly looked after! We dream in our waking moments, and walk in our sleep. Come, good sir, and my dear friend, I pray you let me lead you home!"

"How knewest thou that I was here?" asked the minister, fearfully.

"Verily, and in good faith," answered Roger Chillingworth, "I knew nothing of the matter. I had spent the better part of the night at the bedside of the worshipful Governor Winthrop, doing what my poor skill might to give him ease. He, going home to a better world, I, likewise, was on my way homeward, when this light shone out. Come with me, I beseech you, Reverend sir, else you will be poorly able to do Sabbath duty to-morrow. Aha! see now how they trouble the brain—these books!—these books! You should study less, good sir, and take a little pastime, or these night whimsies will grow upon you."

"I will go home with you," said Mr. Dimmesdale.

With a chill despondency, like one awakening, all nerveless, from an ugly dream, he yielded himself to the physician, and was led away.

The next day, however, being the Sabbath, he preached a discourse which was held to be the richest and most powerful, and the most replete with heavenly influences, that had ever proceeded from his lips. Souls, it is said, more souls than one, were brought to the truth by the efficacy of that sermon, and vowed within themselves to cherish a holy gratitude towards Mr. Dimmesdale throughout the long hereafter. But as he came down the pulpit steps, the grey-bearded sexton met him, holding up a black glove, which the minister recognised as his own.

"It was found," said the Sexton, "this morning on the scaffold where evil-doers are set up to public shame. Satan dropped it there, I take it, intending a scurrilous jest against your reverence. But, indeed, he was blind and foolish, as he ever and always is. A pure hand needs no glove to cover it!"

"Thank you, my good friend," said the minister, gravely, but startled at heart; for so confused was his remembrance, that he had almost brought himself to look at the events of the past night as visionary.

"Yes, it seems to be my glove, indeed!"

"And, since Satan saw fit to steal it, your reverence must needs handle him without gloves henceforward," remarked the old sexton, grimly smiling. "But did your reverence hear of the portent that was seen last night? a great red letter in the sky—the letter A, which we interpret to stand for Angel. For, as our good Governor Winthrop was made an angel this past night, it was doubtless held fit that there should be some notice thereof!"

"No," answered the minister, "I had not heard of it."

COMMENTARY

Falling at the center of the novel, this chapter contains the book's second of three scaffold scenes. While the first presented Hester's pain and humiliation as she stood with baby Pearl before a crowd of unsympathetic spectators, this scene focuses on the minister's guilt, which verges on madness, as he tries to reckon with his cowardice and remorse. Having decided that he has one option for revealing his suffering, Reverend Arthur Dimmesdale dons his worship garb and walks out to the scaffold where Hester and Pearl previously stood. He makes this trip late at night, which raises questions for the reader: Why has he come? Is this a sincere act of repentance? Obviously, no one will see him in the darkness, so his show of penance won't be a public spectacle, as Hester's was. Again, we see that Dimmesdale's sense of remorse is accompanied by an equally strong cowardice, which prevents him from publicly confessing his sin.

In the last chapter we learned that Dimmesdale has become prone to visions, due to his frequent fasting and vigils. These visionary experiences continue in this chapter, and Dimmesdale's meditations border on hallucination. Standing on the scaffold, Dimmesdale feels that the universe is staring at a scarlet letter on his breast, above his heart. Does he actually have a letter on his bare skin?

Is this what Chillingworth saw at the end of Chapter X? Has Dimmesdale engraved a tattoo into his flesh? Or is the letter a mysterious physical manifestation of his guilt? These questions will emerge again in Chapter XXIII, though the novel never provides definite answers. The narrator tells us that Dimmesdale actually suffers from "the gnawing and poisonous tooth of bodily pain" in the region of his heart. So intense are his thoughts related to this letter of shame that he lets out a shriek that sounds as if a "company of devils" is tossing the scream around the village. While Dimmesdale expects the shriek to attract throngs of townspeople to the scaffold, the narrator indicates that if anyone in the town heard the cry, they mistook it for the noise of witches, who could often be heard at night riding through the air with Satan. With this explanation, the narrator connects Dimmesdale with the devil and witches, a connection that Pearl will reiterate later in the novel.

The connection between Dimmesdale and the demonic emerges again in the imagery used to describe the minister's vision of what will happen when his legs stiffen so that he can't descend the scaffold. For example, he thinks of himself as a "ghost," a reference to how insubstantial his body and spirit have become. He believes that the sight of his disgrace will cause a "dusky tumult" to spread the news around town, and everyone will flock into the streets in a nightmarish disorder. There the townspeople will see Dimmesdale bathed in a "red eastern light." This vision is a hellish nightmare, and the red light explicitly connects Dimmesdale with the fires of hell and with Hester's red letter, denoting his shame and sin.

This macabre vision sends the minister into a fit of laughter; he seems to have reached the point of hysteria. His laughter is returned by Pearl, who is walking home with her mother from the mansion of Governor Winthrop, who died that evening. At Dimmesdale's request, Hester and Pearl ascend the scaffold. This scene is important because it offers a repetition and a variation on the initial scaffold scene in which Hester and Pearl stood alone, publicly humiliated. For Dimmesdale, this momentary connection with Hester and Pearl offers vitality. As he holds Pearl's hand, Dimmesdale receives a sudden charge of energy and life that pours into his heart. Hester and Pearl send a "vital warmth to his half-torpid system," and together, the three form an "electric chain." The images of vital energy that light this scene contrast sharply the "dimness" of Dimmesdale's solitary life. His guilt-ridden existence has turned him into a shade—a shadow of a human—but the love of Hester and Pearl could revitalize and rehumanize him, giving him back his lost identity.

With typical psychological acumen, Pearl asks the minister if she and her mother can stand on the scaffold with him again tomorrow, in the daylight. Although she is associated primarily with the natural world, Pearl continually reminds her parents of their moral failings. For Hester, Pearl is the scarlet letter embodied; for Dimmesdale, she is the voice of conscience, pinpointing the discrepancy between his public and private lives. When the minister responds that the three will meet on judgment day, the night sky is suddenly lit with a great meteor shower, as if to expose the fault in the minister's character. The entire sky glows, as if a gigantic lamp is burning.

One of the novel's major symbols, the meteor shower mixes fantasy and reality. Notice that other references to light and lamps in this chapter contribute to our understanding of the meteor. For example, Reverend Wilson's lighted lantern reminds Dimmesdale of the "radiant halo" of the saints in heaven. As he walks, Wilson's light throws a "gleam of recognition" on the world around him. Like Wilson's lantern, the meteor illuminates the town, making familiar objects glow with an "awful" and "unaccustomed" light. For example, in the meteor's light, Roger Chillingworth looks like the devil, because this unfamiliar

The meteor shower.

light exposes his malevolence. According to the narrator, this strange glow gives the world a new and different "moral interpretation"; not only does the meteor's light clearly reveal Dimmesdale's paternity, but by emphasizing the vitality of the link between the three characters, this light suggests that Dimmesdale's relationship with Hester is not necessarily morally tainted. By lighting up the moral darkness, the meteor reveals that their bond could be a source of love and affection. The meteor's "strange and solemn splendor" reveals all secrets and unites these three souls, who belong together.

The townspeople interpret the meteor as a supernatural symbol. The narrator suggests that no important event ever happened to the Puritans without some prior warning coming via a natural spectacle. These "awful hieroglyphics" give the Puritans a sense of security that God is watching them carefully. But as this chapter shows, there is no singular interpretation of these supposedly clear signs from God. For example, in Dimmesdale's eye, the meteor creates an enormous letter "A" in the sky, outlined in red light, which highlights his guilt. The narrator suggests that this vision could be simply an effect of the minister's disordered mind. Another member of the community also sees the meteor creating the letter A in the night sky, but to him the letter stands for "angel," in honor of the death of Governor Winthrop.

Chapter XIII

Hester decides that she should help Dimmesdale because Chillingworth's cure is obviously killing him. Hester has been so generous to the poor in the years since she was released from prison that many people have reinterpreted her "A" as standing for "able" rather than "adultery." Because of her repressed lifestyle, Hester has lost much of her beauty, but she has gained something more important: a free and creative mind.

CHAPTER XIII: ANOTHER VIEW OF HESTER

IN her late singular interview with Mr. Dimmesdale, Hester Prynne was shocked at the condition to which she found the clergyman reduced. His nerve seemed absolutely destroyed. His moral force was abased into more than childish weakness. It grovelled helpless on the ground, even while his intellectual faculties retained their pristine strength, or had perhaps acquired a morbid energy, which disease only could have given them. With her knowledge of a train of circumstances hidden from all others, she could readily infer that, besides the legitimate action of his own conscience, a terrible machinery had been brought to bear, and was still operating, on Mr. Dimmesdale's well-being and repose. Knowing what this poor fallen man had once been, her whole soul was moved by the shuddering terror with which he had appealed to her—the outcast woman—for support against his instinctively discovered enemy. She decided, moreover, that he had a right to her utmost aid. Little accustomed, in her long seclusion from society, to measure her ideas of right and wrong by any standard external to herself, Hester saw—or seemed to see—that there lay a responsibility upon her in reference to the clergyman, which she owed to no other, nor to the whole world besides. The links that united her to the rest of humankind—links of flowers, or silk, or gold, or whatever the material—had all been broken. Here was the iron link of mutual crime, which neither he nor she could break. Like all other ties, it brought along with it its obligations.

Hester Prynne did not now occupy precisely the same position in which we beheld her during the earlier periods of her ignominy. Years had come and gone. Pearl was now seven years old. Her mother, with the scarlet letter on her breast, glittering in its fantastic embroidery, had long been a familiar object to the townspeople. As is apt to be the case when a person stands out in any prominence before the community, and, at the same time, interferes neither with public nor individual interests and convenience, a species of general regard had ultimately grown up in reference to Hester Prynne. It is to the credit of human nature that, except where its selfishness is brought into play, it loves more readily than it hates. Hatred, by a gradual and quiet process, will even be transformed to love, unless the change be impeded by a continually new irritation of the original feeling of hostility. In this matter of Hester Prynne there was neither irritation nor irksomeness. She never battled with the public, but submitted uncomplainingly to its worst usage; she made no claim upon it in requital for what she suffered; she did not weigh upon its sympathies. Then, also, the blameless purity of her life during all these years in which she had been set apart to infamy was reckoned largely in her favour. With nothing now to lose, in the sight of mankind, and with no hope, and seemingly no wish, of gaining anything, it could only be a genuine regard for virtue that had brought back the poor wanderer to its paths.

It was perceived, too, that while Hester never put forward even the humblest title to share in the world's privileges—further than to breathe the common air and earn daily bread for little Pearl and herself by the faithful labour of her hands—she was quick to acknowledge her sisterhood with the race of man whenever benefits were to be conferred. None so ready as she to give of her little substance to every demand of poverty, even though the bitter-hearted pauper threw back a gibe in requital of the food brought regularly to his door, or the garments wrought for him by the fingers that could have embroidered a monarch's robe. None so self-devoted as Hester when pestilence stalked through the town. In all seasons of calamity, indeed, whether general or of individuals, the outcast of society at once found her place. She came, not as a guest, but as a rightful inmate, into the household that was darkened by trouble, as if its gloomy twilight were a medium in which she was entitled to hold intercourse with her fellow-creature. There glimmered the embroidered letter, with comfort in its unearthly ray. Elsewhere the token of sin, it was the taper of the sick chamber. It had even thrown its gleam, in the sufferer's hard extremity, across the verge of time. It had shown him where to set his foot, while the light of earth was fast becoming dim, and ere the light of futurity could reach him. In such emergencies Hester's nature showed itself warm and rich—a well-spring of human tenderness, unfailing to every real demand, and inexhaustible by the largest. Her breast, with its badge of shame, was but the softer pillow for the head that needed one. She was self-ordained a Sister of Mercy, or, we may rather say, the world's heavy hand had so ordained her, when neither the world nor she looked forward to this result. The letter was the symbol of her calling. Such helpfulness was found in her—so much power to do, and power to sympathise—that many people refused to interpret the scarlet A by its original signification. They said that it meant Able, so strong was Hester Prynne, with a woman's strength.

It was only the darkened house that could contain her. When sunshine came again, she was not there. Her shadow had faded across the threshold. The helpful inmate had departed, without one backward glance to gather up the meed of gratitude, if any were in the hearts of those whom she had served so zealously. Meeting them in the street, she never raised her head to receive their greeting. If they were resolute to accost her, she laid her finger on the scarlet letter, and passed on. This might be pride, but was so like humility, that it produced all the softening influence of the latter quality on the public mind. The public is despotic in its temper; it is capable of denying common justice when too strenuously demanded as a right; but quite as frequently it awards more than justice, when the appeal is made, as despots love to have it made, entirely to its generosity. Interpreting Hester Prynne's deportment as an appeal of this nature, society was inclined to show its former victim a more benign countenance than she cared to be favoured with, or, perchance, than she deserved.

The rulers, and the wise and learned men of the community, were longer in acknowledging the influence of Hester's good qualities than the people. The prejudices which they shared in common with the latter were fortified in themselves by an iron frame-work of reasoning, that made it a far tougher labour to expel them. Day by day, nevertheless, their sour and rigid wrinkles were relaxing into something which, in the due course of years, might grow to be an expression of almost benevolence. Thus it was with the men of rank, on whom their eminent position imposed the guardianship of the public morals. Individuals in private life, meanwhile, had quite forgiven Hester Prynne for her frailty; nay, more, they had begun to look upon the scarlet letter as the token, not of that one sin for which she had borne so long and dreary a penance, but of her many good deeds since. "Do you see that woman with the embroidered badge?" they would say to strangers. "It is our Hester—the town's own Hester— who is so kind to the poor, so helpful to the sick, so comfortable to the afflicted!" Then, it is true, the propensity of human nature to tell the very worst of itself, when embodied in the person of another, would constrain them to whisper the black scandal of bygone years. It was none the less a fact, however, that in the eyes of the very men who spoke thus, the scarlet letter had the effect of the cross on a nun's bosom. It imparted to the wearer a kind of sacredness, which enabled her to walk securely amid all peril. Had she fallen among thieves, it would have kept her safe. It was reported, and believed by many, that an Indian had drawn his arrow against the badge, and that the missile struck it, and fell harmless to the ground.

The effect of the symbol—or rather, of the position in respect to society that was indicated by it—on the mind of Hester Prynne herself was powerful and peculiar. All the light and graceful foliage of her character had been withered up by this red-hot brand, and had long ago fallen away, leaving a bare and harsh outline, which might have been repulsive had she possessed friends or companions to be repelled by it. Even the attractiveness of her person had undergone a similar change. It might be partly owing to the studied austerity of her dress, and partly to the lack of demonstration in her manners. It was a sad transformation, too, that her rich and luxuriant hair had either been cut off, or was so completely hidden by a cap, that not a shining lock of it ever once gushed into the sunshine. It was due in part to all these causes, but still more to something else, that there seemed to be no longer anything in Hester's face for Love to dwell upon; nothing in Hester's form, though majestic and statue like, that Passion would ever dream of clasping in its embrace; nothing in Hester's bosom to make it ever again the pillow of Affection. Some attribute had departed from her, the permanence of which had been essential to keep her a woman. Such is frequently the fate, and such the stern development, of the feminine character and person, when the woman has encountered, and lived through, an experience of peculiar severity. If she be all tenderness, she will die. If she survive, the tenderness will either be crushed out of her, or—and the outward semblance is the same—crushed so deeply into her heart that it can never show itself more. The latter is perhaps the truest theory. She who has once been a woman, and ceased to be so, might at any moment become a woman again, if there were only the magic touch to effect the transformation. We shall see whether Hester Prynne were ever afterwards so touched and so transfigured.

Much of the marble coldness of Hester's impression was to be attributed to the circumstance that her life had turned, in a great measure, from passion and feeling to thought. Standing alone in the world—alone, as to any dependence on society, and with little Pearl to be guided and protected—alone, and hopeless of retrieving her position, even had she not scorned to consider it desirable—she cast away the fragment a broken chain. The world's law was no law for her mind. It was an age in which the human intellect, newly emancipated, had taken a more active and a wider range than for many centuries before. Men of the sword had overthrown nobles and kings. Men bolder than these had overthrown and rearranged—not actually, but within the sphere of theory, which was their most real abode—the whole system of ancient prejudice, wherewith was linked much of ancient principle. Hester Prynne imbibed this spirit. She assumed a freedom of speculation, then common enough on the other side of the Atlantic, but which our forefathers, had they known it, would have held to be a deadlier crime than that stigmatised by the scarlet letter. In her lonesome cottage, by the seashore, thoughts visited her such as dared to enter no other dwelling in New England; shadowy guests, that would have been as perilous as demons to their entertainer, could they have been seen so much as knocking at her door.

It is remarkable that persons who speculate the most boldly often conform with the most perfect quietude to the external regulations of society. The thought suffices them, without investing itself in the flesh and blood of action. So it seemed to be with Hester. Yet, had little Pearl never come to her from the spiritual world, it might have been far otherwise. Then she might have come down to us in history, hand in hand with Ann Hutchinson, as the foundress of a religious sect. She might, in one of her phases, have been a prophetess. She might, and not improbably would, have suffered death from the stern tribunals of the period, for attempting to undermine the foundations of the Puritan establishment. But, in the education of her child, the mother's enthusiasm of thought had something to wreak itself upon. Providence, in the person of this little girl, had assigned to Hester's charge, the germ and blossom of womanhood, to be cherished and developed amid a host of difficulties. Everything was against her. The world was hostile. The child's own nature had something wrong in it which continually betokened that she had been born amiss—

the effluence of her mother's lawless passion—and often impelled Hester to ask, in bitterness of heart, whether it were for ill or good that the poor little creature had been born at all.

Indeed, the same dark question often rose into her mind with reference to the whole race of womanhood. Was existence worth accepting even to the happiest among them? As concerned her own individual existence, she had long ago decided in the negative, and dismissed the point as settled. A tendency to speculation, though it may keep women quiet, as it does man, yet makes her sad. She discerns, it may be, such a hopeless task before her. As a first step, the whole system of society is to be torn down and built up anew. Then the very nature of the opposite sex, or its long hereditary habit, which has become like nature, is to be essentially modified before woman can be allowed to assume what seems a fair and suitable position. Finally, all other difficulties being obviated, woman cannot take advantage of these preliminary reforms until she herself shall have undergone a still mightier change, in which, perhaps, the ethereal essence, wherein she has her truest life, will be found to have evaporated. A woman never overcomes these problems by any exercise of thought. They are not to be solved, or only in one way. If her heart chance to come uppermost, they vanish. Thus Hester Prynne, whose heart had lost its regular and healthy throb, wandered without a clue in the dark labyrinth of mind; now turned aside by an insurmountable precipice; now starting back from a deep chasm. There was wild and ghastly scenery all around her, and a home and comfort nowhere. At times a fearful doubt strove to possess her soul, whether it were not better to send Pearl at once to Heaven, and go herself to such futurity as Eternal Justice should provide.

The scarlet letter had not done its office. Now, however, her interview with the Reverend Mr. Dimmesdale, on the night of his vigil, had given her a new theme of reflection, and held up to her an object that appeared worthy of any exertion and sacrifice for its attainment. She had witnessed the intense misery beneath which the minister struggled, or, to speak more accurately, had ceased to struggle. She saw that he stood on the verge of lunacy, if he had not already stepped across it. It was impossible to doubt that, whatever painful efficacy there might be in the secret sting of remorse, a deadlier venom had been infused into it by the hand that proffered relief. A secret enemy had been continually by his side, under the semblance of a friend and helper, and had availed himself of the opportunities thus afforded for tampering with the delicate springs of Mr. Dimmesdale's nature. Hester could not but ask herself whether there had not originally been a defect of truth, courage, and loyalty on her own part, in allowing the minister to be thrown into position where so much evil was to be foreboded and nothing auspicious to be hoped. Her only justification lay in the fact that she had been able to discern no method of rescuing him from a blacker ruin than had overwhelmed herself except by acquiescing in Roger Chillingworth's scheme of disguise. Under that impulse she had made her choice, and had chosen, as it now appeared, the more wretched alternative of the two. She determined to redeem her error so far as it might yet be possible. Strengthened by years of hard and solemn trial, she felt herself no longer so inadequate to cope with Roger Chillingworth as on that night, abased by sin and half-maddened by the ignominy that was still new, when they had talked together in the prison-chamber. She had climbed her way since then to a higher point. The old man, on the other hand, had brought himself nearer to her level, or, perhaps, below it, by the revenge which he had stooped for.

In fine, Hester Prynne resolved to meet her former husband, and do what might be in her power for the rescue of the victim on whom he had so evidently set his gripe. The occasion was not long to seek. One afternoon, walking with Pearl in a retired part of the peninsula, she beheld the old physician with a basket on one arm and a staff in the other hand, stooping along the ground in quest of roots and herbs to concoct his medicine withal.

COMMENTARY

As the title of this chapter suggests, here we are given new insight on Hester's personality. In the years since her public humiliation on the scaffold, Hester has changed significantly due to her constant isolation. Unlike the other members of her community, Hester makes moral judgments based not on external standards, but on internal beliefs. Shocked by the deterioration of Dimmesdale's character in recent years, Hester's conscience convinces her that she has a responsibility to help him. All her links to humanity have been broken, except the one forged through the "iron" bond of crime that chains her to Dimmesdale. (Notice that Hester's "crime" has throughout the book been described as an "iron" manacle, much like the iron in the prison door or the iron chain that keeps her in Boston.)

Believing that Dimmesdale is on the verge of madness, Hester wonders if she made the right decision in vowing to keep Chillingworth's identity a secret. It now appears to her that she may have been wrong. Still, she can redeem herself by revealing the secret now, rather than maintaining a harmful vow of silence. In her opinion, Chillingworth has equaled her sin, perhaps even surpassed it, by seeking malicious revenge. The novel asks readers to consider whose crime is worse: Hester's adultery or Chillingworth's revenge. In the narrator's opinion, Hester's betrayal of her husband is not as wretched as Chillingworth's cruelty in crushing Dimmesdale's psyche.

At this point in the story, Pearl is seven years old and Hester's position within the community has changed.

People have come to regard Hester as an asset to the community due to the "blameless purity" with which she now lives. She always offers as much help to the poor as she can, and when townspeople fall ill or suffer an accident, Hester is able to help because she feels an empathy with their misfortune. In the gloom of a sick room, her scarlet letter loses its symbolism as a token of sin and, instead, becomes a candle that offers solace to the suffering. The narrator suggests that the scarlet letter has helped some dying folk to find their way to the next world, offering its light as the earth becomes dim. From a symbol of her status as outcast, the scarlet letter is slowly becoming a symbol of Hester's tender, rich, warm, and inexhaustible nature. While the letter once stood for "adulterer," it now means "able" to those community members who have benefited from Hester's strength. The scarlet letter has come to act much like the cross on a nun's chest, which imparts sacredness to Hester and supposedly protects her from all harm. Typical of the Puritan tendency toward exaggeration, the community now believes that the letter protects her from arrows and thieves.

Despite these changes in the public's attitude toward her, Hester's attitude toward herself hasn't changed. For example, this chapter shows us that Hester is at home only in darkened houses—during the daytime she keeps to herself. While the townspeople recognize her unfailing good deeds in the years since her sin, Hester does not demonstrate the same level of compassion toward herself. The letter still weighs heavily on her and has even affected her physical appearance. Because for so long it has withered the "light and graceful foliage" of her personality, she now appears "bare and harsh." Although her body is still majestic and statuesque, Hester's beauty has disappeared because her life has been devoid of passion.

Hester has learned to look at life though an intellectual lens, much like the desiccated leaders of the Puritan community. While the townspeople come to recognize Hester's true, admirable nature, the magistrates—supposedly wise and educated men—are much slower to notice her good qualities. Their prejudices are based on their intellectual attainments, the "iron framework of their reasoning." Just as Hester is trapped by the iron chain of her adultery, the magistrates are equally limited by their intellectualizing, which prohibits them from understanding human nature.

But while Hester has learned to live through her intellect rather than her passions, her thinking still differs dramatically from the magistrates'. Earlier in the book, Dimmesdale describes Pearl as representing a "broken law." Echoing that image, in this chapter the narrator explains that Hester has cast aside "the fragments of a broken chain" and has separated herself from the world's laws. Hester's philosophy of life accords more readily

with the Europeans' than with the Puritan fathers, who would find her beliefs—if she chose to make them public—more shocking than her adultery.

Because of her need to protect Pearl, Hester keeps these ideas primarily to herself. Yet the narrator suggests that if she weren't a mother, Hester could easily have been a prophetess or the founder of a new religion, much like Ann Hutchinson. In particular, she might have been the founder of a new society for women. Reflecting on the position of women within Puritan culture, Hester wonders if even the happiest of women have enough options. She believes that society needs to be completely reformed in order for women to assume a fair position and, in addition, women themselves need to undergo a transformation.

The narrator seems to suggest that women can find their true selves only through love; a woman's problems are solved only if "her heart chance to come uppermost." Without the possibility of love, Hester is trapped in "the dark labyrinth of mind," stuck inside her intellectual world, basically homeless. Contemporary readers may disagree with the notion that love is the only road to happiness for women, but they also recognize that Hester's strength and insight are on prominent display in this chapter, proving why many critics have found her to be one of the few true heroines of American literature.

Chapter XIV

Hester visits Chillingworth and tells him that she must reveal his true identity to Dimmesdale. She is shocked by the change in Chillingworth's appearance: His cruelty toward Dimmesdale has transformed him into a devil.

CHAPTER XIV: HESTER AND THE PHYSICIAN

HESTER bade little Pearl run down to the margin of the water, and play with the shells and tangled sea-weed, until she should have talked awhile with yonder gatherer of herbs. So the child flew away like a bird, and, making bare her small white feet went pattering along the moist margin of the sea. Here and there she came to a full stop, ad peeped curiously into a pool, left by the retiring tide as a mirror for Pearl to see her face in. Forth peeped at her, out of the pool, with dark, glistening curls around her head, and an elf-smile in her eyes, the image of a little maid whom Pearl, having no other playmate, invited to take her hand and run a race with her. But the visionary little maid on her part, beckoned likewise, as if to say—"This is a better place; come thou into the pool." And Pearl, stepping in mid-leg deep, beheld her own white feet at the bottom; while, out of a still lower depth, came the gleam of a kind of fragmentary smile, floating to and fro in the agitated water.

Meanwhile her mother had accosted the physician. "I would speak a word with you," said she—"a word that concerns us much."

"Aha! and is it Mistress Hester that has a word for old Roger Chilling-worth?" answered he, raising himself from his stooping posture. "With all my heart! Why, mistress, I hear good tidings of you on all hands! No longer ago than yester-eve, a magistrate, a wise and godly man, was discoursing of your affairs, Mistress Hester, and whispered me that there had been question concerning you in the council. It was debated whether or no, with safety to the commonweal, yonder scarlet letter might be taken off your bosom. On my life, Hester, I made my intreaty to the worshipful magistrate that it might be done forthwith."

"It lies not in the pleasure of the magistrates to take off the badge," calmly replied Hester. "Were I worthy to be quit of it, it would fall away of its own nature, or be transformed into something that should speak a different purport."

"Nay, then, wear it, if it suit you better," rejoined he. "A woman must needs follow her own fancy touching the adornment of her person. The letter is gaily embroidered, and shows right bravely on your bosom!"

All this while Hester had been looking steadily at the old man, and was shocked, as well as wonder-smitten, to discern what a change had been wrought upon him within the past seven years. It was not so much that he had grown older; for though the traces of advancing life were visible he bore his age well, and seemed to retain a wiry vigour and alertness. But the former aspect of an intellectual and studious man, calm and quiet, which was what she best remembered in him, had altogether vanished, and been succeeded by an eager, searching, almost fierce, yet carefully guarded look. It seemed to be his wish and purpose to mask this expression with a smile, but the latter played him false, and flickered over his visage so derisively that the spectator could see his blackness all the better for it. Ever and anon, too, there came a glare of red light out of his eyes, as if the old man's soul were on fire and kept on smouldering duskily within his breast, until by some casual puff of passion it was blown into a momentary flame. This he repressed as speedily as possible, and strove to look as if nothing of the kind had happened.

In a word, old Roger Chillingworth was a striking evidence of man's faculty of transforming himself into a devil, if he will only, for a reasonable space of time, undertake a devil's office. This unhappy person had effected such a transformation by devoting himself for seven years to the constant analysis of a heart full of torture, and deriving his enjoyment thence, and adding fuel to those fiery tortures which he analysed and gloated over.

The scarlet letter burned on Hester Prynne's bosom. Here was another ruin, the responsibility of which came partly home to her.

"What see you in my face," asked the physician, "that you look at it so earnestly?"

"Something that would make me weep, if there were any tears bitter enough for it," answered she. "But let it pass! It is of yonder miserable man that I would speak."

"And what of him?" cried Roger Chillingworth, eagerly, as if he loved the topic, and were glad of an opportunity to discuss it with the only person of whom he could make a confidant. "Not to hide the truth, Mistress Hester, my thoughts happen just now to be busy with the gentleman. So speak freely and I will make answer."

"When we last spake together," said Hester, "now seven years ago, it was your pleasure to extort a promise of secrecy as touching the former relation betwixt yourself and me. As the life and good fame of yonder man were in your hands there seemed no choice to me, save to be silent in accordance with your behest. Yet it was not without heavy misgivings that I thus bound myself, for, having cast off all duty towards other human beings, there remained a duty towards him, and something whispered me that I was betraying it in pledging myself to keep your counsel. Since that day no man is so near to him as you. You tread behind his every footstep. You are beside him, sleeping and waking. You search his thoughts. You burrow and rankle in his heart! Your clutch is on his life, and you cause him to die daily a living death, and still he knows you not. In permitting this I have surely acted a false part by the only man to whom the power was left me to be true!"

"What choice had you?" asked Roger Chillingworth. "My finger, pointed at this man, would have hurled him from his pulpit into a dungeon, thence, peradventure, to the gallows!"

"It had been better so!" said Hester Prynne.

"What evil have I done the man?" asked Roger Chillingworth again. "I tell thee, Hester Prynne, the richest fee that ever physician earned from monarch could not have bought such care as I have wasted on this miserable priest! But for my aid his life would have burned away in torments within the first two years after the perpetration of his crime and thine. For, Hester, his spirit lacked the strength that could have borne up, as thine has, beneath a burden like thy scarlet letter. Oh, I could reveal a goodly secret! But enough. What art can do, I have exhausted on him. That he now breathes and creeps about on earth is owing all to me!"

"Better he had died at once!" said Hester Prynne.

"Yea, woman, thou sayest truly!" cried old Roger Chillingworth, letting the lurid fire of his heart blaze out before her eyes. "Better had he died at once! Never did mortal suffer what this man has suffered. And all, all, in the sight of his worst enemy! He has been conscious of me. He has felt an influence dwelling always upon him like a curse. He knew, by some spiritual sense—for the Creator never made another being so sensitive as this—he knew that no friendly hand was pulling at his heartstrings, and that an eye was looking curiously into him, which sought only evil, and found it. But he knew not that the eye and hand were mine! With the superstition common to his brotherhood, he fancied himself given over to a fiend, to be tortured with frightful dreams and desperate thoughts, the sting of remorse and despair of pardon, as a foretaste of what awaits him beyond the grave. But it was the constant shadow of my presence, the closest propinquity of the man whom he had most vilely wronged, and who had grown to exist only by this perpetual poison of the direst revenge! Yea, indeed,—he did not err,—there was a fiend at his elbow! A mortal man, with once a human heart, has become a fiend for his especial torment."

The unfortunate physician, while uttering these words, lifted his hands with a look of horror, as if he had beheld some frightful shape, which he could not recognise, usurping the place of his own image in a glass. It was one of those moments—which sometimes occur only at the interval of years—when a man's moral aspect is faithfully revealed to his mind's eye. Not improbably he had never before viewed himself as he did now.

"Hast thou not tortured him enough?" said Hester, noticing the old man's look. "Has he not paid thee all?"

"No, no! He has but increased the debt!" answered the physician, and as he proceeded, his manner lost its fiercer characteristics, and subsided into gloom. "Dost thou remember me, Hester, as I was nine years agone? Even then I was in the autumn of my days, nor was it the early autumn. But all my life had been made up of earnest, studious, thoughtful, quiet years, bestowed faithfully for the increase of mine own knowledge, and faithfully, too, though this latter object was but casual to the other— faithfully for the advancement of human welfare. No life had been more peaceful and innocent than mine; few lives so rich with benefits conferred. Dost thou remember me? Was I not, though you might deem me cold, nevertheless a man thoughtful for others, craving little for himself—kind, true, just and of constant, if not warm affections? Was I not all this?"

"All this, and more," said Hester.

"And what am I now?" demanded he, looking into her face, and permitting the whole evil within him to be written on his features. "I have already told thee what I am—a fiend! Who made me so?"

"It was myself," cried Hester, shuddering. "It was I, not less than he. Why hast thou not avenged thyself on me?"

"I have left thee to the scarlet letter," replied Roger Chillingworth. "If that has not avenged me, I can do no more!"

He laid his finger on it with a smile.

"It has avenged thee," answered Hester Prynne.

"I judged no less," said the physician. "And now what wouldst thou with me touching this man?"

"I must reveal the secret," answered Hester, firmly. "He must discern thee in thy true character. What may be the result I know not. But this long debt of confidence, due from me to him, whose bane and ruin I have been, shall at length be paid. So far as concerns the overthrow or preservation of his fair fame and his earthly state, and perchance his life, he is in my hands. Nor do I—whom the scarlet letter has disciplined to truth, though it be the truth of red-hot iron entering into the soul—nor do I perceive such advantage in his living any longer a life of ghastly emptiness, that I shall stoop to implore thy mercy. Do with him as thou wilt! There is no good for him, no good for me, no good for thee. There is no good for little Pearl. There is no path to guide us out of this dismal maze."

"Woman, I could well-nigh pity thee," said Roger Chillingworth, unable to restrain a thrill of admiration too, for there was a quality almost majestic in the despair which she expressed. "Thou hadst great elements. Peradventure, hadst thou met earlier with a better love than mine, this evil had not been. I pity thee, for the good that has been wasted in thy nature."

"And I thee," answered Hester Prynne, "for the hatred that has transformed a wise and just man to a fiend! Wilt thou yet purge it out of thee, and be once more human? If not for his sake, then doubly for thine own! Forgive, and leave his further retribution to the Power that claims it! I said, but now, that there could be no good event for him, or thee, or me, who are here wandering together in this gloomy maze of evil, and stumbling at every step over the guilt wherewith we have strewn our path. It is not so! There might be good for thee, and thee alone, since thou hast been deeply wronged and hast it at thy will to pardon. Wilt thou give up that only privilege? Wilt thou reject that priceless benefit?"

"Peace, Hester, peace!" replied the old man, with gloomy sternness. "It is not granted me to pardon. I have no such power as thou tellest me of. My old faith, long forgotten, comes back to me, and explains all that we do, and all we suffer. By thy first step awry, thou didst plant the germ of evil; but since that moment it has all been a dark necessity. Ye that have wronged me are not sinful, save in a kind of typical illusion; neither am I fiend-like, who have snatched a fiend's office from his hands. It is our fate. Let the black flower blossom as it may! Now, go thy ways, and deal as thou wilt with yonder man."

He waved his hand, and betook himself again to his employment of gathering herbs.

COMMENTARY

This chapter opens with a brief look at Pearl. As she frolics near the edge of the ocean, playing with the shells and seaweed, Pearl seems to have become a water sprite. She's compared again to a bird, flying along the beach. We are reminded of Pearl's active imagination when she peers into an ocean pool and creates an imaginary playmate for herself out of her own reflection. This make-believe activity also suggests that Pearl is a perfect reflection of the natural world, an idea repeated later in the novel. Notice how images of water, birds, and fire seem to cluster around Pearl.

Chapter XIV also offers additional insight on the changes that Roger Chillingworth has undergone. Gone is the calm and intellectual man that Hester married. In his place is an eager, fierce, suspicious demon. Although he tries to hide his new identity, Chillingworth doesn't succeed; his "blackness" is readily apparent. Hester also notices a "red light" emanating from his eyes, which, in the narrator's opinion, makes him look as if his soul is on fire: "In a word, old Roger Chillingworth was a striking evidence of man's faculty of transforming himself into a devil." Chillingworth has assumed a "devil's office" by tediously analyzing Reverend Dimmesdale's tortured heart and thereby contributing to the minister's discomfort. His lack of sympathy and pity has dehumanized the doctor. So pernicious is Chillingworth's task that Hester believes Dimmesdale would have been better off in the gallows than in Chillingworth's clutches.

Chillingworth suggests that he has actually helped Dimmesdale, who lacks Hester's strength and would have collapsed long ago without the doctor's aid. Yet he also appears to recognize his own evil, saying that his human heart has become fiendish in order to torture Dimmesdale. Holding up his hand, Chillingworth momentarily recognizes with horror his own immorality. Chillingworth is also aware that he hasn't always been fiendish. As he contemplates his past life, he remembers his peace and innocence. Coldness was his only fault. He blames Dimmesdale for transforming him into a fiend, but Hester believes the transformation was her fault.

Hester tells the doctor that she can no longer keep her secret from Dimmesdale; she

Hester and Chillingworth in an F.O.C. Darley illustration.
Photo courtesy of The Darley Society, Inc.

must reveal Chillingworth in his "true character"—as her husband. While Dimmesdale has diminished during the years since Pearl's birth, Hester has strengthened, as becomes apparent in this chapter. The scarlet letter has "disciplined" her into the "truth of red-hot iron, entering into the soul." Because of her suffering, Hester recognizes the value of being truthful, even when the truth causes pain. No good emerges from anyone maintaining secrets, especially this secret, which has left Dimmesdale's life a "ghastly emptiness."

Hester's moral strength incites Chillingworth's admiration; he imagines that she would have had an admirable life if she had "earlier met a better love" than his. He pities the wasted talents in her nature, and she pities the waste in his—the transformation of a wise and just man into a devil.

Hester and Chillingworth discuss fate: Do they have any choice in plotting their futures? In Hester's opinion, Chillingworth has the opportunity to do good by pardoning Dimmesdale, but he rejects this option. Chillingworth believes that her first misstep led them both onto the path of evil, but since then everything has happened due to "dark necessity." In the doctor's opinion, fate is responsible, so Hester is not sinful nor is he fiendish; they are simply following in the footsteps laid out for them. In accepting whatever fate has to offer, Chillingworth blithely says, "Let the black flower blossom as it may!," a reference to the black flower described in the opening chapter. The philosophies of Hester and Chillingworth differ greatly. Chillingworth seems to accept the doctrine of predestination: a Calvinist belief that God has preordained which souls will be saved and which will be damned. Hester, on the other hand, believes in accepting responsibility for her actions—in charting her own path rather than following someone else's footsteps.

Chapter XV

While her mother was speaking with Chillingworth, Pearl was playing near a pool of water. Copying the letter on her mother's chest, Pearl puts a green seaweed "A" on her own chest. Hester wonders if Pearl knows what the letter means. Intuitively, Pearl associates her mother's letter with the minister always holding his hand over his heart.

CHAPTER XV: HESTER AND PEARL

SO Roger Chillingworth—a deformed old figure with a face that haunted men's memories longer than they liked—took leave of Hester Prynne, and went stooping away along the earth. He gathered here and there an herb, or grubbed up a root and put it into the basket on his arm. His gray beard almost touched the ground as he crept onward. Hester gazed after him a little while, looking with a half fantastic curiosity to see whether the tender grass of early spring would not be blighted beneath him and show the wavering track of his footsteps, sere and brown, across its cheerful verdure. She wondered what sort of herbs they were which the old man was so sedulous to gather. Would not the earth, quickened to an evil purpose by the sympathy of his eye, greet him with poisonous shrubs of species hitherto unknown, that would start up under his fingers? Or might it suffice him that every wholesome growth should be converted into something deleterious and malignant at his touch? Did the sun, which shone so brightly everywhere else, really fall upon him? Or was there, as it rather seemed, a circle of ominous shadow moving along with his deformity whichever way he turned himself? And whither was he now going? Would he not suddenly sink into the earth, leaving a barren and blasted spot, where, in due course of time, would be seen **deadly nightshade, dogwood, henbane**, and whatever else of vegetable wickedness the climate could produce, all flourishing with hideous luxuriance? Or would he spread bat's wings and flee away, looking so much the uglier the higher he rose towards heaven?

"Be it sin or no," said Hester Prynne, bitterly, as still she gazed after him, "I hate the man!"

She upbraided herself for the sentiment, but could not overcome or lessen it. Attempting to do so, she thought of those long-past days in a distant land, when he used to emerge at eventide from the seclusion of his study and sit down in the firelight of their home, and in the light of her nuptial smile. He needed to bask himself in that smile, he said, in order that the chill of so many lonely hours among his books might be taken off the scholar's heart. Such scenes had once appeared not otherwise than happy, but now, as viewed through the dismal medium of her subsequent life, they classed themselves among her ugliest remembrances. She marvelled how such scenes could have been! She marvelled how she could ever have been wrought upon to marry him! She deemed in her crime most to be repented of, that she had ever endured and reciprocated the lukewarm grasp of his hand, and had suffered the smile of her lips

deadly nightshade, dogwood, henbane: plants associated with witchcraft. All had both deadly and magical powers.

Nightshade, dogwood, and henbane.

and eyes to mingle and melt into his own. And it seemed a fouler offence committed by Roger Chillingworth than any which had since been done him, that, in the time when her heart knew no better, he had persuaded her to fancy herself happy by his side.

"Yes, I hate him!" repeated Hester more bitterly than before. "He betrayed me! He has done me worse wrong than I did him!"

Let men tremble to win the hand of woman, unless they win along with it the utmost passion of her heart! Else it may be their miserable fortune, as it was Roger Chillingworth's, when some mightier touch than their own may have awakened all her sensibilities, to be reproached even for the calm content, the marble image of happiness, which they will have imposed upon her as the warm reality. But Hester ought long ago to have done with this injustice. What did it betoken? Had seven long years, under the torture of the scarlet letter, inflicted so much of misery and wrought out no repentance?

The emotion of that brief space, while she stood gazing after the crooked figure of old Roger Chillingworth, threw a dark light on Hester's state of mind, revealing much that she might not otherwise have acknowledged to herself.

He being gone, she summoned back her child.

"Pearl! Little Pearl! Where are you?"

Pearl, whose activity of spirit never flagged, had been at no loss for amusement while her mother talked with the old gatherer of herbs. At first, as already told, she had flirted fancifully with her own image in a pool of water, beckoning the phantom forth, and—as it declined to venture—seeking a passage for herself into its sphere of impalpable earth and unattainable sky. Soon finding, however, that either she or the image was unreal, she turned elsewhere for better pastime. She made little boats out of birch-bark, and freighted them with snailshells, and sent out more ventures on the mighty deep than any merchant in New England; but the larger part of them foundered near the shore. She seized a live horse-shoe by the tail, and made prize of several five-fingers, and laid out a jelly-fish to melt in the warm sun. Then she took up the white foam that streaked the line of the advancing tide, and threw it upon the breeze, scampering after it with winged footsteps to catch the great snowflakes ere they fell. Perceiving a flock of beach-birds that fed and fluttered along the shore, the naughty child picked up her apron full of pebbles, and, creeping from rock to rock after these small sea-fowl, displayed remarkable dexterity in pelting them. One little gray bird, with a white breast, Pearl was almost sure had been hit by a pebble, and fluttered away with a broken wing. But then the elf-child sighed, and gave up her sport, because it grieved her to have done harm to a little being that was as wild as the sea-breeze, or as wild as Pearl herself.

Her final employment was to gather seaweed of various kinds, and make herself a scarf or mantle, and a head-dress, and thus assume the aspect of a little mermaid. She inherited her mother's gift for devising drapery and costume. As the last touch to her mermaid's garb, Pearl took some eel-grass and imitated, as best she could, on her own bosom the decoration with which she was so familiar on her mother's. A letter—the letter A—but freshly green instead of scarlet. The child bent her chin upon her breast, and contemplated this device with strange interest, even as if the one only thing for which she had been sent into the world was to make out its hidden import.

"I wonder if mother will ask me what it means?" thought Pearl.

Just then she heard her mother's voice, and, flitting along as lightly as one of the little sea-birds, appeared before Hester Prynne dancing, laughing, and pointing her finger to the ornament upon her bosom.

"My little Pearl," said Hester, after a moment's silence, "the green letter, and on thy childish bosom, has no purport. But dost thou know, my child, what this letter means which thy mother is doomed to wear?"

"Yes, mother," said the child. "It is the great letter A. Thou hast taught me in the horn-book."

Hester looked steadily into her little face; but though there was that singular expression which she had so often remarked in her black eyes, she could not satisfy herself whether Pearl really attached any meaning to the symbol. She felt a morbid desire to ascertain the point.

"Dost thou know, child, wherefore thy mother wears this letter?"

"Truly do I!" answered Pearl, looking brightly into her mother's face. "It is for the same reason that the minister keeps his hand over his heart!"

"And what reason is that?" asked Hester, half smiling at the absurd incongruity of the child's observation; but on second thoughts turning pale. "What has the letter to do with any heart save mine?"

"Nay, mother, I have told all I know," said Pearl, more seriously than she was wont to speak. "Ask yonder old man whom thou hast been talking with,—it may be he can tell. But in good earnest now, mother dear, what does this scarlet letter mean?—and why dost thou wear it on thy bosom?—and why does the minister keep his hand over his heart?"

She took her mother's hand in both her own, and gazed into her eyes with an earnestness that was seldom seen in her wild and capricious character. The thought occurred to Hester, that the child might really be seeking to approach her with childlike confidence, and doing what she could, and as intelligently as she knew how, to establish a meeting-point of sympathy. It showed Pearl in an unwonted aspect. Heretofore, the mother, while loving her child with the intensity of a sole affection, had schooled herself to hope for little other return than the waywardness of an April breeze, which spends its time in airy sport, and has its gusts of inexplicable passion, and is petulant in its best of moods, and chills oftener than caresses you, when you take it to your bosom; in requital of which misdemeanours it will sometimes, of its own vague purpose, kiss your cheek with a kind of doubtful tenderness, and play gently with your hair, and then be gone about its other idle business, leaving a dreamy pleasure at your heart. And this, moreover, was a mother's estimate of the child's disposition. Any other observer might have seen few but unamiable traits, and have given them a far darker colouring. But now the idea came strongly into Hester's mind, that Pearl, with her remarkable precocity and acuteness, might already have approached the age when she could have been made a friend, and intrusted with as much of her mother's sorrows as could be imparted, without irreverence either to the parent or the child. In the little chaos of Pearl's character there might be seen emerging and could have been from the very first—the steadfast principles of an unflinching courage—an uncontrollable will—sturdy pride, which might be disciplined into self-respect—and a bitter scorn of many things which, when examined, might be found to have the taint of falsehood in them. She possessed affections, too, though hitherto acrid and disagreeable, as are the richest flavours of unripe fruit. With all these sterling attributes, thought Hester, the evil which she inherited from her mother must be great indeed, if a noble woman do not grow out of this elfish child.

Pearl's inevitable tendency to hover about the enigma of the scarlet letter seemed an innate quality of her being. From the earliest epoch of her conscious life, she had entered upon this as her appointed mission. Hester had often fancied that Providence had a design of justice and retribution, in endowing the child with this marked propensity; but never, until now, had she bethought herself to ask, whether, linked with that design, there might not likewise be a purpose of mercy and beneficence. If little Pearl were entertained with faith and trust, as a spirit messenger no less than an earthly child, might it not be her errand to soothe away the sorrow that lay cold in her mother's heart, and converted it into a tomb?— and to help her to overcome the passion, once so wild, and even yet neither dead nor asleep, but only imprisoned within the same tomb-like heart?

Such were some of the thoughts that now stirred in Hester's mind, with as much vivacity of impression as if they had actually been whispered into her ear. And there was little Pearl, all this while, holding her mother's hand in both her own, and turning her face upward, while she put these searching questions, once and again, and still a third time.

"What does the letter mean, mother? and why dost thou wear it? and why does the minister keep his hand over his heart?"

"What shall I say?" thought Hester to herself. "No! If this be the price of the child's sympathy, I cannot pay it."

Then she spoke aloud.

"Silly Pearl," said she, "what questions are these? There are many things in this world that a child must not ask about. What know I of the minister's heart? And as for the scarlet letter, I wear it for the sake of its gold thread."

In all the seven bygone years, Hester Prynne had never before been false to the symbol on her bosom. It may be that it was the talisman of a stern and severe, but yet a guardian spirit, who now forsook her; as recognising that, in spite of his strict watch over her heart, some new evil had crept into it, or some old one had never been expelled. As for little Pearl, the earnestness soon passed out of her face.

But the child did not see fit to let the matter drop. Two or three times, as her mother and she went homeward, and as often at supper-time, and while Hester was putting her to bed, and once after she seemed to be fairly asleep, Pearl looked up, with mischief gleaming in her black eyes.

"Mother," said she, "what does the scarlet letter mean?"

And the next morning, the first indication the child gave of being awake was by popping up her head from the pillow, and making that other enquiry, which she had so unaccountably connected with her investigations about the scarlet letter:—

"Mother!—Mother!—Why does the minister keep his hand over his heart?"

"Hold thy tongue, naughty child!" answered her mother, with an asperity that she had never permitted to herself before. "Do not tease me; else I shall put thee into the dark closet!"

COMMENTARY

As this chapter opens, Hester watches Chillingworth as he walks away from her down the beach. She feels that even nature must recognize and respond to his evil: Does the earth greet him with poisonous shrubs? Do wholesome plants become malignant through his touch? Does the sun actually shine on him, or is he bathed in shadows? Will deadly nightshade, dogwood, and henbane—all herbs associated with witches' spells—grow from the site of his tomb? Hester can no longer recognize any goodness in this man, who seems to have forfeited all compassion and morality in his efforts to punish Dimmesdale.

Hester and Pearl in an F.O.C. Darley illustration.
Photo courtesy of The Darley Society, Inc.

Chapter XV provides a glimpse into Hester's married life that we haven't seen before. She remembers a time when Chillingworth would bask in her smiles in order to warm himself after the chill of his solitary, scholarly days. Now Hester believes that marrying him was a crime. In light of subsequent events, Chillingworth's desire to marry her seems like an evil in itself. The reader is led to consider whether Chillingworth committed a worse wrong by marrying Hester than she did by loving Dimmesdale. In its portrayal of Hester and Chillingworth, the novel appears to support Hester. While her crime has led her toward a virtuous and compassionate life, his has led only to hatred and destruction.

The connection between Pearl and nature is continued in this chapter. As mentioned previously, Pearl is associated with air and water—with all the changing moods of nature. She is wild and capricious and as wayward as the April breeze, so her mother finds the establishment of any lasting, passionate connection with her daughter difficult. Pearl has an almost inhuman lack of compassion for human emotion. She spends some time pelting sea birds with pebbles, but Pearl soon stops this activity for fear of harming one of the delicate birds, which is described to be as wild as Pearl herself. Instead, she gathers seaweed and drapes it around herself, showing that, like her mother, she has a gift for fashioning costumes. In this garb, Pearl becomes a mermaid, but one adorned with a green letter A. Her letter stands in contrast to her mother's: Green connotes fertility and growth, rather than the sin associated with her mother's scarlet letter.

Seeing Pearl's playful costume, Hester wonders if her daughter understands the meaning of the letter. She seems obsessed with the letter, always toying with it and attempting to discover its meaning. In her role as guardian of her parents' morality, Pearl insightfully connects her mother's letter with the minister putting his hand over his heart. Her very existence reminds her parents of their sins. Being a reminder seems to be her "appointed mission," but is this mission associated with justice and retribution, or might she also offer mercy to her mother's worn heart? The conversation in this chapter focuses primarily on the relationship between Pearl and the letter: Is the girl, like the letter, a punishment to Hester? Does she have any capacity for human emotion and sympathy, or is she as indifferent as the natural world to human troubles? The reader is left to wonder whether Pearl will one day bring comfort to her lonely mother, or if she will forever remind her mother of the pain of her sin.

Chapter XVI

Following her resolution to tell Dimmesdale the truth about Chillingworth, Hester must devise a way to meet the minister privately. She decides to meet him during one of his many walks in the woods. As she and Pearl wander down the path, Pearl is again thinking about her mother's letter and wonders if it will disappear when Pearl is a woman. Her mother tells her that the letter is the Black Man's mark, and Pearl wonders why Dimmesdale doesn't wear the mark of his sin on the outside, as her mother does.

CHAPTER XVI: A FOREST WALK

HESTER Prynne remained constant in her resolve to make known to Mr. Dimmesdale, at whatever risk of present pain or ulterior consequences, the true character of the man who had crept into his intimacy. For several days, however, she vainly sought an opportunity of addressing him in some of the meditative walks which she knew him to be in the habit of taking along the shores of the Peninsula, or on the wooded hills of the neighbouring country. There would have been no scandal, indeed, nor peril to the holy whiteness of the clergyman's good fame, had she visited him in his own study, where many a penitent, ere now, had confessed sins of perhaps as deep a dye as the one betokened by the scarlet letter. But, partly that she dreaded the secret or undisguised interference of old Roger Chillingworth, and partly that her conscious heart imparted suspicion where none could have been felt, and partly that both the minister and she would need the whole wide world to breathe in, while they talked together—for all these reasons Hester never thought of meeting him in any narrower privacy than beneath the open sky.

At last, while attending a sick chamber, whither the Reverend Mr. Dimmesdale had been summoned to make a prayer, she learnt that he had gone, the day before, to visit the **Apostle Eliot**, among his Indian converts. He would probably return by a certain hour in the afternoon of the morrow. Betimes, therefore, the next day, Hester took little Pearl—who was necessarily the companion of all her mother's expeditions, however inconvenient her presence—and set forth.

The road, after the two wayfarers had crossed from the Peninsula to the mainland, was no other than a foot-path. It straggled onward into the mystery of the primeval forest. This hemmed it in so narrowly, and stood so black and dense on either side, and disclosed such imperfect glimpses of the sky above, that, to Hester's mind, it imaged not amiss the moral wilderness in which she had so long been wandering. The day was chill and sombre. Overhead was a gray expanse of cloud, slightly stirred, however, by a breeze; so that a gleam of flickering sunshine might now and then be seen at its solitary play along the path. This flitting cheerfulness was always at the further extremity of some long vista through the forest. The sportive sunlight—feebly sportive, at best, in the predominant pensiveness of the day and scene—withdrew itself as they came nigh, and

Apostle Eliot: John Eliot (1604–1690) emigrated to Massachusetts in 1630. He is famous for preaching to the Native Americans in their own language beginning in 1648. In addition, he translated the Bible into native languages.

left the spots where it had danced the drearier, because they had hoped to find them bright.

"Mother," said little Pearl, "the sunshine does not love you. It runs away and hides itself, because it is afraid of something on your bosom. Now, see! There it is, playing a good way off. Stand you here, and let me run and catch it. I am but a child. It will not flee from me—for I wear nothing on my bosom yet!"

"Nor ever will, my child, I hope," said Hester.

"And why not, mother?" asked Pearl, stopping short, just at the beginning of her race. "Will not it come of its own accord when I am a woman grown?"

"Run away, child," answered her mother, "and catch the sunshine. It will soon be gone."

Pearl set forth at a great pace, and as Hester smiled to perceive, did actually catch the sunshine, and stood laughing in the midst of it, all brightened by its splendour, and scintillating with the vivacity excited by rapid motion. The light lingered about the lonely child, as if glad of such a playmate, until her mother had drawn almost nigh enough to step into the magic circle too.

"It will go now," said Pearl, shaking her head.

"See!" answered Hester, smiling. "Now I can stretch out my hand and grasp some of it."

As she attempted to do so, the sunshine vanished; or, to judge from the bright expression that was dancing on Pearl's features, her mother could have fancied that the child had absorbed it into herself, and would give it forth again, with a gleam about her path, as they should plunge into some gloomier shade. There was no other attribute that so much impressed her with a sense of new and untransmitted vigour in Pearl's nature, as this never failing vivacity of spirits: she had not the disease of sadness, which almost all children, in these latter days, inherit, with the scrofula, from the troubles of their ancestors. Perhaps this, too, was a disease, and but the reflex of the wild energy with which Hester had fought against her sorrows before Pearl's birth. It was certainly a doubtful charm, imparting a hard, metallic lustre to the child's character. She wanted—what some people want throughout life—a grief that should deeply touch her, and thus humanise and make her capable of sympathy. But there was time enough yet for little Pearl.

"Come, my child!" said Hester, looking about her from the spot where Pearl had stood still in the sunshine. "We will sit down a little way within the wood, and rest ourselves."

"I am not aweary, mother," replied the little girl. "But you may sit down, if you will tell me a story meanwhile."

"A story, child!" said Hester. "And about what?"

"Oh, a story about the Black Man," answered Pearl, taking hold of her mother's gown, and looking up, half earnestly, half mischievously, into her face.

"How he haunts this forest, and carries a book with him a big, heavy book, with iron clasps; and how this ugly Black Man offers his book and an iron pen to everybody that meets him here among the trees; and they are to write their names with their own blood; and then he sets his mark on their bosoms. Didst thou ever meet the Black Man, mother?"

"And who told you this story, Pearl," asked her mother, recognising a common superstition of the period.

"It was the old dame in the chimney corner, at the house where you watched last night," said the child. "But she fancied me asleep while she was talking of it. She said that a thousand and a thousand people had met him here, and had written in his book, and have his mark on them. And that ugly tempered lady, old Mistress Hibbins, was one. And, mother, the old dame said that this scarlet letter was the Black Man's mark on thee, and that it glows like a red flame when thou meetest him at midnight, here in the dark wood. Is it true, mother? And dost thou go to meet him in the nighttime?"

"Didst thou ever awake and find thy mother gone?" asked Hester. "Not that I remember," said the child. "If thou fearest to leave me in our cottage, thou mightest take me along with thee. I would very gladly go! But, mother, tell me now! Is there such a Black Man? And didst thou ever meet him? And is this his mark?"

"Wilt thou let me be at peace, if I once tell thee?" asked her mother.

"Yes, if thou tellest me all," answered Pearl.

"Once in my life I met the Black Man!" said her mother. "This scarlet letter is his mark!"

Thus conversing, they entered sufficiently deep into the wood to secure themselves from the observation of any casual passenger along the forest track. Here they sat down on a luxuriant heap of moss; which at some epoch of the preceding century, had been a gigantic pine, with its roots and trunk in the darksome shade, and its head aloft in the upper atmosphere. It was a little dell where they had seated themselves, with a leaf-strewn bank rising gently on either side, and a brook flowing through the midst, over a bed of fallen and drowned leaves. The trees impending over it had flung down great branches from time to time, which choked up the current, and compelled it to form eddies and black depths at some points; while, in its swifter and livelier passages there appeared a channel-way of pebbles, and brown, sparkling sand. Letting the eyes follow along the course of the stream, they could catch the reflected light from its water, at some short distance within the forest, but soon lost all traces of it amid the bewilderment of tree-trunks and underbush, and here and there a huge rock covered over with gray lichens. All these giant trees and boulders of granite seemed intent on making a mystery of the course of this small brook; fearing, perhaps, that, with its never-ceasing loquacity, it should whisper tales out of the heart of the old forest whence it flowed, or mirror its revelations on the smooth surface of a pool. Continually, indeed, as it stole onward, the streamlet kept up a babble, kind, quiet, soothing, but melancholy, like the voice of a young child that was spending its infancy without playfulness, and knew not how to be merry among sad acquaintance and events of sombre hue.

"Oh, brook! Oh, foolish and tiresome little brook!" cried Pearl, after listening awhile to its talk. "Why art thou so sad? Pluck up a spirit, and do not be all the time sighing and murmuring!"

But the brook, in the course of its little lifetime among the forest trees, had gone through so solemn an experience that it could not help talking about it, and seemed to have nothing else to say. Pearl resembled the brook, inasmuch as the current of her life gushed from a well-spring as mysterious, and had flowed through scenes shadowed as heavily with gloom. But, unlike the little stream, she danced and sparkled, and prattled airily along her course.

"What does this sad little brook say, mother?" inquired she.

"If thou hadst a sorrow of thine own, the brook might tell thee of it," answered her mother, "even as it is telling me of mine. But now, Pearl, I hear a footstep along the path, and the noise of one putting aside the branches. I would have thee betake thyself to play, and leave me to speak with him that comes yonder."

"Is it the Black Man?" asked Pearl.

"Wilt thou go and play, child?" repeated her mother. "But do not stray far into the wood. And take heed that thou come at my first call."

"Yes, mother," answered Pearl. "But if it be the Black Man, wilt thou not let me stay a moment, and look at him, with his big book under his arm?"

"Go, silly child!" said her mother impatiently. "It is no Black Man! Thou canst see him now, through the trees. It is the minister!"

"And so it is!" said the child. "And, mother, he has his hand over his heart! Is it because, when the minister wrote his name in the book, the Black Man set his mark in that place? But why does he not wear it outside his bosom, as thou dost, mother?"

"Go now, child, and thou shalt tease me as thou wilt another time," cried Hester Prynne. "But do not stray far. Keep where thou canst hear the babble of the brook."

The child went singing away, following up the current of the brook, and striving to mingle a more lightsome cadence with its melancholy voice. But the little stream would not be comforted, and still kept telling its unintelligible secret of some very mournful mystery that had happened— or making a prophetic lamentation about something that was yet to happen—within the verge of the dismal forest. So Pearl, who had enough of shadow in her own little life, chose to break off all acquaintance with this repining brook. She set herself, therefore, to gathering violets and wood-anemones, and some scarlet columbines that she found growing in the crevice of a high rock.

When her elf-child had departed, Hester Prynne made a step or two towards the track that led through the forest, but still remained under the deep shadow of the trees. She beheld the minister advancing along the path entirely alone, and leaning on a staff which he had cut by the wayside. He looked haggard and feeble, and betrayed a nerveless despondency in his air, which had never so remarkably characterised him in his walks about the settlement, nor in any other situation where he deemed himself liable to notice. Here it was wofully visible, in this intense seclusion of the forest, which of itself would have been a heavy trial to the spirits. There was a listlessness in his gait, as if he saw no reason for taking one step further, nor felt any desire to do so, but would have been glad, could he be glad of anything, to fling himself down at the root of the nearest tree, and lie there passive for evermore. The leaves might bestrew him, and the soil gradually accumulate and form a little hillock over his frame, no matter whether there were life in it or no. Death was too definite an object to be wished for or avoided.

To Hester's eye, the Reverend Mr. Dimmesdale exhibited no symptom of positive and vivacious suffering, except that, as little Pearl had remarked, he kept his hand over his heart.

COMMENTARY

This chapter sets the stage for Hester's revelation to Dimmesdale of Chillingworth's identity. Symbolism abounds, especially references to the forest and the brook, which both reflect Hester's mood. In planning her meeting with Dimmesdale, Hester realizes that she can only speak with him outdoors, where they'll have the "whole wide world to breathe in."

Hester and Pearl walk into the "mystery of the primeval forest," which grows black and dense on either side of the path. For Hester, the forest symbolizes the moral wilderness in which she has been living. To the Puritans, the forest is the home of the devil, who wanders its paths carrying a big book in which he tries to get people to write their names in blood. As they enter the woods, Pearl and Hester discuss the scarlet letter, which Pearl has been told is the symbol of her mother's meeting with the devil.

The dark gloom of the forest is lighted with a "flitting cheerfulness" that always seems a long way off, symbolizing the uncertain possibility of light and happiness coming into Hester's life. Pearl suggests that this sunshine seems to dislike Hester, because it runs and hides whenever she appears. Pearl foreshadows the difficulty Hester will have in overcoming her guilt in order to embrace happiness. As a pure and vivacious spirit, Pearl

is able to play in the light. Hester, shunned by the sun, has rejected her passion in favor of an isolated, intellectual life.

The giant trees and boulders in the dell where Hester and Pearl sit prevent them from seeing where a small brook runs, "fearing, perhaps, that, with its never-ceasing loquacity, it should whisper tales out of the heart of the old forest." The forest itself seems to support the telling and keeping of secrets.

The murmuring brook imparts a feeling of melancholy on the scene that Pearl dislikes, and she asks the brook to cheer up. Connected with nature throughout the novel, Pearl is here compared with the brook: Both of their lives gush from a spring of mystery, and both have flowed through "scenes shadowed as heavily with gloom." As a product of instinct and passion, Pearl has an innate connection with the vitality of the natural world, which blesses her just as the sunshine does at the beginning of the chapter. In rejecting her passion, Hester seems to have lost this connection with nature's energy. Instead, she relates only to the sad message of the brook. While the brook doesn't speak to Pearl, because she hasn't yet suffered—one message of this chapter is that Pearl needs to experience tragedy so that she will be humanized—it echoes the feeling in Hester's heart.

Chapter XVII

Dimmesdale sits with Hester in the forest. After they talk about their feelings of the past seven years, Hester reveals Chillingworth's identity. Dimmesdale is horrified, initially blaming her for his torture but then forgiving her. Hester encourages Dimmesdale to leave Boston—to move further into the wilderness or return to Europe. She vows to go with him.

CHAPTER XVII: THE PASTOR AND HIS PARISHIONER

SLOWLY as the minister walked, he had almost gone by before Hester Prynne could gather voice enough to attract his observation. At length she succeeded.

"Arthur Dimmesdale!" she said, faintly at first, then louder, but hoarsely—"Arthur Dimmesdale!"

"Who speaks?" answered the minister. Gathering himself quickly up, he stood more erect, like a man taken by surprise in a mood to which he was reluctant to have witnesses. Throwing his eyes anxiously in the direction of the voice, he indistinctly beheld a form under the trees, clad in garments so sombre, and so little relieved from the gray twilight into which the clouded sky and the heavy foliage had darkened the noontide, that he knew not whether it were a woman or a shadow. It may be that his pathway through life was haunted thus by a spectre that had stolen out from among his thoughts.

He made a step nigher, and discovered the scarlet letter.

"Hester! Hester Prynne!" said he. "Is it thou? Art thou in life?"

"Even so," she answered. "In such life as has been mine these seven years past! And thou, Arthur Dimmesdale, dost thou yet live?"

It was no wonder that they thus questioned one another's actual and bodily existence, and even doubted of their own. So strangely did they meet in the dim wood that it was like the first encounter in the world beyond the grave of two spirits who had been intimately connected in their former life, but now stood coldly shuddering in mutual dread, as not yet familiar with their state, nor wonted to the companionship of disembodied beings. Each a ghost, and awe-stricken at the other ghost! They were awe-stricken likewise at themselves, because the crisis flung back to them their consciousness, and revealed to each heart its history and experience, as life never does, except at such breathless epochs. The soul beheld its features in the mirror of the passing moment. It was with fear, and tremulously, and, as it were, by a slow, reluctant necessity, that Arthur Dimmesdale put forth his hand, chill as death, and touched the chill hand of Hester Prynne. The grasp, cold as it was, took away what was dreariest in the interview. They now felt themselves, at least, inhabitants of the same sphere.

Without a word more spoken—neither he nor she assuming the guidance, but with an unexpressed consent—they glided back into the shadow of the woods whence Hester had emerged, and sat down on the heap of moss where she and Pearl had before been sitting. When they found voice to speak, it was at first only to utter remarks and inquiries such as any two acquaintances might have made, about the gloomy sky, the threatening storm, and, next, the health of each. Thus they went onward, not boldly, but step by step, into the themes that were brooding deepest in their hearts. So long estranged by fate and circumstances, they needed something slight and casual to run before and throw open the doors of intercourse, so that their real thoughts might be led across the threshold.

After awhile, the minister fixed his eyes on Hester Prynne's.

"Hester," said he, "hast thou found peace?"

She smiled drearily, looking down upon her bosom.

"Hast thou?" she asked.

"None—nothing but despair!" he answered. "What else could I look for, being what I am, and leading such a life as mine? Were I an atheist—a man devoid of conscience—a wretch with coarse and brutal instincts— I might have found peace long ere now. Nay, I never should have lost it. But, as matters stand with my soul, whatever of good capacity there originally was in me, all of God's gifts that were the choicest have become the ministers of spiritual torment. Hester, I am most miserable!"

"The people reverence thee," said Hester. "And surely thou workest good among them! Doth this bring thee no comfort?"

"More misery, Hester!—Only the more misery!" answered the clergyman with a bitter smile. "As concerns the good which I may appear to do, I have no faith in it. It must needs be a delusion. What can a ruined soul like mine effect towards the redemption of other souls?—or a polluted soul towards their purification? And as for the people's reverence, would that it were turned to scorn and hatred! Canst thou deem it, Hester, a consolation that I must stand up in my pulpit, and meet so many eyes turned upward to my face, as if the light of heaven were beaming from it!—must see my flock hungry for the truth, and listening to my words as if a tongue of Pentecost were speaking!—and then look inward, and discern the black reality of what they idolise? I have laughed, in bitterness and agony of heart, at the contrast between what I seem and what I am! And Satan laughs at it!"

"You wrong yourself in this," said Hester gently.

"You have deeply and sorely repented. Your sin is left behind you in the days long past. Your present life is not less holy, in very truth, than it seems in people's eyes. Is there no reality in the penitence thus sealed and witnessed by good works? And wherefore should it not bring you peace?"

"No, Hester—no!" replied the clergyman. "There is no substance in it! It is cold and dead, and can do nothing for me! Of penance, I have had enough! Of penitence, there has been none! Else, I should long ago have thrown off these garments of mock holiness, and have shown myself to mankind as they will see me at the judgment-seat. Happy are you, Hester, that wear the scarlet letter openly upon your bosom! Mine burns in secret! Thou little knowest what a relief it is, after the torment of a seven years' cheat, to look into an eye that recognises me for what I am! Had I one friend—or were it my worst enemy!—to whom, when sickened with the praises of all other men, I could daily betake myself, and known as the vilest of all sinners, methinks my soul might keep itself alive thereby. Even thus much of truth would save me! But now, it is all falsehood!—all emptiness!—all death!"

Hester Prynne looked into his face, but hesitated to speak. Yet, uttering his long-restrained emotions so vehemently as he did, his words here offered her the very point of circumstances in which to interpose what she came to say. She conquered her fears, and spoke:

"Such a friend as thou hast even now wished for," said she, "with whom to weep over thy sin, thou hast in me, the partner of it!" Again she hesitated, but brought out the words with an effort "Thou hast long had such an enemy, and dwellest with him, under the same roof!"

The minister started to his feet, gasping for breath, and clutching at his heart, as if he would have torn it out of his bosom.

"Ha! What sayest thou?" cried he. "An enemy! And under mine own roof! What mean you?"

Hester Prynne was now fully sensible of the deep injury for which she was responsible to this unhappy man, in permitting him to lie for so many years, or, indeed, for a single moment, at the mercy of one whose purposes could not be other than malevolent. The very contiguity of his enemy, beneath whatever mask the latter might conceal himself, was enough to disturb the magnetic sphere of a being so sensitive as Arthur Dimmesdale. There had been a period when Hester was less alive to this consideration; or, perhaps, in the misanthropy of her own trouble, she left the minister to bear what she might picture to herself as a more tolerable doom. But of late, since the night of his vigil, all her sympathies towards him had been both softened and invigorated. She now read his heart more accurately. She doubted not that the continual presence of Roger Chillingworth—the secret poison of his malignity, infecting all the air about him—and his authorised interference, as a physician, with the minister's physical and spiritual infirmities—that these bad opportunities had been turned to a cruel purpose. By means of them, the sufferer's conscience had been kept in an irritated state, the tendency of which was, not to cure by wholesome pain, but to disorganize and corrupt his spiritual being. Its result, on earth, could hardly fail to be insanity, and hereafter, that eternal alienation from the Good and True, of which madness is perhaps the earthly type.

Such was the ruin to which she had brought the man, once—nay, why should we not speak it?—still so passionately loved! Hester felt that the sacrifice of the clergyman's good name, and death itself, as she had

already told Roger Chillingworth, would have been infinitely preferable
to the alternative which she had taken upon herself to choose. And now,
rather than have had this grievous wrong to confess, she would gladly
have laid down on the forest leaves, and died there, at Arthur Dimmesdale's feet.

"Oh, Arthur!" cried she, "forgive me! In all things else, I have striven to
be true! Truth was the one virtue which I might have held fast, and did
hold fast, through all extremity; save when thy good—thy life—thy
fame—were put in question! Then I consented to a deception. But a lie is
never good, even though death threaten on the other side! Dost thou not
see what I would say? That old man!—the physician!—he whom they
call Roger Chillingworth!—he was my husband!"

The minister looked at her for an instant, with all that violence of passion, which—intermixed in more shapes than one with his higher, purer,
softer qualities—was, in fact, the portion of him which the devil claimed,
and through which he sought to win the rest. Never was there a blacker
or a fiercer frown than Hester now encountered. For the brief space that
it lasted, it was a dark transfiguration. But his character had been so
much enfeebled by suffering, that even its lower energies were incapable
of more than a temporary struggle. He sank down on the ground, and
buried his face in his hands.

"I might have known it," murmured he. "I did know it! Was not the
secret told me, in the natural recoil of my heart at the first sight of him,
and as often as I have seen him since? Why did I not understand? Oh,
Hester Prynne, thou little, little knowest all the horror of this thing! And
the shame!—the indelicacy!—the horrible ugliness of this exposure of a
sick and guilty heart to the very eye that would gloat over it! Woman,
woman, thou art accountable for this!—I cannot forgive thee!"

"Thou shalt forgive me!" cried Hester, flinging herself on the fallen leaves
beside him. "Let God punish! Thou shalt forgive!"

With sudden and desperate tenderness she threw her arms around him,
and pressed his head against her bosom, little caring though his cheek
rested on the scarlet letter. He would have released himself, but strove in
vain to do so. Hester would not set him free, lest he should look her
sternly in the face. All the world had frowned on her—for seven long
years had it frowned upon this lonely woman—and still she bore it all,
nor ever once turned away her firm, sad eyes. Heaven, likewise, had
frowned upon her, and she had not died. But the frown of this pale,
weak, sinful, and sorrow-stricken man was what Hester could not bear,
and live!

"Wilt thou yet forgive me?" she repeated, over and over again. "Wilt
thou not frown? Wilt thou forgive?"

"I do forgive you, Hester," replied the minister at length, with a deep
utterance, out of an abyss of sadness, but no anger. "I freely forgive you
now. May God forgive us both. We are not, Hester, the worst sinners in

the world. There is one worse than even the polluted priest! That old man's revenge has been blacker than my sin. He has violated, in cold blood, the sanctity of a human heart. Thou and I, Hester, never did so!"

"Never, never!" whispered she. "What we did had a consecration of its own. We felt it so! We said so to each other. Hast thou forgotten it?"

"Hush, Hester!" said Arthur Dimmesdale, rising from the ground. "No; I have not forgotten!"

They sat down again, side by side, and hand clasped in hand, on the mossy trunk of the fallen tree. Life had never brought them a gloomier hour; it was the point whither their pathway had so long been tending, and darkening ever, as it stole along—and yet it unclosed a charm that made them linger upon it, and claim another, and another, and, after all, another moment. The forest was obscure around them, and creaked with a blast that was passing through it. The boughs were tossing heavily above their heads; while one solemn old tree groaned dolefully to another, as if telling the sad story of the pair that sat beneath, or constrained to forbode evil to come.

And yet they lingered. How dreary looked the forest-track that led backward to the settlement, where Hester Prynne must take up again the burden of her ignominy and the minister the hollow mockery of his good name! So they lingered an instant longer. No golden light had ever been so precious as the gloom of this dark forest. Here seen only by his eyes, the scarlet letter need not burn into the bosom of the fallen woman! Here seen only by her eyes, Arthur Dimmesdale, false to God and man, might be, for one moment true!

He started at a thought that suddenly occurred to him.

"Hester!" cried he, "here is a new horror! Roger Chillingworth knows your purpose to reveal his true character. Will he continue, then, to keep our secret? What will now be the course of his revenge?"

"There is a strange secrecy in his nature," replied Hester, thoughtfully; "and it has grown upon him by the hidden practices of his revenge. I deem it not likely that he will betray the secret. He will doubtless seek other means of satiating his dark passion."

"And I!—how am I to live longer, breathing the same air with this deadly enemy?" exclaimed Arthur Dimmesdale, shrinking within himself, and pressing his hand nervously against his heart—a gesture that had grown involuntary with him. "Think for me, Hester! Thou art strong. Resolve for me!"

"Thou must dwell no longer with this man," said Hester, slowly and firmly. "Thy heart must be no longer under his evil eye!"

"It were far worse than death!" replied the minister. "But how to avoid it? What choice remains to me? Shall I lie down again on these withered leaves, where I cast myself when thou didst tell me what he was? Must I sink down there, and die at once?"

"Alas! what a ruin has befallen thee!" said Hester, with the tears gushing into her eyes. "Wilt thou die for very weakness? There is no other cause!"

"The judgment of God is on me," answered the conscience-stricken priest. "It is too mighty for me to struggle with!"

"Heaven would show mercy," rejoined Hester, "hadst thou but the strength to take advantage of it."

"Be thou strong for me!" answered he. "Advise me what to do."

"Is the world, then, so narrow?" exclaimed Hester Prynne, fixing her deep eyes on the minister's, and instinctively exercising a magnetic power over a spirit so shattered and subdued that it could hardly hold itself erect. "Doth the universe lie within the compass of yonder town, which only a little time ago was but a leaf-strewn desert, as lonely as this around us? Whither leads yonder forest-track? Backward to the settlement, thou sayest! Yes; but, onward, too! Deeper it goes, and deeper into the wilderness, less plainly to be seen at every step; until some few miles hence the yellow leaves will show no vestige of the white man's tread. There thou art free! So brief a journey would bring thee from a world where thou hast been most wretched, to one where thou mayest still be happy! Is there not shade enough in all this boundless forest to hide thy heart from the gaze of Roger Chillingworth?"

"Yes, Hester; but only under the fallen leaves!" replied the minister, with a sad smile.

"Then there is the broad pathway of the sea!" continued Hester. "It brought thee hither. If thou so choose, it will bear thee back again. In our native land, whether in some remote rural village, or in vast London—or, surely, in Germany, in France, in pleasant Italy—thou wouldst be beyond his power and knowledge! And what hast thou to do with all these iron men, and their opinions? They have kept thy better part in bondage too long already!"

"It cannot be!" answered the minister, listening as if he were called upon to realise a dream. "I am powerless to go. Wretched and sinful as I am, I have had no other thought than to drag on my earthly existence in the sphere where Providence hath placed me. Lost as my own soul is, I would still do what I may for other human souls! I dare not quit my post, though an unfaithful sentinel, whose sure reward is death and dishonour, when his dreary watch shall come to an end!"

"Thou art crushed under this seven years' weight of misery," replied Hester, fervently resolved to buoy him up with her own energy. "But thou shalt leave it all behind thee! It shall not cumber thy steps, as thou treadest along the forest-path: neither shalt thou freight the ship with it, if thou prefer to cross the sea. Leave this wreck and ruin here where it hath happened. Meddle no more with it! Begin all anew! Hast thou exhausted possibility in the failure of this one trial? Not so! The future is yet full of trial and success. There is happiness to be enjoyed! There is good to be done! Exchange this false life of thine for a true one. Be, if thy spirit summon thee to such a mission, the teacher and apostle of the red men. Or, as is more thy nature, be a scholar and a sage among the wisest and the most renowned of the cultivated world. Preach! Write! Act! Do anything, save to lie down and die! Give up this name of Arthur Dimmesdale, and make thyself another, and a high one, such as thou canst wear without fear or shame. Why shouldst thou tarry so much as one other day in the torments that have so gnawed into thy life? that have made thee feeble to will and to do? that will leave thee powerless even to repent? Up, and away!"

"Oh, Hester!" cried Arthur Dimmesdale, in whose eyes a fitful light, kindled by her enthusiasm, flashed up and died away, "thou tellest of running a race to a man whose knees are tottering beneath him! I must die here! There is not the strength or courage left me to venture into the wide, strange, difficult world alone!"

It was the last expression of the despondency of a broken spirit. He lacked energy to grasp the better fortune that seemed within his reach.

He repeated the word. "Alone, Hester!"

"Thou shall not go alone!" answered she, in a deep whisper. Then, all was spoken!

COMMENTARY

Meeting in the shadowy world of the forest, Hester and Dimmesdale question each other's physical existence. The narrator likens their encounter to that of two spirits meeting in the world beyond the grave. Like Chillingworth, Dimmesdale seems to have lost all his best characteristics in the aftermath of the adultery, saying that "whatever of good capacity there originally was in me, all of God's gifts that were the choicest have become the ministers of spiritual torment." Because he is so aware of the contrast between what he is and what he appears to be, Dimmesdale cannot accept that he is doing any good work for his parishioners. Hester offers him the truth—that he has repented adequately, and

Dimmesdale and Hester in the forest, in an F.O.C. Darley illustration. Photo courtesy of The Darley Society, Inc.

his life is as holy as people give him credit for. But because he has been living a lie, Dimmesdale sees nothing but falsehood, emptiness, and death in his world. This conception of himself shows that Chillingworth's plan to "disorganize and corrupt" Dimmesdale's spiritual being is working. Dimmesdale's morbid thoughts seem to indicate that he is on the verge of insanity.

Although we don't learn much about the past relationship between Dimmesdale and Hester, the narrator does tell us that she passionately loves him still, despite all their hardships. She kept his secret to save his reputation and his life, but now she realizes that a lie is never profitable—that truth is preferable even when it leads to death. Learning the secret of Chillingworth's identity, Dimmesdale claims that the old man's sin is greater than theirs because he has "violated, in cold blood, the sanctity of a human heart," while their act, as Hester reminds him, had "a consecration of its own." This is a message repeated throughout the book: Chillingworth's deliberate destruction of Dimmesdale's life makes him more culpable than the lovers, whose sin consisted of following their natural passion.

While they are together in the forest, away from society and its rules, the former lovers can be authentic: Hester does not have to play the role of the fallen woman, and Dimmesdale does not have to lie. But as their true natures emerge, the differences between Dimmesdale and Hester become apparent. While she has grown stronger through adversity, he has grown weaker. He is now incapable of even thinking for himself; he needs Hester to advise him on a plan to avoid Chillingworth.

Hester offers Dimmesdale two suggestions. Critiquing the "iron men" of the New World community—the Puritan fathers whose inflexibility does not allow them to see beyond simple dichotomies of right and wrong—Hester suggests that a brief journey could take them deeper into the wilderness, to places that have no interaction with the Puritans. On the other hand, they could return to England, where the minister could put his intellectual attainments to good use. Why should either Dimmesdale or Hester choose to live any longer under the Puritans' domination? But despite the obvious solution of leaving Boston, the question lingers whether they can escape the laws created by these iron men. Is Dimmesdale too immersed in the Puritan way of thinking to free himself from his guilt? Can the minister attain freedom if he doesn't confess his sin, or will he be forever immersed in remorse? The novel asks whether it is better to run away from troubles or to face them directly, and it doesn't offer a definitive answer to the question.

Dimmesdale confesses that he has remained in Boston in part because he still hopes to do God's work, but mostly because of fear and apathy: He lacks the energy or the courage to venture into the world alone. Hester encourages him to leave the old, false life for a new one somewhere else, some place where happiness may be possible: "Do any thing, save to lie down and die!" This message of strength seems to be Hester's motto. She even suggests that Dimmesdale give up his current name and choose another, one that he can wear without shame. But her suggestion raises the question of whether, in relinquishing his identity, Dimmesdale would be as false as Chillingworth. Wouldn't this action dim his identity even more? In Hester's opinion, their suffering has served to cleanse them both from their sin, so they are free to begin life again. During their interaction, Hester's long dormant love for Dimmesdale is reawakened, and she vows to accompany him wherever he might go.

Chapter XVIII

Taking courage from Hester's strength, Dimmesdale decides that leaving the Puritan colony will be his best option, but only if she accompanies him. Hester feels so free in the beauty of the forest that she removes her scarlet letter and throws it on the ground. She also lets down her hair, and her beauty is restored. Now that they are reunited, Hester wants Dimmesdale to meet Pearl.

CHAPTER XVIII: A FLOOD OF SUNSHINE

ARTHUR Dimmesdale gazed into Hester's face with a look in which hope and joy shone out, indeed, but with fear betwixt them, and a kind of horror at her boldness, who had spoken what he vaguely hinted at, but dared not speak.

But Hester Prynne, with a mind of native courage and activity, and for so long a period not merely estranged, but outlawed from society, had habituated herself to such latitude of speculation as was altogether foreign to the clergyman. She had wandered, without rule or guidance, in a moral wilderness, as vast, as intricate, and shadowy as the untamed forest, amid the gloom of which they were now holding a colloquy that was to decide their fate. Her intellect and heart had their home, as it were, in desert places, where she roamed as freely as the wild Indian in his woods. For years past she had looked from this estranged point of view at human institutions, and whatever priests or legislators had established; criticising all with hardly more reverence than the Indian would feel for the clerical band, the judicial robe, the pillory, the gallows, the fireside, or the church. The tendency of her fate and fortunes had been to set her free. The scarlet letter was her passport into regions where other women dared not tread. Shame, Despair, Solitude! These had been her teachers—stern and wild ones—and they had made her strong, but taught her much amiss.

The minister, on the other hand, had never gone through an experience calculated to lead him beyond the scope of generally received laws; although, in a single instance, he had so fearfully transgressed one of the most sacred of them. But this had been a sin of passion, not of principle, nor even purpose. Since that wretched epoch, he had watched with morbid zeal and minuteness, not his acts—for those it was easy to arrange—but each breath of emotion, and his every thought. At the head of the social system, as the clergymen of that day stood, he was only the more trammelled by its regulations, its principles, and even its prejudices. As a priest, the framework of his order inevitably hemmed him in. As a man who had once sinned, but who kept his conscience all alive and painfully sensitive by the fretting of an unhealed wound, he might have been supposed safer within the line of virtue than if he had never sinned at all.

Thus we seem to see that, as regarded Hester Prynne, the whole seven years of outlaw and ignominy had been little other than a preparation for this very hour. But Arthur Dimmesdale! Were such a man once more to fall, what plea could be urged in extenuation of his crime? None; unless it avail him somewhat that he was broken down by long and exquisite suffering; that his mind was darkened and confused by the very remorse which harrowed it; that, between fleeing as an avowed criminal, and remaining as a hypocrite, conscience might find it hard to strike the balance; that it was human to avoid the peril of death and infamy, and the inscrutable machinations of an enemy; that, finally, to this poor pilgrim, on his dreary and desert path, faint, sick, miserable, there appeared a glimpse of human affection and sympathy, a new life, and a true one, in exchange for the heavy doom which he was now expiating. And be the stern and sad truth spoken, that the breach which guilt has once made into the human soul is never, in this mortal state, repaired. It may be watched and guarded, so that the enemy shall not force his way again into the citadel, and might even in his subsequent assaults, select some other avenue, in preference to that where he had formerly succeeded. But there is still the ruined wall, and near it the stealthy tread of the foe that would win over again his unforgotten triumph.

The struggle, if there were one, need not be described. Let it suffice that the clergyman resolved to flee, and not alone.

"If in all these past seven years," thought he, "I could recall one instant of peace or hope, I would yet endure, for the sake of that earnest of Heaven's mercy. But now—since I am irrevocably doomed—wherefore should I not snatch the solace allowed to the condemned culprit before his execution? Or, if this be the path to a better life, as Hester would persuade me, I surely give up no fairer prospect by pursuing it! Neither can I any longer live without her companionship; so powerful is she to sustain—so tender to soothe! O Thou to whom I dare not lift mine eyes, wilt Thou yet pardon me?"

"Thou wilt go!" said Hester calmly, as he met her glance.

The decision once made, a glow of strange enjoyment threw its flickering brightness over the trouble of his breast. It was the exhilarating effect—upon a prisoner just escaped from the dungeon of his own heart—of breathing the wild, free atmosphere of an unredeemed, unchristianised, lawless region. His spirit rose, as it were, with a bound, and attained a nearer prospect of the sky, than throughout all the misery which had kept him grovelling on the earth. Of a deeply religious temperament, there was inevitably a tinge of the devotional in his mood.

"Do I feel joy again?" cried he, wondering at himself. "Methought the germ of it was dead in me! Oh, Hester, thou art my better angel! I seem to have flung myself—sick, sin-stained, and sorrow-blackened—down upon these forest leaves, and to have risen up all made anew, and with new powers to glorify Him that hath been merciful! This is already the better life! Why did we not find it sooner?"

"Let us not look back," answered Hester Prynne. "The past is gone! Wherefore should we linger upon it now? See! With this symbol I undo it all, and make it as if it had never been!"

So speaking, she undid the clasp that fastened the scarlet letter, and, taking it from her bosom, threw it to a distance among the withered leaves. The mystic token alighted on the hither verge of the stream. With a hand's-breadth further flight, it would have fallen into the water, and have given the little brook another woe to carry onward, besides the unintelligible tale which it still kept murmuring about. But there lay the embroidered letter, glittering like a lost jewel, which some ill-fated wanderer might pick up, and thenceforth be haunted by strange phantoms of guilt, sinkings of the heart, and unaccountable misfortune.

The stigma gone, Hester heaved a long, deep sigh, in which the burden of shame and anguish departed from her spirit. O exquisite relief! She had not known the weight until she felt the freedom! By another impulse, she took off the formal cap that confined her hair, and down it fell upon her shoulders, dark and rich, with at once a shadow and a light in its abundance, and imparting the charm of softness to her features. There played around her mouth, and beamed out of her eyes, a radiant and tender smile, that seemed gushing from the very heart of womanhood. A crimson flush was glowing on her cheek, that had been long so pale. Her sex, her youth, and the whole richness of her beauty, came back from what men call the irrevocable past, and clustered themselves with her maiden hope, and a happiness before unknown, within the magic circle of this hour. And, as if the gloom of the earth and sky had been but the effluence of these two mortal hearts, it vanished with their sorrow. All at once, as with a sudden smile of heaven, forth burst the sunshine, pouring a very flood into the obscure forest, gladdening each green leaf, transmuting the yellow fallen ones to gold, and gleaming adown the gray trunks of the solemn trees. The objects that had made a shadow hitherto, embodied the brightness now. The course of the little brook might be traced by its merry gleam afar into the wood's heart of mystery, which had become a mystery of joy.

Such was the sympathy of Nature—that wild, heathen Nature of the forest, never subjugated by human law, nor illumined by higher truth—with the bliss of these two spirits! Love, whether newly-born, or aroused from a death-like slumber, must always create a sunshine, filling the heart so full of radiance, that it overflows upon the outward world. Had the forest still kept its gloom, it would have been bright in Hester's eyes, and bright in Arthur Dimmesdale's!

Hester looked at him with a thrill of another joy.

"Thou must know Pearl!" said she. "Our little Pearl! Thou hast seen her—yes, I know it!—but thou wilt see her now with other eyes. She is a strange child! I hardly comprehend her! But thou wilt love her dearly, as I do, and wilt advise me how to deal with her!"

"Dost thou think the child will be glad to know me?" asked the minister, somewhat uneasily. "I have long shrunk from children, because they often show a distrust—a backwardness to be familiar with me. I have even been afraid of little Pearl!"

"Ah, that was sad!" answered the mother. "But she will love thee dearly, and thou her. She is not far off. I will call her. Pearl! Pearl!"

"I see the child," observed the minister. "Yonder she is, standing in a streak of sunshine, a good way off, on the other side of the brook. So thou thinkest the child will love me?"

Hester smiled, and again called to Pearl, who was visible at some distance, as the minister had described her, like a bright-apparelled vision in a sunbeam, which fell down upon her through an arch of boughs. The ray quivered to and fro, making her figure dim or distinct—now like a real child, now like a child's spirit—as the splendour went and came again. She heard her mother's voice, and approached slowly through the forest.

Pearl had not found the hour pass wearisomely while her mother sat talking with the clergyman. The great black forest—stern as it showed itself to those who brought the guilt and troubles of the world into its bosom—became the playmate of the lonely infant, as well as it knew how. Sombre as it was, it put on the kindest of its moods to welcome her. It offered her the partridge-berries, the growth of the preceding autumn, but ripening only in the spring, and now red as drops of blood upon the withered leaves. These Pearl gathered, and was pleased with their wild flavour. The small denizens of the wilderness hardly took pains to move out of her path. A partridge, indeed, with a brood of ten behind her, ran forward threateningly, but soon repented of her fierceness, and clucked to her young ones not to be afraid. A pigeon, alone on a low branch, allowed Pearl to come beneath, and uttered a sound as much of greeting as alarm. A squirrel, from the lofty depths of his domestic tree, chattered either in anger or merriment—for the squirrel is such a choleric and humorous little personage, that it is hard to distinguish between his moods—so he chattered at the child, and flung down a nut upon her head. It was a last year's nut, and already gnawed by his sharp tooth. A fox, startled from his sleep by her light footstep on the leaves, looked inquisitively at Pearl, as doubting whether it were better to steal off, or renew his nap on the same spot. A wolf, it is said—but here the tale has surely lapsed into the improbable—came up and smelt of Pearl's robe, and offered his savage head to be patted by her hand. The truth seems to be, however, that the mother-forest, and these wild things which it nourished, all recognised a kindred wilderness in the human child.

And she was gentler here than in the grassy-margined streets of the settlement, or in her mother's cottage. The flowers appeared to know it, and one and another whispered as she passed, "Adorn thyself with me, thou beautiful child, adorn thyself with me!"—and, to please them, Pearl gathered the violets, and anemones, and columbines, and some twigs of the freshest green, which the old trees held down before her eyes. With these she decorated her hair and her young waist, and became a nymph child, or an infant dryad, or whatever else was in closest sympathy with the antique wood. In such guise had Pearl adorned herself, when she heard her mother's voice, and came slowly back.

Slowly—for she saw the clergyman!

COMMENTARY

Arthur Dimmesdale is shocked by Hester's boldness: In suggesting that they leave the Puritan colony, she spoke the words he only dared think. The beginning of Chapter XVIII develops more fully the differences between these two characters. Hester has courage and a longing for freedom that Dimmesdale seems to lack. Her courage has been strengthened by her long isolation, which has led her to develop ideas the minister cannot even imagine. Hester has become critical of all "human institutions"—legal, religious, and otherwise—viewing them with disdain and distrust in much the same way any disenfranchised person might. As the narrator tells us, "The scarlet letter was her passport into regions where other women dared not tread." Her thoughts demonstrate that she wanders a moral wilderness, where she has gone without guidance and without the rules of the Puritan fathers to guide her. Her ideas have become as vast, complicated, and shadowy as the forest itself.

While Hester's intellect roams through wild places, Dimmesdale's remains in the relative security of conventional thoughts and ideas. Even though these ideas have resulted in his guilt and suffering, he refuses to relinquish them. The narrator emphasizes that Dimmesdale's one transgression emerged from passion, which is somewhat better than if the sin was fueled by principle. How, then, given Dimmesdale's guilt over a sin of passion, could he justify to himself a second fall from grace—the deliberate choice of a lifestyle he considers sinful? The narrator provides a voice of compassion and human sympathy that contrasts with Dimmesdale's harsh judgments of himself. In the narrator's opinion, all humans need affection and sympathy, and everyone needs to live in a way that feels true. The question hanging in the air is which seems to be the better option for Dimmesdale: pursuing a loving life with Hester and Pearl, or continuing on the path he has chosen for himself in Boston?

Realizing that no hope or peace is available to him in the colony, Dimmesdale resolves to leave with Hester, partially because he recognizes that her strength will soothe and sustain him. The imagery used to describe Dimmesdale's emotions after making this decision suggests that he has chosen wisely. Thinking about the possibility of beginning a new life, Dimmesdale feels he is breathing a "wild, free atmosphere of an unredeemed, unchristianized, lawless region." Earlier in the book, he had felt a similar sense of fresh air when discussing Chillingworth's radical ideas. But here these feelings lead him to visions of the sky, heaven, and joy. Hester has become

Hester removes the letter for the first time in the novel.

his "angel," as the meaning of her scarlet A is transformed again. Ironically, through the "wild lawless" air of Hester's ideas, Dimmesdale's powers are renewed, and he is enabled to praise God more fully.

For the first time in the novel, Hester removes the scarlet letter from her breast. She throws it into the withered leaves, as if the natural world could somehow erase its evil. It lies on the ground like a "lost jewel," but one that no one would want to discover because the letter can cause only guilt and misfortune. After removing the heavy weight of this talisman, Hester experiences a symbolic rebirth that seems to match Dimmesdale's. In honor of this change, she lets her hair down, and her beauty is renewed. Even nature shows its sympathy for these lovers, as gloominess disappears and the sun shines down. Having resumed her passionate nature, Hester is again entitled to enjoy the sun's blessings. Like Pearl, she is now "bright-apparelled" by the sun. In the view of the narrator, love always creates sunshine by filling the heart with radiance that overflows into the world. While the laws of the Puritans blight passion and imagination, nature renews the human capacity for joy and creativity. The novel takes the side of vivacity over austerity, as is seen through the dichotomy it establishes between human institutions and the natural world—between Pearl's lawless energy and the dull, dreary Puritan leaders.

Although the forest is associated with guilt and sin to those who bring their own troubles to it, for innocent Pearl, it is a welcoming playmate. The birds and animals seem to recognize her as one of themselves. In the fairy-tale ending of this chapter, the animals of the forest each greet Pearl in some way; even the wolf supposedly allows her to pat its head. By creating this fairy-tale moment, the narrator surrounds Pearl in difference, symbolically demonstrating that wild inhabitants of the "mother-forest" seem to recognize a similar wildness in Pearl. When in the woods, Pearl's personality grows gentle, and even the flowers call out to her, asking her to enhance her beauty with theirs. In a previous chapter, Pearl wrapped herself with seaweed, showing her affinity with the mermaids; in this chapter, she adorns herself with the flowers growing in the forest, like a wood nymph. This time she doesn't add the letter A to her costume, perhaps reflecting her pure affinity with the natural world in this scene. After enjoying the bounties of nature, Pearl is not anxious to return to the civilized world, represented by her mother and the clergyman. She returns to them slowly, primarily because of the Puritan mistrust of nature that Dimmesdale represents.

Chapter XIX

Dimmesdale believes that children dislike him, so he is anxious before meeting Pearl. Seeing Hester's scarlet letter on the ground and her hair down, Pearl becomes hysterical. Hester understands that children are often frightened by change, so she quickly replaces the letter on her dress. Pearl tells Dimmesdale that she would like him to acknowledge her in public, but Hester tells her this can't happen immediately. When Dimmesdale kisses her, Pearl rushes to the brook to wash the kiss away.

CHAPTER XIX: THE CHILD AT THE BROOK-SIDE

"THOU will love her dearly," repeated Hester Prynne, as she and the minister sat watching little Pearl. "Dost thou not think her beautiful? And see with what natural skill she has made those simple flowers adorn her! Had she gathered pearls, and diamonds, and rubies in the wood, they could not have become her better! She is a splendid child! But I know whose brow she has!"

"Dost thou know, Hester," said Arthur Dimmesdale, with an unquiet smile, "that this dear child, tripping about always at thy side, hath caused me many an alarm? Methought—oh, Hester, what a thought is that, and how terrible to dread it!—that my own features were partly repeated in her face, and so strikingly that the world might see them! But she is mostly thine!"

"No, no! Not mostly!" answered the mother, with a tender smile. "A little longer, and thou needest not to be afraid to trace whose child she is. But how strangely beautiful she looks with those wild flowers in her hair! It is as if one of the fairies, whom we left in dear old England, had decked her out to meet us."

It was with a feeling which neither of them had ever before experienced, that they sat and watched Pearl's slow advance. In her was visible the tie that united them. She had been offered to the world, these seven past years, as the living hieroglyphic, in which was revealed the secret they so darkly sought to hide—all written in this symbol—all plainly manifest—had there been a prophet or magician skilled to read the character of flame! And Pearl was the oneness of their being. Be the foregone evil what it might, how could they doubt that their earthly lives and future destinies were conjoined when they beheld at once the material union, and the spiritual idea, in whom they met, and were to dwell immortally together; thoughts like these—and perhaps other thoughts, which they did not acknowledge or define—threw an awe about the child as she came onward.

"Let her see nothing strange—no passion or eagerness—in thy way of accosting her," whispered Hester. "Our Pearl is a fitful and fantastic little elf sometimes. Especially she is generally intolerant of emotion, when she does not fully comprehend the why and wherefore. But the child hath strong affections! She loves me, and will love thee!"

"Thou canst not think," said the minister, glancing aside at Hester Prynne, "how my heart dreads this interview, and yearns for it! But, in truth, as I already told thee, children are not readily won to be familiar with me. They will not climb my knee, nor prattle in my ear, nor answer to my smile, but stand apart, and eye me strangely. Even little babes, when I take them in my arms, weep bitterly. Yet Pearl, twice in her little lifetime, hath been kind to me! The first time—thou knowest it well! The last was when thou ledst her with thee to the house of yonder stern old Governor."

"And thou didst plead so bravely in her behalf and mine!" answered the mother. "I remember it; and so shall little Pearl. Fear nothing. She may be strange and shy at first, but will soon learn to love thee!"

By this time Pearl had reached the margin of the brook, and stood on the further side, gazing silently at Hester and the clergyman, who still sat together on the mossy tree-trunk waiting to receive her. Just where she had paused, the brook chanced to form a pool so smooth and quiet that it reflected a perfect image of her little figure, with all the brilliant picturesqueness of her beauty, in its adornment of flowers and wreathed foliage, but more refined and spiritualized than the reality. This image, so nearly identical with the living Pearl, seemed to communicate somewhat of its own shadowy and intangible quality to the child herself. It was strange, the way in which Pearl stood, looking so steadfastly at them through the dim medium of the forest gloom, herself, meanwhile, all glorified with a ray of sunshine, that was attracted thitherward as by a certain sympathy. In the brook beneath stood another child—another and the same—with likewise its ray of golden light. Hester felt herself, in some indistinct and tantalizing manner, estranged from Pearl, as if the child, in her lonely ramble through the forest, had strayed out of the sphere in which she and her mother dwelt together, and was now vainly seeking to return to it.

There were both truth and error in the impression; the child and mother were estranged, but through Hester's fault, not Pearl's. Since the latter rambled from her side, another inmate had been admitted within the circle of the mother's feelings, and so modified the aspect of them all, that Pearl, the returning wanderer, could not find her wonted place, and hardly knew where she was.

"I have a strange fancy," observed the sensitive minister, "that this brook is the boundary between two worlds, and that thou canst never meet thy Pearl again. Or is she an elfish spirit, who, as the legends of our childhood taught us, is forbidden to cross a running stream? Pray hasten her, for this delay has already imparted a tremor to my nerves."

"Come, dearest child!" said Hester encouragingly, and stretching out both her arms. "How slow thou art! When hast thou been so sluggish before now? Here is a friend of mine, who must be thy friend also. Thou wilt have twice as much love henceforward as thy mother alone could give thee! Leap across the brook and come to us. Thou canst leap like a young deer!"

Pearl, without responding in any manner to these honey-sweet expressions, remained on the other side of the brook. Now she fixed her bright wild eyes on her mother, now on the minister, and now included them both in the same glance, as if to detect and explain to herself the relation which they bore to one another. For some unaccountable reason, as Arthur Dimmesdale felt the child's eyes upon himself, his hand—with that gesture so habitual as to have become involuntary—stole over his heart. At length, assuming a singular air of authority, Pearl stretched out her hand, with the small forefinger extended, and pointing evidently towards her mother's breast. And beneath, in the mirror of the brook, there was the flower-girdled and sunny image of little Pearl, pointing her small forefinger too.

"Thou strange child! why dost thou not come to me?" exclaimed Hester.

Pearl still pointed with her forefinger, and a frown gathered on her brow—the more impressive from the childish, the almost baby-like aspect of the features that conveyed it. As her mother still kept beckoning to her, and arraying her face in a holiday suit of unaccustomed smiles, the child stamped her foot with a yet more imperious look and gesture. In the brook, again, was the fantastic beauty of the image, with its reflected frown, its pointed finger, and imperious gesture, giving emphasis to the aspect of little Pearl.

"Hasten, Pearl, or I shall be angry with thee!" cried Hester Prynne, who, however, inured to such behaviour on the elf-child's part at other seasons, was naturally anxious for a more seemly deportment now. "Leap across the brook, naughty child, and run hither! Else I must come to thee!"

But Pearl, not a whit startled at her mother's threats any more than mollified by her entreaties, now suddenly burst into a fit of passion, gesticulating violently, and throwing her small figure into the most extravagant contortions She accompanied this wild outbreak with piercing shrieks, which the woods reverberated on all sides, so that, alone as she was in her childish and unreasonable wrath, it seemed as if a hidden multitude were lending her their sympathy and encouragement. Seen in the brook once more was the shadowy wrath of Pearl's image, crowned and girdled with flowers, but stamping its foot, wildly gesticulating, and, in the midst of all, still pointing its small forefinger at Hester's bosom.

"I see what ails the child," whispered Hester to the clergyman, and turning pale in spite of a strong effort to conceal her trouble and annoyance, "Children will not abide any, the slightest, change in the accustomed aspect of things that are daily before their eyes. Pearl misses something that she has always seen me wear!"

"I pray you," answered the minister, "if thou hast any means of pacifying the child, do it forthwith! Save it were the cankered wrath of an old witch like Mistress Hibbins," added he, attempting to smile, "I know nothing that I would not sooner encounter than this passion in a child. In Pearl's young beauty, as in the wrinkled witch, it has a preternatural effect. Pacify her if thou lovest me!"

Hester turned again towards Pearl with a crimson blush upon her cheek, a conscious glance aside at the clergyman, and then a heavy sigh, while, even before she had time to speak, the blush yielded to a deadly pallor.

"Pearl," said she sadly, "look down at thy feet! There!—before thee!—on the hither side of the brook!"

The child turned her eyes to the point indicated, and there lay the scarlet letter so close upon the margin of the stream that the gold embroidery was reflected in it.

"Bring it hither!" said Hester.

"Come thou and take it up!" answered Pearl.

"Was ever such a child!" observed Hester aside to the minister. "Oh, I have much to tell thee about her! But, in very truth, she is right as regards this hateful token. I must bear its torture yet a little longer—only a few days longer—until we shall have left this region, and look back hither as to a land which we have dreamed of. The forest cannot hide it! The mid-ocean shall take it from my hand, and swallow it up for ever!"

With these words she advanced to the margin of the brook, took up the scarlet letter, and fastened it again into her bosom. Hopefully, but a moment ago, as Hester had spoken of drowning it in the deep sea, there was a sense of inevitable doom upon her as she thus received back this deadly symbol from the hand of fate. She had flung it into infinite space!—she had drawn an hour's free breath! and here again was the scarlet misery glittering on the old spot! So it ever is, whether thus typified or no, that an evil deed invests itself with the character of doom. Hester next gathered up the heavy tresses of her hair and confined them beneath her cap. As if there were a withering spell in the sad letter, her beauty, the warmth and richness of her womanhood, departed like fading sunshine, and a gray shadow seemed to fall across her.

When the dreary change was wrought, she extended her hand to Pearl.

"Dost thou know thy mother now, child?" asked she, reproachfully, but with a subdued tone. "Wilt thou come across the brook, and own thy mother, now that she has her shame upon her—now that she is sad?"

"Yes; now I will!" answered the child, bounding across the brook, and clasping Hester in her arms. "Now thou art my mother indeed! and I am thy little Pearl!"

In a mood of tenderness that was not usual with her, she drew down her mother's head, and kissed her brow and both her cheeks. But then—by a kind of necessity that always impelled this child to alloy whatever comfort she might chance to give with a throb of anguish—Pearl put up her mouth and kissed the scarlet letter, too.

"That was not kind!" said Hester. "When thou hast shown me a little love, thou mockest me!"

"Why doth the minister sit yonder?" asked Pearl.

"He waits to welcome thee," replied her mother. "Come thou, and entreat his blessing! He loves thee, my little Pearl, and loves thy mother, too. Wilt thou not love him? Come he longs to greet thee!"

"Doth he love us?" said Pearl, looking up with acute intelligence into her mother's face. "Will he go back with us, hand in hand, we three together, into the town?"

"Not now, my child," answered Hester. "But in days to come he will walk hand in hand with us. We will have a home and fireside of our own; and thou shalt sit upon his knee; and he will teach thee many things, and love thee dearly. Thou wilt love him—wilt thou not?"

"And will he always keep his hand over his heart?" inquired Pearl.

"Foolish child, what a question is that!" exclaimed her mother. "Come, and ask his blessing!"

But, whether influenced by the jealousy that seems instinctive with every petted child towards a dangerous rival, or from whatever caprice of her freakish nature, Pearl would show no favour to the clergyman. It was only by an exertion of force that her mother brought her up to him, hanging back, and manifesting her reluctance by odd grimaces; of which, ever since her babyhood, she had possessed a singular variety, and could transform her mobile physiognomy into a series of different aspects, with a new mischief in them, each and all. The minister—painfully embarrassed, but hoping that a kiss might prove a talisman to admit him into the child's kindlier regards—bent forward, and impressed one on her brow. Hereupon, Pearl broke away from her mother, and, running to the brook, stooped over it, and bathed her forehead, until the unwelcome kiss was quite washed off and diffused through a long lapse of the gliding water. She then remained apart, silently watching Hester and the clergyman; while they talked together and made such arrangements as were suggested by their new position and the purposes soon to be fulfilled.

And now this fateful interview had come to a close. The dell was to be left in solitude among its dark, old trees, which, with their multitudinous tongues, would whisper long of what had passed there, and no mortal be the wiser. And the melancholy brook would add this other tale to the mystery with which its little heart was already overburdened, and whereof it still kept up a murmuring babble, with not a whit more cheerfulness of tone than for ages heretofore.

COMMENTARY

As Pearl walks toward her mother and Dimmesdale in the forest, Hester emphasizes Pearl's beauty and points out her artistic ability to adorn herself in flowers. Dimmesdale, however, feels only fear. Pearl threatens him partly because her energy seems wild to the sedate, unhealthy minister, and partly because he fears that he— and everyone else—can recognize his own features in her face. As Dimmesdale notes, Pearl is primarily Hester's child; her wild, creative nature seems scarcely to reflect her paternity. The only characteristic she appears to have inherited from Dimmesdale is his animal passion, the one trait he stridently tries to repress.

Pearl's appearance at the beginning of this chapter, when she is decked with wild flowers, again points to a contrast between the old and the new worlds as she is compared to one of the fairies that the Puritans thought to have left back in old England. The narrator's differentiation between Old and New Worlds suggests that the Old World has a vibrancy and artistry lacking in the colonies. England appears to be a safe haven for free spirits—a magical, mystical world in which the forbidden love of Hester and Dimmesdale can flourish.

Pearl is also described as the "living hieroglyphic" that reveals the secret union between Hester and Dimmesdale. Fortunately, no prophet or magician is available to read this "character of flame," a character of passion and energy, except perhaps for the novel's resident magician, Chillingworth. But even Chillingworth cannot pin down exactly what Pearl represents. As Hawthorne emphasizes in the meteor shower scene, symbols do not contain a singular, umambiguous message. Instead, their meaning is created through the interaction of viewer and symbol. Although Pearl is the symbol of her parents' union, the meaning of this union is open for interpretation. Is she a sign of evil, as the Puritans believe? Or does she symbolize the beauty of love and passion?

Just as Pearl's image was reflected in a pool of water when she played near the ocean, her image is now reflected in a calm pool formed by the babbling brook. In this mirror, Pearl appears almost identical to her real life self, except for the addition of a "shadowy and intangible quality" emerging from the water itself. This image emphasizes Pearl's almost perfect affinity with the natural world, from which she seems inseparable. Hester feels "estranged" from her child, as if Pearl has become somehow isolated during her walk through the woods— so purely a part of the natural world that she cannot return to the human. Dimmesdale notices this distance, defining the brook as a boundary between worlds that separate Pearl from her mother.

But the narrator reminds us that the estrangement is Hester's fault, not Pearl's: The presence of the minister has separated Pearl from her mother. The absence of the scarlet letter from her mother's breast also accounts for some of Pearl's anxiety. She will not cross the brook until her mother reattaches the letter to her breast. Thus, although Pearl appears as an embodiment of nature, she acts also as a curb to her mother's passion, insisting that her mother resume her place as a woman marked for her sin.

In this F.O.C. Darley illustration, Pearl insists that Hester reattach the letter. Photo courtesy of The Darley Society, Inc.

Fastening the letter back into place, Hester sees that her daughter is correct: Hester cannot discard the letter as long as she remains in a part of the New World, because even the forest will not hide her sin. Only the ocean is vast enough to swallow the letter's negative energy and hide it forever. Yet while Hester recognizes the need to return to the Old World, when she places the letter back on her breast, the hand of fate seems to be nixing all of Dimmesdale's and Hester's plans of escape. The letter has taken on "the character of doom," and it prevents Hester from starting life anew.

After putting the letter back on her chest, Hester also tucks her hair back under her cap, and her beauty disappears. Now that Hester is sad and gray as before, Pearl accepts her as a mother. After kissing her, Pearl kisses the letter also, an action that angers Hester who feels that her daughter is mocking her. Here, as in the rest of the novel, Pearl seems to have little sympathy for her mother's pain.

Equally painful to Hester is Pearl's rejection of her father. Pearl's anger toward him could be explained simply as the natural anxiety of a child who recognizes that change is imminent in her life, and who resents the presence of an outsider in her sheltered relationship with her mother. However, it seems apparent that Pearl recognizes and despises Dimmesdale's insincerity. She wonders aloud if the minister will walk back to town with her and her mother hand in hand, echoing her question in Chapter XII about whether Dimmesdale would stand on the scaffold with Hester and Pearl in broad daylight. Hester answers for Dimmesdale, saying that the minister will not walk in public with them now. Because he is dishonest about their relationship, Pearl refuses to acknowledge him. Pearl's negative reaction to Dimmesdale, together with the narrator's suggestion that this tale will be added to the sad stories told by the babbling brook, foreshadows the sad ending of the novel.

Chapter XX

Following his meeting with Hester and Pearl in the forest, Dimmesdale feels a new energy. He also sees the world differently: Three times he meets people from his congregation and is tempted to say terrible things to them. Content with Hester's plan of moving to Europe, Dimmesdale prepares his final Election Day sermon.

CHAPTER XX: THE MINISTER IN A MAZE

AS the minister departed, in advance of Hester Prynne and little Pearl, he threw a backward glance, half expecting that he should discover only some faintly traced features or outline of the mother and the child, slowly fading into the twilight of the woods. So great a vicissitude in his life could not at once be received as real. But there was Hester, clad in her gray robe, still standing beside the tree-trunk, which some blast had overthrown a long antiquity ago, and which time had ever since been covering with moss, so that these two fated ones, with earth's heaviest burden on them, might there sit down together, and find a single hour's rest and solace. And there was Pearl, too, lightly dancing from the margin of the brook—now that the intrusive third person was gone—and taking her old place by her mother's side. So the minister had not fallen asleep and dreamed!

In order to free his mind from this indistinctness and duplicity of impression, which vexed it with a strange disquietude, he recalled and more thoroughly defined the plans which Hester and himself had sketched for their departure. It had been determined between them that the Old World, with its crowds and cities, offered them a more eligible shelter and concealment than the wilds of New England or all America, with its alternatives of an Indian wigwam, or the few settlements of Europeans scattered thinly along the sea-board. Not to speak of the clergyman's health, so inadequate to sustain the hardships of a forest life, his native gifts, his culture, and his entire development would secure him a home only in the midst of civilization and refinement; the higher the state the more delicately adapted to it the man. In futherance of this choice, it so happened that a ship lay in the harbour; one of those unquestionable cruisers, frequent at that day, which, without being absolutely outlaws of the deep, yet roamed over its surface with a remarkable irresponsibility of character. This vessel had recently arrived from the Spanish Main, and within three days' time would sail for Bristol. Hester Prynne—whose vocation, as a self-enlisted Sister of Charity, had brought her acquainted with the captain and crew—could take upon herself to secure the passage of two individuals and a child with all the secrecy which circumstances rendered more than desirable.

The minister had inquired of Hester, with no little interest, the precise time at which the vessel might be expected to depart. It would probably be on the fourth day from the present. "This is most fortunate!" he had then said to himself. Now, why the Reverend Mr. Dimmesdale considered it so very fortunate we hesitate to reveal. Nevertheless—to hold nothing back from the reader—it was because, on the third day from the present, he was to preach the **Election Sermon**; and, as such an occasion formed an honourable epoch in the life of a New England Clergyman, he could not have chanced upon a more suitable mode and time of terminating his professional career. "At least, they shall say of me," thought this exemplary man, "that I leave no public duty unperformed or ill-performed!" Sad, indeed, that an introspection so profound and acute as this poor minister's should be so miserably deceived! We have had, and may still have, worse things to tell of him; but none, we apprehend, so pitiably weak; no evidence, at once so slight and irrefragable, of a subtle disease that had long since begun to eat into the real substance of his character. No man, for any considerable period, can wear one face to himself and another to the multitude, without finally getting bewildered as to which may be the true.

The excitement of Mr. Dimmesdale's feelings as he returned from his interview with Hester, lent him unaccustomed physical energy, and hurried him townward at a rapid pace. The pathway among the woods seemed wilder, more uncouth with its rude natural obstacles, and less trodden by the foot of man, than he remembered it on his outward journey. But he leaped across the plashy places, thrust himself through the clinging underbush, climbed the ascent, plunged into the hollow, and overcame, in short, all the difficulties of the track, with an unweariable activity that astonished him. He could not but recall how feebly, and with what frequent pauses for breath he had toiled over the same ground, only two days before. As he drew near the town, he took an impression of change from the series of familiar objects that presented themselves. It seemed not yesterday, not one, not two, but many days, or even years ago, since he had quitted them. There, indeed, was each former trace of the street, as he remembered it, and all the peculiarities of the houses, with the due multitude of gable-peaks, and a weather-cock at every point where his memory suggested one. Not the less, however, came this importunately obtrusive sense of change. The same was true as regarded the acquaintances whom he met, and all the well-known shapes of human life, about the little town. They looked neither older nor younger now; the beards of the aged were no whiter, nor could the creeping babe of yesterday walk on his feet to-day; it was impossible to describe in what respect they differed from the individuals on whom he had so recently bestowed a parting glance; and yet the minister's deepest sense seemed to inform him of their mutability. A similar impression struck him most remarkably a he passed under the walls of his own church. The edifice had so very strange, and yet so familiar an aspect, that Mr. Dimmesdale's mind vibrated between two ideas; either that he had seen it only in a dream hitherto, or that he was merely dreaming about it now.

This phenomenon, in the various shapes which it assumed, indicated no external change, but so sudden and important a change in the spectator of the familiar scene, that the intervening space of a single day had operated on his consciousness like the lapse of years. The minister's own will, and Hester's will, and the fate that grew between them, had wrought

Election Sermon: the sermon preached at the inauguration of the colonial governor.

this transformation. It was the same town as heretofore, but the same minister returned not from the forest. He might have said to the friends who greeted him—"I am not the man for whom you take me! I left him yonder in the forest, withdrawn into a secret dell, by a mossy tree trunk, and near a melancholy brook! Go, seek your minister, and see if his emaciated figure, his thin cheek, his white, heavy, pain-wrinkled brow, be not flung down there, like a cast-off garment!" His friends, no doubt, would still have insisted with him—"Thou art thyself the man!"—but the error would have been their own, not his. Before Mr. Dimmesdale reached home, his inner man gave him other evidences of a revolution in the sphere of thought and feeling. In truth, nothing short of a total change of dynasty and moral code, in that interior kingdom, was adequate to account for the impulses now communicated to the unfortunate and startled minister. At every step he was incited to do some strange, wild, wicked thing or other, with a sense that it would be at once involuntary and intentional, in spite of himself, yet growing out of a profounder self than that which opposed the impulse. For instance, he met one of his own deacons. The good old man addressed him with the paternal affection and patriarchal privilege which his venerable age, his upright and holy character, and his station in the church, entitled him to use and, conjoined with this, the deep, almost worshipping respect, which the minister's professional and private claims alike demanded. Never was there a more beautiful example of how the majesty of age and wisdom may comport with the obeisance and respect enjoined upon it, as from a lower social rank, and inferior order of endowment, towards a higher. Now, during a conversation of some two or three moments between the Reverend Mr. Dimmesdale and this excellent and hoary-bearded deacon, it was only by the most careful self-control that the former could refrain from uttering certain blasphemous suggestions that rose into his mind, respecting the communion-supper. He absolutely trembled and turned pale as ashes, lest his tongue should wag itself in utterance of these horrible matters, and plead his own consent for so doing, without his having fairly given it. And, even with this terror in his heart, he could hardly avoid laughing, to imagine how the sanctified old patriarchal deacon would have been petrified by his minister's impiety.

Again, another incident of the same nature. Hurrying along the street, the Reverend Mr. Dimmesdale encountered the eldest female member of his church, a most pious and exemplary old dame, poor, widowed, lonely, and with a heart as full of reminiscences about her dead husband and children, and her dead friends of long ago, as a burial-ground is full of storied gravestones. Yet all this, which would else have been such heavy sorrow, was made almost a solemn joy to her devout old soul, by religious consolations and the truths of Scripture, wherewith she had fed herself continually for more than thirty years. And since Mr. Dimmesdale had taken her in charge, the good grandam's chief earthly comfort—which, unless it had been likewise a heavenly comfort, could have been none at all—was to meet her pastor, whether casually, or of set purpose, and be refreshed with a word of warm, fragrant, heaven-breathing Gospel truth, from his beloved lips, into her dulled, but rapturously attentive ear. But, on this occasion, up to the moment of putting his lips to the old woman's ear, Mr. Dimmesdale, as the great enemy of souls would have it, could recall no text of Scripture, nor aught else, except a brief, pithy, and, as it then appeared to him, unanswerable argument against the immortality of the human soul. The instilment thereof into her mind would probably have caused this aged sister to drop down dead, at once, as by the effect of an intensely poisonous infusion. What he really did whisper, the minister could never afterwards recollect. There was, perhaps, a fortunate disorder in his utterance, which failed to impart any distinct idea to the good widow's comprehension, or which Providence interpreted after a method of its own. Assuredly, as the minister looked back, he beheld an expression of divine gratitude and ecstasy that seemed like the shine of the celestial city on her face, so wrinkled and ashy pale.

Again, a third instance. After parting from the old church member, he met the youngest sister of them all. It was a maiden newly-won—and won by the Reverend Mr. Dimmesdale's own sermon, on the Sabbath after his vigil—to barter the transitory pleasures of the world for the heavenly hope that was to assume brighter substance as life grew dark around her, and which would gild the utter gloom with final glory. She was fair and pure as a lily that had bloomed in Paradise. The minister knew well that he was himself enshrined within the stainless sanctity of her heart, which hung its snowy curtains about his image, imparting to religion the warmth of love, and to love a religious purity. Satan, that afternoon, had surely led the poor young girl away from her mother's side, and thrown her into the pathway of this sorely tempted, or—shall we not rather say?—this lost and desperate man. As she drew nigh, the arch-fiend whispered him to condense into small compass, and drop into her tender bosom a germ of evil that would be sure to blossom darkly soon, and bear black fruit betimes. Such was his sense of power over this virgin soul, trusting him as she did, that the minister felt potent to blight all the field of innocence with but one wicked look, and develop all its opposite with but a word. So—with a mightier struggle than he had yet sustained—he held his Geneva cloak before his face, and hurried onward, making no sign of recognition, and leaving the young sister to digest his rudeness as she might. She ransacked her conscience—which was full of harmless little matters, like her pocket or her work-bag—and took herself to task, poor thing! for a thousand imaginary faults, and went about her household duties with swollen eyelids the next morning.

Before the minister had time to celebrate his victory over this last temptation, he was conscious of another impulse, more ludicrous, and almost as horrible. It was—we blush to tell it—it was to stop short in the road, and teach some very wicked words to a knot of little Puritan children who were playing there, and had but just begun to talk. Denying himself this freak, as unworthy of his cloth, he met a drunken seaman, one of the ship's crew from the **Spanish Main**. And here, since he had so valiantly forborne all other wickedness, poor Mr. Dimmesdale longed at least to shake hands with the tarry black-guard, and recreate himself with a few improper jests, such as dissolute sailors so abound with, and a volley of good, round, solid, satisfactory, and heaven-defying oaths! It was not so much a better principle, as partly his natural good taste, and still more his buckramed habit of clerical decorum, that carried him safely through the latter crisis.

"What is it that haunts and tempts me thus?" cried the minister to himself, at length, pausing in the street, and striking his hand against his forehead.

"Am I mad? or am I given over utterly to the fiend? Did I make a contract with him in the forest, and sign it with my blood? And does he now summon me to its fulfilment, by suggesting the performance of every wickedness which his most foul imagination can conceive?"

At the moment when the Reverend Mr. Dimmesdale thus communed with himself, and struck his forehead with his hand, old Mistress Hibbins, the reputed witch-lady, is said to have been passing by. She made a very grand appearance, having on a high head-dress, a rich gown of velvet, and a ruff done up with the famous yellow starch, of which **Anne Turner**, her especial friend, had taught her the secret, before this last good lady had been hanged for Sir Thomas Overbury's murder. Whether the witch had read the minister's thoughts or no, she came to a full stop, looked shrewdly into his face, smiled craftily, and—though little given to converse with clergymen—began a conversation.

"So, reverend sir, you have made a visit into the forest," observed the witch-lady, nodding her high head-dress at him. "The next time I pray you to allow me only a fair warning, and I shall be proud to bear you company. Without taking overmuch upon myself my good word will go far towards gaining any strange gentleman a fair reception from yonder potentate you wot of."

"I profess, madam," answered the clergyman, with a grave obeisance, such as the lady's rank demanded, and his own good breeding made imperative—"I profess, on my conscience and character, that I am utterly bewildered as touching the purport of your words! I went not into the forest to seek a potentate, neither do I, at any future time, design a visit thither, with a view to gaining the favour of such personage. My one sufficient object was to greet that pious friend of mine, the Apostle Eliot, and rejoice with him over the many precious souls he hath won from heathendom!"

"Ha, ha, ha!" cackled the old witch-lady, still nodding her high head-dress at the minister. "Well, well! we must needs talk thus in the daytime! You carry it off like an old hand! But at midnight, and in the forest, we shall have other talk together!"

She passed on with her aged stateliness, but often turning back her head and smiling at him, like one willing to recognise a secret intimacy of connexion.

Spanish Main: a sea route through the Caribbean that was used by Spanish galleons and pirates.

Anne Turner: a keeper of a house of prostitution who brought the poison to the Tower of London that was used to kill Thomas Overbury.

"Have I then sold myself," thought the minister, "to the fiend whom, if men say true, this yellow-starched and velveted old hag has chosen for her prince and master?"

The wretched minister! He had made a bargain very like it! Tempted by a dream of happiness, he had yielded himself with deliberate choice, as he had never done before, to what he knew was deadly sin. And the infectious poison of that sin had been thus rapidly diffused throughout his moral system. It had stupefied all blessed impulses, and awakened into vivid life the whole brotherhood of bad ones. Scorn, bitterness, unprovoked malignity, gratuitous desire of ill, ridicule of whatever was good and holy, all awoke to tempt, even while they frightened him. And his encounter with old Mistress Hibbins, if it were a real incident, did but show its sympathy and fellowship with wicked mortals, and the world of perverted spirits.

He had by this time reached his dwelling on the edge of the burial ground, and, hastening up the stairs, took refuge in his study. The minister was glad to have reached this shelter, without first betraying himself to the world by any of those strange and wicked eccentricities to which he had been continually impelled while passing through the streets. He entered the accustomed room, and looked around him on its books, its windows, its fireplace, and the tapestried comfort of the walls, with the same perception of strangeness that had haunted him throughout his walk from the forest dell into the town and thitherward. Here he had studied and written; here gone through fast and vigil, and come forth half alive; here striven to pray; here borne a hundred thousand agonies! There was the Bible, in its rich old Hebrew, with Moses and the Prophets speaking to him, and God's voice through all.

There on the table, with the inky pen beside it, was an unfinished sermon, with a sentence broken in the midst, where his thoughts had ceased to gush out upon the page two days before. He knew that it was himself, the thin and white-cheeked minister, who had done and suffered these things, and written thus far into the Election Sermon! But he seemed to stand apart, and eye this former self with scornful pitying, but half-envious curiosity. That self was gone. Another man had returned out of the forest—a wiser one—with a knowledge of hidden mysteries which the simplicity of the former never could have reached. A bitter kind of knowledge that!

While occupied with these reflections, a knock came at the door of the study, and the minister said, "Come in!"—not wholly devoid of an idea that he might behold an evil spirit. And so he did! It was old Roger Chillingworth that entered. The minister stood white and speechless, with one hand on the Hebrew Scriptures, and the other spread upon his breast.

"Welcome home, reverend sir," said the physician. "And how found you that godly man, the Apostle Eliot? But methinks, dear sir, you look pale, as if the travel through the wilderness had been too sore for you. Will not my aid be requisite to put you in heart and strength to preach your Election Sermon?"

"Nay, I think not so," rejoined the Reverend Mr. Dimmesdale. "My journey, and the sight of the holy Apostle yonder, and the free air which I have breathed have done me good, after so long confinement in my study. I think to need no more of your drugs, my kind physician, good though they be, and administered by a friendly hand."

All this time Roger Chillingworth was looking at the minister with the grave and intent regard of a physician towards his patient. But, in spite of this outward show, the latter was almost convinced of the old man's knowledge, or, at least, his confident suspicion, with respect to his own interview with Hester Prynne. The physician knew then that in the minister's regard he was no longer a trusted friend, but his bitterest enemy. So much being known, it would appear natural that a part of it should he expressed. It is singular, however, how long a time often passes before words embody things; and with what security two persons, who choose to avoid a certain subject, may approach its very verge, and retire without disturbing it. Thus the minister felt no apprehension that Roger Chillingworth would touch, in express words, upon the real position which they sustained towards one another. Yet did the physician, in his dark way, creep frightfully near the secret.

"Were it not better," said he, "that you use my poor skill tonight? Verily, dear sir, we must take pains to make you strong and vigorous for this occasion of the Election discourse. The people look for great things from you, apprehending that another year may come about and find their pastor gone."

"Yes, to another world," replied the minister with pious resignation. "Heaven grant it be a better one; for, in good sooth, I hardly think to tarry with my flock through the flitting seasons of another year! But touching your medicine, kind sir, in my present frame of body I need it not."

"I joy to hear it," answered the physician. "It may be that my remedies, so long administered in vain, begin now to take due effect. Happy man were I, and well deserving of New England's gratitude, could I achieve this cure!"

"I thank you from my heart, most watchful friend," said the Reverend Mr. Dimmesdale with a solemn smile. "I thank you, and can but requite your good deeds with my prayers."

"A good man's prayers are golden recompense!" rejoined old Roger Chillingworth, as he took his leave. "Yea, they are the current gold coin of the New Jerusalem, with the King's own mint mark on them!"

Left alone, the minister summoned a servant of the house, and requested food, which, being set before him, he ate with ravenous appetite. Then flinging the already written pages of the Election Sermon into the fire, he forthwith began another, which he wrote with such an impulsive flow of thought and emotion, that he fancied himself inspired; and only wondered that Heaven should see fit to transmit the grand and solemn music of its oracles through so foul an organ pipe as he. However, leaving that mystery to solve itself, or go unsolved for ever, he drove his task onward with earnest haste and ecstasy.

Thus the night fled away, as if it were a winged steed, and he careering on it; morning came, and peeped, blushing, through the curtains; and at last sunrise threw a golden beam into the study, and laid it right across the minister's bedazzled eyes. There he was, with the pen still between his fingers, and a vast, immeasurable tract of written space behind him!

COMMENTARY

This chapter documents Dimmesdale's psychological and spiritual battle with himself following his meeting with Hester in the woods. Although he feels renewed physical strength after this meeting, Dimmesdale also seems to have suffered from a moral loss.

Hester and Dimmesdale have decided to return to Europe because only there will the minister be able to fully express his intellect and the trio of Hester, Pearl, and Dimmesdale be able to build new lives together. Hester will book passage on a ship to England that is docked near Boston, and the trio will depart in four days. The narrator intrudes obviously in Chapter XX, claiming at first that he doesn't want to expose Dimmesdale's joy about not leaving for four days: "[W]e hesitate to reveal." But because he wants to "hold nothing back from the reader," the narrator tells us that the minister will be preaching an Election Sermon three days from now, which Dimmesdale believes will be a fitting end to his career in Boston.

Following his encounter with Hester, the minister is filled with an unusual physical energy, as if she has imparted some of her vivacity to him. As Dimmesdale walks through the forest on the way back to town, the pathway seems wilder than it was previously, signaling perhaps the moral wilderness he is becoming entangled in. Yet he is able to make it energetically through: The narrator explains that Dimmesdale "leaped," "thrust," "climbed," and "plunged" through the forest—words that some critics see as connoting a newfound sexual energy.

The world and people of Boston seem different to him when he returns, so that he wonders if he was or is now entrapped in a dream. The narrator interprets this change by saying that the fate that has grown up between Hester and Dimmesdale altered him: "[T]he same minister returned not from the forest." He threw away his emaciated figure like a worn-out garment. His entire moral code changed following the interaction in the woods, as if he was infected with some wild energy that incites him to do strange and wicked things. Has Hester's lawless, irreverent view of life infused the minister? Or did the Black Man find him as he wandered through the woods? For example, while on the path back to town, Dimmesdale feels the power of corrupting an innocent young girl with a simple look and word, or of teaching naughty words to a group of Puritan children. Now that the iron wall of his repression has been broken, Dimmesdale is overcome with childishly wicked impulses. The fantastical element of Dimmesdale's new personality is heightened by his conversation with the witch Mistress Hibbins, who instinctively seems to know of his visit to the forest.

In order to fulfill his dream of happiness with Hester, the minister has deliberately chosen to commit a sin, and it appears that the poison of this sin has spread throughout his moral system. Because his previous adultery with Hester was not calculated, it pales in comparison with the deliberate plan to leave the colonies with Hester, a married woman. Gone is the minister's simplicity; he now has an understanding of life's "hidden mysteries." Again, this comment suggests that the minister retained his innocence during his affair with Hester but has now lost it. This implication raises some questions that are never fully answered in the novel: Is the pursuit of happiness really such an evil undertaking? Would the minister really be better off if he remained in the colonies?

The new energy Dimmesdale found in the forest has the effect of inspiring him with an excess of creativity. He works feverishly upon his return to Boston and finishes his Election Sermon in an almost dream-like state, producing "a vast, immeasurable tract of written space." His energy also provides him with the courage to converse with Chillingworth, a conversation filled with double-entendres at the end of the chapter. For example, when Chillingworth says the minister's parishioners will miss him if he dies, Dimmesdale admits that he will soon be gone to "another world" and hopes it will be "a better one."

Chapter XXI

Election Day has arrived, and Boston is as festive as a Puritan town ever gets. Hester and Pearl stand in the crowd, watching the procession of elected officials pass by. The captain of the Bristol-bound ship on which Hester has booked passages for herself, Dimmesdale, and Pearl walks over to talk with her. He reveals that Chillingworth has also booked a berth on the ship.

CHAPTER XXI: THE NEW ENGLAND HOLIDAY

BETIMES in the morning of the day on which the new Governor was to receive his office at the hands of the people, Hester Prynne and little Pearl came into the market-place. It was already thronged with the craftsmen and other plebeian inhabitants of the town, in considerable numbers, among whom, likewise, were many rough figures, whose attire of deer-skins marked them as belonging to some of the forest settlements, which surrounded the little metropolis of the colony.

On this public holiday, as on all other occasions for seven years past, Hester was clad in a garment of coarse gray cloth. Not more by its hue than by some indescribable peculiarity in its fashion, it had the effect of making her fade personally out of sight and outline; while again the scarlet letter brought her back from this twilight indistinctness, and revealed her under the moral aspect of its own illumination. Her face, so long familiar to the townspeople, showed the marble quietude which they were accustomed to behold there. It was like a mask; or, rather like the frozen calmness of a dead woman's features; owing this dreary resemblance to the fact that Hester was actually dead, in respect to any claim of sympathy, and had departed out of the world with which she still seemed to mingle.

It might be, on this one day, that there was an expression unseen before, nor, indeed, vivid enough to be detected now; unless some preternaturally gifted observer should have first read the heart, and have afterwards sought a corresponding development in the countenance and mien. Such a spiritual seer might have conceived, that, after sustaining the gaze of the multitude through several miserable years as a necessity, a penance, and something which it was a stern religion to endure, she now, for one last time more, encountered it freely and voluntarily, in order to convert what had so long been agony into a kind of triumph. "Look your last on the scarlet letter and its wearer!"—the people's victim and lifelong bondslave, as they fancied her, might say to them. "Yet a little while, and she will be beyond your reach! A few hours longer and the deep, mysterious ocean will quench and hide for ever the symbol which ye have caused to burn on her bosom!" Nor were it an inconsistency too improbable to be assigned to human nature, should we suppose a feeling of regret in Hester's mind, at the moment when she was about to win her freedom from the pain which had been thus deeply incorporated with her being. Might there not be an irresistible desire to quaff a last, long, breathless draught of the cup of wormwood and aloes, with which nearly all her years of womanhood had been perpetually flavoured. The wine of life, henceforth to be presented to her lips, must be indeed rich, delicious, and exhilarating, in its chased and golden beaker, or else leave an inevitable and weary languor, after the lees of bitterness wherewith she had been drugged, as with a cordial of intensest potency.

Pearl was decked out with airy gaiety. It would have been impossible to guess that this bright and sunny apparition owed its existence to the shape of gloomy gray; or that a fancy, at once so gorgeous and so delicate as must have been requisite to contrive the child's apparel, was the same that had achieved a task perhaps more difficult, in imparting so distinct a peculiarity to Hester's simple robe. The dress, so proper was it to little Pearl, seemed an effluence, or inevitable development and outward manifestation of her character, no more to be separated from her than the many-hued brilliancy from a butterfly's wing, or the painted glory from the leaf of a bright flower. As with these, so with the child; her garb was all of one idea with her nature. On this eventful day, moreover, there was a certain singular inquietude and excitement in her mood, resembling nothing so much as the shimmer of a diamond, that sparkles and flashes with the varied throbbings of the breast on which it is displayed. Children have always a sympathy in the agitations of those connected with them: always, especially, a sense of any trouble or impending revolution, of whatever kind, in domestic circumstances; and therefore Pearl, who was the gem on her mother's unquiet bosom, betrayed, by the very dance of her spirits, the emotions which none could detect in the marble passiveness of Hester's brow.

This effervescence made her flit with a bird-like movement, rather than walk by her mother's side.

She broke continually into shouts of a wild, inarticulate, and sometimes piercing music. When they reached the market-place, she became still more restless, on perceiving the stir and bustle that enlivened the spot; for it was usually more like the broad and lonesome green before a village meeting-house, than the centre of a town's business.

"Why, what is this, mother?" cried she. "Wherefore have all the people left their work to-day? Is it a play-day for the whole world? See, there is the blacksmith! He has washed his sooty face, and put on his Sabbath-day clothes, and looks as if he would gladly be merry, if any kind body would only teach him how! And there is Master Brackett, the old jailer, nodding and smiling at me. Why does he do so, mother?"

"He remembers thee a little babe, my child," answered Hester.

"He should not nod and smile at me, for all that—the black, grim, ugly-eyed old man!" said Pearl.

"He may nod at thee, if he will; for thou art clad in gray, and wearest the scarlet letter. But see, mother, how many faces of strange people, and Indians among them, and sailors! What have they all come to do, here in the market-place?"

"They wait to see the procession pass," said Hester. "For the Governor and the magistrates are to go by, and the ministers, and all the great people and good people, with the music and the soldiers marching before them."

"And will the minister be there?" asked Pearl. "And will he hold out both his hands to me, as when thou led'st me to him from the brook-side?"

"He will be there, child," answered her mother, "but he will not greet thee to-day, nor must thou greet him."

"What a strange, sad man is he!" said the child, as if speaking partly to herself. "In the dark nighttime he calls us to him, and holds thy hand and mine, as when we stood with him on the scaffold yonder! And in the deep forest, where only the old trees can hear, and the strip of sky see it, he talks with thee, sitting on a heap of moss! And he kisses my forehead, too, so that the little brook would hardly wash it off! But, here, in the sunny day, and among all the people, he knows us not; nor must we know him! A strange, sad man is he, with his hand always over his heart!"

"Be quiet, Pearl—thou understandest not these things," said her mother. "Think not now of the minister, but look about thee, and see how cheery is everybody's face to-day. The children have come from their schools, and the grown people from their workshops and their fields, on purpose to be happy, for, to-day, a new man is beginning to rule over them; and so—as has been the custom of mankind ever since a nation was first gathered—they make merry and rejoice: as if a good and golden year were at length to pass over the poor old world!"

It was as Hester said, in regard to the unwonted jollity that brightened the faces of the people. Into this festal season of the year—as it already was, and continued to be during the greater part of two centuries—the Puritans compressed whatever mirth and public joy they deemed allowable to human infirmity; thereby so far dispelling the customary cloud, that, for the space of a single holiday, they appeared scarcely more grave than most other communities at a period of general affliction.

But we perhaps exaggerate the gray or sable tinge, which undoubtedly characterized the mood and manners of the age. The persons now in the market-place of Boston had not been born to an inheritance of Puritanic gloom. They were native Englishmen, whose fathers had lived in the sunny richness of the **Elizabethan epoch**; a time when the life of England, viewed as one great mass, would appear to have been as stately, magnificent, and joyous, as the world has ever witnessed. Had they followed their hereditary taste, the New England settlers would have illustrated all events of public importance by bonfires, banquets, pageantries, and processions. Nor would it have been impracticable, in the observance of majestic ceremonies, to combine mirthful recreation with solemnity, and give, as it were, a grotesque and brilliant embroidery to the great robe of state, which a nation, at such festivals, puts on. There was some shadow of an attempt of this kind in the mode of celebrating the day on

Elizabethan epoch: a period in the late 1500s marked by the reign of Queen Elizabeth I. Called the Golden Age, it is known for its artistic, political, and scientific growth.

which the political year of the colony commenced. The dim reflection of a remembered splendour, a colourless and manifold diluted repetition of what they had beheld in proud old London—we will not say at a royal coronation, but at a Lord Mayor's show—might be traced in the customs which our forefathers instituted, with reference to the annual installation of magistrates. The fathers and founders of the commonwealth—the statesman, the priest, and the soldier—seemed it a duty then to assume the outward state and majesty, which, in accordance with antique style, was looked upon as the proper garb of public and social eminence. All came forth to move in procession before the people's eye, and thus impart a needed dignity to the simple framework of a government so newly constructed.

Then, too, the people were countenanced, if not encouraged, in relaxing the severe and close application to their various modes of rugged industry, which at all other times, seemed of the same piece and material with their religion. Here, it is true, were none of the appliances which popular merriment would so readily have found in the England of Elizabeth's time, or that of James—no rude shows of a theatrical kind; no minstrel, with his harp and legendary ballad, nor gleeman with an ape dancing to his music; no juggler, with his tricks of mimic witchcraft; no **Merry Andrew**, to stir up the multitude with jests, perhaps a hundred years old, but still effective, by their appeals to the very broadest sources of mirthful sympathy. All such professors of the several branches of jocularity would have been sternly repressed, not only by the rigid discipline of law, but by the general sentiment which give law its vitality. Not the less, however, the great, honest face of the people smiled—grimly, perhaps, but widely too. Nor were sports wanting, such as the colonists had witnessed, and shared in, long ago, at the country fairs and on the village-greens of England; and which it was thought well to keep alive on this new soil, for the sake of the courage and manliness that were essential in them. Wrestling matches, in the different fashions of Cornwall and Devonshire, were seen here and there about the market-place; in one corner, there was a friendly bout at quarterstaff; and—what attracted most interest of all—on the platform of the pillory, already so noted in our pages, two masters of defence were commencing an exhibition with the buckler and broadsword. But, much to the disappointment of the crowd, this latter business was broken off by the interposition of the **town beadle**, who had no idea of permitting the majesty of the law to be violated by such an abuse of one of its consecrated places.

It may not be too much to affirm, on the whole, (the people being then in the first stages of joyless deportment, and the offspring of sires who had known how to be merry, in their day), that they would compare favourably, in point of holiday keeping, with their descendants, even at so long an interval as ourselves. Their immediate posterity, the generation next to the early emigrants, wore the blackest shade of Puritanism, and so darkened the national visage with it, that all the subsequent years have not sufficed to clear it up. We have yet to learn again the forgotten art of gaiety.

Merry Andrew: a clown, fool.

town beadle: a minor parish official, who kept order in church.

The picture of human life in the market-place, though its general tint was the sad gray, brown, or black of the English emigrants, was yet enlivened by some diversity of hue. A party of Indians—in their savage finery of curiously embroidered deerskin robes, wampum-belts, red and yellow ochre, and feathers, and armed with the bow and arrow and stone-headed spear—stood apart with countenances of inflexible gravity, beyond what even the Puritan aspect could attain. Nor, wild as were these painted barbarians, were they the wildest feature of the scene. This distinction could more justly be claimed by some mariners—a part of the crew of the vessel from the Spanish Main—who had come ashore to see the humours of Election Day. They were rough-looking desperadoes, with sun-blackened faces, and an immensity of beard; their wide short trousers were confined about the waist by belts, often clasped with a rough plate of gold, and sustaining always a long knife, and in some instances, a sword. From beneath their broad-brimmed hats of palm-leaf, gleamed eyes which, even in good-nature and merriment, had a kind of animal ferocity. They transgressed without fear or scruple, the rules of behaviour that were binding on all others: smoking tobacco under the beadle's very nose, although each whiff would have cost a townsman a shilling; and quaffing at their pleasure, draughts of wine or aqua-vitae from pocket flasks, which they freely tendered to the gaping crowd around them. It remarkably characterised the incomplete morality of the age, rigid as we call it, that a licence was allowed the seafaring class, not merely for their freaks on shore, but for far more desperate deeds on their proper element. The sailor of that day would go near to be arraigned as a pirate in our own. There could be little doubt, for instance, that this very ship's crew, though no unfavourable specimens of the nautical brother-hood, had been guilty, as we should phrase it, of depredations on the Spanish commerce, such as would have perilled all their necks in a modern court of justice.

But the sea in those old times heaved, swelled, and foamed very much at its own will, or subject only to the tempestuous wind, with hardly any attempts at regulation by human law. The buccaneer on the wave might relinquish his calling and become at once if he chose, a man of probity and piety on land; nor, even in the full career of his reckless life, was he regarded as a personage with whom it was disreputable to traffic or casually associate. Thus the Puritan elders in their black cloaks, starched bands, and steeple-crowned hats, smiled not unbenignantly at the clamour and rude deportment of these jolly seafaring men; and it excited neither surprise nor animadversion when so reputable a citizen as old Roger Chillingworth, the physician, was seen to enter the market-place in close and familiar talk with the commander of the questionable vessel.

The latter was by far the most showy and gallant figure, so far as apparel went, anywhere to be seen among the multitude. He wore a profusion of ribbons on his garment, and gold lace on his hat, which was also encircled by a gold chain, and surmounted with a feather. There was a sword

animadversion: criticism.

at his side and a sword-cut on his forehead, which, by the arrangement of his hair, he seemed anxious rather to display than hide. A landsman could hardly have worn this garb and shown this face, and worn and shown them both with such a **galliard** air, without undergoing stern question before a magistrate, and probably incurring a fine or imprisonment, or perhaps an exhibition in the stocks. As regarded the shipmaster, however, all was looked upon as pertaining to the character, as to a fish his glistening scales.

galliard: a lively French dance in triple time.

After parting from the physician, the commander of the Bristol ship strolled idly through the market-place; until happening to approach the spot where Hester Prynne was standing, he appeared to recognise, and did not hesitate to address her. As was usually the case wherever Hester stood, a small vacant area—a sort of magic circle—had formed itself about her, into which, though the people were elbowing one another at a little distance, none ventured or felt disposed to intrude. It was a forcible type of the moral solitude in which the scarlet letter enveloped its fated wearer; partly by her own reserve, and partly by the instinctive, though no longer so unkindly, withdrawal of her fellow-creatures. Now, if never before, it answered a good purpose by enabling Hester and the seaman to speak together without risk of being overheard; and so changed was Hester Prynne's repute before the public, that the matron in town, most eminent for rigid morality, could not have held such intercourse with less result of scandal than herself.

"So, mistress," said the mariner, "I must bid the steward make ready one more berth than you bargained for! No fear of scurvy or ship fever this voyage. What with the ship's surgeon and this other doctor, our only danger will be from drug or pill; more by token, as there is a lot of apothecary's stuff aboard, which I traded for with a Spanish vessel."

"What mean you?" inquired Hester, startled more than she permitted to appear. "Have you another passenger?"

"Why, know you not," cried the shipmaster, "that this physician here—Chillingworth he calls himself—is minded to try my cabin-fare with you? Ay, ay, you must have known it; for he tells me he is of your party, and a close friend to the gentleman you spoke of—he that is in peril from these sour old Puritan rulers."

"They know each other well, indeed," replied Hester, with a mien of calmness, though in the utmost consternation. "They have long dwelt together."

Nothing further passed between the mariner and Hester Prynne. But at that instant she beheld old Roger Chillingworth himself, standing in the remotest corner of the market-place and smiling on her; a smile which—across the wide and bustling square, and through all the talk and laughter, and various thoughts, moods, and interests of the crowd—conveyed secret and fearful meaning.

COMMENTARY

As Hester wanders through the crowd on Election Day, her face is mask-like, similar to "the frozen calmness of a dead woman's features." And in a sense, she is dead while in this community, because she is unable to claim any sympathy from the people around her. The narrator notes that although the average viewer may not recognize any change in Hester on this day, a more spiritual seer may recognize a subtle difference in her demeanor—a sense of freedom that provides a clue that she will soon leave the colony. Realizing the often contradictory impulses of human nature, the narrator also says that Hester feels regret at this moment of escape: Perhaps the richness of happiness will be almost disappointing to her after her long years of bitter suffering.

As in previous chapters, Pearl's attire contrasts with her mother's, offering insight on Hester's own repressed nature. While Hester suppresses her personality inside a coarse gray dress, Pearl wears a multi-colored gown that is as bright as a butterfly's wing or the brilliant leaf of a flower: "her garb was all of one idea with her nature." Her walk is again "bird-like," and she shouts with "wild, inarticulate, and sometimes piercing music." Her mood is also sparkling, and the narrator compares it with the flash and color of a diamond, as if Pearl reflects the emotions that Hester must hide. Thus, in both appearance and mood, Pearl reflects her mother's repressed imagination and emotions.

In describing the Election Day festivities, the narrator again creates a contrast between the Old and New Worlds that offers insight into seventeenth-century life. While the colony is colored by a "gray or sable tinge," its inhabitants are descendents of Englishmen who lived through the "sunny richness" of the Elizabethan era, when the world was regal, dazzling, and joyous. Despite their efforts to the contrary, the Puritans retain some elements of this splendid world for which the narrator obviously feels nostalgic.

Making an implicit connection with Hester's needlecraft, the narrator writes that this English pageantry combined "mirthful recreation with solemnity" that added "a grotesque and brilliant embroidery to the great robe of state." The Puritan festival lacks many elements of the English pageant: the theatre, the music, and the magicians. These are repressed due to the rigid legal discipline of the colonies, a rigidity condoned and supported by popular

sentiment. And the narrator claims that American life will become more sober, rather than less, as generations pass. He explains that these earliest Puritans, immigrants from England, maintain many festivities that would be erased by the next generation, a much more severe, "blacker" variety of Puritan, from whom our nation has inherited its soberness. Again, the narrator implicitly critiques the attributes of American culture inherited from the Puritans: our work ethic and our soberness.

Although the Puritans dominate the marketplace on Election Day, some diversity among the crowd adds color to the scene, from the embroidered deer-skin robes of the Native American contingent to the wild garb of the sailors from the Spanish ship. The sailors transgress, without punishment, all the Puritan's rules, drinking and smoking in front of the magistrates. The narrator points this behavior out as an example of the "incomplete morality of the age": Because the sailors lead difficult lives, they seem free from all regulation by human laws. Whereas the sea captain freely wears his gaudy clothing and sword, a Puritan would be fined or imprisoned for dressing in a similar manner. This example shows the relativity of all human laws of morality and good conduct.

The ill-fated nature of Hester and Dimmesdale's plan, foreshadowed by Pearl's tantrum in the forest when her mother introduced her to the minister, comes to fruition in Chapter XXI. The child's comments in this chapter add to this sense of doom. Pearl notices what a "strange, sad" man the minister is, and wonders why he can only greet them in the dark or in the depths of the forest: Why can't he acknowledge them in this sunny, public place? Pearl's innocent comments and unwitting queries serve as a potent critique of Dimmesdale's lack of moral honesty, showing her mother how unworthy this holy man is and how severely his public and private selves differ. Unless he confesses his sin, Dimmesdale will never enjoy the happiness promised by Hester. Therefore, it does not seem surprising that Chillingworth, Dimmesdale's ruthless conscience, has somehow discovered the plan to sail to Europe and has booked passage on the same ship. The "secret and fearful" meaning conveyed by his smile suggests the impossibility of escape: Dimmesdale will be free from this pernicious man only through confession or death.

Chapter XXII

Dimmesdale walks past Hester and Pearl in the Election Day procession. His spiritual, remote energy distances him from them. Later in the day, as she listens to Dimmesdale's sermon, Hester hears the sadness and despair in his voice. Pearl runs up to her mother with a message that Chillingworth has booked spaces on the ship for himself and Dimmesdale.

CHAPTER XXII: THE PROCESSION

BEFORE Hester Prynne could call together her thoughts, and consider what was practicable to be done in this new and startling aspect of affairs, the sound of military music was heard approaching along a contiguous street. It denoted the advance of the procession of magistrates and citizens on its way towards the meeting-house: where, in compliance with a custom thus early established, and ever since observed, the Reverend Mr. Dimmesdale was to deliver an Election Sermon.

Soon the head of the procession showed itself, with a slow and stately march, turning a corner, and making its way across the market-place. First came the music. It comprised a variety of instruments, perhaps imperfectly adapted to one another, and played with no great skill; but yet attaining the great object for which the harmony of drum and clarion addresses itself to the multitude—that of imparting a higher and more heroic air to the scene of life that passes before the eye. Little Pearl at first clapped her hands, but then lost for an instant the restless agitation that had kept her in a continual effervescence throughout the morning; she gazed silently, and seemed to be borne upward like a floating sea-bird on the long heaves and swells of sound. But she was brought back to her former mood by the shimmer of the sunshine on the weapons and bright armour of the military company, which followed after the music, and formed the honorary escort of the procession. This body of soldiery— which still sustains a corporate existence, and marches down from past ages with an ancient and honourable fame—was composed of no mercenary materials. Its ranks were filled with gentlemen who felt the stirrings of martial impulse, and sought to establish a kind of **College of Arms**, where, as in an association of **Knights Templars**, they might learn the science, and, so far as peaceful exercise would teach them, the practices of war. The high estimation then placed upon the military character might be seen in the lofty port of each individual member of the company. Some of them, indeed, by their services in the **Low Countries** and on other fields of European warfare, had fairly won their title to assume the name and pomp of soldiership. The entire array, moreover, clad in burnished steel, and with plumage nodding over their bright **morions**, had a brilliancy of effect which no modern display can aspire to equal.

And yet the men of civil eminence, who came immediately behind the military escort, were better worth a thoughtful observer's eye. Even in outward demeanour they showed a stamp of majesty that made the warrior's haughty stride look vulgar, if not absurd. It was an age when what

College of Arms: founded in the 15th century to record titles and coats of arms for the British aristocracy. Critics believe that Hawthorne used it incorrectly here to denote a military college.

Knights Templars: a military and religious order founded in 1118 by nine knights, whose original mission was to guide pilgrims making trips to Jerusalem. The group was banned by the Church in 1312 when it became too powerful.

Low Countries: an area that is now the Netherlands.

morions: a hatlike, crested helmet.

we call talent had far less consideration than now, but the massive materials which produce stability and dignity of character a great deal more. The people possessed by hereditary right the quality of reverence, which, in their descendants, if it survive at all, exists in smaller proportion, and with a vastly diminished force in the selection and estimate of public men. The change may be for good or ill, and is partly, perhaps, for both. In that old day the English settler on these rude shores—having left king, nobles, and all degrees of awful rank behind, while still the faculty and necessity of reverence was strong in him—bestowed it on the white hair and venerable brow of age—on long-tried integrity—on solid wisdom and sad-coloured experience—on endowments of that grave and weighty order which gave the idea of permanence, and comes under the general definition of respectability. These primitive statesmen, therefore—**Bradstreet, Endicott, Dudley, Bellingham**, and their compeers—who were elevated to power by the early choice of the people, seem to have been not often brilliant, but distinguished by a ponderous sobriety, rather than activity of intellect. They had fortitude and self-reliance, and in time of difficulty or peril stood up for the welfare of the state like a line of cliffs against a tempestuous tide. The traits of character here indicated were well represented in the square cast of countenance and large physical development of the new colonial magistrates. So far as a demeanour of natural authority was concerned, the mother country need not have been ashamed to see these foremost men of an actual democracy adopted into the **House of Peers**, or made the **Privy Council of the Sovereign**.

Next in order to the magistrates came the young and eminently distinguished divine, from whose lips the religious discourse of the anniversary was expected. His was the profession at that era in which intellectual ability displayed itself far more than in political life; for—leaving a higher motive out of the question it offered inducements powerful enough in the almost worshipping respect of the community, to win the most aspiring ambition into its service. Even political power—as in the case of **Increase Mather**—was within the grasp of a successful priest.

It was the observation of those who beheld him now, that never, since Mr. Dimmesdale first set his foot on the New England shore, had he exhibited such energy as was seen in the gait and air with which he kept his pace in the procession. There was no feebleness of step as at other times; his frame was not bent, nor did his hand rest ominously upon his heart. Yet, if the clergyman were rightly viewed, his strength seemed not of the body. It might be spiritual and imparted to him by angelical ministrations. It might be the exhilaration of that potent cordial which is distilled only in the furnace-glow of earnest and long-continued thought. Or perchance his sensitive temperament was invigorated by the loud and piercing music that swelled heaven-ward, and uplifted him on its ascending wave. Nevertheless, so abstracted was his look, it might be questioned whether Mr. Dimmesdale ever heard the music. There was his body, moving onward, and with an unaccustomed force. But where was his mind? Far and deep in its own region, busying itself, with preternatural

Bradstreet, Endicott, Dudley, Bellingham: several of the first settlers in the Massachusetts Bay Colony, all of whom served terms as the colonial governor.

House of Peers: Also known as the House of Lords, this is the upper house of Britain's Parliament.

Privy Council of the Sovereign: a group of advisors to the British king or queen.

Increase Mather: (1639–1723) A distinguished early New England Puritan minister, in 1685, Mather became President of Harvard College. He retained the position until 1701.

activity, to marshal a procession of stately thoughts that were soon to issue thence; and so he saw nothing, heard nothing, knew nothing of what was around him; but the spiritual element took up the feeble frame and carried it along, unconscious of the burden, and converting it to spirit like itself. Men of uncommon intellect, who have grown morbid, possess this occasional power of mighty effort, into which they throw the life of many days and then are lifeless for as many more.

Hester Prynne, gazing steadfastly at the clergyman, felt a dreary influence come over her, but wherefore or whence she knew not, unless that he seemed so remote from her own sphere, and utterly beyond her reach. One glance of recognition she had imagined must needs pass between them. She thought of the dim forest, with its little dell of solitude, and love, and anguish, and the mossy tree-trunk, where, sitting hand-in-hand, they had mingled their sad and passionate talk with the melan-choly murmur of the brook. How deeply had they known each other then! And was this the man? She hardly knew him now! He, moving proudly past, enveloped as it were, in the rich music, with the procession of majestic and venerable fathers; he, so unattainable in his worldly posi-tion, and still more so in that far vista of his unsympathizing thoughts, through which she now beheld him! Her spirit sank with the idea that all must have been a delusion, and that, vividly as she had dreamed it, there could be no real bond betwixt the clergyman and herself. And thus much of woman was there in Hester, that she could scarcely forgive him—least of all now, when the heavy footstep of their approaching Fate might be heard, nearer, nearer, nearer!—for being able so completely to withdraw himself from their mutual world—while she groped darkly, and stretched forth her cold hands, and found him not.

Pearl either saw and responded to her mother's feelings, or herself felt the remoteness and intangibility that had fallen around the minister. While the procession passed, the child was uneasy, fluttering up and down, like a bird on the point of taking flight. When the whole had gone by, she looked up into Hester's face—

"Mother," said she, "was that the same minister that kissed me by the brook?"

"Hold thy peace, dear little Pearl!" whispered her mother. "We must not always talk in the marketplace of what happens to us in the forest."

"I could not be sure that it was he—so strange he looked," continued the child. "Else I would have run to him, and bid him kiss me now, before all the people, even as he did yonder among the dark old trees. What would the minister have said, mother? Would he have clapped his hand over his heart, and scowled on me, and bid me begone?"

"What should he say, Pearl," answered Hester, "save that it was no time to kiss, and that kisses are not to be given in the market-place? Well for thee, foolish child, that thou didst not speak to him!"

Another shade of the same sentiment, in reference to Mr. Dimmesdale, was expressed by a person whose eccentricities—insanity, as we should term it—led her to do what few of the townspeople would have ventured on—to begin a conversation with the wearer of the scarlet letter in public. It was Mistress Hibbins, who, arrayed in great magnificence, with a triple ruff, a broidered stomacher, a gown of rich velvet, and a gold-headed cane, had come forth to see the procession. As this ancient lady had the renown (which subsequently cost her no less a price than her life) of being a principal actor in all the works of necromancy that were continually going forward, the crowd gave way before her, and seemed to fear the touch of her garment, as if it carried the plague among its gorgeous folds. Seen in conjunction with Hester Prynne—kindly as so many now felt towards the latter—the dread inspired by Mistress Hibbins had doubled, and caused a general movement from that part of the market-place in which the two women stood.

"Now, what mortal imagination could conceive it?" whispered the old lady confidentially to Hester. "Yonder divine man! That saint on earth, as the people uphold him to be, and as—I must needs say—he really looks! Who, now, that saw him pass in the procession, would think how little while it is since he went forth out of his study—chewing a Hebrew text of Scripture in his mouth, I warrant—to take an airing in the forest! Aha! we know what that means, Hester Prynne! But truly, forsooth, I find it hard to believe him the same man. Many a church member saw I, walking behind the music, that has danced in the same measure with me, when Somebody was fiddler, and, it might be, an Indian powwow or a Lapland wizard changing hands with us! That is but a trifle, when a woman knows the world. But this minister. Couldst thou surely tell, Hester, whether he was the same man that encountered thee on the forest path?"

"Madam, I know not of what you speak," answered Hester Prynne, feeling Mistress Hibbins to be of infirm mind; yet strangely startled and awe-stricken by the confidence with which she affirmed a personal connexion between so many persons (herself among them) and the Evil One. "It is not for me to talk lightly of a learned and pious minister of the Word, like the Reverend Mr. Dimmesdale."

"Fie, woman, fie!" cried the old lady, shaking her finger at Hester. "Dost thou think I have been to the forest so many times, and have yet no skill to judge who else has been there? Yea, though no leaf of the wild garlands which they wore while they danced be left in their hair! I know thee, Hester, for I behold the token. We may all see it in the sunshine! and it glows like a red flame in the dark. Thou wearest it openly, so there need be no question about that. But this minister! Let me tell thee in thine ear! When the Black Man sees one of his own servants, signed and sealed, so shy of owning to the bond as is the Reverend Mr. Dimmesdale, he hath a way of ordering matters so that the mark shall be disclosed, in open daylight, to the eyes of all the world! What is that the minister seeks to hide, with his hand always over his heart? Ha, Hester Prynne?"

"What is it, good Mistress Hibbins?" eagerly asked little Pearl. "Hast thou seen it?"

"No matter, darling!" responded Mistress Hibbins, making Pearl a profound reverence. "Thou thyself wilt see it, one time or another. They say, child, thou art of the lineage of the **Prince of Air**! Wilt thou ride with me some fine night to see thy father? Then thou shalt know wherefore the minister keeps his hand over his heart!"

Prince of Air: Satan (Ephesians 2:2).

Laughing so shrilly that all the market-place could hear her, the weird old gentlewoman took her departure.

By this time the preliminary prayer had been offered in the meeting-house, and the accents of the Reverend Mr. Dimmesdale were heard commencing his discourse. An irresistible feeling kept Hester near the spot. As the sacred edifice was too much thronged to admit another auditor, she took up her position close beside the scaffold of the pillory. It was in sufficient proximity to bring the whole sermon to her ears, in the shape of an indistinct but varied murmur and flow of the minister's very peculiar voice.

This vocal organ was in itself a rich endowment, insomuch that a listener, comprehending nothing of the language in which the preacher spoke, might still have been swayed to and fro by the mere tone and cadence. Like all other music, it breathed passion and pathos, and emotions high or tender, in a tongue native to the human heart, wherever educated. Muffled as the sound was by its passage through the church walls, Hester Prynne listened with such intenseness, and sympathized so intimately, that the sermon had throughout a meaning for her, entirely apart from its indistinguishable words. These, perhaps, if more distinctly heard, might have been only a grosser medium, and have clogged the spiritual sense. Now she caught the low undertone, as of the wind sinking down to repose itself; then ascended with it, as it rose through progressive gradations of sweetness and power, until its volume seemed to envelop her with an atmosphere of awe and solemn grandeur. And yet, majestic as the voice sometimes became, there was for ever in it an essential character of plaintiveness. A loud or low expression of anguish—the whisper, or the shriek, as it might be conceived, of suffering humanity, that touched a sensibility in every bosom! At times this deep strain of pathos was all that could be heard, and scarcely heard sighing amid a desolate silence. But even when the minister's voice grew high and commanding—when it gushed irrepressibly upward—when it assumed its utmost breadth and power, so overfilling the church as to burst its way through the solid walls, and diffuse itself in the open air—still, if the auditor listened intently, and for the purpose, he could detect the same cry of pain. What was it? The complaint of a human heart, sorrow-laden, perchance guilty, telling its secret, whether of guilt or sorrow, to the great heart of mankind; beseeching its sympathy or forgiveness,—at every moment,—in each accent,—and never in vain! It was this profound and continual undertone that gave the clergyman his most appropriate power.

During all this time, Hester stood, statue-like, at the foot of the scaffold. If the minister's voice had not kept her there, there would, nevertheless, have been an inevitable magnetism in that spot, whence she dated the first hour of her life of ignomiy. There was a sense within her—too ill-defined to be made a thought, but weighing heavily on her mind—that her whole orb of life, both before and after, was connected with this spot, as with the one point that gave it unity.

Little Pearl, meanwhile, had quitted her mother's side, and was playing at her own will about the market-place. She made the sombre crowd cheerful by her erratic and glistening ray, even as a bird of bright plumage illuminates a whole tree of dusky foliage by darting to and fro, half seen and half concealed amid the twilight of the clustering leaves. She had an undulating, but oftentimes a sharp and irregular movement. It indicated the restless vivacity of her spirit, which to-day was doubly indefatigable in its tip-toe dance, because it was played upon and vibrated with her mother's disquietude. Whenever Pearl saw anything to excite her ever active and wandering curiosity, she flew thitherward, and, as we might say, seized upon that man or thing as her own property, so far as she desired it, but without yielding the minutest degree of control over her motions in requital. The Puritans looked on, and, if they smiled, were none the less inclined to pronounce the child a demon offspring, from the indescribable charm of beauty and eccentricity that shone through her little figure, and sparkled with its activity. She ran and looked the wild Indian in the face, and he grew conscious of a nature wilder than his own. Thence, with native audacity, but still with a reserve as characteristic, she flew into the midst of a group of mariners, the swarthy-cheeked wild men of the ocean, as the Indians were of the land; and they gazed wonderingly and admiringly at Pearl, as if a flake of the sea-foam had taken the shape of a little maid, and were gifted with a soul of the sea-fire, that flashes beneath the prow in the night-time.

One of these seafaring men—the shipmaster, indeed, who had spoken to Hester Prynne—was so smitten with Pearl's aspect, that he attempted to lay hands upon her, with purpose to snatch a kiss. Finding it as impossible to touch her as to catch a humming-bird in the air, he took from his hat the gold chain that was twisted about it, and threw it to the child. Pearl immediately twined it around her neck and waist with such happy skill, that, once seen there, it became a part of her, and it was difficult to imagine her without it.

"Thy mother is yonder woman with the scarlet letter," said the seaman, "Wilt thou carry her a message from me?"

"If the message pleases me, I will," answered Pearl.

"Then tell her," rejoined he, "that I spake again with the black-a-visaged, hump shouldered old doctor, and he engages to bring his friend, the gentleman she wots of, aboard with him. So let thy mother take no thought, save for herself and thee. Wilt thou tell her this, thou witch-baby?"

"Mistress Hibbins says my father is the Prince of the Air!" cried Pearl, with a naughty smile. "If thou callest me that ill-name, I shall tell him of thee, and he will chase thy ship with a tempest!"

Pursuing a zigzag course across the marketplace, the child returned to her mother, and communicated what the mariner had said. Hester's strong, calm steadfastly-enduring spirit almost sank, at last, on beholding this dark and grim countenance of an inevitable doom, which at the moment when a passage seemed to open for the minister and herself out of their labyrinth of misery—showed itself with an unrelenting smile, right in the midst of their path.

With her mind harassed by the terrible perplexity in which the shipmaster's intelligence involved her, she was also subjected to another trial. There were many people present from the country round about, who had often heard of the scarlet letter, and to whom it had been made terrific by a hundred false or exaggerated rumours, but who had never beheld it with their own bodily eyes. These, after exhausting other modes of amusement, now thronged about Hester Prynne with rude and boorish intrusiveness. Unscrupulous as it was, however, it could not bring them nearer than a circuit of several yards. At that distance they accordingly stood, fixed there by the centrifugal force of the repugnance which the mystic symbol inspired. The whole gang of sailors, likewise, observing the press of spectators, and learning the purport of the scarlet letter, came and thrust their sunburnt and desperado-looking faces into the ring. Even the Indians were affected by a sort of cold shadow of the white man's curiosity and, gliding through the crowd, fastened their snake-like black eyes on Hester's bosom, conceiving, perhaps, that the wearer of this brilliantly embroidered badge must needs be a personage of high dignity among her people. Lastly, the inhabitants of the town (their own interest in this worn-out subject languidly reviving itself, by sympathy with what they saw others feel) lounged idly to the same quarter, and tormented Hester Prynne, perhaps more than all the rest, with their cool, well-acquainted gaze at her familiar shame. Hester saw and recognized the selfsame faces of that group of matrons, who had awaited her forthcoming from the prison-door seven years ago; all save one, the youngest and only compassionate among them, whose burial-robe she had since made. At the final hour, when she was so soon to fling aside the burning letter, it had strangely become the centre of more remark and excitement, and was thus made to sear her breast more painfully, than at any time since the first day she put it on.

While Hester stood in that magic circle of ignominy, where the cunning cruelty of her sentence seemed to have fixed her for ever, the admirable preacher was looking down from the sacred pulpit upon an audience whose very inmost spirits had yielded to his control. The sainted minister in the church! The woman of the scarlet letter in the marketplace! What imagination would have been irreverent enough to surmise that the same scorching stigma was on them both!

COMMENTARY

In Chapter XXII, the narrator offers another mini-lesson on life in the colonies. We learn, for example, that the music presented during the procession before Dimmesdale's sermon is offered by a military group. This honorable company is composed primarily of gentlemen who established their military prowess in European battles. Their brilliant outfits give them an elegant appearance unmatched by the modern military. Even more impressive are the civilians following behind these military men: They have an aura of "majesty" and "reverence" that the narrator feels has disappeared from modern life. During the festival and procession scenes, we are given a new look at the culture of seventeenth-century America as interpreted by the narrator. The early colonists admired solidity, fortitude, integrity, and respectability more than intelligence, so these were the characteristics that typified their leaders. Priests, unlike politicians, were more renowned for their intellectual gifts, and they often discovered that religious and political power coexisted in colonial life.

The changes in Dimmesdale's appearance and vitality following his conversation with Hester in the forest are still apparent. In particular, he shows more energy and firmness than ever before, but the narrator describes this as a spiritual rather than a physical energy. He doesn't seem to be fully present at the procession, as if his body and mind have become separated.

Seeing the minister in this new state of being disheartens Hester, who feels that Dimmesdale has moved so far out of her reach that she barely recognizes him; he no longer seems to be the man she sat in the forest with just days ago. Enveloped in the music and in the movement of the procession, he becomes unattainable and intangible. Hester's strong spirit flags: Was she deluded to imagine that a passionate connection existed between her and Dimmesdale? Is the minister capable of sustaining a deep physical bond, or does his guilt make him inaccessible to human connection? Continuing in his failure to acknowledge Hester or Pearl, the minister has again withdrawn himself, so that Hester receives neither comfort nor guidance from him.

Pearl also recognizes the difference in Dimmesdale's appearance; she wonders if this is the same minister who kissed her by the brook. Pointing to the vast divide between public and private space, Hester tells Pearl that she can't speak in the marketplace of things that happened in the forest. Mistress Hibbins reiterates this gap between public and private selves by noting that Dimmesdale looks like a saint yet passes sinful moments in the forest. Unlike many of the supposedly faithful people who Mistress Hibbins has seen in the woods, Dimmesdale is able to completely disguise the hidden aspect of his personality. This discrepancy in his appearance—the fundamental lie on which his identity is built—seems to be the minister's biggest sin, the one that renders him "dim," a mere shadow. Foreshadowing Dimmesdale's actions in the next chapter, Mistress Hibbins suggests that guilty secrets are always eventually revealed, as in the minister's case by his habit of always placing his hand over his heart. Many of Mistress Hibbins' comments are similar to Pearl's, as if they both have an inherent understanding of the shadowy side of human behavior.

While Dimmesdale has become emotionally and spiritually remote, his words still carry passion and eloquence so that his sermon finds the hidden places in the human heart. Although Hester can't hear his exact words, the sound of Dimmesdale's voice offers a message to her. With her deep understanding of his character, Hester recognizes the nuances of his tone. No matter how majestic his voice becomes, it still carries an undertone of suffering and anguish, almost as if his voice is asking for forgiveness. The undercurrent of pain is what connects the minister to his listeners and gives his sermon its emotional power.

The wildness of Pearl's nature is highlighted again in this chapter. She is described as a hummingbird and as a "bird of bright plumage." In her movements, she darts, glistens, illuminates, undulates, dances, flies, and sparkles—all words that capture her indefatigable energy and eccentricity. To the Native American onlookers, she has a wildness of spirit that seems out of place among Puritan rigidity. To the sailors, she appears to be a "flake of the sea-foam," filled with the "sea-fire" that flashes under the prow of a ship at night. When the sea captain tries to kiss her, he finds her as impossible to grasp as a bird in flight. Notice the recurrent associations of Pearl with birds, the sea, and fire: All these associations are gathered together in this chapter to form a composite picture of the wild and indefatigable Pearl.

Hester and Pearl are the object of public attention in this F.O.C. Darley illustration. Photo courtesy of The Darley Society, Inc.

Hester seems to be functioning as a circus act to strangers at the festival who flock around her to view the infamous scarlet letter. Ironically, just as she was about to escape from the tribulations associated with the letter, it assumes even greater significance in her life. Hester feels as if she's been returned to the scaffold on that first day after being released from prison, a notion that foreshadows the events of the next chapter. The "magic circle of ignominy" has Hester locked in its iron grip, and the chances of escape seem remote.

While Pearl's spirit seems unleashed in its full glory in this chapter, Hester's spirit is weakening under the knowledge that her plans to escape with Dimmesdale will fail. The "dark and grim" face of an unavoidable doom is blocking her path to happiness and freedom. In addition, Both Dimmesdale and Hester are thus the objects of the crowd's gaze, but the minister is at the height of his spiritual prowess, while Hester is the height of her torment over the scarlet letter. The minister's lack of courage seems to have left Hester isolated and friendless, an unhappy spectacle amid the curious crowd.

Chapter XXIII

Dimmesdale learns that he can escape Chillingworth only on the scaffold. With all the Election Day crowd as witnesses, he mounts the scaffold and calls Hester and Pearl to him. The minister declares his guilt, then falls, soon uttering his dying words: "Praise be his name! His will be done! Farewell!"

CHAPTER XXIII: THE REVELATION OF THE SCARLET LETTER

THE eloquent voice, on which the souls of the listening audience had been borne aloft as on the swelling waves of the sea, at length came to a pause. There was a momentary silence, profound as what should follow the utterance of oracles. Then ensued a murmur and half-hushed tumult, as if the auditors, released from the high spell that had transported them into the region of another's mind, were returning into themselves, with all their awe and wonder still heavy on them. In a moment more the crowd began to gush forth from the doors of the church. Now that there was an end, they needed more breath, more fit to support the gross and earthly life into which they relapsed, than that atmosphere which the preacher had converted into words of flame, and had burdened with the rich fragrance of his thought.

In the open air their rapture broke into speech. The street and the market-place absolutely babbled, from side to side, with applauses of the minister. His hearers could not rest until they had told one another of what each knew better than he could tell or hear.

According to their united testimony, never had man spoken in so wise, so high, and so holy a spirit, as he that spake this day; nor had inspiration ever breathed through mortal lips more evidently than it did through his. Its influence could be seen, as it were, descending upon him, and possessing him, and continually lifting him out of the written discourse that lay before him, and filling him with ideas that must have been as marvellous to himself as to his audience. His subject, it appeared, had been the relation between the Deity and the communities of mankind, with a special reference to the New England which they were here planting in the wilderness. And, as he drew towards the close, a spirit as of prophecy had come upon him, constraining him to its purpose as mightily as the old prophets of Israel were constrained, only with this difference, that, whereas the Jewish seers had denounced judgments and ruin on their country, it was his mission to foretell a high and glorious destiny for the newly gathered people of the Lord. But, throughout it all, and through the whole discourse, there had been a certain deep, sad undertone of pathos, which could not be interpreted otherwise than as the natural regret of one soon to pass away. Yes; their minister whom they so loved— and who so loved them all, that he could not depart heavenward without a sigh—had the foreboding of untimely death upon him, and would soon leave them in their tears. This idea of his transitory stay on earth

gave the last emphasis to the effect which the preacher had produced; it
was if an angel, in his passage to the skies, had shaken his bright wings
over the people for an instant—at once a shadow and a splendour—and
had shed down a shower of golden truths upon them.

Thus, there had come to the Reverend Mr. Dimmesdale—as to most
men, in their various spheres, though seldom recognised until they see it
far behind them—an epoch of life more brilliant and full of triumph
than any previous one, or than any which could hereafter be. He stood,
at this moment, on the very proudest eminence of superiority, to which
the gifts or intellect, rich lore, prevailing eloquence, and a reputation of
whitest sanctity, could exalt a clergyman in New England's earliest days,
when the professional character was of itself a lofty pedestal. Such was the
position which the minister occupied, as he bowed his head forward on
the cushions of the pulpit at the close of his Election Sermon. Meanwhile
Hester Prynne was standing beside the scaffold of the pillory, with the
scarlet letter still burning on her breast!

Now was heard again the clamour of the music, and the measured tramp
of the military escort issuing from the church door. The procession was
to be marshalled thence to the town hall, where a solemn banquet would
complete the ceremonies of the day.

Once more, therefore, the train of venerable and majestic fathers were
seen moving through a broad pathway of the people, who drew back rev-
erently, on either side, as the Governor and magistrates, the old and wise
men, the holy ministers, and all that were eminent and renowned,
advanced into the midst of them. When they were fairly in the market-
place, their presence was greeted by a shout. This—though doubtless it
might acquire additional force and volume from the child-like loyalty
which the age awarded to its rulers—was felt to be an irrepressible out-
burst of enthusiasm kindled in the auditors by that high strain of eloquence which was yet reverberating in their ears. Each felt the impulse in
himself, and in the same breath, caught it from his neighbour. Within
the church, it had hardly been kept down; beneath the sky it pealed
upward to the zenith. There were human beings enough, and enough of
highly wrought and symphonious feeling to produce that more impressive sound than the organ tones of the blast, or the thunder, or the roar
of the sea; even that mighty swell of many voices, blended into one great
voice by the universal impulse which makes likewise one vast heart out of
the many. Never, from the soil of New England had gone up such a
shout! Never, on New England soil had stood the man so honoured by
his mortal brethren as the preacher!

How fared it with him, then? Were there not the brilliant particles of a
halo in the air about his head? So etherealised by spirit as he was, and so
apotheosised by worshipping admirers, did his footsteps, in the procession, really tread upon the dust of earth?

As the ranks of military men and civil fathers moved onward, all eyes
were turned towards the point where the minister was seen to approach

among them. The shout died into a murmur, as one portion of the crowd after another obtained a glimpse of him. How feeble and pale he looked, amid all his triumph! The energy—or say, rather, the inspiration which had held him up, until he should have delivered the sacred message that had brought its own strength along with it from heaven—was withdrawn, now that it had so faithfully performed its office. The glow, which they had just before beheld burning on his cheek, was extinguished, like a flame that sinks down hopelessly among the late decaying embers. It seemed hardly the face of a man alive, with such a death-like hue: it was hardly a man with life in him, that tottered on his path so nervously, yet tottered, and did not fall!

One of his clerical brethren—it was the venerable John Wilson—observing the state in which Mr. Dimmesdale was left by the retiring wave of intellect and sensibility, stepped forward hastily to offer his support. The minister tremulously, but decidedly, repelled the old man's arm. He still walked onward, if that movement could be so described, which rather resembled the wavering effort of an infant, with its mother's arms in view, outstretched to tempt him forward. And now, almost imperceptible as were the latter steps of his progress, he had come opposite the well-remembered and weather-darkened scaffold, where, long since, with all that dreary lapse of time between, Hester Prynne had encountered the world's ignominious stare. There stood Hester, holding little Pearl by the hand! And there was the scarlet letter on her breast! The minister here made a pause; although the music still played the stately and rejoicing march to which the procession moved. It summoned him onward—inward to the festival!—but here he made a pause.

Bellingham, for the last few moments, had kept an anxious eye upon him. He now left his own place in the procession, and advanced to give assistance judging, from Mr. Dimmesdale's aspect that he must otherwise inevitably fall. But there was something in the latter's expression that warned back the magistrate, although a man not readily obeying the vague intimations that pass from one spirit to another. The crowd, meanwhile, looked on with awe and wonder. This earthly faintness, was, in their view, only another phase of the minister's celestial strength; nor would it have seemed a miracle too high to be wrought for one so holy, had he ascended before their eyes, waxing dimmer and brighter, and fading at last into the light of heaven!

He turned towards the scaffold, and stretched forth his arms.

"Hester," said he, "come hither! Come, my little Pearl!"

It was a ghastly look with which he regarded them; but there was something at once tender and strangely triumphant in it. The child, with the bird-like motion, which was one of her characteristics, flew to him, and clasped her arms about his knees. Hester Prynne—slowly, as if impelled by inevitable fate, and against her strongest will—likewise drew near, but paused before she reached him. At this instant old Roger Chillingworth thrust himself through the crowd—or, perhaps, so dark, disturbed, and evil was his look, he rose up out of some nether region—to snatch back his victim from what he sought to do! Be that as it might, the old man rushed forward, and caught the minister by the arm.

"Madman, hold! what is your purpose?" whispered he. "Wave back that woman! Cast off this child! All shall be well! Do not blacken your fame, and perish in dishonour! I can yet save you! Would you bring infamy on your sacred profession?"

"Ha, tempter! Methinks thou art too late!" answered the minister, encountering his eye, fearfully, but firmly. "Thy power is not what it was! With God's help, I shall escape thee now!"

He again extended his hand to the woman of the scarlet letter.

"Hester Prynne," cried he, with a piercing earnestness, "in the name of Him, so terrible and so merciful, who gives me grace, at this last moment, to do what—for my own heavy sin and miserable agony—I withheld myself from doing seven years ago, come hither now, and twine thy strength about me! Thy strength, Hester; but let it be guided by the will which God hath granted me! This wretched and wronged old man is opposing it with all his might!—with all his own might, and the fiend's! Come, Hester, come! Support me up yonder scaffold."

The crowd was in a tumult. The men of rank and dignity, who stood more immediately around the clergyman, were so taken by surprise, and so perplexed as to the purport of what they saw—unable to receive the explanation which most readily presented itself, or to imagine any other—that they remained silent and inactive spectators of the judgement which Providence seemed about to work. They beheld the minister, leaning on Hester's shoulder, and supported by her arm around him, approach the scaffold, and ascend its steps; while still the little hand of the sin-born child was clasped in his. Old Roger Chillingworth followed, as one intimately connected with the drama of guilt and sorrow in which they had all been actors, and well entitled, therefore to be present at its closing scene.

"Hadst thou sought the whole earth over," said he looking darkly at the clergyman, "there was no one place so secret—no high place nor lowly place, where thou couldst have escaped me—save on this very scaffold!"

"Thanks be to Him who hath led me hither!" answered the minister.

Yet he trembled, and turned to Hester, with an expression of doubt and anxiety in his eyes, not the less evidently betrayed, that there was a feeble smile upon his lips.

"Is not this better," murmured he, "than what we dreamed of in the forest?"

"I know not! I know not!" she hurriedly replied. "Better? Yea; so we may both die, and little Pearl die with us!"

"For thee and Pearl, be it as God shall order," said the minister; "and God is merciful! Let me now do the will which He hath made plain before my sight. For, Hester, I am a dying man. So let me make haste to take my shame upon me!"

Partly supported by Hester Prynne, and holding one hand of little Pearl's, the Reverend Mr. Dimmesdale turned to the dignified and venerable rulers; to the holy ministers, who were his brethren; to the people, whose great heart was thoroughly appalled yet overflowing with tearful sympathy, as knowing that some deep life-matter—which, if full of sin, was full of anguish and repentance likewise—was now to be laid open to them. The sun, but little past its meridian, shone down upon the clergyman, and gave a distinctness to his figure, as he stood out from all the earth, to put in his plea of guilty at the bar of Eternal Justice.

"People of New England!" cried he, with a voice that rose over them, high, solemn, and majestic—yet had always a tremor through it, and sometimes a shriek, struggling up out of a fathomless depth of remorse and woe—"ye, that have loved me!—ye, that have deemed me holy!—behold me here, the one sinner of the world! At last—at last!—I stand upon the spot where, seven years since, I should have stood, here, with this woman, whose arm, more than the little strength wherewith I have crept hitherward, sustains me at this dreadful moment, from grovelling down upon my face! Lo, the scarlet letter which Hester wears! Ye have all shuddered at it! Wherever her walk hath been—wherever, so miserably burdened, she may have hoped to find repose—it hath cast a lurid gleam of awe and horrible repugnance round about her. But there stood one in the midst of you, at whose brand of sin and infamy ye have not shuddered!"

It seemed, at this point, as if the minister must leave the remainder of his secret undisclosed. But he fought back the bodily weakness—and, still more, the faintness of heart—that was striving for the mastery with him. He threw off all assistance, and stepped passionately forward a pace before the woman and the children.

"It was on him!" he continued, with a kind of fierceness; so determined was he to speak out tile whole. "God's eye beheld it! The angels were for ever pointing at it! (The Devil knew it well, and fretted it continually with the touch of his burning finger!) But he hid it cunningly from men, and walked among you with the mien of a spirit, mournful, because so pure in a sinful world!—and sad, because he missed his heavenly kindred! Now, at the death-hour, he stands up before you! He bids you look again at Hester's scarlet letter! He tells you, that, with all its mysterious horror, it is but the shadow of what he bears on his own breast, and that even this, his own red stigma, is no more than the type of what has seared his inmost heart! Stand any here that question God's judgment on a sinner! Behold! Behold, a dreadful witness of it!"

With a convulsive motion, he tore away the ministerial band from before his breast. It was revealed! But it were irreverent to describe that revelation. For an instant, the gaze of the horror-stricken multitude was concentrated on the ghastly miracle; while the minister stood, with a flush of triumph in his face, as one who, in the crisis of acutest pain, had won a victory. Then, down he sank upon the scaffold! Hester partly raised him, and supported his head against her bosom. Old Roger Chillingworth knelt down beside him, with a blank, dull countenance, out of which the life seemed to have departed.

"Thou hast escaped me!" he repeated more than once. "Thou hast escaped me!"

"May God forgive thee!" said the minister. "Thou, too, hast deeply sinned!"

He withdrew his dying eyes from the old man, and fixed them on the woman and the child.

"My little Pearl," said he, feebly and there was a sweet and gentle smile over his face, as of a spirit sinking into deep repose; nay, now that the burden was removed, it seemed almost as if he would be sportive with the child—"dear little Pearl, wilt thou kiss me now? Thou wouldst not, yonder, in the forest! But now thou wilt?"

Pearl kissed his lips. A spell was broken. The great scene of grief, in which the wild infant bore a part had developed all her sympathies; and as her tears fell upon her father's cheek, they were the pledge that she would grow up amid human joy and sorrow, nor forever do battle with the world, but be a woman in it. Towards her mother, too, Pearl's errand as a messenger of anguish was fulfilled.

"Hester," said the clergyman, "farewell!"

"Shall we not meet again?" whispered she, bending her face down close to his. "Shall we not spend our immortal life together? Surely, surely, we have ransomed one another, with all this woe! Thou lookest far into eternity, with those bright dying eyes! Then tell me what thou seest!"

"Hush, Hester, hush!" said he, with tremulous solemnity. "The law we broke!—the sin here awfully revealed!—let these alone be in thy thoughts! I fear! I fear! It may be, that, when we forgot our God—when we violated our reverence each for the other's soul—it was thenceforth vain to hope that we could meet hereafter, in an everlasting and pure reunion. God knows; and He is merciful! He hath proved his mercy, most of all, in my afflictions. By giving me this burning torture to bear upon my breast! By sending yonder dark and terrible old man, to keep the torture always at red-heat! By bringing me hither, to die this death of triumphant ignominy before the people! Had either of these agonies been wanting, I had been lost for ever! Praised be His name! His will be done! Farewell!"

That final word came forth with the minister's expiring breath. The multitude, silent till then, broke out in a strange, deep voice of awe and wonder, which could not as yet find utterance, save in this murmur that rolled so heavily after the departed spirit.

COMMENTARY

The Election Day crowd feels that Dimmesdale's sermon was spoken with "words of flame," an allusion to the flaming tongues with which the apostles spoke at Pentecost. This phrase reminds the reader of the narrator's remarks in Chapter XI, when he emphasized Dimmesdale's ability to speak a universal language because he himself knows the effects of sin. With the Election Sermon, Dimmesdale has attained the true spirit of Christian doctrine in his language. The crowd labels his words "wise," "high," and "holy," believing that inspiration has rarely, if ever, been so clearly articulated by human lips.

The subject of his sermon is the relation between God and humanity, and he offers a flattering prophecy to the community: They will have a mighty and glorious future. But there's a duality in Dimmesdale's speech, as there is in his personality; a tone of sadness underlies his speech, which his listeners interpret as his recognition of impending death. Again he is compared to an angel, which has brought both its shadow and splendor into this human community.

Dimmesdale is at the peak of his power during the sermon, poised at the moment before his fall. Highlighting the contrast between the minister and Hester, the narrator juxtaposes the image of a glorious Dimmesdale with that of Hester standing beside the scaffold with the scarlet letter still burning into her breast. The narrator exaggerates the extent of the public's adoration of Dimmesdale in order to make this contrast even more apparent. For example, he claims that at this moment of Dimmesdale's power, all the voices of New England seem joined together to praise him; the narrator assures us that never before on New England soil "has stood the man so honored by his mortal brethren as the preacher!" But the glow of inspiration that has guided Dimmesdale since his conversation with Hester in the woods is suddenly extinguished following the sermon. In a description that foreshadows the chapter's end, the narrator describes him as feeble and worn, almost death-like. While the members of the crowd expect to see Dimmesdale fade up into the light of heaven at any moment, the loss of his powers also signals the end of Hester's plans for a new and better life. The moment of truth has finally, irrevocably arrived for the spirit-worn minister.

In this Lantern slide wash drawing, Dimmesdale ascends the scaffold.
©Bettmann/CORBIS

The novel's action culminates in this third and final scaffold scene, in which Dimmesdale, Hester, and Pearl together ascend the scaffold in broad daylight. As they make their ascent, Chillingworth rushes forth, like a demon from hell, promising that he will save the minister's reputation if he does not climb the scaffold steps. But Dimmesdale has realized that the only way for him to truly attain peace is to declare his guilt, so that his public and private selves can be united. As he makes his way to the scaffold, both Reverend Wilson and Governor Bellingham attempt to help him walk, but he rejects their assistance, symbolically showing that he will not find salvation through the church or the state. Only with Hester's strength is he able to walk up the steps of the scaffold. Fighting for Dimmesdale's soul, Hester and God pit their strength against the opposing powers of Chillingworth and the devil. Hester wins. Only on the scaffold can Dimmesdale escape from Chillingworth—only by publicly admitting his guilt.

*Dimmesdale collapses on the scaffold in this F.O.C. Darley illustration.
Photo courtesy of The Darley Society, Inc.*

At the moment of revelation, Dimmesdale rips open his shirt to show his chest. What do the spectators see? The narrator doesn't reveal this detail. Just as in Chapter X, when Chillingworth saw something wondrous on Dimmesdale's chest, the reader is left to guess exactly what that "something" is. More important than any physical manifestation of the minister's guilt is the fact that Pearl kisses Dimmesdale, and a spell is broken. Through her presence at this tragic moment, Pearl is symbolically humanized, becoming one with human joy and sorrow. No longer will she be her mother's reminder of the scarlet letter; she is released to be simply the object of Hester's affection. Showing the differences between himself and Chillingworth, Dimmesdale blesses his tormentor, proving that forgiveness is always preferable to revenge. Thus, this scene which began with Dimmesdale's triumphant sermon ends with the "triumphant ignominy" of his death. Ironically, only through public disgrace does Dimmesdale finally attain peace.

Chapter XXIV

Among the townspeople, opinions diverge about what happened on the scaffold: Many people think they saw an "A" imprinted on Dimmesdale's chest. Chillingworth dies soon after Dimmesdale, leaving a fortune to Pearl. She and Hester move away to Europe, and many years later Hester returns, alone, to Boston. Again, she lives alone in her seaside cottage with the letter still affixed to her chest, but it has become a symbol of compassion and comfort rather than a stigma.

CHAPTER XXIV: CONCLUSION

AFTER many days, when time sufficed for the people to arrange their thoughts in reference to the foregoing scene, there was more than one account of what had been witnessed on the scaffold.

Most of the spectators testified to having seen, on the breast of the unhappy minister, a SCARLET LETTER—the very semblance of that worn by Hester Prynne—imprinted in the flesh. As regarded its origin there were various explanations, all of which must necessarily have been conjectural. Some affirmed that the Reverend Mr. Dimmesdale, on the very day when Hester Prynne first wore her ignominious badge, had begun a course of penance—which he afterwards, in so many futile methods, followed out—by inflicting a hideous torture on himself. Others contended that the stigma had not been produced until a long time sub-sequent, when old Roger Chillingworth, being a potent necromancer, had caused it to appear, through the agency of magic and poisonous drugs. Others, again and those best able to appreciate the minister's pecu-liar sensibility, and the wonderful operation of his spirit upon the body—whispered their belief, that the awful symbol was the effect of the ever-active tooth of remorse, gnawing from the inmost heart outwardly, and at last manifesting Heaven's dreadful judgment by the visible pres-ence of the letter. The reader may choose among these theories. We have thrown all the light we could acquire upon the portent, and would gladly, now that it has done its office, erase its deep print out of our own brain, where long meditation has fixed it in very undesirable distinctness.

It is singular, nevertheless, that certain persons, who were spectators of the whole scene, and professed never once to have removed their eyes from the Reverend Mr. Dimmesdale, denied that there was any mark whatever on his breast, more than on a new-born infant's. Neither, by their report, had his dying words acknowledged, nor even remotely implied, any—the slightest—connexion on his part, with the guilt for which Hester Prynne had so long worn the scarlet letter. According to these highly-respectable witnesses, the minister, conscious that he was dying—conscious, also, that the reverence of the multitude placed him already among saints and angels—had desired, by yielding up his breath in the arms of that fallen woman, to express to the world how utterly nugatory is the choicest of man's own righteousness. After exhausting life in his efforts for mankind's spiritual good, he had made the manner of his death a parable, in order to impress on his admirers the mighty and mournful lesson, that, in the view of Infinite Purity, we are sinners all alike. It was to teach them, that the holiest amongst us has but attained so far above his fellows as to discern more clearly the Mercy which looks down, and repudiate more utterly the phantom of human merit, which would look aspiringly upward. Without disputing a truth so momentous, we must be allowed to consider this version of Mr. Dimmesdale's story as only an instance of that stubborn fidelity with which a man's friends— and especially a clergyman's—will sometimes uphold his character, when proofs, clear as the mid-day sunshine on the scarlet letter, establish him a false and sin-stained creature of the dust.

The authority which we have chiefly followed—a manuscript of old date, drawn up from the verbal testimony of individuals, some of whom had known Hester Prynne, while others had heard the tale from contemporary witnesses fully confirms the view taken in the foregoing pages. Among many morals which press upon us from the poor minister's miserable experience, we put only this into a sentence:—"Be true! Be true! Be true! Show freely to the world, if not your worst, yet some trait whereby the worst may be inferred!"

Nothing was more remarkable than the change which took place, almost immediately after Mr. Dimmesdale's death, in the appearance and demeanour of the old man known as Roger Chillingworth. All his strength and energy—all his vital and intellectual force—seemed at once to desert him, insomuch that he positively withered up, shrivelled away and almost vanished from mortal sight, like an uprooted weed that lies wilting in the sun. This unhappy man had made the very principle of his life to consist in the pursuit and systematic exercise of revenge; and when, by its completest triumph and consummation that evil principle was left with no further material to support it—when, in short, there was no more Devil's work on earth for him to do, it only remained for the unhumanised mortal to betake himself whither his master would find him tasks enough, and pay him his wages duly. But, to all these shadowy beings, so long our near acquaintances—as well Roger Chillingworth as his companions—we would fain be merciful. It is a curious subject of observation and inquiry, whether hatred and love be not the same thing at bottom. Each, in its utmost development, supposes a high degree of intimacy and heart-knowledge; each renders one individual dependent for the food of his affections and spiritual fife upon another: each leaves the passionate lover, or the no less passionate hater, forlorn and desolate by the withdrawal of his subject. Philosophically considered, therefore, the two passions seem essentially the same, except that one happens to be seen in a celestial radiance, and the other in a dusky and lurid glow. In the spiritual world, the old physician and the minister—mutual victims as they have been—may, unawares, have found their earthly stock of hatred and antipathy transmuted into golden love.

Leaving this discussion apart, we have a matter of business to communicate to the reader. At old Roger Chillingworth's decease, (which took place within the year), and by his last will and testament, of which Governor Bellingham and the Reverend Mr. Wilson were executors, he bequeathed a very considerable amount of property, both here and in England to little Pearl, the daughter of Hester Prynne.

So Pearl—the elf child—the demon offspring, as some people up to that epoch persisted in considering her—became the richest heiress of her day in the New World. Not improbably this circumstance wrought a very material change in the public estimation; and had the mother and child remained here, little Pearl at a marriageable period of life might have mingled her wild blood with the lineage of the devoutest Puritan among them all. But, in no long time after the physician's death, the wearer of the scarlet letter disappeared, and Pearl along with her. For many years, though a vague report would now and then find its way across the sea—like a shapeless piece of driftwood tossed ashore with the initials of a name upon it—yet no tidings of them unquestionably authentic were received. The story of the scarlet letter grew into a legend. Its spell, however, was still potent, and kept the scaffold awful where the poor minister had died, and likewise the cottage by the sea-shore where Hester Prynne had dwelt. Near this latter spot, one afternoon some children were at play, when they beheld a tall woman in a gray robe approach the cottage-door. In all those years it had never once been opened; but either she unlocked it or the decaying wood and iron yielded to her hand, or she glided shadow-like through these impediments—and, at all events, went in.

On the threshold she paused—turned partly round—for perchance the idea of entering alone and all so changed, the home of so intense a former life, was more dreary and desolate than even she could bear. But her hesitation was only for an instant, though long enough to display a scarlet letter on her breast.

And Hester Prynne had returned, and taken up her long-forsaken shame! But where was little Pearl? If still alive she must now have been in the flush and bloom of early womanhood. None knew—nor ever learned with the fulness of perfect certainty—whether the elf-child had gone thus untimely to a maiden grave; or whether her wild, rich nature had been softened and subdued and made capable of a woman's gentle happiness. But through the remainder of Hester's life there were indications that the recluse of the scarlet letter was the object of love and interest with some inhabitant of another land. Letters came, with armorial seals upon them, though of bearings unknown to English heraldry. In the cottage there were articles of comfort and luxury such as Hester never cared to use, but which only wealth could have purchased and affection have imagined for her. There were trifles too, little ornaments, beautiful tokens of a continual remembrance, that must have been wrought by delicate fingers at the impulse of a fond heart. And once Hester was seen embroidering a baby-garment with such a lavish richness of golden fancy as would have raised a public tumult had any infant thus apparelled, been shown to our sober-hued community.

In fine, the gossips of that day believed—and Mr. Surveyor Pue, who made investigations a century later, believed—and one of his recent successors in office, moreover, faithfully believes—that Pearl was not only alive, but married, and happy, and mindful of her mother; and that she would most joyfully have entertained that sad and lonely mother at her fireside.

But there was a more real life for Hester Prynne, here, in New England, than in that unknown region where Pearl had found a home. Here had been her sin; here, her sorrow; and here was yet to be her penitence. She had returned, therefore, and resumed of her own free will, for not the sternest magistrate of that iron period would have imposed it—resumed the symbol of which we have related so dark a tale. Never afterwards did it quit her bosom. But, in the lapse of the toilsome, thoughtful, and self-devoted years that made up Hester's life, the scarlet letter ceased to be a stigma which attracted the world's scorn and bitterness, and became a type of something to be sorrowed over, and looked upon with awe, yet with reverence too. And, as Hester Prynne had no selfish ends, nor lived in any measure for her own profit and enjoyment, people brought all their sorrows and perplexities, and besought her counsel, as one who had herself gone through a mighty trouble. Women, more especially—in the continually recurring trials of wounded, wasted, wronged, misplaced, or erring and sinful passion—or with the dreary burden of a heart unyielded, because unvalued and unsought—came to Hester's cottage, demanding why they were so wretched, and what the remedy! Hester comforted and counselled them, as best she might. She assured them, too, of her firm belief that, at some brighter period, when the world should have grown ripe for it, in Heaven's own time, a new truth would be revealed, in order to establish the whole relation between man and woman on a surer ground of mutual happiness. Earlier in life, Hester had vainly imagined that she herself might be the destined prophetess, but had long since recognised the impossibility that any mission of divine and mysterious truth should be confided to a woman stained with sin, bowed down with shame, or even burdened with a life-long sorrow. The angel and apostle of the coming revelation must be a woman, indeed, but lofty, pure, and beautiful, and wise; moreover, not through dusky grief, but the ethereal medium of joy; and showing how sacred love should make us happy, by the truest test of a life successful to such an end.

So said Hester Prynne, and glanced her sad eyes downward at the scarlet letter. And, after many, many years, a new grave was delved, near an old and sunken one, in that burial-ground beside which King's Chapel has since been built. It was near that old and sunken grave, yet with a space between, as if the dust of the two sleepers had no right to mingle. Yet one tomb-stone served for both. All around, there were monuments carved with armorial bearings; and on this simple slab of slate—as the curious investigator may still discern, and perplex himself with the purport—there appeared the semblance of an engraved **escutcheon**. It bore a device, a herald's wording of which may serve for a motto and brief description of our now concluded legend; so sombre is it, and relieved only by one ever-glowing point of light gloomier than the shadow:—

"ON A FIELD, SABLE, THE LETTER A, **GULES**."

escutcheon: a shield or shield-shaped surface on which a coat of arms is displayed.

GULES: in heraldry, the color red.

COMMENTARY

This final chapter ties up all the loose ends left after the scaffold scene, but with a vagueness and ambiguity typical of Hawthorne. What exactly was imprinted on the minister's chest remains unclear. Rather than giving us a single answer, the narrator offers a variety of viewpoints. Many spectators believe it was an exact replica of Hester's scarlet letter, created by self-mutilation or by Chillingworth's spells or by the minister's gnawing "tooth of remorse." Others refuse to admit that any marking was on Dimmesdale's chest or even that he confessed to being Pearl's father. For these people, Dimmesdale simply wanted to make his death a parable, one proving that all humans are sinners. In their view, as with the minister's previous attempts at confession, this one only offers further proof of his humility and saintliness.

The narrator leaves room for interpretation regarding what exactly happened on the scaffold, asking the reader to accept the answer that seems most reasonable to him or her. Perhaps it doesn't matter. The most important lesson to be drawn from the story is: "Be true! Be true! Be true! Show freely to the world, if not your worst, yet some trait whereby the worst may be inferred!" Does this maxim seem true in terms of this story? How does truth relate to suffering in the novel?

With Dimmesdale's death, Chillingworth loses his purpose and soon dies. The narrator asks us to be merciful, even upon this sinner, because sometimes hate and love are essentially the same thing. He also suggests that Chillingworth and Dimmesdale may be joined together in heaven.

In death, Chillingworth atones for some of the damage done to Hester by leaving all his property to Pearl, who becomes the richest person in the colony. With this inheritance, the town's estimation of Pearl and her mother changes, and the narrator suggests that if she had remained in Boston, Pearl could probably have married one of the devout Puritans. Again emphasizing the hypocrisy of this community, the narrator indicates that money will wash away even the taint of witchcraft and illegitimacy. Pearl seems to find a happier, more fulfilling life away from the colonies, although we don't know this for certain. Rumor and research join to suggest that Pearl moved abroad and is happily married. That her presence on the scaffold at the moment of Dimmesdale's death humanized Pearl seems apparent: The gifts Hester regularly receives from abroad seem to be evidence of her daughter's continuing love and esteem. The narrator even

suggests that Pearl would love to have her mother live with her in Europe, but Hester has another agenda.

Having initially left Boston with Pearl, Hester eventually returns to her cottage by the sea. Why would she return to this site of infamy and suffering? Perhaps because so much of her life was lived here. Perhaps because she is still serving penance for her sins. Why does she still wear the scarlet letter? Is it a sign of her acceptance of Puritan morality? This doesn't seem likely, based on the narrator's earlier description of Hester's irreverent thinking. Does it perhaps signal her difference? Hawthorne never tells. Like so much in this chapter, the answers to these questions remain ambiguous and are left for the reader to decide. What we do know for certain is that the meaning of the letter has changed completely by the novel's end, becoming an object of awe and reverence rather than disdain. Hester provides solace to all sufferers, but, in particular, to women who have been wronged in love. In Hester's opinion, the world will one day change so that men and women can relate to each other happily. She also believes that an apostle of truth will one day come and that this visionary will be a woman, one who is beautiful and true. By associating Hester with this apostle, the novel implicitly valorizes her ideas over those of the other characters.

The tombstone that Hester and Dimmesdale share.

After her death, Hester is buried in a plot next to Dimmesdale, though far enough away so that their ashes will not mingle. Was Dimmesdale perhaps correct in prophesying that he and Hester would not be together in the afterlife? While their remains don't touch, though, they do share a tombstone that contains the motto of their mutual sin, implying that together they will bear the weight of the scarlet letter into eternity.

Notes

CLIFFSCOMPLETE REVIEW

Use this CliffsComplete Review to gauge what you learned and to build confidence in your understanding of the original text. After you work through the review questions, the problem-solving exercises and the suggested activities, you're well on your way to understanding and appreciating *The Scarlet Letter*.

TRUE / FALSE

1. T F One of Hawthorne's ancestors was a judge in the Salem witch trials.

2. T F When Roger Chillingworth arrives in Boston and discovers his wife, Hester, disgraced on the scaffold, his face writhes in horror like a snake.

3. T F Hester and her husband were once deeply in love, until he deserted her by moving west.

4. T F The needlework Hester does to support herself and Pearl is plain and ordinary, in typical Puritan fashion.

5. T F Some members of the town want to take Pearl away from Hester because they think she is too poor to support a child.

6. T F Pearl is associated with elves, mermaids, and the Lord of Misrule.

7. T F Arthur Dimmesdale asks Roger Chillingworth to come live with him because he feels guilty for falling in love with Chillingworth's wife.

8. T F "The Black Man" was another name for the devil in Puritan times.

9. T F After she's been wearing the scarlet letter for a while, it imparts a sacredness to Hester, much like a cross on a nun's chest.

10. T F Pearl intuitively equates the minister's habit of holding his hand over his chest with her mother's scarlet letter.

11. T F Hester hates Arthur Dimmesdale because he is too cowardly to reveal to the town that he is Pearl's father.

12. T F Chillingworth learns of Arthur and Hester's plan to sail to England, so he books a passage on the same ship.

13. T F Dimmesdale, Hester, and Pearl manage to escape from Chillingworth and live happily ever after in England.

14. T F The subject of Dimmesdale's Election Day speech is the relationship between God and humanity.

15. T F While Hester's mind is free and creative, Arthur's thinking is limited by the boundaries of traditional Christian doctrine.

MULTIPLE CHOICE

1. The narrator supposedly found the narrative that is the basis for *The Scarlet Letter* in

   a. a shoebox under his bed.

   b. a file cabinet at the Essex Historical Society.

   c. a rubbish heap in a corner of the custom house.

   d. a box filled with his father's papers.

2. Hawthorne suggests that the wild rosebush that grows outside the prison door is a symbol of
   a. a sweet moral blossom that could relieve this tale of human frailty and suffering.
   b. the loss of love.
   c. the beauty of youth.
   d. the thorny road that life often takes.

3. What does the scarlet letter look like?
   a. Very plain and severe, like most Puritan decorations
   b. Artistically done, with elaborate embroidery and flourishes of gold thread
   c. A plain A, twined with a thorny rosebush
   d. Small and understated, so that it blends into Hester's dress

4. Hester's husband, Roger Chillingworth, is
   a. much younger than she is.
   b. her soul mate.
   c. much older than she is.
   d. the minister of the town of Salem.

5. After she is released from prison, Hester remains in Boston because
   a. the townspeople won't let her go.
   b. she and Pearl's father can live together, giving Pearl a more stable lifestyle.
   c. she has neither money nor friends to support her if she moves.
   d. every other place on earth would feel foreign to her, so she is bound, psychologically, to stay.

6. To support herself and Pearl, Hester sells needlework for all public ceremonies except
   a. weddings.
   b. funerals.
   c. ordinations of new ministers.
   d. baptisms.

7. When asked who created her, Pearl says it was
   a. God.
   b. her parents.
   c. the wild rosebush outside the prison door.
   d. the Lord of Misrule.

8. Following an impressive meteor shower, the people of Boston see a symbol in the sky: a huge letter A. They interpret this A as standing for
   a. adultery.
   b. able.
   c. angel.
   d. Arthur (as in Arthur Dimmesdale).

9. Hester decides to reveal Chillingworth's true identity to Dimmesdale because
   a. she realizes that Chillingworth is literally killing Dimmesdale.
   b. she wants to hurt Dimmesdale by revealing her love for Chillingworth.
   c. she wants Pearl to meet her real father.
   d. otherwise Chillingworth will reveal the secret himself.

10. Hester explains the scarlet letter to Pearl by saying it is
    a. a symbol of her membership in a secret society of women.
    b. a family heirloom, given to her by her grandmother.
    c. a sample of her craftsmanship.
    d. a mark left from her one meeting with the Black Man.

FILL IN THE BLANK

1. Hester's daughter's name is _____.

2. The novel is set in _____, Massachusetts in the _____ century.

3. When Hester is released from prison, a wild _____ is growing just outside the prison door.

4. _____ is the name of Hester's husband.

5. The "A" of the scarlet letter originally stands for _____, but the townspeople later interpret it as _____, instead, because Hester is so strong.

6. The opening section of the novel, which gives some of Hawthorne's personal history, is called _____.

7. Dimmesdale, Hester, and Pearl plan to run away from Massachusetts on a ship bound for _____.

8. Roger Chillingworth is Dimmesdale's doctor, or, to use the seventeenth century word for doctor, his _____.

9. As Dimmesdale, Hester, and Pearl stand on the scaffold in the second scaffold scene, a _____ illuminates the sky.

10. On _____ Day, Dimmesdale reveals to the town that he is Pearl's father.

IDENTIFY THE QUOTATION

Identify these quotes by answering the following questions:

* Who is the speaker?
* Who is being spoken to?
* What is the context of the quote (what's just happened, what's just about to happen)?
* What important themes, images, or symbols are contained in the quote?
* How does this quote relate to the rest of the novel?

1. I have a strange fancy that this brook is the boundary between two worlds, and that thou canst never meet thy Pearl again. Or is she an elfish spirit, who, as the legends of our childhood taught us, is forbidden to cross a running stream? Pray hasten her; for this delay has already imparted a tremor to my nerves.

2. This envelope had the air of an official record of some period long past, when clerks engrossed their stiff and formal chirography on more substantial materials than at present. There was something about it that quickened an instinctive curiosity, and made me undo the faded red tape, that tied up the package, with the sense that a treasure would here be brought to light.

3. What do we talk of marks and brands, whether on the bodice of her gown, or the flesh of her forehead? This woman has brought shame upon us all, and ought to die. Is there not law for it? Truly there is, both in the scripture and the statute-book. Then let the magistrates, who have made it of no effect, thank themselves if their own wives and daughters go astray!

4. He has been conscious of me. He has felt an influence dwelling always upon him like a curse. He knew, by some spiritual sense,—for the Creator never made another being so sensitive as this,—he knew that no friendly hand was pulling at his heart-strings, and that an eye was looking curiously into him, which sought only evil, and found it.

5. Her final employment was to gather sea-weed, of various kinds, and make herself a scarf, or mantle, and a head-dress, and thus assume the aspect of a little mermaid. She inherited her mother's gift for devising drapery and costume.

6. And so it is! And, mother, he has his hand over his heart! Is it because, when the minister wrote his name in the book, the Black Man set his mark in that place? But why does he not wear it outside his bosom, as thou dost, mother?

7. After putting her fingers in her mouth, with many ungrateful refusals to answer Mr. Wilson's question, the child finally announced that she had not been made at all, but had been plucked by her mother off the bush of wild roses that grew by the prison-door.

8. But she named the infant 'Pearl,' as being of great price—purchased with all she had—her mother's only pleasure!

9. What we did had a consecration of its own. We felt it so! We said so to each other! Hast thou forgotten it?

10. It may serve, let us hope, to symbolize some sweet moral blossom, that may be found along the track, or relieve the darkening close of a tale of human frailty and sorrow.

DISCUSSION

1. In the "Custom-House" section of the novel, Hawthorne critiques his ancestors for their bitter prosecution of the Quakers and other disenfranchised members of their community. What seems to be his overall attitude toward Puritanism in the novel? How does the novel relate to traditional Puritan beliefs such as original sin, guilt, or discipline? Which characters in the novel embody the beliefs of Puritanism? Which characters critique them?

2. Commenting on Hester's superiority to other female characters in nineteenth-century fiction, Charles F. Richardson in 1886 wrote: "When the heroines of other story-tellers were bursting into tears every page or two, Hawthorne's Hester Prynne was walking in the loneliness and silence of majestic sorrow and voiceless remorse." How does Hester compare with the heroines of other novels you've read? Describe Hester's physical appearance: How does this influence our response to her? What are her strengths and her weaknesses? Is she a feminist? Could she be a role model for women today?

3. Discuss the symbolism of the scarlet letter. How does its meaning change as the novel develops? What different meanings does it hold for Pearl, for Roger Chillingworth, for Arthur Dimmesdale, and for the townspeople? What does it mean to Hester? What color and style is the letter? Why are these details important? Does American culture still use symbols to signal difference? What other significant symbols do you see in the text? For example, how do colors function symbolically?

4. Hawthorne had originally intended to publish *The Scarlet Letter* as a story in the collection *Old-Time Legends*. After deciding to publish it on its own, Hawthorne added the "Custom-House" section as an introduction. Discuss the importance of this section to the themes and ideas discussed later in the novel. What do we learn about Hawthorne and his family in this section? How does he feel about Salem? Readers have often viewed this section as reflecting Hawthorne's bitterness after losing his job at the custom house—does this section have a "sour grapes" tone? What do we learn about Puritan society? Based on this section, what do we learn about Hawthorne's theory of romance?

5. The novel contains three scaffold scenes, in Chapters 1, 12, and 23. Analyze each of them, looking for similarities and differences in the imagery in each. Hester, Pearl, Chillingworth, and Dimmesdale are present in each scaffold scene: Describe their attitudes in each. How do they change? What does the scaffold itself symbolize?

6. Analyze each of the novel's four main characters: Hester, Pearl, Chillingworth, and Dimmesdale. What strengths and weaknesses do you find in each character? Which character do you most admire? Which do you most dislike?

7. Many of the early readers of *The Scarlet Letter* criticized its immorality. The Episcopal bishop Arthur Cleveland Coxe, for example, condemned the story for transforming "a lady's frailty" into "a natural and necessary result of the Scriptural law of marriage." What seems to be Hawthorne's view toward the relationship of Hester and Dimmesdale? Does he condone their adultery, or does he criticize it?

8. Hawthorne is careful to set his story in a very specific time and place, yet in the "Custom-House" essay he tells us the tale exists in "a neutral territory, somewhere between the real world and fairy-land, where the Actual and the Imaginary may meet, and each imbue itself with the nature of the other." Discuss the setting. First, think about the historical framework of the novel. What elements of reality do you find? Of fairytale? What does the forest symbolize here? Do you see any contrasts between the world of the town and of the forest?

9. Analyze the narrator of the story. What seem to be his views of the characters and the action in the novel? Does the narrator seem to have nineteenth-century views or Puritanical views? What details reveal the narrator's point of view?

(Keep in mind that the narrator is not Hawthorne; he is a fictional element, just like the characters in the novel.)

10. This novel introduces numerous themes, such as the clash between individuals and society, women and men, the past and the present, nature and culture, science and imagination, and so on. Analyze one or more of these themes, or identify some of your own. How does an analysis of theme enrich your understanding of the novel? Of American culture in general?

ACTIVITIES

1. Draw, paint, or embroider your vision of the scarlet letter.

2. Read some of Hawthorne's short stories, such as "Young Goodman Brown" or "The Minister's Black Veil." What similarities and differences do you notice between the themes and ideas presented in the novel and in the stories?

3. Enact a scene from the novel, such as the final scaffold scene or Dimmesdale and Hester's discussion in the forest.

4. Research the life and culture of seventeenth-century Puritan New England. What was daily life like in Hester's time? What would a normal day be like for a Puritan teenager? What could people living in this historical moment expect their lives to be like?

5. Keep a dialectical journal as you're reading the novel. Purchase a dialectical notebook or divide some paper you already have into two columns. On the left side of the paper, record general movements in the plot and interesting quotations. On the right side, write your responses to what you just read. For example, you may note questions or ideas that occur to you as you work through the text.

6. Using an electronic search engine, find Internet sites related to the novel or to Hawthorne. Compile a list of sites, with brief annotations of what's available at each site and a critical evaluation of the site.

7. As a follow-up to question 6, create an electronic study guide for the novel. Include interesting quotations, background information about Hawthorne, illustrations, student responses to the text, short essays about the novel, and a list of the top ten Web sites you found during your electronic search. You may also include historical information about Puritanism and Boston, and about other nineteenth-century American authors.

8. Watch two or more film adaptations of the novel. Notice how specific scenes are presented by different directors. You might also analyze differences in actors, costumes, music, scenery, and so on: How do these different choices influence your opinion of the story?

9. Pretend to take on the persona of one of the characters in the novel. Write an autobiographical sketch of yourself: What motivates you? Why did you make some of the choices you made? What changes would you like to make in your character? What was your life like before the novel began? What have you been doing since the book ended? You might draw a picture of yourself to accompany the written sketch.

10. Create a visual representation of the novel (a drawing, painting, sculpture, or collage, for example). What types of colors and images best capture the tone and feeling of the novel? You could also create visual representations of individual elements of the novel: the characters, setting, or symbols.

ANSWERS

True / False

1. T, 2. T, 3. F, 4. F, 5. F, 6. T, 7. F, 8. T, 9. T, 10. T, 11. F, 12. T, 13. F, 14. T, 15. T

Multiple Choice

1. c, 2. a, 3. b, 4. c, 5. d, 6. a, 7. c, 8. c, 9. a, 10. d

Fill in the Blank

1. Pearl 2. Boston, seventeenth 3. rosebush 4. Roger Chillingworth 5. adultery, able 6. The Custom-House 7. Bristol 8. leech 9. meteor 10. Election

Identify the Quotation

1. Dimmesdale, from Ch. XIX.
2. Narrator, from "The Custom-House."
3. One of the female townswomen, from Ch. II.
4. Roger Chillingworth, in Ch. XIV.
5. Narrator speaking of Pearl, from Ch. XV.
6. Pearl, from Ch. XVI.
7. Narrator speaking of Pearl when she's being questioned on theology at the Governor's Hall, in Ch. VIII.
8. Narrator, from Ch. VI.
9. Hester to Dimmesdale, from Ch. XVII.
10. Narrator, in Ch. I.

CLIFFSCOMPLETE RESOURCE CENTER

The learning doesn't need to stop here. Cliffs-Complete Resource Center shows you the best of the best: great links to information in print, on film, and online. And the following aren't all the great resources available to you; visit www.cliffsnotes.com for tips on reading literature, writing papers, giving presentations, locating other resources, and testing your knowledge.

BOOKS AND ARTICLES

Barlowe, Jamie. "Rereading women: Hester Prynne-ism and the scarlet mob of scribblers." *American Literary History.* Vol. 9, No. 2 (1997): pp. 197–226.

This feminist reading of the novel critiques male scholarship of *The Scarlet Letter* for reinforcing gender stereotypes. For many male critics, Hester's silence and acceptance of her exiled position within Boston society make her a prototype for all women. This essay argues that Hester must be abandoned as a model in women's scholarship, although she's still a good example of how sexism is reinforced within our culture and within literary studies.

Baym, Nina. The Scarlet Letter: *A Reading* (Twayne Masterwork Studies, No. 1). Boston: Twayne, 1986.

This book offers a close and insightful reading of the novel. In her analysis, Baym considers the plot, setting, characters, symbols, and themes. She also provides a comprehensive bibliography and an overview of the critical reception to the novel.

Bigsby, Christopher W. *Hester: A Novel about the heroine of* The Scarlet Letter. New York: Viking Penguin, 1995.

In this novel, Bigsby offers his vision of Hester's life before *The Scarlet Letter* begins, including her efforts to avoid her unhappy marriage with Chillingworth, her early life in Boston, and her love affair with Arthur Dimmesdale.

Bloom, Harold and William Golding, eds. *Nathaniel Hawthorne's* The Scarlet Letter: *Bloom's Notes* (Contemporary Literary Views). Broomall, PA: Chelsea House, 1996.

This collection features seven critical essays on the novel, arranged in chronological order. Written in a highly accessible style, these essays offer first-time readers a comprehensive look at the critical issues surrounding the novel.

Egan, Ken, Jr. "The adulteress in the market-place: Hawthorne and *The Scarlet Letter.*" *Studies in the Novel.* Vol. 27, No. 1 (1995): pp. 26–42.

Egan argues that *The Scarlet Letter* is an allegory of the author's place in society, proving that the artist can triumph over oppression. In his opinion, Hawthorne, the oppressed artist, is represented by Hester. Her adultery is seen as a creative act, much like artistic ability. The connection between art and adultery is made clear in the "Custom-House" essay, which celebrates the individual artist prevailing over oppression. *The Scarlet Letter's* allegory of art justifies the need for romantic art in a culture dominated by utilitarian concerns.

Kreger, Erika M. "Depravity Dressed Up in a Fascinating Garb: Sentimental Motifs and the Seduced Hero(ine) in *The Scarlet Letter*." *Nineteenth-Century Literature.* Vol. 54, No. 3 (1999): pp. 308–335.

Although many critics have argued that *The Scarlet Letter* transgresses social norms, this author says that when it is placed within the context of the literary debates of the 1840s and 1850s, the novel appears conventional, rather than radical. As part of this conservative message, the novel reminds readers of the need for self-denial and social responsibility. The essay analyzes the novel in terms of antebellum views of morality and gender in fiction to show readers the context in which it was written.

Morey, Eileen, ed. *Readings on* The Scarlet Letter. San Diego: Greenhaven Press, 1997.

Essays in this collection examine the major aspects of the novel: characters, style, use of allegory, Puritan culture, and symbolism of the scarlet "A." They also offer modern insights into the historical context in which Hawthorne was working. Written in an easy-to-understand style, this book should be accessible to most high school students.

Murfin, Ross C., ed. The Scarlet Letter: *A Case Study in Contemporary Criticism*. Boston: Bedford, 1991.

This book provides five critical essays, especially commissioned for a student audience, that look at the novel from five contemporary theoretical perspectives: psychoanalysis, reader-response, feminism, deconstruction, and new historicism. In addition, this volume offers a survey of the critical responses to the novel from the time of its publication to the present.

Reed, J.D. "Can he write, or what?" *People Weekly.* 30 Oct. 1995: pp. 54–55.

This comical mock interview with Nathaniel Hawthorne asks him to comment on the 1995 film version of the novel. In the interview, the fake Hawthorne says he's not upset about the negative reviews of the film because the book also received bad reviews when it was first published.

Reeves, W.J. "Will zealots spell the doom of great literature?" *USA Today.* Sept. 1996: pp. 68–69.

This opinionated article looks at the current censorship of literature in high schools and colleges. The author argues that political correctness is the McCarthyism of contemporary society and criticizes current attacks on classics such as *Moby Dick*, *The Scarlet Letter*, and other books that don't fit into a politically correct agenda. For example, *The Scarlet Letter* has been critiqued by feminists because of its sexual double standard. The essay forces the reader to consider whether the classics are still valuable reading for today's students.

Reiss, John. "Hawthorne's *The Scarlet Letter*." *The Explicator.* Vol. 53, No. 4 (1995): pp. 200–202.

Reiss analyzes the allegorical significance of the novel's main characters, discovering that they each represent an important philosophical or religious concept. For example, Hester symbolizes free will, Chillingworth represents predestation, and Dimmesdale signifies Puritanical predestation.

Scharnhorst, Gary, ed. *The Critical Response to Nathaniel Hawthorne's* The Scarlet Letter, *Vol. 2.* Westport, CT: Greenwood, 1992.

The documents in this collection illustrate the changes in Hawthorne's literary reputation over the years. Documents reprinted include news reports of Hawthorne's dismissal from the Salem custom house, the publisher James T. Fields's story of the book's composition, and numerous reviews from both American and British newspapers following the novel's publication in March 1850.

INTERNET

Campbell, Donna. "Nathaniel Hawthorne."

www.gonzaga.edu/faculty/campbell/enl311/hawthor.htm

This site offers links to texts, bibliographies, and study questions. In addition to links specifically related to the novel, it also includes links to general sites dealing with American literature and offering information about the historical period in which Hawthorne was writing and about contemporary authors, such as Herman Melville or Ralph Waldo Emerson.

Fisher, Edward. "Nathaniel Hawthorne."

www.enteract.com/~gleam/bio.html

A valuable addition to Hawthorne studies, this site includes links to images of Hawthorne, a short biography (from *The Cambridge Biographical Dictionary*), letters, places of interest, and documents related to Herman Melville's relationship with Hawthorne.

Eldred, Eric. "Nathaniel Hawthorne (1804-1864)." Home Page from Eldritch Press.

eldred.ne.mediaone.net/nh/hawthorne.html

Probably the most comprehensive Hawthorne-related site, this one has links to all aspects of Hawthorne studies, including complete html versions of all Hawthorne's texts. It also includes critical responses—both early and recent—to his works, a bibliography, a list of places from Hawthorne's life, and a timeline of dates and events.

FILMS

Hauser, Rick, dir. *The Scarlet Letter*. WGBH Video, 1979.

Performed by Kevin Conway, Meg Foster, and John Heard. Produced by Boston public television, this four-hour adaptation of the novel is considered to be an insightful and accurate rendition. The simple costumes and scenery allow the viewer to focus on the characters. The film includes three behind-the-scenes interludes featuring discussions of set design and the filming of the market scene as well as an interview with Kevin Conway (the actor who plays Roger Chillingworth).

Jaffe, Roland, dir. *The Scarlet Letter*. Hollywood Pictures, 1995.

Performed by Demi Moore, Gary Oldman, and Robert Duvall. A modernized version of the book that has received uniformly poor reviews, this film is little more than a soap opera. Through Demi Moore's erotic appeal, this film capitalizes on Hester's sexuality, while erasing the moral issues that structure Hawthorne's text. A tacked-on happy ending and plenty of violent action scenes make this film an almost unrecognizable rendition of the novel.

Vignola, Robert G., dir. *The Scarlet Letter*. Timeless Video, Inc., 1934.

Performed by Colleen Moore, Hardie Albright, and Henry B. Walthall. Reviews say this is an interesting adaptation of the novel but somewhat slow and poorly directed. It does offer an interesting historical perspective on the novel and is enlightening when compared with the other film versions of the novel.

CLIFFSCOMPLETE READING GROUP DISCUSSION GUIDE

Use the following questions and topics to enhance your reading group discussions. The discussion can help get you thinking—and hopefully talking—about *The Scarlet Letter* in a whole new way.

DISCUSSION QUESTIONS

1. If you were the casting director for a new film version of *The Scarlet Letter,* consider which actors you would cast in the key roles and why. What characteristics would an actress playing Hester need to have? What about an actor playing Dimmesdale or Chillingworth?

2. Consider Hester's child-rearing practices with Pearl. Are our methods of disciplining children largely the same as Hester's? Or are they very different? If Pearl were your child, would you behave differently toward her than Hester does?

3. Why doesn't Hester move to a new town after she's released from prison at the beginning of the novel? Do you think that she makes a good choice in returning to Boston at the end of the novel? Why or why not?

4. Hawthorne doesn't tell us exactly what happens to Pearl after she and Hester leave Boston. What do you think Pearl's future life is like? Does she marry? Does she have children? Where does she live?

5. Hawthorne also doesn't tell us much about Hester and Dimmesdale's relationship before the novel begins. Why do you think he chose to keep this information from the reader? What do you suppose these characters' lives were like before Hester was sent to prison?

6. What do you think Dimmesdale felt as he watched Hester on the pillory after she was released from prison? Imagine that he kept a diary. What do you think he might have written on that day?

7. In your opinion, which character deserves the harsher judgment: Chillingworth for tormenting Dimmesdale, or Dimmesdale for not publicly accepting responsibility for his actions?

8. What did you learn about American history from this novel? Does Hawthorne depict seventeenth-century America in the way you would expect, based on your previous knowledge about American history?

9. In addition to reading the book, watch any film version of the story. Does it depict the novel in the same way you would have? What did you like or dislike about the film? If you were the director, what would you have changed? Are there scenes you would have added or cut? What would you change about the scenery or the clothing?

10. If you were Roger Chillingworth, what would you do if you arrived in Boston and saw your wife standing on a public scaffold being shamed for her adultery? Are Chillingworth's actions justified?

Index

continued

9 780764 587245